JENNIFER SNOW

Under an
Alaskan
Sky

A
WILD RIVER

D0035367

ISBN-13: 978-1-335-04536-2

Praise for Jennifer Snow's Wild River series

An Alaskan Christmas

"The big-city girl choosing between her career and loving a small-town boy is a romance staple, but the nail-biting search-and-rescue scenes save Erika and Reed from being a cliché. Readers will enjoy the mix of sexy love scenes, tense missions, and amiable banter. This entertaining introduction to Wild River will encourage fans of small-town contemporaries to follow the series."

—*Publishers Weekly*

"*An Alaskan Christmas*, the first book in the Wild River series, drew me in from the first page to the last. I tried to read slower so that I could savor the story and feel every emotion. I reveled in every nuance, felt the cold, the wind and snow, and loved the small town and the mountains... I can't wait to return to Wild River."

—*Romance Junkies*

"This first title in A Wild River series is passionate, sensual, and very sexy. The freezing, winter-cold portrayal of the Alaskan ski slopes is not the only thing sending chills through one's body as Erika and Reed's connection heats up."

—*New York Journal of Books*

"Set in the wilds of Alaska, the beauty of winter and the cold shines through in this romance."

—*Fresh Fiction*

"Jennifer Snow's Alaska setting and search-and-rescue element are interesting twists, and the romance is generally smart and sexy... An exciting contemporary series debut with a wildly unique Alaskan setting."

—*Kirkus Reviews*

**Also available from
Jennifer Snow**

Wild River

An Alaskan Christmas

JENNIFER SNOW

Under an Alaskan Sky

HQN

HQN

ISBN-13: 978-1-335-04536-2

Recycling programs
for this product may
not exist in your area.

Under an Alaskan Sky

Copyright © 2020 by Jennifer Snow

This edition published by arrangement with Harlequin Books S.A.

For questions and comments about the quality of this book,
please contact us at CustomerService@Harlequin.com.

HQN
22 Adelaide St. West, 40th Floor
Toronto, Ontario M5H 4E3, Canada
www.Harlequin.com

Printed in U.S.A.

To the four-legged members of
all search-and-rescue crews.

"Until they are home, until you have closure, until you can rest, I will not rest... I am K-9 search and rescue." —Buckeye Search and Rescue Dogs

Acknowledgments

I'm grateful for so many people, from my agent, Jill Marsal, and editors Dana Grimaldi and Susan Swinwood, who make every book stronger with their feedback, to my husband and son, who keep me sane and fed during deadlines. A big thank you to SARDAA (Search and Rescue Dogs Association of Alberta) for all their research help with this book. All mistakes are my own, and I hope they would be proud of the S & R dog that Diva becomes.

Under an
Alaskan
Sky

CHAPTER ONE

WOULD HER OBITUARY read *brave* or *crazy*?

Cassie Reynolds stared down the steep slope of packed snow that ramped at the end, sending Slush Cup contestants across a wide pond onto a crash pad on the other side.

Few had actually made it to the soft, dry landing. Most were shivering human popsicles standing on the sidelines, hoping they'd sailed far enough, fast enough, to advance to Wild River's Slush Cup finals later that day.

Hoping? Okay, she was definitely crazy.

"No wonder it's free to enter this event," her best friend, Erika Sheraton, said, bouncing next to her to stay warm in the damp, cool April weather.

"I wouldn't exactly say free. I think we're paying with our pride," Cassie's brother, Reed, said, trying to cover his lower region in the skintight silver spandex one-piece body-con suit with the SnowTrek Tours logo on the back.

Cassie shot her brother a look. Each team that entered the Slush Cup was required to wear matching costumes. On the sidelines, there was a group dressed as hippies with wide-leg jeans and peace symbols on their tie-dyed shirts, a group of Spartans wearing short brown leather kilts and sashes over their bare bodies, and a group of werewolves in white fuzzy onesies… Cassie had planned her company-logo'd silver body-con costumes, thinking strategically.

They were more aerodynamic all dressed up like silver rockets, right?

"Oh, come on, guys," she said. "Where's the spirit? Tank's not complaining." Neither was she. Her brother in the skintight suit was something she could do without seeing, but Tank, affectionately nicknamed for his six-foot-five, two-hundred-seventy-pound solid muscle frame, on the other hand…she could stare at his shiny silver ass all day.

"I tried complaining. It didn't work," Tank said, checking over their DIY craft—a dune buggy on skis that Cassie would use to attempt her flight across the slushy twenty-by-forty-foot pond in three minutes. This year, contestants had a choice of how they wanted to cross the pond: skis, snowboards or a homemade dune buggy. After breaking her foot in an avalanche accident months before, Cassie had opted for the buggy.

"I still can't believe you signed us up for this," Erika said, wrapping her sweater around her own shiny costume. Technically, she was missing the point, covering up Cassie's company logo by wearing the big bulky sweater, but when Cassie had pointed that out, Erika had told her she could technically kiss her ass.

"Yeah, I'm pretty sure none of us volunteered," Reed said.

"You were each *selected* for a reason," Cassie said. "Tank is the muscle…" And boy, did he have muscles. She eyed her friend's solid, sculpted chest in the suit. His pectoral muscles should have been deemed illegal, and his abs gave way to oblique muscles that had her drooling. She lost her train of thought. They had to start having sex soon. It was five years overdue, in fact.

A few months before, they'd finally started moving away from friend territory, but Tank moved at the pace of a military vehicle. And damn, her patience was certainly being tried. His fear of commitment and his unwavering dedication to the only permanent woman in his life—his daughter, Kaia—kept her lusting from afar.

"And the rest of us? How did we make the cut?" Erika asked.

Cassie turned to her brilliant surgeon friend. "You're here to fix my face if this goes horribly wrong…"

"Which it most likely will," Reed said.

"Shhh…and you, big brother, are here to film it all," she said, handing Reed her cell phone. She readjusted her GoPro camera on her helmet as she climbed into the craft. Various angles would make a more compelling video. "Be sure to get a good, clear shot. One I can use for promotion." Bookings at her company, SnowTrek Tours, were down since winter ended, and with the opening of North Mountain Sports Company in a few weeks, a rival chain store, Cassie was desperate to drive more tourists to the mountains. People just needed to see how fun Alaska could be in the spring and how much her company was part of this wild and adventurous community. Adding footage of their participation in the Spring Carnival and the annual Slush Cup competition would definitely help.

Looking down the steep slope, she almost lost her nerve. Every competitor so far had been swallowed up by the half-frozen pond. Could she make it across in one piece?

Thousands of spectators watched from the sidelines,

waving signs in support of their favorite team. It was one of the busiest weekends in Wild River. Cassie's goal was to turn some of these extreme sports fans into customers.

If she survived.

She took a deep breath, putting on her goggles.

With the man of her dreams watching, she couldn't wimp out now.

"Come on, Cass! You got this." Tank's daughter Kaia waved from her position at the base of the slope, camera poised and ready to take the still shots for the social media promo. Cassie's Siberian husky sat at Kaia's feet, trying to be obedient, but the panting and wiggling of her tail betrayed her. Diva would happily be in the pond if Kaia wasn't holding tight to her leash.

Cassie climbed into the craft. There was nothing to worry about. She had a surgeon and two of Alaska Search and Rescue's best on her team, and they'd designed a foolproof...

The craft's steering lever broke off in her hand as she tested it.

"Well, that's unfortunate." Was it too late to make adjustments to the dune buggy? Like maybe install an airbag?

"Okay, so we're out?" Erika said, looking more than happy to call it a day. "This means we're out, right?"

Reed shook his head. "Don't get your hopes up. She's insane."

Cassie gave him the middle finger.

"Don't worry. You don't need it," Tank said, taking the steering lever from her. "You're only going in one direction." He bent next to her, getting ready for push off, as the official signaled for them to get into position. "Ready? Let's get this stunt of yours over with."

His dark charcoal-colored eyes revealed his concern. They held that emotion a lot. On rescues with S & R, he was always tense, worried until the mission was over, and as a single dad, he was constantly concerned about Kaia…whether she was safe, whether he was making the right parenting decisions, whether he was successfully fulfilling the role of father *and* mother… It was a big part of what attracted Cassie to Tank—his thoughtful, serious nature, fierce loyalty and protectiveness. She was carefree and always up for adventure, but having someplace safe to land and someone to have her back as she adventured her way through life was a good feeling. And she had that in Tank.

As a friend.

He brushed her hair out of her eyes, and the feel of his cool hand against her sweating skin made her shiver. Maybe she should kiss him just in case she died without getting the chance… How many times over the years had she wanted to? But she always came to her senses before taking the plunge over that line. Once she crossed it, there'd be no going back, and there was a lot at stake. Everyone in Wild River thought the two of them were perfect together…everyone except Tank. He either ignored the whispers and looks they got from everyone, or he was actually that obtuse.

Would a kiss finally make him realize they could be more than just friends? She stared at his mouth. Tempting Tom Hardy lips…

He grinned. "Can you focus, please?"

Damn, he could always read her mind.

She tore her eyes away from him. "Okay. Ready," she said, gripping the sides of the buggy.

Reed gave the wave to the official at the bottom of the hill and the five-second countdown started.

"I can't believe I'm helping you do this," Tank muttered, giving her a shove. "Please don't die."

The dune buggy tipped over the edge of the slope and Cassie clenched her eyes tightly shut as the craft picked up speed, descending a lot faster than she'd anticipated. Wet snow flew up from beneath the skis, hitting her in the face and sticking to her hair. The craft shook and the sound of rattling confirmed that screws were coming loose.

Maybe they weren't essential ones.

She struggled to hold on as the craft soared over several small ramps—added for more "fun." Who the hell came up with this event in the first place? She was a thrill seeker, but this was just violent, the way her body bumped and thumped on the way down the slope.

Tossed around like a rag doll, she white-knuckled it as she neared the big final ramp that would launch her across the pond.

Or into it…

"Open your eyes for the pics, Cass!"

Forget the promo pics, she was going to die.

She held on even tighter as she neared the end of the slope and felt the craft lift over the packed-down ice and snow.

Airborne lasted far too long. Each second felt as though someone had hit a pause button.

Please make it to the mat. Please make it to the mat.

Crashing hard onto the pad a second later, she inhaled sharply as she was thrown from the dune buggy. But she was on the other side.

She'd made it. She was alive. Definitely would be bruised to shit, but alive.

Cheering from the crowd made her smile as she opened her eyes and removed the goggles.

Reed, Erika, Tank and Kaia all ran toward her. Diva, her narcolepsy getting the better of the puppy in all the excitement, was asleep in Tank's arms.

"Jesus, sis, you must have hit a new height on the jump," Reed said.

Impressing her older brother took some doing, so Cassie shook off the rattled feeling in her brain. "Just tell me you got it on camera," she said.

"You bet. I'll upload the video later today."

Erika approached and took her face between her hands. "You good?" She scanned her eyes for signs of concussion.

Cassie laughed. "Yes, I'm fine." She hugged her friend, feeling better than ever. A good adrenaline rush did that to her. Made her feel invincible. Once there was no turning back and the initial danger was over, of course.

"You advanced to the finals!" Kaia looked to be the only one excited about that.

"Yeah, you know, I think maybe we'll forfeit. Quit while we're ahead?" Tank said.

Damn, that sounded good. Why tempt fate? But Kaia's look of disappointment made Cassie put on her bravest face. The little girl had been looking forward to this for weeks, had helped paint the dune buggy with the SnowTrek Tours logo and had gone shopping with Cassie for the silver body-con suits…

"No way! Kaia's right. We've made it this far and we're totally going to win this thing."

But first she needed an ice pack for her ass.

TANK ARRIVED AT the training clearance field five minutes behind schedule. The Alaska Search and Rescue Dogs van was already there. Parking his truck next to it, he grabbed his Search and Rescue jacket. "Diva, we're late."

Through the rearview, he caught the dog's look that said, "Not my fault this time."

"For once, it's all on me." Peeling off that bodysuit and washing the silver sparkle paint off his face had taken forever. There was no way to get all that shit off. He'd be glistening for months.

Opening the back of his truck, he let Diva out and gathered her leash and training gear.

She danced at his feet, eager to start that day's training. She'd been sitting next to Cassie's apartment door when he'd picked her up. Her tail wagged so fast it blurred, and the tiny whining noises coming from her meant she had energy to burn.

Usually they arrived early enough to play catch, but today they'd have to play later. "Ready to go to work?"

She sat obediently, though Tank knew it was a struggle.

He suppressed a grin and forced authority into his voice. "Alright, let's go."

Diva walked alongside him to the training area. He varied his pace several times and she matched him. After four months of training together, they were well synchronized as a team.

"Hey, man… I was hoping you'd still be in your silver bodysuit," Frank Jennings, head trainer at ASARD, called to him. The older man had helped train and certify over fifty search and rescue dogs for the organization in his thirty-year career. They were lucky to have his assistance training Diva, their first attempt at adding a tracking dog to the team.

"I'm burning that thing," Tank said. He still couldn't believe Cassie had talked him into wearing it, but when had he ever successfully said no to her?

How could he? She was his best friend, someone he could trust and rely on to help him with his ten-year-old daughter, Kaia, and man, he was crazy about her. So much so, he'd resisted a relationship with her for five years. Kaia was his focus, his priority, and until he was sure they were both prepared for a life with someone else, he couldn't take that leap.

But watching Cassie that day in her tight, body-hugging silver suit had driven him wild. Her athletic, rock-hard body containing her adventurous, fearless spirit was tempting as fuck… But the way she'd looked like she was about to kiss him at the top of that suicide slope had made him panic. He knew she had feelings for him that went far beyond friendship and he sensed her patience with him was running out. His patience with himself was running out. How much longer could he keep his attraction to her in check? Chemistry wasn't the problem—they had plenty of that. It was commitment he wasn't ready for. It wasn't just himself he had to think about.

Was Cassie really prepared take on the role of stepmom to Kaia? She'd been his daughter's primary female role model for years and the two of them were really close, but while Kaia had learned to have Cassie in their life as someone she could depend on, learn from…his little girl knew at the end of the day, it was just the two of them, that his loyalties were with her.

Cassie's chosen lifestyle made it difficult for Tank to see her in their lives on a full-time basis. Her adventurous, no-fear attitude and zest for life both attracted Tank and repelled him. As lead adventure guide of her company, SnowTrek Tours, Cassie took on the most challenging expeditions through the Alaska wilderness and sometimes took calculated risks that other, more inexperienced guides wouldn't even consider. Tank worried about her.

He struggled with his involvement on the search and rescue team because of the guilt that if something happened to him out on a mission, Kaia would be on her own. It was the reason he hadn't committed to becoming a full member yet. So Cassie having a similarly risky career, going out into the wilderness on adventure-seeking trips year-round, made her someone Tank wasn't sure he could fully commit to…

He'd been down that road before with Kaia's mother.

"I saw the events this morning," said Jimmy, Frank's son and their volunteer training "target," joining them. "Your girl soared over that pond. What the hell kind of jacked-up motor was in that dune buggy?"

"It met regulations and Cass is just a friend." And he was a major asshole saying it. She deserved more from him…and damn, he wished he could give it.

Jimmy glanced at Diva. "But isn't your partner here her dog?"

"Yes."

"And I saw her leave your place really early the other morning…like walk-of-shame early."

Small towns and their assumptions. "There was nothing shameful about it. She stays over sometimes to watch Kaia when I have night shift duty at the station."

"She stays over when you're *not* there?"

"Correct."

Jimmy and Frank exchanged looks that suggested Tank was indeed an asshole. Was he crazy or was even Diva judging him?

"Can we get started?"

"Sure thing," Frank said, checking his chart. "You know, I think we're ready for phase five... Diva's been tracking for several weeks now without treats."

Tank hesitated. Phase five was the final stage before they were eligible for certification. He'd hoped to stay in phase four a little longer, but Diva was an unexpected superstar. Despite her narcolepsy, she was proving to be a lot tougher and smarter than her sequined collar and pampered paws suggested. "Are you sure? Don't want to shake her confidence, you know..."

Jimmy laughed. "I've never seen a dog with more confidence. She wears pink booties and a winter coat when she isn't training and struts around town like a Chihuahua."

"Jimmy's right," Frank said, putting on his hat and gloves as a cold wind blew through the clearing. "Diva's ready for this."

But was *he*? It was shitty to have doubted the dog in the first place, but now he needed more time. Their certification to full search and rescue members meant a lot of changes Tank wasn't quite ready for yet. This had been Kaia's idea. Since Diva was a pup, she'd been desperate for the dog to be the first four-legged member of the S & R team. Tank hadn't believed Diva could pull off the demanding obedience training and commitment to their tracking practice. Her condition—unpredictably falling asleep without cause or warning—would make her a liability, he'd argued.

Diva's vet disagreed. Dr. Jose believed that training for a greater purpose might help Diva have fewer episodes, keep her focused. And so far, the dog was performing better than anyone had expected.

"Holding her back wouldn't be fair," Frank warned. "That would do more damage to her confidence than trying and failing. You need to show her you believe in her and that it's okay to try."

When they put it that way… "Okay, I guess we'll give it a shot," he said.

Tank moved aside and Jimmy took over interacting with the eager puppy. He played with her and allowed her to sniff him, his clothing and skin. Then, handing Tank his sweatshirt, he headed off with Frank toward the thick forested area at the end of the clearing.

The two men would walk so far together, then they'd break off and go in different directions. Diva's test was to follow and track Jimmy and not let herself get distracted by Frank. The "distraction" element of phase five proved the most challenging for most dogs.

"Okay, girl, you ready?" Tank asked, reattaching Diva's leash and letting her sniff Jimmy's sweater.

Diva took her job seriously. She sniffed and pawed at the garment, then sat at attention, satisfied she had the scent.

"Find!"

On Tank's command, Diva headed in the direction the two men had walked. As in phase four, she wasn't rewarded at intervals…just kept going until the target was found. She led Tank past the clearing and into the trees. Mud from the thawing ground caked his boots as he followed. Spring weather meant the trees were blooming, and the damp floral scent in the air made tracking a little tougher. Each season provided its own challenges, but winter months would be the hardest.

Diva followed Jimmy's scent to the marking where the men had separated.

Could the dog get this right on her first try?

She sat at Tank's feet, looking up at him.

"Find!"

She sniffed the air, but remained seated.

Confused by the two scents and not wanting to get this wrong, she wouldn't move any further. Her tail wagged against the ground and she let out a little whimper. She was clearly discouraged by this new challenge.

He tried again. "Find!"

Diva stared in the right direction, where Jimmy was hiding forty feet away, out of sight, but she refused to go to him.

Tank knelt beside her and pet her soft gray-and-white fur. "Good girl. You almost got us there."

Diva whimpered and looked disappointed. Overachiever complex. Like her owner. "It's okay. You did good." Standing, he led the dog down the correct trail to Jimmy.

Seeing him, Diva barked her alert, then sat again, ears down. She knew she'd failed this test.

Tank unhooked her leash as Jimmy praised her for her assistance, but Diva still looked at Tank for his approval.

He took a treat from his pocket and Diva's favorite ball. Her tail wagged happily, reminding him that she was still just a pup. Work time was over. Time to play. "Fetch!" Tank said, throwing the ball back toward the clearing.

Diva dashed after it.

"Well, it was a good first attempt," Frank said, returning to them.

"Yeah…not bad." For a second, Tank had thought Diva would get it right. It wouldn't take many more attempts for Diva to pass this stage of the process too… and that had him nervous as hell.

An hour later, after he'd exhausted his right arm throwing the ball, they'd packed it in and headed to SnowTrek Tours. "We're back," he called as they entered Cassie's office.

"Hey, how did she do?" Cassie asked, standing on her office chair, peering through her window blinds.

"She attempted phase five today." Tank removed Diva's leash and hung it on a hook near the door. The dog immediately passed out on her cushion near the front window.

"Really? That's great," Cassie said, barely glancing his way. Her attention still on the window.

Closing the blinds, Tank moved her away from it, lifting her into his arms and off the chair. He set her feet on the floor. "You have to stop stressing. That company is opening whether we want it to or not." Not that they hadn't tried to prevent North Mountain Sports Company from buying the building across the street the year before. They'd started petitions and talked to the mayor, but ultimately it had been decided that the big chain adventure company was a positive addition to the community.

Even if it meant driving out some of the smaller competitors, like Cass.

Cassie sighed. "I just wish they weren't being so secretive."

Part of their grand opening launch depended on a great storefront reveal. Therefore, no one other than the work crews renovating the building were allowed inside, and everyone involved had signed NDAs. Large black tarps draped over the exterior and big fences blocked any external views of the construction.

"Look, your company has survived competition before. You have a great reputation. Stop stressing." He rubbed her arms and her expression changed.

He'd wanted to comfort her, but damn if the feel of her arms beneath the thin fabric of her sweater didn't make him long to keep touching her. Everywhere. This was the problem with being alone with her. Without anyone around, he felt his guard slipping a little. He forgot that he had responsibilities to Kaia…and to Cassie, not to act hastily and put the situation they had working for them at risk. An impulsive kiss could throw off the balance they had in their lives.

Could being with her make things better? Absolutely. As long as everything worked out, but he wasn't prepared to take the chance that it wouldn't.

"Would you be feeling as confident if there was an internationally well-known bar moving into that space?" she asked.

Competition for his own bar on Main Street, The Drunk Tank? Absolutely not. "I feel you, I do." More than was safe, really. "But the locals here have your back. I have your back."

Damn, her blue eyes were mesmerizing. Most days

they held him captive because of the excitement there that never seemed to die, but today, they held a concerning hint of worry.

"Listen, they are a chain store. They might have a big flashy opening that draws a crowd for a few weeks, but it won't take long before everyone realizes that they are simply selling overpriced name-brand equipment and clothing and that the tours they offer aren't up to your standard. You've gotten permits from Wild River to explore backwoods areas this company has never even heard of."

"That's true…"

"And their guides are probably some pretty boys from Aspen who have never experienced wilderness like this."

Cassie cocked her head to the side. "Some tourists like pretty boys from Aspen… I can't compete with the eye candy."

Tank laughed. That just might be the other company's edge over her. Cassie's male guides were Alaskan-tough with mountain man beards and muscles built for function, not fashion. If tourists were looking to fulfill some romantic fantasy on their vacation, they'd best stick to North Mountain Sports Company, but if they wanted an authentic outback experience, they couldn't do better than SnowTrek Tours.

"Unless, of course, you and I cross-promote and I send them into the bar for a free cocktail, served by Alaska's hottest bartender," she said.

Damn, when she flirted, it erased every cautionary reason he relied on for keeping things PG between them. Instances like now, when they were alone, Kaia wasn't around and he was touching her, it was hard as hell not to take the plunge and let everything work itself out.

At first, when they'd met, he'd had Reed as enough of a cockblock not to act on his crazy lust-filled attraction to Cassie. They were on the search and rescue team together, he was Reed's boss at the bar...there were far too many lines that would be crossed, but over the years Reed had more than given his blessing for Tank to go for his sister. It was like that here in Wild River. No bro codes broken when one guy fell for another guy's sister...or ex-girl... Love was love and they could all act mature about things.

After that, his hesitation was Kaia. And his daughter's best interests were more than enough for him to put on the brakes. Kaia loved Cassie, but he wasn't sure how his daughter would feel about having Cassie in their life full-time. Having to share his attention with someone else. And if things fell apart, his daughter would be devastated to lose Cassie, as well.

There was too much at stake.

"The free cocktail I'll happily provide, but you can't be pimping me out to tourists," he said.

"Why not? I mean, how long is your vow of celibacy anyway?" The teasing glint in her eyes should have had him retreating, but his betraying body just stepped closer.

"Don't tempt me, Cass..."

She stood on tiptoe and still only came below his chin, but her attempt at intimidation was cute. "That's exactly what I've been trying to do..." Her glaze flitted between his lips and his eyes as she slowly raised her arms, wrapping them around his neck.

"Cassie..." It came out more as a groan, his entire

body tensing. Hard. Could they cross the line to physical without actually entering into a real relationship? Best friends with benefits sounded like the perfect situation to him…but he knew she wanted more and he couldn't give her that. He was already taking so much from her and not giving nearly enough back.

Diva's bark alerted them to the presence of another person before the door chimed.

Tank cleared his throat and stepped back as Bobby Taylor entered, struggling to carry the large, awkwardly shaped Slush Cup trophy that Cass had naturally secured that year. No other competitor had even been a challenge. The woman had a no-fail drive to succeed. "Where do you want this, Cass?"

"Oh…um…" She looked annoyed at the interruption, but Tank was relieved.

"How about right here next to the Business of the Year Award?" Tank suggested, raised eyebrows implying she was giving North Mountain Sports Company far too much power. Wild River didn't give out the Business of the Year Award for arbitrary conditions or who spent the most in advertising in their monthly newsletter.

Cassie should know that based on how many years she'd come up just shy, one year losing it to his bar.

That had certainly made things interesting for a while.

Bobby set the award on the shelf near Cassie's desk. "Don't get too attached. It's headed back to Bobby's Delicates next year."

Tank didn't doubt that it would. Bobby's Delicates had claimed the Slush Cup title for six years running. Cassie's unexpected win that year had been an upset. While Bobby had inherited the lingerie store from his mother—also named Bobby—his true passion was his mechanic's shop, and he stayed as far away from women's underwear as he could. Both professionally and personally.

"She's all yours again next year," Cassie said. "I just needed to borrow her for a while."

He actually looked teary eyed as he glanced at the trophy before leaving the store.

"So that means we're not entering again next year?" Tank was hopeful.

Cassie turned her office chair around to show him the soft, inflated donut she was using as a cushion. "Not unless someone else is flying over that pond. The bruises on my ass are no joke."

"That's a hard pass, then," he said with a forced laugh.

Unfortunately, now all he could think about was how much he'd like to kiss away her injuries.

CHAPTER TWO

"Hey, man. How'd it go?" Reed asked as Tank entered the Search and Rescue station later that day.

"Training was amazing. Diva is a superstar. Didn't quite make it past phase five today, but I'm sure it will take her no time…"

"You're talking a lot, which means you're diverting from my *actual* question—you and Cass still haven't discussed Diva moving in with you, have you?"

Tank hung his training equipment on a hook. "Nope." Cassie knew that in order for Diva to be an official member of ASARD, the dog would have to live with him, but so far they'd both skirted the issue. Diva was *her* pet and she adored the dog. She'd rescued her from the side of the highway the year before. Someone had abandoned an entire litter of Siberian husky pups and Cassie would have kept them all if she'd had the space in her condo.

She kept Diva because of her narcolepsy. A puppy with a medical condition would be harder to find a home for.

"You know you two won't get certified as a team unless Diva lives with you. They are letting it slide for now because you two spend so much time together," Reed, stater of the obvious, said.

"Explain to me how I'm supposed to have that conversation with Cass." Hands on his hips, Tank waited. He'd welcome the other man's suggestions on the matter.

Reed could talk a big game, but disappointing his sister wasn't something the guy did often either.

"You know, if you and Cass lived together, you wouldn't need to have this conversation at all."

Where the hell had Erika come from with her wisdom?

Tank shot his buddy a look as Erika entered the room and plunked herself down on Reed's lap.

Reed shrugged. "What? She has a point. It would save you from having to steal my sister's dog."

"I'm not stealing her dog." But he wasn't making the leap to live with Cassie either. That would be insane. They hadn't even gone on a date. Not a real one anyway.

Four months ago, he'd finally grown a set big enough to take a chance with her. They'd planned a real date for New Year's Eve—just the two of them—but then Reed almost died on a rescue mission and well…their rescheduled date hadn't quite happened.

His balls had shrunk right back up into his body.

Reed's accident had only served as a reminder that things here in Wild River could be dangerous with his choice to be on the S & R team, and he relied on Cassie to be there for Kaia…if anything were to happen to him. If they took a chance on a relationship and things didn't work out, what then?

He knew it was selfish, but he needed Cassie in his life; he wouldn't know what to do without her. Having her as a best friend was better than not at all…on so many levels.

"Besides, this training wasn't exactly my idea." Kaia

was the one insisting on this. She'd done all the research and filled out the paperwork herself. She'd been the one to reach out to Frank Jennings. His little girl was a go-getter when there was something she wanted. He slid his arms into his reflective jacket. "You two ready to go?"

They had wilderness training that evening and then he had to get to the bar. He ran a hand over his chin and blinked exhaustion from his eyes.

Man, he felt old. And not just because he was a week away from his thirty-fifth birthday.

Thirty-five.

Shit.

He liked his life. He had everything he wanted—his bar on Main Street was successful, Kaia was happy and healthy, he had great friends…but life was speeding past. Ten years ago, after a challenging childhood and teen years, he'd thought he'd had all aspects figured out. His life had finally gotten on track. And things still were… So, he couldn't quite explain the unset-tling feeling in his gut that at any time, the life he'd created could be swept out from under him. He knew how easily life could change. He never took anything for granted and he continued to work his ass off to make sure he and Kaia would always be okay, have every-thing they needed.

Thirty-five.

He was suddenly feeling every one of those years. He just hoped that no one knew about his upcoming birth-day and he could slip into the other side of his thirties without acknowledging it.

THE THREE-LAYER CHOCOLATE, strawberry and vanilla cake would be perfect. Dark green fondant wrapped over the cake and the words *Happy Birthday Tank* on top were understated, like Tank, yet the flavors were sure to please the over two hundred guests scheduled to arrive at The Drunk Tank the following Tuesday night for his surprise party.

Keeping the birthday event a secret in a town like Wild River was a feat in itself, but somehow, with Kaia's help, Cassie hoped to pull it off. It was the little girl who'd done the recon to find out when Tank's birthday was, claiming she needed the information for a school project. For years, no one knew, and it was something he refused to talk about. But now they did, and just in time for his thirty-fifth!

"You sure you're not too busy to get this done in time?" she asked. She wasn't giving the bakery much notice.

But Mrs. Carly waved a hand. "Absolutely not."

"Good, because an event is only as good as its food and everyone loves your cakes," Cassie said, surveying the baked goods in the display case and savoring the scent of fresh cinnamon bagels coming from the oven.

Mad Batter had been in the same location on Main Street for over forty years. Mrs. Carly had owned and worked there all her life, and the now-seventy-year-old didn't seem to age at all. Her tiny waistline was still the most talked about mystery among the women in Wild River. The woman had won countless baking contests in Alaska throughout the years. She'd been featured in a bunch of cooking magazines and had come in second place on the *Halloween Cake-Bake* challenge the year before. All of Wild River had tuned in to the popular seasonal edition of the reality television show out of LA to cheer her on.

"You're coming to the party, right?" she asked Mrs. Carly.

"Wouldn't miss it, dear. After all, I've been trying to catch that boy's eye for years," she said with a wink.

You and me both, Mrs. Carly.

After paying for the cake and leaving the bakery, Cassie headed south on Main Street toward her office. With only a week until the party, there was so much to do—decorations to finish, caterers to book, and she still needed a gift for Tank…

As she passed what would soon be the new North Mountain Sports Company, she slowed her pace. There were no work crews there that early in the morning.

Just keep walking.

A broken piece of fence surrounding the construction site caught her eye and she deemed it an act of fate. Really, what were the chances that she'd be practically alone on the street with no workers around and that piece of fence conveniently broken, allowing viewing access?

It was kismet, really.

Crossing the street, she approached the fence and looked around before moving the broken piece of wood aside.

Just a quick peek couldn't hurt anything.

It was still dusk, so visibility wasn't great, but she could make out several grand opening signs, boasting deals. Okay, that wasn't unusual…and she could offer special pricing of her own that week. Half-price tours, two-for-one deals, discounts on equipment rentals…

She leaned in further, squinting to see through the tinted glass windows of the lower level. She spotted a full-size, cardboard cutout…a guy holding a snowboard… Holy shit! Lance Baker! Announcing that he would be there for their grand opening event.

How the hell had they gotten him to agree to that? The professional gold-medalist Alaskan native never did endorsements. Ever. Cassie had certainly tried…

"Whatcha doing, Cass?"

She jumped, bumping her head on the fence. Turning, she released a sigh, relieved to see it was just a friend of hers from high school. "Shit, Eddie, I thought you were a cop."

"I am a cop."

"You know what I mean."

"Not really." He gestured to the very real-looking gun and handcuffs on his utility belt… Cassie's eyes widened, taking in his crisp new state trooper's uniform.

"Oh my God, you passed your police entrance exam!"

He beamed, then cleared his throat, hiding his smile. "Don't change the subject. Trespassing here is illegal, Cass."

"I wasn't trespassing. This fence was broken already, I swear. I was just taking a peek."

He bent to pick up the broken shards of wood. "Taking a peek is illegal too."

Cassie huffed as she stepped back out through the fence. "Well, I didn't see anything anyway." Except their surprise grand opening guest. Lance Baker, seriously? "And I think *this* should be illegal." She gestured around her. "This eyesore they've constructed right here on Main Street."

"It's just temporary and apparently it's the standard for this company. They like their opening day launches to be big. Secrecy leading up to the day adds buzz."

Cassie bit her lip. *She* needed buzz. Something great and exciting and better than Lance freaking Baker!

Eddie set the wood back into place, wrapping a piece of caution tape around it to hold it in place and block any other *peekers*. "Sorry, Cass, I know this is tough for SnowTrek Tours..."

"Ah, I'm not worried." She'd moved beyond worried... to contemplating new career choices. Truth was, she'd never wanted to do anything else. When she was growing up, school was challenging for her, mostly because she didn't care. She craved the outdoors and found herself daydreaming of rock climbing and exploring areas of the outback that were untamed and uncharted. Her family were outdoor enthusiasts and spent their summers camping, fishing and kayaking on the river. The school year dragged on for her, and Cassie had longed for adulthood so she could escape the confines of a classroom and homework for good and get out into the real world.

After high school, she'd traveled all over the world, hiking mountains in Japan and New Zealand. She'd never felt more free.

Fulfilling her wanderlust, settling back in Wild River and opening SnowTrek Tours had been a dream come true, and she'd worked her butt off to make it a success.

What would she do if North Mountain Sports Company made it impossible to keep her business's doors open?

"So, no more trying to get a look, okay, or I'll have to fine you," Eddie said.

Cassie scoffed. "You've been a cop all of five minutes."

"And I'd like to stay that way."

Despite her own troubles, she smiled. "It's really great, Eddie." He'd worked so hard to get to this point. He was dyslexic, so school had never been easy for him either, and he'd worked as a security guard for ten years after graduation, applying to the academy as often as he could. He'd passed the physical components of the application process, but the written tests had always challenged him.

He hadn't given up.

Cassie wouldn't either. Someway, she'd figure out how to compete with the big chain store.

"Hey, you'll be at Tank's party next Tuesday night, right?"

He nodded. "I've heard most of Wild River will be there. You are adhering to the bar's maximum capacity regulations, right?"

Cassie walked away. "Cop Eddie's not invited. Leave the gun and handcuffs at home."

His laugh followed her down the street. "Always a rule breaker."

TANK FINISHED MAKING Kaia's lunch for school and put the Wonder Woman–themed lunch bag inside the matching backpack. "Hey Kaia! You're going to miss the bus," he called out as he left the kitchen and headed down the hall toward his daughter's room.

"Be there in a sec!" she called back through the bedroom door, which was slightly ajar.

Tank paused outside when he heard her laugh. She was talking to someone. "Okay, I gotta go…talk again soon? Okay…bye."

Tank moved away from the door quickly as Kaia opened it. "Hi…ready to go?" he asked.

"Yeah. Sorry, I was just Skyping with Mom," she said.

He nodded, shoving his hands deep into his pockets. These Skype chats were new. Before a few months ago, there had only been phone calls a few times a year and birthday and Christmas gifts from Kaia's mother, Montana.

After suffering a brain injury and returning to her hometown in Colorado when Kaia was a baby, the woman hadn't been back to Wild River since, content to leave the parenting of their daughter to him. They both agreed it was for the best, but naturally, as a result, the relationship between mother and daughter had always been slightly tense and practically nonexistent.

Up until recently. This was the third Skype chat in a month. Tank was desperately trying to hide how he felt about Montana's sudden increase in contact because Kaia seemed happy about it…but he just hoped his little girl didn't get her hopes up for more. Montana hadn't been the most reliable before her head injury had taken her out of their lives.

"No problem," he said, in what he hoped was a casual tone. "Everything okay?"

Kaia smiled as she took her backpack from him. "Everything's great. Is my soccer uniform in here?"

And she changes the subject.

Kaia was tight-lipped about the conversations with her mother. Tank wasn't sure why, but he suspected she was trying to protect him and his feelings, which made him feel guilty as shit, because the conversations did worry him and obviously Kaia could sense that. He nodded. "Yes it is. I'll meet you at the field at four. Walk straight over there after school."

"I know, Dad."

"And..."

"No talking to strangers and say no to drugs. Yes, I got it," she said, putting her baseball hat on over her thick, dark hair.

Tank laughed. She was such a smartass sometimes. "I was going to say, no more arguing with that ref."

Kaia rolled her eyes. "But he's horrible. You know that call against me in the last game was bull..." she stopped just short of the inappropriate word "...was wrong."

"I don't make the calls." He paused. "But yes, it was bullshit."

She grinned.

"Go, before you miss the bus."

"I'll see you at the game."

"Okay..." He gave her a quick hug and sighed as the door shut behind her.

Going into her bedroom, he collected dirty clothes from her hamper and picked up a pair of socks from the floor. He opened the bedroom blinds and picked up her stuffed unicorn and placed it on her bed.

He paused, seeing the photo of Montana on her bedside table.

Three Skype chats in a month.

More contact than *he'd* had with his ex in years. They'd met when she was visiting Wild River with a team of BASE jumpers. The town had been home to one of the few legal jumping sites in the world and Montana was an extreme athlete, a professional jumper. Unfortunately, some of the other jumpers in their group weren't as skilled, and Tank had assisted on the search and rescue mission when one of them got injured.

He'd immediately been attracted to Montana. Adventurous, smart, funny, stunning... Montana had quickly broken through walls Tank had thought were impenetrable.

Then she'd quickly broken his heart as well, leaving Wild River three months later. For her, the relationship had been a fling. For him, it had been everything. The first time he'd let his guard down since his parents' death. She'd been his first love and the scar she'd left behind had been deep.

For years, she'd barely been a part of their lives, but it seemed she wanted that to change. Tank was doing his best to be supportive. Contact between them was good for Kaia. She'd had so many questions over the years and Tank had done his best to answer them. Now, the little girl had a chance to develop a relationship with her mother.

He just hoped Montana didn't disappoint their little girl, the way she'd disappointed him.

CHAPTER THREE

THEY'D ADDED AN official countdown.

Cassie closed her office window blinds to block the view of North Mountain Sports Company's new live billboard on the street in front of their store, the digital display counting down the remaining twenty days, four hours, thirty-three minutes and ten seconds until their grand opening.

The huge billboard was an eyesore on Main Street. How on earth had they gotten approval for it?

Hell, she'd had to file a ton of paperwork just to be allowed to extend the overhang outside her shop by three centimeters to accommodate her logo.

No special treatment my ass.

And now she was stuck with an in-your-face constant reminder of the potential lifespan of her own company. Unless...she could come up with something quick.

Scanning her reservations system made her even more uneasy. Winter was always busy for her company—ski and snowmobiling tours, winter camping, corporate retreats and holiday tourists had her working her butt off during those months. Spring always slowed a little; the weather wasn't ideal with the thawing ground and high probability of rain, but summer always picked up again, so normally she wouldn't be so worried, but this year, North Mountain Sports Company would be there, stealing her business.

She hadn't had a big group booking in weeks, but luckily there was one coming up. A two-night couples' retreat at the base of Snowcrest Mountain. Eight couples confirmed for teepees along the river was at least a decent payday. It would cover her operating costs and payroll for the month. But then what?

She sat back in her chair and scanned the details of the booking. The retreat was being hosted by a new holistic therapy counselor in town…the woman had just opened her practice a few weeks ago. Her website advertised sex therapy, gender expression, couples' counseling and intimacy…

Maybe Cassie should invite Tank along on this retreat. Did this counselor work with noncouples who were clearly meant for one another, but one partner was too much of a commitment-phobe?

She wasn't sure anyone could help them move past this stalemate—the friend zone.

As if sensing her anxiety, Diva curled up at her feet, resting her soft fur against Cassie's legs. Cassie sighed, reaching down to pet the dog. Diva's certification with ASARD was another issue weighing on her mind. She knew what needed to happen for Tank and Diva to be a team, but just the thought of her dog not living with her anymore broke her heart.

Her phone chimed with a text from her mother and Diva's ears immediately perked, recognizing the personalized tone.

Cassie smiled. "Yes, Diva, it's Grandma."

Opening the text, she read,

Hey darlin' dinner at my place some night soon?

Her mother still lived in the next community over, Willow Lake, where she and Reed had grown up and lived until they'd both relocated to the resort town for more opportunities. It was smaller than Wild River, but her mother loved it there. She knew everyone, having owned the small pub in town for many years, and she had her friends that she played cribbage with on Friday nights and hosted a book club with on Tuesdays. Cassie and Reed had suggested her moving to Wild River several times, but her mother was happy and comfortable in the family home she'd lived in for almost thirty-five years.

But Willow Lake was a short enough drive that they saw each other at least once a month and her mother came to visit several times a year. Despite not seeing one another all the time, they were super close. The sale of her mother's pub had helped fund SnowTrek Tours years before and the support Cassie had received from both her mother and Reed during that first year of her new business venture had kept her sane and pushing forward whenever things were most challenging.

She suspected her mother knew she needed that support again now. They always had a sort of uncanny connection, where her mother's timing was spot-on. She could really use her mother's advice on a lot of things right now.

I'll be there. Just let me know when. Xo

She sent the text as the door opened and a man entered.

At least, she assumed by his height and build that it was a man... She couldn't be sure with the amount of winter gear the person was wearing.

Full ski suit, boots, thick gloves, hat and balaclava. Oversized ski sunglasses covering their eyes. Obviously not from Wild River. The temperature outside that day was balmy for locals. Five minutes ago, she'd seen two joggers pass the window wearing shorts. Forty degrees was the forecasted low, yet this person looked ready to take on an arctic freeze.

"Hi, can I help you?"

Diva was full-on alert now, sitting obediently by Cassie's side.

The guy removed his sunglasses and looked around, before lowering the balaclava away from his mouth, letting it bunch around his neck. "Nippy out there, isn't it? That windchill…brrrr…"

Cassie suppressed a grin and nodded. "You wouldn't like it here in December."

"Probably not…but I'm hoping I'll get used to it… gradually…" He shivered.

So not a local, but also not a tourist. "New in town?"

He nodded, removing the gloves. Stepping forward, he extended a hand toward her. "Miller Hartwell, and you are?"

Shocked.

Miller Hartwell. The owner of North Mountain Sports Company was standing in her store. Not one of the many executives she'd read about online or seen around town in the last four months overseeing the construction and being interviewed by all of the local media outlets, but the *actual* owner of the chain of stores.

What was he doing in Wild River? She'd expected maybe he'd make a quick cameo on the grand opening day, then fly back to their corporate offices in

Arizona—back to heat…which he obviously preferred to this weather.

Diva nudged her leg.

Realizing she still hadn't responded or accepted the outstretched hand, she shook her head. "Sorry… I'm Cassie Reynolds," she said, shaking his hand, which was surprisingly freezing.

At least he'd picked a good day to stop by. The office was neat and tidy…though it was empty. The retail section was really only for impulse buys or last-minute gear if someone forgot something. She had three separate wholesalers and brands she carried, but the revenue from merchandise sales was almost nothing. Therefore, unless there was a tour group, the place was usually quiet. Her staff only came in when they were leading a tour or during their monthly meetings. Otherwise, it was just her.

If only he'd stopped by an hour earlier, he'd have seen the twenty-two students from Wild River High School boarding the SnowTrek Tour vans for their spring hiking and orienteering lesson that day. Of course, she offered this to the local high school for free every year… but he didn't need to know that.

"You're the owner, right?" he asked.

He'd checked out her company? Her stomach twisted. She'd already turned down a buyout offer from North Mountain Sports Company the year before, when one of the executives stopped by with a form letter and boilerplate contract. The guy had assumed she'd say yes and was surprised she'd turned down their very reasonable offer.

At the time she still had a ton of business and a fighting spirit keeping her confidence high.

What would she do if Mr. Hartwell presented her with another opportunity right now?

No. Nope. The answer was still no. Their fancy billboard that broke several of Wild River business association regulations didn't scare her that much.

"Yes, I'm the owner. How may I help you?" She'd be polite but firm. He wouldn't intimidate her. Money and power weren't everything. He was still the new kid on the block around here.

He walked around the office, taking in the photos of various tour groups and her own opening day. Not nearly as grandiose as the one he was planning, but it had been an amazing day for her. She'd never felt such pride, and the support of the community who'd come out for hot dogs and free balloons had meant everything to her. She refused to let this man steal how that day had validated so much for her. She tried again. "Is there something I can help you with, Mr. Hartwell?"

He still didn't answer, turning his attention to the Business of the Year award on the shelf.

That's right. Be intimidated.

Instead, he pointed to the Slush Cup trophy. "Impressive win."

He'd been at the Slush Cup competition? He'd been in town for a while? "Thank you."

"Maybe North Mountain Sports Company can give you some healthy competition next year."

So he wasn't there to offer to buy her out and he assumed she'd still be in business a year from now. Good. "We look forward to the challenge," she said, meeting his gaze square on.

"You have a nice setup here. And your reputation in town is great." He glanced at Diva, who'd assessed he wasn't a threat and had gone back to sleep. "What's his name?" he asked.

"It's a she. Diva. Um…was there a reason you stopped by?"

"Oh, yes." He opened his jacket and reached inside for an envelope. He handed it to her and she saw her name embossed in gold on the front. "It's an invitation to our private event before the official grand opening… in…" He leaned toward the window, opened the blinds and read, "Twenty days, three hours, and forty-eight minutes."

Cassie forced a smile. These personalized envelopes alone probably cost more than her monthly marketing budget. But, whatever, she didn't need fancy to be effective. "Great. Thank you."

"The event is by invite only for the business owners in Wild River. An opportunity to get to know one another. Show you all that we're not a big corporate monster, trying to wipe out the small shops—such as yours—that are the spirit of this community."

Right. That's why they'd tried to buy her out before. If he was trying to soften her up, just to take her out when she let her guard down, he'd be disappointed. She hadn't made it this far in life by being susceptible to manipulation. "Well, thank you for the invite."

He smiled, before the bottom half of his face disappeared beneath the balaclava and he lowered his sunglasses back down over his eyes. "I hope to see you then," he said as he left the store.

I wouldn't count on it.

And she'd be surprised if any of the other business owners attended either… Mr. Hartwell could say what he wanted, but his company was already different from the rest around here. And in Wild River the small business owners stuck together. Of course, she wouldn't fault anyone who did decide to go…

She tossed the invite into the trash can beneath her desk and turned her attention to the new marketing brochures awaiting design approval on the screen.

Of course, getting an early inside look at the store only made sense. And learning more about Mr. Hartwell and the company could help her…

Retrieving the invite, she slid it into her purse and inserted the event into her Outlook calendar just as the door opened again and Tank rushed in.

"Hey, I came to give you a heads-up. There's some douchebag dressed like he's ready for the blizzard of '87 going around handing these out." He held an invite to the VIP party like the one she'd received, but personalized with his name in gold lettering.

Cassie nodded, forcing her heartbeat to steady at the sight of him. Dressed in tight-fitting jeans that hugged his thighs and a black T-shirt with The Drunk Tank logo on it, he always made her pulse pound. "He was just here. And that *douchebag* happens to be the owner of North Mountain Sports Company—Mr. Hartwell."

Tank ripped his invite in half.

"What are you doing?"

He frowned. "We're not actually going to the party… are we?"

Cassie nodded slowly. "I think I will…"

Tank reached for the tape on her desk. "Guess I should have clarified that first."

Cassie smiled. "You don't have to go."

"Of course I do, if you're going. I told you. I'm here. For support." He taped the invite. "We will go together."

Together. Of course they'd go together. They did everything together. Unfortunately, she knew enough not to think of it as a real date. "Great," she said.

If Tank could sense it wasn't actually great, he didn't show it. "Are you coming to Kaia's soccer game today?"

She nodded. "I'll be there. I hope it's a different ref this time. That call against her in the last game was bullshit."

Tank raised an eyebrow. "So that's where she got it."

"Got what?"

"The potty mouth," Tank said with a grin.

Cassie felt her cheeks flush. Okay, so maybe she wasn't always the best influence on the little girl. Which was one of the reasons why Tank doubted her ability to be in Kaia's life full-time. She wanted to prove to him that she could handle the responsibility of being a caregiver to Kaia…but she refused to change who she was. "Sorry about that."

Tank waved it off, but his expression grew serious. "Hey…has Kaia mentioned anything about her mom to you?"

Cassie frowned, her heart racing at the mention of Tank's ex. He never brought her up. Like, ever. "No… She showed me the unicorn stuffie she sent for her birthday, but she hasn't said much else. Why do you ask?"

Tank shoved his hands in his pockets and rocked back on his heels. "No reason. They've just been Skyping lately and I… Never mind. I'm sure everything's fine."

They're Skyping now? The last Cassie had heard, they spoke several times a year at most. Birthday gifts… Christmas gifts. She didn't know the full story, but Tank and his ex had agreed that was for the best. Apparently, Kaia's mother decided to change their arrangement. Cassie could tell by Tank's expression, it hadn't been his idea. "Do you want me to ask her about it?"

Tank shook his head. "No. I'm sure she will talk to me about it when she's ready." He headed toward the door.

Funny, that's what Cassie always thought about Tank. In five years of friendship, he'd barely mentioned Kaia's mom. From what Cassie had gathered, Kaia kept in contact, but Tank had no relationship with his ex. They didn't need to. They weren't sharing custody of Kaia or having to coparent.

But Tank's silence regarding their history had always spoken volumes. Cassie suspected there was a good reason Tank was worried about this increasing contact between his daughter and her mother now.

Would he ever open up about it?

He hesitated at the door, but then opened it. "I'll see you at the game," he said as he left the store.

Obviously not today.

CHAPTER FOUR

INSIDE THE DRUNK TANK the following Tuesday afternoon, Erika knotted off a blue balloon with the number 30 on it. "I thought Tank was turning thirty-five. Why do all the balloons say thirty?"

"I could only find thirty or forty, and I didn't think he'd appreciate the latter," Cassie said from her perch on the bar where she was hanging the Happy Birthday banner.

"I thought he didn't like to celebrate his birthday," Erika said, slightly out of breath from another balloon.

"That's just because he's never had a party."

"Like ever?"

"Like ever." The thought of Tank as a kid never having a party had brought tears to Cassie's eyes when he'd told her. His upbringing had been difficult and lonely from the tiniest bits that he'd actually revealed over the years. His dad had died when he was a baby—a motorcycle accident—and his single mother had been too wrapped up in her own grief to look after her son, taking her own life six months later. Tank didn't like to talk about his past and Cassie respected him enough not to push him. He'd open up when he was ready... she hoped. They were so close, yet sometimes she felt like she didn't know him at all. Not when it came to the things that really mattered. Without him trusting her enough to share all of himself, a real relationship could never develop between them. Since the day in her office a week ago, he hadn't brought up his ex again either and as usual, she didn't ask.

It was their *thing*. Along with not having sex and repressing all confessions of feelings.

"He grew up in foster care," she told Erika. "He said he remembers a smashed cake once, but it was for him and two other kids with birthdays that month, and that's it. So I want to do this for him."

Erika gave her a look. The one that said she wasn't completely on board, that this whole thing could backfire, blow up in Cassie's face, but she kept blowing up balloons.

That was all Cassie needed.

Cassie knew the risk she was taking. When Tank said he wanted to ignore his birthday, he might very well mean it…*or* he might appreciate the gesture for what it was—a chance for others to celebrate him. Tank was one of the best guys in Wild River. Everyone loved The Drunk Tank and the man who owned it. That night, the bar would be at maximum capacity as everyone came to wish him the best. He deserved that. It was long overdue.

And after a couple of shots, he'd be fine…

"So, I meant to tell you, a few days ago, one of the workers on the new store construction came in with a nail gun injury to his leg…"

"How does that even happen?"

"You wouldn't believe the shit we see in emergency… Anyway, I asked him a few questions…"

"Right there—this is why you're my best friend. What did he say?"

Erika held up a finger as she emptied her lungs into another balloon. She tied it and sent it flying into the air as she said, "He was fairly tight-lipped. They've all signed confidentiality agreements. But I pushed him for details on how he got the injury and he said he'd been building a skiing simulator...whatever that is. He said the technology attached to North Mountain Sports Company's displays is insane—virtual reality combined with actual motion to give an authentic skiing experience, right there in the store. Tourists won't have to even go outside."

Was it Cassie's look of horror or the one of disgust that had Erika's smile fading fast?

"I mean, that's horrible..." Erika said, stretching another balloon.

Cassie sighed. "What's horrible is the fact that this is the world we live in now. People would rather have a simulated version instead of the actual thrill of racing down a slope, exertion and adrenaline making their cheeks red...snow flying up all around them..."

"Actually, the simulator has snow, apparently."

Typical Erika. Cassie loved her blunt, straightforward friend, but Erika was still working on her ability to "read a room." "Unbelievable. I really am screwed, aren't I?"

"I think you're going to have some competition for sure."

Cassie shot her a look.

"Sorry. I'll reserve my air for the balloons." Her face disappeared behind the inflating rubber.

Hearing the truth was hard, but she could count on Erika not to sugarcoat things. That was good. Everyone else was trying to reassure her that things would be fine, but Erika was helping her prepare for the challenges ahead. "No, it's okay. You're right. The worst thing is that I have no idea what's going on over there and it's killing me. Those black drapes covering the windows are blocking any view…"

"Tell me you aren't the person who vandalized the fence."

"Of course not." She paused. "Did I try to peek inside once the damage was done? Absolutely. But it wasn't me. And besides, I saw nothing." North Mountain Sports Company took up a full corner of Main Street and was three stories high. Based on their other locations, Cassie knew the top floor was the reservations office and the bottom two were retail and "experiences." The sheer size of the place was intimidating compared to her small overhang beneath her condo on Main Street.

"I guess I'll know soon enough though—they invited the local business owners to a private party before their official grand opening to the public."

"Do you want me to come with you? For moral support?" she asked.

"Actually, Tank was invited too…so we'll just go together."

Erika raised an eyebrow. "Like a real date? Finally?"

"No. Just two friends and local business owners."

Erika's balloon popped. "When are you going to give him an ultimatum? Either take things to the next level or…" Her voice trailed off.

Exactly. Or what? If the choice was having Tank in her life as a friend or not at all, she'd have to choose this friend zone she was locked in. "Believe me, I want to," she said. "But the truth is, I don't think he's ready. I'm not sure he'll ever be ready."

"Everyone can see you two are perfect together. He

obviously adores you. Do you really think he'd shut you down if you went for it?"

That was the fear. "I'm not sure…"

"Well, he better smarten up soon before he loses you," Erika said.

Cassie was silent. What could she say without sounding pathetic? Tank would never lose her. No matter how long it took, she'd wait. She'd loved him for five years, her feelings only getting stronger, her attraction never fizzling out—not even a little bit. He was the only man she wanted, the only one she could ever see a future with. Love wasn't always perfect, but she'd rather have this situation with Tank than all the fairy tales in the world.

Erika's pager sounded and she released a half-inflated balloon as she reached for it. Then, after she dialed the hospital, Cassie listened to one side of her conversation. "This is Dr. Sheraton. I was paged…right…okay… moron, okay. I'll be there right away." She disconnected the call. "Sorry, Cass. I have to go." She slid into her coat. "Apparently some kid attempted the Slush Cup run this morning on an old crazy carpet. I'll be resetting the bones in his arm all day."

Cassie winced. "Better you than me." Unfortunately, having a surgeon best friend who was constantly rushing off to save lives and limbs put Cassie's problems into perspective.

"I'll be back as soon as I can," Erika said, leaving the bar.

Which meant, for now, Cassie was on balloon duty, alone. Left with her own questioning thoughts about whether this party was a mistake.

Ten hours later, she was about to get her answer. Guests started pouring into The Drunk Tank right on time and Reed was scheduled to arrive with Tank in minutes. Unfortunately, her brother wasn't calling to report good news.

"Cass, I'll warn you—he's in a shitty mood," Reed said as Cassie answered his call. "Tyler said happy birthday to him earlier and he nearly snapped."

"Tank doesn't snap." Never in her years of knowing him had Tank even come close to "snapping."

"Exactly my point," Reed said.

"Just get him here. People are showing up now."

"You sure this is a good…"

She disconnected the call, not wanting to hear the rest of Reed's question. It was too late now.

"Hey, Cass, where should we hide?" Wade, another member of the search and rescue team, asked as he finished his drink at the bar. He and his wife, Alison, had arrived an hour early. Together for almost twenty years, the two were relationship goals before it became a hashtag, but like for most young couples, a night out with kids at home was a rare occasion.

"Anywhere you'd like… He will be here in about ten minutes." If her brother was successful in dragging his cranky butt there. It was just after seven, and the bar technically opened that evening at eight, so Tank would have to show up eventually…

Heading into the kitchen, Cassie filled a large bucket with ice. Then took several deep breaths. Caterers were here. Cake had been delivered. The decorations were over-kill but on point. She'd managed to keep the party a secret. She was worrying for nothing. Everything was going to be fine. It was a party Tank was walking into…not a beheading.

"Head count out there is already at two hundred and eight."

A voice behind her made her jump. "Shit, Eddie, quit sneaking up on me like that," Cassie said, hand to her chest. She hadn't even heard him come into the kitchen. He was no longer in uniform, but his disapproving frown was still in place.

"Quit breaking the law." He picked up the ice bucket for her and followed her back out into the front. "There's far too many people here... Maximum capacity is..."

Seeing the front door open and her brother walking in, Cassie grabbed Eddie by the shirtsleeve and ducked behind the bar. "Shit, they are early... Shhhh..."

"This conversation's not over," Eddie hissed, but a second later, the lights turned on, everyone popped out at Tank, yelling "Happy Birthday," and Cassie slipped away into the crowd, away from Eddie's lecture unnoticed.

But as she walked toward the shocked-looking man of the hour, already surrounded by friends...her heart started to race.

Tank did not look happy.

HE'D NEVER LET Cass know how depressing this was for him. She'd obviously gone through a lot of trouble, but the sight of the balloons, the Happy Birthday banner, the number of people who'd given up their free time on a Tuesday night to come just made him feel like hiding out in his office.

He'd never told anyone when his birthday was for this exact reason. He didn't want a big deal made of it. Never celebrating a real birthday, he'd never known what he'd been missing. Moving foster homes frequently as a kid meant never having that traditional upbringing. No one cared about him enough to make sure he came home every day after school, let alone spend any money on throwing a party.

Besides, his friends back then weren't exactly the balloons and party-game type. Stealing cars and smoking up were more their speed.

He'd come a long way since then. Now he was surrounded by good, caring people he considered extended family. Looking around the bar, he recognized every face—he'd served them celebratory champagne and mourning shots of whiskey. He'd kicked some of them out for being underage and asked for ID from those that were old enough to be his grandmother.

He was lucky. And he hadn't needed a party to realize that.

Thirty-five.

Shit.

He'd accomplished a lot in his life so far, but each and every day of that thirty-five years had been a struggle, and celebrating it felt anticlimactic in a way.

"You're not exactly loving this, are you?" Cassie said, finding him hiding out near the back inventory room an hour into the party. He'd needed a breather from the crowd.

She looked so nervous, he wanted to reassure her, but fuck if he could find the right words. "It's a little overwhelming, that's all."

"I'm sorry… I just thought…"

Damn, he was an asshole. *Thank you*. He should have just said *thank you*. He wrapped an arm around her shoulders and pulled her closer. "It's great, Cass. Really. I appreciate all the work you did." He forced a smile and a lighter tone. "I have no idea how you managed to keep it a secret."

She relaxed a little. "It wasn't easy. Kaia was a fantastic help."

Tank glanced toward the bar, where Kaia was serving cake. "She didn't say a word… You two make quite a team."

Cassie's expression when she tilted her head to look up at him spoke volumes. They did make a good team. All of them. Together. He desperately wished he could let go and give in to what he knew Cassie wanted, what she deserved.

She'd done all of this for him.

She did so much for him. Without her help with Kaia over the years, he didn't know what he would have done. With no other family nearby, there were few people Tank could have trusted with his little girl. Cassie had saved his ass more times than he could count. And she asked for nothing in return. She never pressured him for more and he knew what that must be costing her.

Impulsively, he lowered his lips to her forehead. His intent was a quick, soft kiss like so many forehead kisses before it, but when she turned into him and reached up to capture the back of his head, his mouth was on hers before he realized what was happening.

Then there was no turning back. The first taste of her coconut-flavored lip balm and he was all in. Tightening his hold on her waist, he backed her up until they pressed against the stone wall in the dimly lit hallway in the back of the pub. He tilted his head to the side, and his mouth continued its hungry, desperate pursuit of satisfaction. Years of teasing, tempting touches, long, loaded silent stares and their shared fear of "what if" all came out in one long overdue, passionate kiss.

His tongue slowly traced her bottom lip, and the

soft moan that escaped her had him gripping her body tighter. His hands starting at her hips, moving upward over her waist and then higher over her ribs, had his body reacting in record time. How many times had he wanted to run his hands all over her like this? Forcing himself to be satisfied with long, body-to-body hugs, playful "wrestling" and fantasizing when he was alone.

Now it was all real. The feel of her body pressed against his and her mouth responding to his kiss with all of the energy and passion that was his best friend.

His best friend…and now instantly so much more…

Out of breath, she pulled back sharply, a look of surprise that must have mirrored his own in her gorgeous eyes.

"Happy birthday…" he murmured against her lips, pink and slightly swollen.

"It's your birthday, not mine," Cassie whispered.

"I was talking to me," he said, kissing her again as her mouth curled into a smile.

The back door of the bar down the hallway opened and he could see the silhouette of a woman as she entered.

Tank instinctively moved to stand in front of Cassie. "Hey, no one's allowed to enter the bar through that door…" Why was it even unlocked? Had Cassie not locked it after bringing in birthday party supplies that day?

"I know I locked that door," Cassie said behind him.

The woman didn't answer. Just the sound of her heeled boots echoed against the stone walls of the hallway as she approached, her face eventually illuminating in the neon lights.

It took a second to register… No fucking way. "Montana?"

Kaia's mother was standing right there in his bar.

CHAPTER FIVE

TEN YEARS DISAPPEARED like a shot of whiskey as Montana walked toward him, looking exactly the same as she had the first time he'd seen her. Tall, athletic with wide shoulders, she was a born athlete. Built for adventure and challenges. Short dark hair and midnight-blue eyes, high cheekbones and arched eyebrows, she belonged on every advertisement for extreme sports. The thing that surprised him most and drew him in was the shine of excitement in her expression. The same one that had always been there...except for those first few months after her accident, when she'd left the mountains.

Left him and Kaia.

"Hi, Theo," she said, stopping in front of him and Cassie.

Cassie's head snapped toward him, her jaw dropping at the use of his real name. Had he ever told anyone else? Had he ever told *Cassie*?

Nope, and that was one hundred percent going to bite him in the ass.

But there was a hell of a lot he hadn't told anyone, and now time had run out on his secrecy. With Montana's arrival, there would be a ton of questions flying his way, from all directions.

He wasn't sure which he was more terrified of—Cassie's or Kaia's.

His gaze landed on his daughter out in the bar and he was relieved that she was preoccupied, playing a game of darts with Reed, and hadn't noticed Montana walk in. Had she known her mother was coming to Wild River?

"Montana," he said again, unsure of exactly how long he'd just been standing there. He cleared his throat, remembering Cassie's arm around him...which was no longer there. He hadn't even felt her moving away. "This is Cassie Reynolds."

"Hi..." Cassie looked uncomfortable and slightly dejected.

Of course she did. He hadn't said *This is Cassie Reynolds, my girlfriend.* They weren't quite there yet, so how could he? They'd literally just had their first kiss. Real kiss, anyway. And she'd probably punch him in the face if he'd called her his *friend,* Cassie... Damn it!

"Nice to meet you," Montana said, looking around them into the bar.

"Um...why don't we go into the office and talk?" Tank said. He had to get her out of the hallway in case Kaia noticed. Already Reed and Erika were looking in their direction with curious stares.

"Good idea," Montana said.

Tank turned to Cassie. Her cheeks were still flushed, but the fire in her expression had definitely changed from lust-filled attraction to murderous. "Um..." He had no idea what to say. He could still taste her coconut lip balm, and while his hard-on had evaporated at the sight of his ex-girlfriend, his palms were still sweaty and his heart pounded in his chest. To be fair, a lot had happened in the last two-and-a-half minutes, so he wasn't sure which things were the cause of the physiological reactions.

"Go ahead. I'll hold down the fort." Cassie extended a hand.

He glanced at it awkwardly, shot a look at Montana, who was watching closely, then tentatively touched Cassie's palm.

She yanked back. "Keys. I'll need the register keys."

Jesus. He was a moron. "Right." He handed them to her and ran a hand through his hair. "Thank you. I won't be long." He had to say something. In truth, he expected this conversation to last for an eternity. Far too much to say and absolutely nothing he wanted to say, at the same time.

"Take your time," Cassie called after him as he led the way to the back office.

Montana's heeled boots kept time with his throbbing head. His birthday had been looking up; now it couldn't get worse.

He opened the office door and held it for her to enter first. He followed, then closed it behind them.

"The place looks great," she said, walking around the office. "I stopped by last night, but you were really busy behind the bar..."

So she hadn't timed her arrival perfectly to ruin his birthday. Good to know. But she'd been there the night before. She'd seen him...seen the bar... He felt even more at a disadvantage.

She scanned the photos on the wall. Him and the search and rescue team. Him and Cassie. Him and Kaia.

He folded his arms, then unfolded them and shoved his hands in his pockets. He didn't like her being in his personal space. Looking at photos of his life. Too familiar. Too unsettling having her standing there at all.

"Why are you here, Montana?" No sense shooting

the shit. If she'd shown up unannounced like this it was because she wanted to catch him off guard.

She'd succeeded.

"I want to be a part of Kaia's life again."

Shot delivered. A bullet to the chest couldn't have packed such a solid punch. He'd known it the moment he'd seen her walk in, but hearing the words made it all that much more real.

She was real. Standing in his office. Looking exactly as she had years ago. Wanting her daughter—their daughter—back. "I wish you'd called."

"I was going to. I tried. I decided this conversation needed to happen face-to-face." She unzipped her coat.

He resisted the urge to zip it back up and send her on her way. "I would have appreciated a heads-up."

"I do apologize for the shock. I just knew if I didn't come here, let you see for yourself, you wouldn't hear what I had to say."

"See what for myself?"

"That I'm better. Or getting better, at least."

"What do you mean?"

"The brain injury. Over the last three years, I've been working with a specialist in Denver. They were testing a few trial drugs and they've been working. My short-term memory loss is getting better. I'm able to remember things for longer periods now. I can retain the new memories after I go to sleep, which was a problem before. I'm not forgetting important things as often…"

"As often. But you still do." He had to grab on to that. She couldn't walk into his life and claim to be cured, if she still wasn't completely better. He'd taken that chance once. He wouldn't again. There was far too much at stake.

She paced in front of his desk, her words picking up steam along with her determined stride. "I'm not perfect. The memory loss is still an issue, yes, but it's become a lot less of one lately. My doctor says my brain scans are showing considerable improvement." She paused, "I'm really getting better, Theo."

"Tank."

"What?"

"My name. No one uses my real name around here.' No one had used his real name in years. He was named after his dad, and just hearing it jabbed at his heart. For a long time now, he'd been Tank.

"I always did."

He couldn't breathe. The soft intimacy in her voice stole his ability to inhale. How dare she walk in here after so long and act like she knew him. They didn't know each other anymore. They'd barely known one another back then.

Well, enough for him to tell her his real name.

"It's Tank now."

She nodded. "Right. Of course."

"Look, you can't just come here and claim to be miraculously better..."

"Hey! There was nothing miraculous about it. I've worked hard to get to this point. I've taken advantage of every holistic therapy and healing method I could get my hands on. I've subjected myself to every clinical trial I qualified for, sometimes taking drugs that had damaging effects on other parts of my body. I've read about my condition every day and researched anything I could to help myself heal." Hands on her hips, she wasn't backing down.

What had he expected? The Montana he remembered

was strong, stubborn and determined. When she wanted something, she got it.

His palms were really sweating now.

"I didn't mean to say that you haven't gone through a lot. I just meant that you have to understand what you showing up means for me...for Kaia... What it will do to our life."

"I know. And I'm not here to disrupt things."

"You crashed my birthday party."

"You hate your birthday. I never in a million years would have expected to walk in here to a party going on. Sorry for that, but come on... The Theo I knew..." She stopped. "You know what, it's been a long time. I shouldn't have made assumptions."

He stared at his boots. "You're right, though. This is not my idea of a good time. Cassie..."

"Your girlfriend?"

"It's complicated."

"Is that what your Facebook status says?" She grinned, but the note of jealousy in her voice stunned him momentarily.

"My life *is* complicated and Cassie and I are friends." Damn, he hated saying that. "Actually she's a lot more than a friend. She has been here for Kaia and me for a long time. She and I are close, but we are taking things slow."

Montana nodded. "You always put Kaia first. You're an amazing dad, Th...Tank. I never had to worry about that."

"So why, all of a sudden, the need to be in her life?"

Her nostrils actually flared and he took a quick step back.

"Are you shitting me? I'm her mother! I've *always* wanted to be in her life. Every single day, I've missed her and thought of her. You know that. I didn't walk away for me. I walked away when it was clear that I was a danger to her. We both know that. But I'm not a danger anymore."

Brain injuries like hers weren't just something that healed... Her accident had nearly killed her.

"That's why I came. To prove it to you."

"How?"

"I'm staying. Here in Wild River. I just rented a furnished apartment and I want to slowly integrate back into Kaia's life. I'm not asking for a lot at the beginning, just a chance to get to know her. A chance for her to know me." Her voice held a note of sadness, but the determination was still there. She wouldn't be deterred from this. She'd obviously given this whole thing a lot of thought if she already had a place here in town.

Yet nowhere in her planning had she called or texted or emailed him her plans.

"You're moving here? You show up, drop this bomb... You could have told me all of this. Allowed me to...adjust." He ran a hand over his face and chin. Too much to process.

"Maybe it's not you I'm concerned for. Maybe I'm thinking about Kaia and the fact that she might actually want her mother beyond cards and Skype chats. We've really been connecting these last few months and she seems open to that. And I'm thinking about me. For so long I wasn't able to have a relationship with her. Now I can." She leaned against the desk and folded her arms across her chest. She was in the driver's seat and she knew it.

And how was that fair? He'd been the one raising Kaia all this time and now Montana could simply waltz back into her life full-time? He wasn't stupid enough to think he could stop it and deep down, he knew that wouldn't be the right thing.

"What if she's not open to it? What if she doesn't want that? What if the Skype chats are enough—all she's comfortable with?" The distance and the computer screen between them had given Kaia a safety blanket in dealing with the emotional impact of having her mother in her life... This would be different. Full-on and complicated.

"I'll respect her wishes and her pace...but I think we both know she will want that." She paused, studying him. "I think that's the part that bothers you the most."

She headed toward the door when he didn't respond. "Look, I'm not in a rush for any of this. I've waited this long. I just wanted to let you know my intent. I'll text you my new address in town. Let this sink in...and we'll talk in a few days."

"I guess I don't really have a choice, do I?"

"No." She opened the door. "The place really does look great. So do you," she said, closing the door behind her.

What the hell was he supposed to do with that?

Tank collapsed onto his sofa and stared at the ceiling.

In thirty-five years of shitty birthdays, this one was the worst one ever.

CHAPTER SIX

IN THE LIGHT of day, it looked like a bomb had gone off inside the bar. Deflated balloons, drooping banners, confetti all over the floor, and empty paper plates with half-eaten cake needing to be cleaned up. But at least it gave Cassie an outlet for her anxious energy.

"His name is Theo. I had no idea." Cassie stabbed a balloon with her pocket knife.

The loud sound made Erika jump. "None of us did. Even Reed didn't know."

"I'd like to think…" *POP!* "That I might rank slightly higher…" *Pop!* "Than my brother when it comes to Tank's—oh, excuse me, *Theo's*—confidences." *Pop!*

"Okay, give me that," Erika said, taking the knife from her friend. "You are on banner duty."

"I like stabbing things," Cassie said.

"Clearly, and I get it and I appreciate that you're not stabbing Tank right now, but just try not to stress just yet. You haven't had a chance to talk to him… You don't know why Montana's here."

"I know exactly why she's here. She wants her family back." And damn if Cassie could compete with that. Compete with *her*. The woman looked like a fitness model. Perfect body, perfect hair, perfect bone structure. Next to Montana, Cassie looked like a child. Classic sophistication oozed from Tank's ex-girlfriend. Kaia's mom... Her thirty-second interaction with her had been intimidating.

Usually so self-assured and confident, Cassie hated these feelings of inadequacy she'd been battling for the last twelve hours. She'd left the party shortly after Tank had rejoined the event, looking devastated and confused. Maybe not the best hostess, but after the kiss they'd shared, followed by the intrusion that was Montana's arrival, Cassie hadn't been able to stay any longer. Keeping up a brave front had been impossible.

Thank God for Erika and Reed taking over and making sure guests had a good time while she'd crawled into bed with Diva, and lain awake all night.

Erika offered a sympathetic look. "What do you know about their situation? Reed says Tank barely talks about her. She left when Kaia was a baby?"

Cassie nodded. "All I know is pieced together from fragmented conversations with Tank. He never likes to talk about her or their situation. Getting Tank to open up about anything is a challenge." She looked around for more balloons to pop, but Erika had taken her knife away. She collapsed onto a stool and lifted her sunglasses up over her hair. Erika wouldn't judge her puffy eyes.

"I know they met on a rescue. She was an extreme BASE jumper from Colorado, here teaching a three-month course, and one of her trainees had an accident. Tank and the guys assisted on the rescue and he and Montana...hooked up." Damn, that was a hard thing to say about the man she was in love with.

"So, Kaia was the result of their fling?"

Cassie cringed. "Yes. No... I'm not sure. Tank makes

it sound that way, but I think he might have actually been in love with her."

"Might explain why he's reluctant to get into a new relationship."

Damn, why did Erika always make so much sense? "That would explain it." Tank hid behind his concern over Kaia and what a new relationship would do to them and their lifestyle…but maybe a part of him was concerned about what a real relationship, opening himself up, would do to him.

"Anyway, Montana broke things off and went back to Colorado but then found out she was pregnant. She came back and they tried to make a go of it but then she had an accident just after Kaia was born and she moved back to Denver again. That's it. I know she sends birthday and Christmas gifts to Kaia…and Tank mentioned that they've been chatting more lately." Cassie paused. "Do you think Kaia invited her mom to come here?"

Erika shook her head. "I'm sure Kaia would have told you if she did. You two are so close."

Tears gathered in Cassie's eyes and she desperately tried to blink them back. They were close. She was Kaia's main female role model. The two of them got along great and Kaia was everything to her.

What happened now that her mother was back? Would Kaia still need Cassie?

Cassie understood complicated relationships with parents. Her own father had disappeared from their lives when they were teens and his semiregular reappearances through invoices from a rehab clinic were the only real contact she had with him. But she was an adult now. She was able to deal with it, see it for what it was… Kaia was still a child.

One who would be thrilled to have her mother back.

Standing, Cassie tore the Happy Birthday banner down from above the bar and folded it. "I just don't know what to do. Should I question Tank about everything? Or just give him time and space to tell me when he's ready?"

"As your friend, I want to tell you to demand answers and get a commitment from him once and for all…but as Tank's friend too, I think we need to give him a break. For now. I can't imagine having his ex show up out of the blue is easy for him…"

"You're right and besides, forcing Tank to open up will only send him recoiling further." Cassie tucked the banner into a drawer behind the bar. "I thought we were so close to finally figuring things out." She wanted to tell Erika about the kiss, but how could she now? This conversation with her best friend should have been a juicy retelling of the best kiss of her life.

One that had left her breathless and hopeful…

One she'd probably never experience again.

That one moment had been incredible. The kiss had been so overdue, but had delivered on all levels. She'd felt the passion and commitment in Tank, even though he was reluctant to verbalize it. She'd sensed the deep connection only best friends acting on attraction could feel. Their bodies had melted into one, setting off metaphorical fireworks all around them. In that moment, everything had been perfect. Before it all went to shit.

Now she was just left with more questions. So many questions.

Where had Montana stayed the night before? Why was she in town? To win Tank's heart again or simply to reconnect with Kaia? And what the hell did it mean for all of them?

All of *them*. Not her. Right now, she could only assume she was lost somewhere on Tank's peripheral radar, and how could she fault him for that? His life had gotten completely upended in a matter of minutes… in the middle of a birthday party he hated.

The door to the bar opened and Tank entered. Both women stopped and turned to look at him. His exhausted expression made Cassie's heart ache for him… but she squared her shoulders and lowered her sunglasses back down over her eyes.

"I think I'll head out," Erika said, grabbing her coat and hurrying toward the door. "Cassie, I'll talk to you tomorrow." She paused next to Tank, giving his arm a quick, awkward hug/squeeze kind of thing. "Good luck."

He nodded. "Yeah, thanks for…everything."

Erika glanced at Cassie and offered an encouraging smile before leaving the bar.

An awkward silence fell over them once they were alone. Tank looked pained as his gaze locked with hers. Full of hurt and confusion and zero reassurance. The air in the bar was thick and stuffy. Uncertainty and awkwardness surrounded her.

Cassie grabbed the garbage bag they'd been filling with the old decorations. "Well, cleanup is done. I'll just bring this out back as I leave," she said, busying herself with tying the knot in the bag. Her hands refused to cooperate, the slight tremble made worse by her desperation to escape.

"You didn't have to do this. I was coming in to do it."

"It's fine. No problem. This was my dumb idea anyway." What the fuck was with this garbage bag?

Tank's hand on hers stopped the attempt. "Cassie…"

She glanced up at him. Waiting. Expecting.

He stared at her, his eyes begging her to understand what he couldn't verbalize.

As usual.

She wouldn't fall apart. He had far too much going on right now to deal with drama from her, as well. And she didn't trust herself to be strong enough to get through the unavoidable conversation they'd eventually have. A breakup before they'd even really gotten together.

"I don't know what to say."

That's it? That's all he had? "It's fine. I'll talk to you…sometime." She wasn't sure when they'd get a chance to talk. She was leaving that evening for the two-night couples' retreat with her company.

Perfect fucking timing on that.

How on earth was she going to survive being away now—not knowing what was going on with Tank and Montana and Kaia…and surrounded by couples trying to make their relationships stronger? She'd never been as tempted to cancel a booking last-minute, but unfortunately her company was depending on her.

She grabbed the bag and her coat and headed for the back door. Though getting out of town might be a good thing. Being out in the wilderness might help give her some clarity, some perspective, 'cause right now, she had none. Being away from Tank might help her come to terms with things. Being this close to him was torture.

"Cass, I…"

She stopped. *Say something. Anything. Give me something to hold on to.*

"Thank you for the party," he said.

Opening the back door, Cassie went outside and tossed the bag into the dumpster. Then she leaned her head against the brick exterior of the building and released a long sigh that held countless unrealized expectations.

"Shit."

HE'D MESSED THINGS up and he had no idea how to fix them.

Watching Cassie walk out of the bar had been hard, knowing she was hurt and upset and just as confused as he was, but he had to let her go. Nothing he could say that morning would be the right thing.

The kiss the night before had complicated the hell out of everything. It had been impulsive and in the moment. But it had also felt passionate and right. Kissing his best friend had both thrown him off balance and centered him. Would he have regretted it? Montana's arrival hadn't given him the opportunity to process it one way or another.

Obviously Cassie had felt things coming to a halt the second Montana interrupted their moment, as well.

Two women, each wanting something from him that he wasn't completely sure he was ready for, but that they each deserved, had him reeling. Cassie deserved a real relationship. Montana deserved one with her daughter. Both left him vulnerable and open to having his life turned upside down.

Going into his office, he grabbed his darts from his dartboard and backed up as far as the space allowed.

This bar was his safe place. He knew what he was doing here. He had control. These four walls represented the ones he'd put up around his heart for so many years.

What did he do now?

He threw the red darts, missing the bullseye by a mile.

Normally, he'd turn to Cassie for advice…but that was out of the question. The pained expression on her face that morning had broken him. But he had no idea what would happen next, and not having full control terrified him.

His life and circumstances had always been in someone else's hands. Strangers' hands. Twelve foster homes in sixteen years had him on unstable ground from the moment his parents died. Some were better than others, but they all shared one thing—they had no desire to become a forever home for him. He supposed he should be grateful that none of the places they put him had kept him much longer than a year. There were always other kids and teens coming and going and it was easy to get attached to the other orphans like himself, if he let himself get close. He never made that mistake with the foster parents though.

He knew better than to unpack his few belongings from the old, worn duffel bag he'd carried around. The entirety of his worldly possessions—mostly hand-me-downs from older kids, an old stuffed toy that he'd had since birth and a family photo of the three of them when he was a few days old. He'd been too young when his father died in the motorcycle crash to understand the significance of the tragedy and he'd still only been a toddler when, six months later, his mother took her own life. There had been no grandparents or relatives willing to step up to take him in, so he'd never really known where he came from. Being told about his parents' deaths from strangers as he grew old enough to ask questions was a soul-sucking experience in itself. None of these people had known his parents, and without any contact with extended family over the years, he'd never been able to get any of his questions answered.

Eventually he stopped asking or looking for family.

Being a child in the system was hard enough, but there were times he wasn't sure he would even survive his teen years growing up in poverty in Kotzebue. Trouble was never too far away and often it seemed like the best of the shitty choices he had laid out in front of him.

He threw the black darts and started to feel the stress seep from his tight shoulders.

Other people had meditation or yoga or vigorous exercise to relieve stress or let off steam... He had his dartboard.

The guys always shit on him about it, but it was his therapy. Always had been.

At seventeen, when he'd narrowly escaped a detention center, ditching his "friends" before they could destroy any chance he had at a future, but with nowhere else to go, he found himself living in a temporary youth center. With no money and no hope, and limited nights in the overcrowded facility, he'd discovered the anger management therapy of dart throwing.

He'd been shit at first. Zero aim. All anger. But days of whipping the sharp, pointy things at the dartboard in the center's game room had helped to ease the burning tension and anxiety that gnawed at him, and as a side benefit to the hours of practice, he'd eventually gotten better.

And then good.

Good enough that the youth center's guidance counselor, Mr. Marcus, noticed and invited him to join his weekly dart league.

Tank's distrust of adults and the oversized chip on his shoulder had him turning down the offer, but eventually the promise of a free meal at least once a week had him agreeing.

It was the best decision he'd ever made. The first one that set in motion a chain of events that changed his life for the better.

Reluctantly, he got to know the other men in the league. They were all middle-aged husbands and fathers, but they never treated him like a child—just another member of their team. No one lectured him or preached at him, the way he'd been expecting. Before long, he found himself couch surfing at their places, having dinner with their families… He was still so grateful for their kindness back then. Trust was slow in coming, but he appreciated them. Appreciated their food and shelter, but more than that, appreciated the connection to nice, decent people who weren't helping him for anything in return. He was desperate to repay their kindness, so he shoveled their driveways, mowed their lawns, helped out with minor construction projects, anything to feel like he was giving a little something back.

Six months into dart league, there was a tournament in Wild River. He couldn't afford to go, but Mr. Marcus sponsored him and smoothed the way for him to participate in the tournament, despite it being in a bar while he was still underage.

They'd won the tournament's ten-grand prize and for the first time in his life, Tank had cash in his pocket. He insisted on paying back every cent Mr. Marcus had given him, leaving him with little over a thousand dollars to live on, but instead of going back to Kotzebue with the team, he'd stayed in Wild River.

The ski resort town was small, but the opportunities there far outweighed any waiting for him back in his hometown with its higher crime rate and chances of falling back in with the wrong crowds. And the energetic vibe around town was something he'd never experienced before. It was where he wanted to be.

Every day for two weeks, he begged Mr. O'Neilly for a job at the bar that had hosted the dart tournament. He offered to clean after hours so he wasn't there during operation… He suggested he could go in early mornings to take inventory. Anything.

He finally wore the old man down and the bar became his first real job. With his dart tournament winnings, he bought a small tent, sleeping bag, water cooler and stove and he learned to survive any weather in the Wild River outback, showering at the community's rec center after a morning workout. His membership fee there was worth the cost for a place to get cleaned up and also meet some of the other guys around town.

Everyone knew he was too young to be on his own, but they also must have seen his strength and determination. He wasn't causing any trouble, so they left him alone to make his own way.

And he did. Wild River became his permanent home. He made great friends and connections within the community. And for eight years, things were going better than he could have ever expected. He saved enough for a down payment on a condo and lived modestly, but by his own means, his own hard work… Buying the bar from Mr. O'Neilly had given him confidence in his future. During those days, he often wondered if his parents would be proud of the way he'd turned out.

Then he realized the only pride he needed was the pride he felt for himself and what he'd been able to accomplish.

He'd made his way before. He'd made a life for himself when all odds were stacked against him. He had to believe he'd be okay now.

CHAPTER SEVEN

CASSIE COULD BARELY keep her eyes open as she parked her van in front of SnowTrek Tours three days later and climbed out.

Three days. Felt like a lifetime.

She went around to the back, opened the doors, and started unloading her camping gear as her newest guide, Mike, exited the store to help her.

His eyes watered and he wrinkled his nose. "Don't take this the wrong way, but you stink," he said, taking the sleeping bag from her.

"That's what three days in the woods will do to a person." The campsite shower facilities hadn't been operational. Something they'd conveniently forgotten to mention when Cassie had booked the site for the couples' therapy retreat.

Funnily enough, none of the couples had cared about the lack of hygiene options. Not enough to prevent them from having sex in their individual teepees the night before. Apparently, their unplugging to reconnect experiment had worked.

Unfortunately, Cassie had only been reminded of the sex she wasn't having. And the conversations she needed to have with Tank. Mike had texted to let her know that Tank had stopped by SnowTrek to see her and he'd let him know she was out with the retreat. Shortly after, she'd received Tank's customary stay safe out there, don't make me have to come save your ass text, which had both made her smile and broken her heart at the same time. Could they really just act normally around one another now? After the kiss that had changed everything? For her at least. She'd waited so long for that kiss. And it had delivered. Tank had to have felt the connection between them explode in the best possible way, as well.

Could they go back to being just friends while he figured everything out? Had he already figured things out with Montana while she'd been away?

Trying to stay focused on keeping a tour group alive when her mind and heart were back here in town, wondering what the hell was going on with Tank and his ex, was near impossible.

In her imagination she envisioned the worst case scenario—that the two had reconciled. Images of the two of them together had plagued her dreams for the last two nights, and combined with the noises from the teepees, sleep had been nonexistent.

Shutting the van door, she followed Mike inside.

"So, how was it?" he asked, carrying the sleeping bag into the back storage room.

"Horrible."

He frowned. "Really? Positive reviews are already starting to come in from the retreaters."

"I meant for me. The retreat was great for the couples. They certainly reconnected…"

Cassie had learned a lot too. More than she'd wanted to, really. The couples' therapist on the retreat had really put things into perspective. Cassie's lack of setting boundaries in her relationship with Tank hadn't done either of them any favors over the years. She'd set a precedent of always being there for him and he'd continued to be emotionally unavailable. They'd both accepted things the way they were, and changing the pattern now would be tough.

Or it would have been tough. Things had changed dramatically in the last forty-eight hours. Now, changing their friendship to something more might never happen at all.

Cassie yawned as she unpacked her backpack.

Mike stopped her. "Seriously, boss, you need to shower. I'll put all of this away."

"Okay…okay, I'm going," she said, leaving the storage room.

"And don't forget you have that private VIP event tonight at North Mountain Sports Company," he called after her.

Cassie groaned. "Damn! I forgot all about it. I'm exhausted. This is the last thing I want to do tonight."

"Go shower and take a nap. You'll feel much better," Mike said, pushing her toward the door.

Trudging upstairs to her apartment, Cassie unlocked the door and went inside. It was dark, quiet and empty. Reed and Erika were puppy-sitting Diva. Normally, Cassie would have left her with Tank and Kaia, but she hadn't been prepared to drop the dog off three days ago out of fear of seeing a family reunion that would have destroyed her. She still had no idea what Montana's intentions were, but the woman's connection with Tank had been arguably stronger than hers—they had a child together and had tried to make a relationship work…or at least that's how the pieces of the puzzle fell into place in her mind. If Montana was back in Wild River, Cassie was willing to bet there was a strong motivation for it.

She tossed her keys onto the kitchen counter and stared at the VIP event invite stuck to her fridge with a promotional magnet in the shape of skis.

She really wasn't in the headspace for this right now. Kissing Tank had been the first time in months that her thoughts hadn't been consumed by her company and North Mountain Sports Company. For a brief respite, things hadn't felt so uncertain. Now she was in danger of losing not only her company but her best friend, the man she loved, as well.

Going to this event would only make her feel worse. Taking the invite from the fridge, she tossed it into the trash.

Then retrieved it. She really should go.

But first a shower and a nap.

By six thirty, she'd talked herself in and out of going four times. Lying on her bed, one leg in a stocking, her head in hot rollers, she suddenly wished she was a coffee drinker.

A hot shower had helped alleviate the smell, but the nap had only made her groggier. Her eyes flitted closed…

The sound of her doorbell made her jump an undeterminable length of time later as her eyes flew open.

Shit, she'd fallen asleep.

Pulling off the pantyhose, she grabbed a robe and headed downstairs, opening the door a second later to find Tank.

He was dressed in a pair of tight-fitting jeans that hugged his thighs and a black crewneck sweater that displayed the toned chest and shoulders she'd been fantasizing about for two nights out in the wilderness, alone in a teepee. Normally, he'd be a sight for sore, exhausted eyes, but right now, with her conflicted state of heart, she hadn't been ready to see him. Not yet. Especially looking so freaking hot. Her mouth felt like sandpaper and her pulse raced. "Hi."

"Welcome back." His smile was slow…nervous.

"Um…thanks. What are you doing here?" *Have you talked to your ex since the party? Have the two of you reconciled? Have you told her anything about me?*

So many questions and she couldn't find the courage to ask any of them.

"I came to pick you up for the VIP party. Did you forget?"

Cassie sighed. "No. I've just decided to go and then not go so many times, I think I was just hoping I'd run out of time while trying to decide." She stepped back to let him in.

"Well, if you're not up for it, I can go and do recon for you…"

Did he sound relieved at the prospect of going alone?

Still nothing about Montana and anything that may or may not have happened in the last few days. He had to know she was aching for answers. She shook her head, sending one of the hot rollers across the room in the process. "No. I should go. I guess I just wasn't expecting…" *Him* to still be available that evening, *him* to still want to go. He had to have a million other things on his mind right now.

"You thought I'd bail on you?" he asked.

Well, yes, actually.

Tank picked up the hot roller and handed it to her. His fingers lingering on hers a fraction too long. Tingles shot up her arm and radiated through her body… His timing really sucked. She was completely vulnerable in that moment. Barely dressed, after nights of missing him and thinking about him, listening to other couples have sex in neighboring teepees, replaying their passionate kiss in her mind, and now he was standing there looking so incredibly hot with his hair gelled to one side, his beard trimmed just the way she loved it and smelling like cologne...which he never wore.

"You know I'd never do that," he said in her silence.

Why? Because he cared about her or because he'd feel guilty letting her down right now, when he was no doubt going to let her down about other things...more important things.

She pulled her hand back. "Make yourself comfortable. I'll be ready in ten minutes," she said, hurrying back upstairs, to safety. She took a deep breath and stared at her reflection in the mirror.

He was here. He hadn't forgotten. He hadn't stood her up. He wasn't avoiding her...for better or worse.

She yanked the rollers out and ran her fingers through the curls. She stuffed her legs into the pantyhose and pulled a simple yet classy black dress over her head. Two-inch heels and a red cardigan completed her outfit and she headed back downstairs.

"Wow, you look amazing," Tank said, turning at the sound of her footsteps on the stairs.

"I wear this exact same thing to every formal event I don't want to go to," she said with a tired laugh.

"And you look amazing each time. I should have told you that before." His expression was pained. His words suggesting it was already over between them. He cleared his throat. "Cassie..."

For the first time ever, she wasn't ready to talk, to know where his head and heart were, to know that once again she was nothing more than his best friend. "We should get going," she interrupted.

And as usual, Tank looked relieved to avoid the conversation. "After you," he said, opening the door for her.

NOT UNTIL HE was standing right beside her did it fully hit him how much he'd missed seeing Cassie the last few days. Holding himself back from a relationship with her over the years, he'd been successful in keeping his emotions in check, his feelings pushed way down, knowing he couldn't act on them. Now that he'd kissed her, his heart and mind had been in constant conflict since the party.

He always worried about her when she was out on adventure tours, but they usually texted constantly. This time had been different. Her brief reply of thanks to his usual text may as well have said fuck off and he couldn't blame her.

He'd almost lost his nerve on the drive to her condo that evening. He knew she was upset and she was waiting for answers, deserved answers…but right now he didn't have any, and being there with her, *for her*, that evening was as close as he could get to trying to make it up to her, to showing her that he was still here…no matter what happened with Montana.

He'd yet to talk to his ex. True to her word, Montana was giving him time and space to process, but he knew that reprieve was short-lived.

He parked his truck in the lot of North Mountain Sports Company and turned to Cassie. "Ready?"

"No, but let's go before I change my mind," she said, opening the door and climbing out.

Entering the main showroom of North Mountain Sports Company was definitely an experience. The three-story, open concept building boasted a six-thousand-square-foot sales floor, a room full of virtual reality experiences and a floor of sales and booking offices for their real outdoor adventures. Unlike most businesses in Wild River, this one screamed high-end, upscale luxury. Even the mannequins were the full body ones complete with heads featuring makeup or five o'clock stubble.

And Cassie looked devastated, taking it all in.

"It's actually not that great," he said.

"Nice try," she said, looking around at the expansive space that housed all of the top-end suppliers. "Look at those mannequins! Jesus—they look like real people."

"I think they're creepy."

"Compared to the headless ones?" Cassie shook her head. "How on earth am I supposed to compete with this?"

Unfortunately, he had no idea. Luckily, he knew she wasn't expecting an answer. He'd prefer her no-frills, no-nonsense company any day, but North Mountain Sports Company would be new and shiny and it cast a huge shadow.

"Hey…welcome! You're The Drunk Tank owner, right?" Mr. Hartwell said, approaching them with a tray of champagne.

Odd that he was serving at his own event. "Yes, hi again…"

The store owner/billionaire/server for the evening turned to Cassie. "And owner of SnowTrek Tours, Cassie Reynolds."

"Hello Mr. Hartwell." Cassie offered a polite smile. "This place is incredible."

"Please call me Miller." He nodded, scanning his store. "We're very proud of it. Have you taken a tour yet?"

"No, we just arrived."

"Perfect! Let me escort you two throughout the building."

Cassie's eyes widened. "Oh no, that's okay. You have so many guests here…"

It was true. There were a lot of familiar faces in the room. Even those originally opposed to the town allowing the big chain store to open. "Yeah, we can look around on our own," Tank said, sensing Cassie's intense unease. And now he was only partially to blame for it.

"Nonsense. Follow me," Miller said, setting the tray of champagne glasses on a nearby table. "Would you both like to grab some food first?" He gestured toward an hors d'oeuvres table on the right and a dessert table on the left.

"No, thank you. I'm good," Cassie said. She glanced at Tank, but he shook his head. An act of solidarity only—he was actually starving. Leftover birthday cake the morning after the party was the last thing he remembered eating in days, but they couldn't eat at the enemy's table.

"Okay, well, this is the main showroom. Our brands include all of the best-known names in sports, as well as some local designers…" He gestured to a section of the display room that consisted of all local products from hand-knitted hats and gloves to a line of skincare ointments Tank recognized from the apothecary shop on Main Street.

So the guy was living up to his promise of carrying these items and helping other business owners. Though Tank suspected it was all for show and once the items weren't top sellers—the markup he noticed on the price tags would send customers directly to the source—they would disappear from the shelves at North Mountain Sports Company.

Unfortunately, beside him, Cassie didn't seem to have the same train of thought. "I wish I had thought of that," she whispered as they moved along.

"In here, we have our virtual reality experiences." Miller handed them both a set of glasses as they entered the room filled with machines that simulated skiing, snowboarding, tobogganing. Nature backdrop scenes were set up so people could take photos of themselves to post to Instagram… They'd literally thought of everything.

Most of them were in use and everyone seemed to be enjoying them. He glanced at Cassie. He gave her credit for trying, but her expression revealed that she'd already mentally packed up her office and permanently closed up shop.

He couldn't let her get discouraged. "These are interesting, but we find most tourists prefer the actual outdoors." Tank placed his glasses back in the basket.

Miller laughed. "Most do—sure. We just like to be able to offer something for those who prefer something less cold, with less exertion…less risk," he said, staring pointedly at Cassie. "But you both are most definitely the outdoorsy type, so let's head upstairs to the offices…"

Did they have a choice? He wasn't one to be rude, but the minute they'd appeased Mr. Hartwell, he was getting Cassie out of here. She looked more defeated every second they were inside the building. He hated that his actions had hurt her a few days ago, and he planned to do everything in his power to make it up to her, but this stranger making her feel shitty wasn't acceptable.

They rode the escalator in silence and he quickly squeezed her hand…just a friendly gesture. But she surprised him by gripping his right back and holding on tight.

The gesture both gave him hope and terrified the shit out of him.

At the top, Mr. Hartwell gestured toward the long line of booking offices. "Each tour guide will have their own office, and we operate on a rotating system…"

"Aren't the guides better suited for one type of adventure or another?" Cassie's crew all boasted specialization in different areas, and she always sent out the best person for each adventure tour.

"We hire very versatile staff. Only the best make it through a rigorous selection and interview process," Mr. Hartwell said. "Follow me, there's just one more thing I'd like to show you."

His impressive corner office, no doubt.

Tank's prediction wasn't too far off. The owner of the store did stop outside a beautifully decorated corner office, but it wasn't his name on the nameplate beside the door. It was Cassie's.

He frowned, swinging around to look at her. Had she accepted a job from this guy without telling him?

Clearly, this was as much of a surprise to her. Her jaw nearly reached the floor and the hand holding his went slack.

"So, what do you think?" Mr. Hartwell asked. "Any chance I could convince you to come work for me?"

Cassie's jaw dropped. "Um…I'm sorry?"

"I'm offering you a job. Not just any job. Head of corporate tours and adventures…or director or whatever official title you'd like."

"She's already *owner* of SnowTrek Tours," Tank said, his protective instincts kicking in. Though he knew to stand down. Cass could handle this on her own.

"Yes, Tank's right. I'm quite comfortable with my

company, but thank you for the offer." Her voice wavered slightly, though.

Was she actually considering this?

"Cassie, look at this place. We will be able to offer tourists and locals so many opportunities on a much bigger scale. Your reputation in Wild River as the best tour guide for experience and safety makes you invaluable. You could name your salary."

Cassie's eyes widened. A tiny flicker of interest appeared in her expression. Hell, who wouldn't be tempted? The offer was incredibly enticing and when she was already faced with the possibility that her own company might struggle as a result of this store opening, Tank would understand completely if she said yes right now.

"That's very generous, but no. My company will be fine," Cassie said, a lot more strength in her voice this time. "We have our own plans for future growth even in your store's enormous shadow," she said as kindly as possible.

He knew he couldn't kiss her anymore, but damn he wanted to kiss her.

Mr. Hartwell shook his head. "You're ambitious, I'll give you that. But darlin', if your company hopes to stay in business with mine offering everything you do and more, be prepared for an uphill battle."

Cassie's confidence appeared to fade a little and Tank took his cue. "Sir, if you're planning for a long future here in Wild River, it's best if you understand something right from the beginning—life here is always uphill. And Cassie's been climbing it a lot longer than you have. If she says her company is not only going to survive, but *thrive*, despite North Mountain Sports Company, the insane thing would be to count her out." Turning to see her slightly flushed, appreciative expression, he said, "Seen all you needed to see?"

"Absolutely," Cassie said. "Good night, Mr. Hartwell."

Miller Hartwell nodded, looking slightly disappointed but not at all deterred. "Have a good evening."

They turned to leave, but Cassie stopped. "Just a sec," she told Tank.

Going back to the office, she slid the nameplate out of the holder. "You won't be needing this."

"Unfortunately not," Mr. Hartwell said as they walked away.

In his truck three minutes later, he turned to her. "Stealing the nameplate thing was epic." Damn, she was amazing. So many other people in her shoes would have considered selling her business months before or accepting the amazing job offer now…not Cassie. She was strong and ambitious and so sexy with her flushed expression.

She turned slightly in the seat to face him. "Thank you…for what you said in there," she said softly.

He reached across the seat and gently touched her cheek. "It was true. Mr. Hartwell doesn't have a clue what he's up against."

Her hesitant expression turned to one of determination when her gaze met his and his mouth went dry. "You're right," she said. "I never let go of the things that matter to me…not without a fight."

CHAPTER EIGHT

WATCHING HERSELF SOAR over the pond and crash into the pad on the other side would normally have her laughing, but that morning, the event felt like it happened months ago—a different lifetime. After uploading the video Reed had captured into her app on her computer, Cassie spliced the footage with shots from her GoPro and in minutes, the promotional video was on to her website and YouTube and all of SnowTrek Tours' social media sites.

She just hoped it helped.

Miller Hartwell's words played repeatedly through her mind. She was determined to fight for her business's future, but taking on his company was going to be tough. No other bookings had been made while she was on the retreat and the phones weren't ringing that day either. Her staff were on call, since there was nothing for them to do. But she knew she wouldn't keep them for long. It wasn't fair to expect them to stay loyal to her and SnowTrek Tours when she didn't have steady employment for them.

She hated the thought of losing her guides to North Mountain Sports Company, but she wouldn't fault any of them if they were spending their days off interviewing for positions with the other company.

She glanced at the name card on her desk. Miller

Hartwell had totally thought he could poach her from her own company.

Unbelievable. It would never happen. Never.

At least the leftover birthday cake was still delicious. She forked a huge chunk into her mouth, hoping the sugary icing and chocolate would help to make her feel better.

Reaching into her in-tray on her desk, she filed away several folders from the most recent tour groups, entered her payroll into her accounting system…then stared at the recent invoice from the Anchorage Addiction Treatment Center. Her father was back for his third attempt at their program to find sobriety and try to get his life on track. This time he was enrolled in a ninety-day stint. After two failed attempts at the thirty-day program, Cassie was happy that he'd just passed the eighty-day mark. He was really doing great this time.

She was his only outside contact and she happily paid the addiction treatment's invoices. After so many years of not having him in her life, she was hopeful that this might be a step toward bringing him home. Her mother and brother knew that he was getting help and while no one talked about it much, everyone was counting down the days on the calendar, same as she was. She'd been fifteen when he'd left for work and never come home. She'd known her dad had demons he was constantly battling and despite their parents' best attempts, she and Reed had felt the tension at home. Her father walking away, choosing alcohol over his family, had hit them all hard—Reed most of all. For years her brother hadn't believed their father had just walked away and he'd never given up searching for him…until the truth couldn't be denied when her father started seeking help.

Families could certainly be complicated. That was something she understood better than most people. As much as her situation with Tank frustrated her, she didn't envy what he must be going through now. Tank liked his life simple, nonmessy, uncomplicated…one of the main reasons he'd avoided a new relationship. But there was no avoiding this. The night before he'd been so supportive of her…she'd wanted to reassure him that things would be okay, but she wasn't sure what okay looked like.

Things were definitely going to change, but how?

The door chimed as Cassie finished paying the invoice online. "Welcome to SnowTrek Tours… Oh, hi." She ran a hand through her flyaway staticky hair and licked the corner of her lips free of cake as the woman she'd spent the last few days obsessing over walked in.

"Hi… Cassie, right?" Montana said, hovering near the still open door, as though unsure whether or not to enter. "I didn't know you worked here…"

Owned the place, actually.

Cassie was still too surprised to see her standing there to verbalize a response, so she nodded.

"I…um… Does this need to be weird?" Montana asked, obviously deciding it was too late to back out of whatever mission she was on. She let the door close behind her and walked toward Cassie's desk. "Me and you, I mean?"

"No!" Too much. Dial it back a little. "I mean, no, of course not. Why should it?" The woman was just the ex-girlfriend of the man she was in love with. No reason for this to be awkward in the slightest. She tossed the paper plate and plastic fork into the trash can under her desk and sat straighter. "What can I help you with?"

Please, please don't tell me to leave Tank and Kaia alone.

Why else would Tank's ex-girlfriend be there first thing in the morning?

Dressed in a body-hugging spring ski jacket and hiking boots, she looked a little less intimidating that day, but her dark hair, slicked back away from her stunning face, and the look of determination in her dark blue eyes—or were they gray?—suggested she was still a force to be reckoned with.

Was Cassie strong enough to take on Montana and win? Was she even still in the running? Had she ever been?

Maybe Tank's resistance to a relationship with her was partly because he'd expected this—Montana's return someday. Was hoping for it?

Damn, that made her chest hurt.

Just focus on why Montana is in your office. One thing at a time.

Montana sat and took a deep breath. "Actually, I was wondering about a job."

She was *staying*? "A job here in Wild River?"

"Yes. I guess Theo…sorry, Tank—calling him that is going to be hard to get used to—he didn't tell you I plan to stay in town for a while?"

So far, he'd told her absolutely nothing, but she wasn't ready to reveal that to Montana. "That's great."

"I can tell you don't really think so, and I get it. I know what it must look like…me leaving, being away so long, but I'm here hoping to have a relationship with Kaia."

That made sense. What mother wouldn't want a relationship with her daughter? It was normal. It was overdue. Cassie refused to judge. Obviously Montana had reasons for staying away. But was she just looking to rebuild a relationship with Kaia, or Tank too? The guy made every female tourist—married and single alike—drool. Montana had already had him. She knew how awesome he was. And if she was back in Wild River looking for family, Tank was family.

Cassie shifted uncomfortably, an image of Montana and Tank flashing in her mind. Obviously they'd had sex…because there was Kaia. But had it been more than that? Had they been in love? She preferred to believe it had been simply a physical attraction, but even that made her stomach drop.

Cassie had the friendship with Tank, the close intimacy of depending on each other and the deep trust that he reserved for few people, but she'd never gotten the physical intimacy she'd been craving. She'd been so close… That kiss had had her anticipating so much more. They'd finally crossed over the line and she'd been ready to go all in…

"Cassie?"

Shit. How long had she fallen down the rabbit hole of her own despair? "Oh sorry, um, I'm sure Kaia and Tank are happy you're here."

Montana's laugh sounded slightly nervous. "Well, Kaia doesn't know yet and *happy* is not the word I'd use to describe Tank's reaction to my showing up unannounced."

Why did that make Cassie feel just a little better? Knowing they hadn't picked up where they'd left off or fallen back into bed together was a relief. Though she should give Tank more credit than that—he respected Cassie enough to let her know if he was still in love with his ex and planned to play house before he went ahead and did it.

Did they have a gas leak in here? She felt dizzy. Hard to breathe.

"He was pissed, actually," Montana said when Cass was silent, trying to find air.

Again, a tad better. Although…pissed wasn't a mood Tank often displayed, so if Montana had spurred such an intense reaction from him, did that mean something? Man, overthinking was going to be the death of her. "I'm sure he was just…surprised." Who wouldn't be? Had Montana pictured the reunion differently?

Nope…she refused to fall into that rabbit hole.

"Yeah… Anyway, the reason I came by…"

"A job. Right. Have you checked out the community job posting board? It's outside the post office and it's updated regularly. Opportunities are scarce around here…but I'm sure there's something that could hold you over until you found something more suitable." Though Cassie had no idea what that even meant for Montana. She had zero knowledge about the skills the woman might possess, other than in the context of extreme sports.

"I was actually hoping to get a job here."

Cassie blinked. "Here? At SnowTrek Tours?" Man, she sounded like a moron. Of course that's what the other woman had meant when she'd walked in and specifically said she was looking for a job.

"I wasn't sure if you were hiring, but it doesn't even have to be a regular full-time position."

"My staff are all casual employees."

"That's okay. I can work with that."

"Well, we don't really offer excursions like the ones

you are trained for. We cater more to the average adventurer. We get a few extremists but mainly just tourists looking for some wildlife fun—hikes, camping, skiing, that kind of thing…" She hadn't spent the night googling Montana Banks for nothing. She'd learned the woman was an experienced BASE jumper from Tank, but what Tank had failed to mention was that she was a superstar within the tight-knit, closed group. With over a hundred skydiving jumps to her résumé, she'd completed the shortest free fall jump on record ten years ago, here in Wild River.

BASE jumping was illegal at almost all national parks and obviously in most US cities, but Wild River had been home to one of three US legal jump sites. Two deaths in recent years had the town shutting down the site on the peak of Canyon Ridge.

Montana nodded. "Right now that's all you offer, but what if you had a trained, expert BASE jumper on staff? You could look at offering those other experiences for the more extreme athlete."

"Oh, I don't know if we'd have enough business." Wild River locals prided themselves on their mountain ruggedness and love of the outdoors, but few of them would be eager to jump off the side of a mountain.

"I guarantee you would. There are currently one thousand and forty-eight BASE jumpers across the US with very few options for legal jumping. Most travel to other countries for an experience they could get here in Wild River. One they used to get here in Wild River. One email blast and you'd have hundreds here this year."

"But the jump site closed down." Thank God for the easy out. Not having to come up with her own excuses was good right now.

"We could apply to have a new one opened."

We. Wow. This had escalated fast. "I don't think so…" The woman was in town less than a week and she was already launching a far-reaching plan of attack?

"Just hear me out…"

Did she really have any other option? She sat back. "Okay, I'm listening."

"The Canyon Ridge site became dangerous because of erosion over time. The jumping platform had eroded to the point where jumpers really had to propel themselves off of the side and 'fly' away from the edge to avoid hitting the mountain further below."

Cassie winced. Montana seemed unfazed by her depiction of just how dangerous this sport was, as she continued, "And, the site was a challenging one at only a thousand feet. Only extremely skilled jumpers can pull off that short of a free fall."

Cassie nodded, knowing there was more.

"I've done my research and I've found a better, safer location just west of Chugach Mountain."

How had she discovered a new site without even being here?

"I'd love to show it to you so you can see for yourself."

Cassie hesitated. The idea was crazy. But hadn't she built her business by promising to offer adventures for all levels of athletes…what about the hard-core extremists? She currently offered nothing that appealed to them or reached that market.

Shut up, voice of reason, this is not happening.

"Unfortunately, I don't think I could afford the liability insurance."

"No need. BASE jumpers have their own and you'd ask for proof before they jumped."

Shit. Montana really came prepared.

"But if a site was legalized again, and that's a huge 'if,' and these athletes could jump on their own, why would they book with me?" What value could her company add to their experience?

"You'd provide transportation—getting to the site will require ATVs or at least a good day's hike."

So she could also add on hiking tours and fees.

"And you'll also provide a safety demo on site, lunch, equipment and gear..."

There was one problem. "Equipment and gear are expensive."

"Most jumpers have their own, but a few backup parachutes and wingsuits on hand would just help legitimize things, that's all. Most jumpers wouldn't trust their life on a rental unit that they haven't personally cared for and inspected anyway. It's all just about perception."

Cassie shook her head. As intriguing as the idea was, she liked her company's safety rating and reputation. BASE jumping was dangerous and she didn't want a death or serious injury on her hands.

Speaking of serious injury...

"Um, didn't you get really hurt doing this?"

"Yes."

"And you want to do it again?"

Montana shifted uncomfortably. "I haven't jumped in ten years. It used to be the only thing I lived for." She paused before continuing. "I did three months in jail when I was nineteen..."

"For jumping off of a building in downtown Denver." Embarrassed, Cassie shrugged. "I may have googled you."

Montana nodded. "That stunt was a dumb mistake. I'm older now and I realize illegal jumping is not the way to go. The truth is, I just need to start getting my life back. One piece at a time and other things might be out of my control, but this is something I can control."

Other things like a relationship with Tank and Kaia. "I understand that, I do. But I'm not sure SnowTrek Tours is ready to do something like this."

"It's a crazy idea, I know. It's extreme and out of the comfort zone, I get it."

Cassie heard a "but" coming.

"But, I know you must be worried about North Mountain Sports Company opening up soon. I can promise you, they wouldn't be offering this, but they will be offering everything else you do."

Way to play on her insecurities.

"This would give you that edge I know you must be looking for."

Cassie bit her lip. Montana was right. North Mountain Sports Company would be offering everything her company did, with bigger numbers, name-brand recognition to draw in customers. Steal hers away. She had been looking for something different, unique...

But this was really different and unique. Maybe too much so.

And the bigger issue was, could she really hire Montana? The woman who had already complicated things further for her and Tank? Someone who could very well take Tank and Kaia away from her? What would Tank say if she hired his ex?

Cassie hesitated. "The idea is really tempting…"

"But this is awkward. I get it. Like I said, I didn't know that you were the owner here, but it's only awkward if we make it that way. I know you and Tank are... friends and you're loyal to him, but I promise you, Cassie, I'm not here to mess up Tank's life. I'm really not."

But she was—whether it was her intention or not, Montana's arrival had Tank in a tailspin. Cassie hadn't spoken to him about everything yet, but she knew the man she loved and his expression at just the sight of Montana had revealed he was conflicted. Over which things, Cassie wasn't sure.

What if Montana could have it all again—Tank, Kaia and a career doing something she loved?

Could Cassie help give her all of that when it would come at such a loss for herself?

"Can I think about it?" Montana was suggesting a solution she'd been looking for, and she may not have any control over what happened between her and Tank, but she could continue to focus on saving her company.

"Absolutely. Take your time and just let me know," Montana said, heading toward the door. "Thanks, Cassie." She paused. "According to Tank, I already have a lot to thank you for." She smiled and closed the door behind her.

Cassie stared after her, but all she saw was the dark plastic wrapping on the exterior of the big box store chain across the street, their Opening Soon sign making her seriously contemplate the dumbest idea ever.

"WE NEED THE litter brought around to the west side of the peak... Tank? You there?" He heard Reed's voice over the radio, but all his attention was focused on the text message he'd just received from Montana.

I'd like to see Kaia. Think about it.

Oh, he had been. In fact, he'd thought of little else for three days. Every time he tried to summon the courage to break the news to his little girl, he chickened out. He wasn't sure what to say. The mother you've barely known over the years is suddenly back in town, wanting a relationship?

What would his daughter say? How would she feel?

So far, he'd succeeded in not finding out. What if Kaia was upset? What if it was too much, too fast? Alternatively, what if his ex was right when she said he was afraid of other outcomes, as well?

Afraid was an understatement. He'd never had to share his daughter's time, love or attention with another parent or guardian. No one else had weighed in on important decisions like whether or not to vaccinate—of course he did—or where she attended school or the restrictions on screen time. House rules, bedtimes, extracurricular activities, appropriate behaviors... It had all been on him. He'd figured it out. Now someone else wanted input on all of that? What if they disagreed on how to raise Kaia? Disagreed on when she could date, future curfews, whether or not she should be allowed to pierce any part of her body...

Tank shuddered, staring at the text.

Things had been simple. Not easy, but simple.

Now they were a complicated mess.

"Tank? You coming with that litter?" Reed asked, sounding impatient. "Tyler...what's going on?"

Tyler reached for the litter. "You still with us, man? You look like you've seen a ghost."

Nope, just received his first text message from one.

"I'm fine." Tank put the phone away and helped drag the litter toward the west of the peak, where the search and rescue crew had located a missing hiker, just a few hours after he'd been reported missing by his friends. The well-worn hiking trail was an easy in and out. And the weather that day was mild and dry. An easy excursion. Unfortunately, the guy had been smoking pot and had had a little too much to drink from his water cooler containing straight vodka before wandering off the trail to take a leak without reappearing.

His friends had explained he'd been going through a breakup and they were worried about him. Tank could empathize about the woman issues. Several times over the last few days, he'd wanted to run away into the woods too.

"We're coming…" he radioed back.

"Seriously, you okay?" Tyler asked, matching his steps. "I heard about Montana."

Everyone on the crew must have by now. "Honestly, I'm a shit show…but I'll be fine."

"Okay, well, if you need someone to throw darts with…"

Tank nodded. His team knew him well. Unfortunately, throwing darts wouldn't make this issue disappear. He couldn't ignore it and hoped it (Montana) just went away. He had to face this…and answering her text was the first step. Later. "I'll let you know."

Arriving at the site where the other three crew members were waiting, he placed the litter next to the intoxicated, stoned hiker. "Any injuries we need to be careful of?" he was asking Reed, but the hiker answered.

"Does a broken heart count?"

"Absolutely," Reed answered. Then to Tank, "He's fine…physically."

Tank nodded as he helped Reed lift the man onto the litter. It would take forever to get him out of there if they allowed him to walk. They said vodka had no smell, so clearly it wasn't the man's first or only poison that day. And his bloodshot eyes and the scent of weed lingering on his hair and clothes confirmed what the friends had said about the drugs.

Even though he was uninjured, the best plan was to bring him back to the station to make sure there was nothing else in his system, then let him sleep this off.

"She was everything to me...the sun, the moon... the sun," the guy rambled as they covered him with a blanket.

Tank shot a look at Reed.

Reed shrugged. "She was the sun."

"Apparently," Tank mumbled. He readjusted his gear as he and Reed lifted the litter and they hiked the three miles back to town.

"Is he okay?" the guy's friend asked as they carried him into the station and set him on the cot in the corner an hour later.

"He's fine. Just needs to sleep this off. No more drinking and hiking, okay?" Reed said to the group. "And while it's legal, pot can seriously mess with your awareness, so that's not the best idea either...unless you've set up camp and plan to stay overnight."

Tank let Reed give the lecture, slipping outside to wash their search and rescue vans. He needed to keep his hands busy so he had an excuse not to respond to the text.

How long could he put this off?

Reed joined him outside a few minutes later, pushing up the sleeves of his search and rescue sweatshirt and filling a bucket of water. "Other than the obvious, what's up with you?"

Tank retrieved his phone and showed Reed the text.

"Shit. Already? She's only been here a few days." He glared at the phone as though personally offended and it made Tank feel a little better. He really wasn't alone in this. Thank God for his buddy.

"It's too soon, right? I mean I've barely spoken to her." What happened to not wanting to rush things? This was supposed to be at his pace. Kaia's pace.

"Yes, of course." Reed paused, still staring at the message. "I mean, I don't know... Does Kaia want to see her? Finally meet her face-to-face? Your feelings aside, I think that should be the consideration here."

Tank tucked the phone into his back pocket and sprayed the van at full blast. "I haven't told her yet." His voice was barely audible above the water.

"Tank, man, avoidance can only go so far." Reed bent and soaped up a sponge, attacking the van doors.

"Do you want to tell Kaia?"

"Hell, no. But she needs to know. Deserves to know."

Of course Reed could be biased in his opinion. His own father disappearing when he was a teen might be clouding his friend's judgment, but unfortunately, Reed was right.

Countless variations of responses in his mind and two sparkling clean vans later, he climbed into his truck and sat staring at the message.

There was really only one way to answer that made any sense.

Okay. How do you suggest we do this?

If Montana was going to be in Kaia's life, she could start helping him make the tough decisions. Starting with this one.

A GOOD RUN with Diva usually helped to clear her mind and help her refocus. But that day, it had only made Cassie more anxious. North Mountain Sports Company had doubled their efforts in promoting their grand opening. Flyers were posted all over town, even in the storefront windows of local companies whose owners had petitioned against the store opening in the first place.

Can't beat them, join them, I guess.

But Cassie wouldn't. No matter how bad things got, she refused to work for the big chain store. Closing her business, selling her condo and moving back in with her mother in Willow Lake wasn't the worst thing, was it?

She slowed her pace as her storefront came into view on Main Street. Diva's excited bark and tail wag revealed the dog had noticed Tank sitting on the bottom step leading to her condo just as she did.

Great. Perfect timing. She hadn't showered yet and she was sweaty and no doubt looked like shit. He stood and waved nervously as she approached.

Diva ran straight for him and Tank bent to pet the dog affectionately.

Would Tank ever be that excited to see her?

Right now, he looked scared.

"Hey…what are you doing here?" she asked, fighting to catch her breath.

"Needed to talk and I was hoping…"

That she was available. Of course. What else was new? "Come on up," she said, climbing the stairs to her condo. She unlocked the door and he followed her inside.

Then started silently pacing her living room.

What should she say? Should she ask about Montana? Tell him his ex had come to see her and pitched a crazy idea? Did he know about that already? Was that why he was here? She cleared her throat. "So...how are you?" Translation: *How are we? Have you thought at all about the kiss or have you been preoccupied with thoughts of your ex? Are we still moving forward or are the brakes on temporarily...or permanently?*

He looked exhausted as he ran a hand over his beard. "I don't know."

Seemed to be the answer she was expecting to all her unvoiced questions. She nodded. But although she'd love to not know, she had to ask, "Have you spoken to Montana since the other night?" *Have you hugged her? Touched her? Kissed her? Planned to get back together?*

"Only through texts."

Cassie released a sigh of relief, then tried to hide it behind a cough.

"She's asking to meet Kaia."

"Already?"

"It's too soon, right?" He searched her expression for validation for his feelings and she would have liked to give him some, but...

A meeting was ten years overdue, more likely. "Maybe not. I mean, she's been here a few days. Wild River is a small town. The last thing you want is for Kaia to run into her when you're not around. That would be much harder." Kaia seeing her mom unexpectedly could be traumatic for her...or impactful in some negative way, and she'd definitely be upset that Tank hadn't told her.

Tank nodded. "I know she will be upset if I don't tell

her about Montana and she finds out that her mom's been here for a while."

"Exactly. You can't keep them apart forever," she said softly. And he was a good man, so she knew he'd never want to. Montana not being in Kaia's life was never his fault or intention. Sure, over the years, it had become the norm and changing that now would be difficult, but deep down, he had to know this would ultimately benefit Kaia.

Tank's shoulders fell. "Yeah, you're right. You usually are."

Not that he always listened. Particularly when it came to how fantastic the two of them could be together.

He must have read where her thoughts had wandered. "And I just wanted to say, I really am sorry about the other night…the kiss and Montana."

Not just Montana…but the kiss too. So he was regretting it. That hurt, but she'd learned to keep a protective layer when dealing with Tank and any kind of emotion. Her self-preservation was second to none. She squared her shoulders as she dismissed the conversation. "Hey, who's watching the bar right now?"

He sighed. Either annoyed that she'd skirted the issue or relieved; she'd put money on the latter. "No one. I expect all of my top shelf liquor will be gone by the time I get back."

His attempt at a joke spoke volumes about where they were, so, as usual, she played along. It was really the only thing she could do. "Then you better go before they take the cheap stuff too."

CHAPTER NINE

So THEY WERE really doing this. Montana's response had luckily echoed how he felt about this first meeting. They both agreed the best option was to tell Kaia face-to-face. Together. In a safe space—her home. That way, everything was on her turf. A public place seemed too inappropriate for what was sure to be an emotional event, one way or another... This was the right thing.

Damn, he hoped.

"Alexa, lights on," Tank said as the sun dipped lower in the sky and the house darkened. Too bright? "Alexa, dim the lights." Too much of a weird ambience? "Alexa, more light."

He had ten minutes before Montana's arrival and clearly he was losing his mind.

"Alexa, lights off." He opened all the living room curtains instead.

Going into the hallway, he opened the linen closet and retrieved a set of throw cushions Cassie's mother had made him and added them to the sofa. Throw cushions were homey, right?

Going into the hall bathroom, he quickly scanned the sink and toilet to make sure everything was spotless. Even the toothbrush holder had been scrubbed and he'd replaced the shower curtain and bath mat earlier that day. He sniffed, then he blew the dust off of a cinnamon-scented candle and lit it.

The timer on the oven chimed and he hurried to the kitchen to retrieve the batch of brownies he'd made. Just a single dad baking brownies in the middle of the afternoon. That was normal, right?

If things went well, they'd have a snack to enjoy… And if things went sideways, Kaia would have enough chocolate to stuff her face with.

God, he hoped things went well. Though he wasn't certain what constituted "well."

Placing the brownies on the stove, he scanned the kitchen.

Everything was neat. Counters weren't cluttered. Dishes were all put away in the dishwasher…the hard-wood floors gleamed.

Man, what was he so stressed about?

It was just Montana coming over. Not child services. But damn, he felt like he was going to be under close inspection. Why did he feel the need to prove himself? According to Kaia, he was a great dad. He tried his best. Their home wasn't a million-dollar mansion, but it was safe and comfortable. He provided everything Kaia needed…

The doorbell rang exactly nine minutes later and his pep talk to himself went to hell as he quickly surveyed the house again. "No turning back," he muttered as he went to the front door.

"Hi," Montana said. "Thanks for inviting me over."

Did he really have a choice? After his quick chat with Cassie earlier that day, he knew the best thing to do was get this introductory meeting out of the way as quickly and hopefully as painlessly as possible. Then they could all move forward. Whatever way that was.

Seeing Cassie that day and still not having any answers for her had been torture. He'd seen the questions she refused to ask and he'd cowardly taken the break she'd given him. Truth was, he had no answers right now, but as soon as he had any clarity, she'd be the first one he owed them to.

"Come in," Tank said, moving away from the door to let Montana enter. "Kaia should be home in a few minutes. The school bus usually arrives between three twelve and three fifteen. I always offer to pick her up from school, but she likes the socialization aspect of taking the bus with her friends..." Why was he explaining himself?

"Yeah, that totally makes sense. And I'm sure it's an independence thing," Montana said.

Great. So she got it. Maybe a little too well. He'd assumed she knew absolutely nothing about kids and parenting... Had been hoping, maybe.

She scanned the interior of the house. "Great place."

"Thank you. Coffee? Tea? Whiskey?"

She laughed, the sound immediately bringing him back to when they first met. Her vibrancy, her passion and energy had been what had attracted him most. The same qualities that attracted him now to Cassie. No one could say he didn't have a type. Someone who was his complete opposite, someone who made him enjoy life just by surrounding him with that energy.

He'd never had anyone in his life like that growing up, so he seemed addicted to it now. For better or worse.

"I'm okay for now, but maybe keep the whiskey close by," she said.

"You got it."

Removing her hat and winter coat, she hesitated… "What should I do with this?"

"I'll take it," he said, hanging it in the closet near the door. "Make yourself at home. Living room is to the right."

He followed her into it and stood awkwardly, checking the time. Just twelve more minutes. Montana sat on the couch, then stood again, wiping her palms against the legs of her jeans.

At least he wasn't the only one sweating. And the combination of smells— cinnamon from the bathroom candle and chocolate from the brownies and Pine-Sol from all his cleaning was making him slightly nauseous.

Maybe he'd overdone it a little.

Montana approached the wall and scanned the variety of framed pictures. Kaia's school pictures from each grade lined one wall. "Thank you for sending me copies of these, by the way. I looked forward to seeing how much she'd grown from year to year."

"Yeah. Of course." He'd sent the photos along with a copy of her school report card. Other than Christmas cards and birthday gifts every year, it was really the only contact between them until recently. Montana had claimed that too much contact was difficult for her, and he'd agreed that maybe the minimal communications helped to keep things simple.

But that had changed in recent months and now, Tank wasn't so sure they'd made the right call. Montana was a huge mystery to Kaia…so that could backfire now in a dozen different ways.

She studied the pictures of Kaia with Diva from the winter before. It was a promotional shoot for Cassie's company and the photographer had taken some breathtaking shots of his daughter and the puppy playing in the snow with the mountains in the background. Kaia's dark hair against her red snowsuit and the radiant look of happiness on her face made the pictures his favorite.

"These are beautiful. Do you have a dog?" She glanced around.

"No. That's Diva. Cassie's dog." In his latest crisis, he'd forgotten about his other dilemma with the dog. "Kaia's very attached."

"Right…" Montana's gaze fell to the set of photos with Cassie in them. Hiking in Canyon Ridge, Halloween when they all dressed as characters from *Guardians of the Galaxy*, Cassie's birthday dinner at Meat & More Steakhouse a few months before, New Year's Eve at The Drunk Tank, skiing, hiking trips, camping… Shit, there were a lot of photos. Maybe he should have taken some of them down…

No. This was his house. If Montana was uncomfortable seeing the life she was missing out on, that wasn't on him. And Cassie was a big part of their lives.

Montana turned to look at him. "Maybe we shouldn't be doing this here. I mean, she might feel like I'm invading her space. Maybe a restaurant or a park…"

Tank glanced at his watch at the sound of school bus brakes outside. "Too late. This is it." His heart pounded as he glanced out the window and saw her getting off the bus a block away. Coat open, flapping in the wind, her scarf dragging on the ground, she lugged a heavy-looking backpack over one shoulder. "So, she might be upset, angry, confused at first… I mean, until recently, there's been little contact…"

"I know." She sounded slightly defensive, but then her tone softened. "I'm prepared for that."

At least someone was.

"We haven't given her a heads-up. She's probably going to be shocked." He certainly had been. "She might just go into her room and refuse to come out." She'd been spending a lot more time in her room lately and Tank had no idea how to deal with her suddenly constantly changing moods. She was ten. He'd wrongfully assumed he'd have another couple of years before the moody teenage years.

He'd been wondering how Kaia and he would get through those years without a mother to teach her woman stuff. But he'd told himself they would make it through as they had every other stage. He'd been nervous when she'd been a baby. He was so big and she was so little, he was afraid of holding her too tight or crushing her whenever she'd fall asleep in his bed. School had terrified him—he had no fashion sense and no idea what a little girl would like as far as clothes and hair stuff. She preferred her plaid shirts and jeans to dresses and skirts and she liked the outdoors and being active. They were a lot alike and Tank had been grateful for that.

Would she change now with her mom here, influencing her?

One thing at a time.

The sound of the door opening had him taking a deep breath. Tension in his shoulders had him aching worse than if he was on hour twenty of a rescue mission.

Concern for his daughter and how she was going to react had him in knots.

"Dad, do you want me to check the mail?" she called out.

He heard her backpack being tossed into the closet. "No, I did that already. Um…come on into the living room. We have a…guest."

"Are Cassie and Diva here?" she asked, excitement in her voice.

Tank caught the look of nervous disappointment in Montana's expression.

"Nope, someone else who wants to see you," Tank said as his daughter appeared in the living room.

She stopped, her tiny face revealing nothing as she stared at Montana.

Silence was ear-shattering. Was Montana even breathing? Was he?

No one spoke. No one moved.

Guess he better say something. "Kaia, your mom decided to come for a visit…" He still wasn't sure how long she planned to stay. She said she was here to make a life in Wild River, but he wasn't sure how he felt about that yet and he wasn't prepared to fully accept the news. And if she changed her mind, he didn't want to disappoint Kaia.

Montana wiped the palms of her hands against the legs of her jeans again and cleared her throat. "Hi, Kaia." Caution, hesitancy in her voice.

Kaia continued to stare.

"I'm sorry to surprise you like this. I probably should have called first or told you last week during our Skype chat." Montana looked uncomfortable as the silence continued from the little girl.

Tank held a breath, waiting for his daughter to say something. Get angry, get upset, run to her bedroom. Her silence and expressionless face were so much worse. What was going on in there?

Did he say something?

"I missed you so much," Montana said, barely above a whisper, but the words seemed to echo off the walls around them and wake Kaia from her trance.

She ran across the living room and wrapped her arms around Montana's waist, and Montana's sharp inhale was in sync with his own.

"I missed you too," Kaia whispered against Montana's stomach. "I'm so glad you're here."

Montana's arms went around Kaia and Tank looked away, the emotions suddenly choking him a complete surprise. His chest was tight, his stomach twisted in a knot and his palms were sweating.

This was a good thing. Kaia was happy to see her mom. There was no crying or anger. This reunion had gone a lot better than he'd expected.

So, why was there an empty, hollow feeling in his core?

CASSIE OPENED THE front door of her family home, and caught the handle in her gut as she came up short. The door was blocked. "Mom!" she called through the opening. "Let me in, it's pouring!" Sudden, unforecasted rain came down in sheets around her and she pushed harder on the door. Just running from the truck, she was drenched. "Mom!"

"Coming... I'm coming...hang on," Arlene said. She struggled to slide several boxes away from the front door to allow Cassie to enter.

She shivered and shook rain from her hair as she surveyed the stack of cardboard boxes that extended all the way down the hallway. "What's all this?" Cassie removed her wet jacket and hung it near the door on the hook labeled with her name. A home-economics project of Reed's from seventh grade. It even had their dad's name on it...

Arlene took a second to catch her breath. "Some old

things of yours and Reed's. Finally getting around to cleaning out the attic… You know, I've been reading a lot about decluttering lately," she said, picking up a book from a table near the door. "You should read this."

"I'm typically not a hoarder." Her open concept apartment left little room for clutter. And she had little storage space in her loft-style condo above SnowTrek Tours. Nowhere to put all of these boxes labeled with her name.

"I'll help you carry these to your truck." Her mother put on her rain boots and grabbed her raincoat from a hook near the door.

"It's a torrential downpour out there," Cassie said.

"Ah…it's just a little rain. When you were a kid, you would go outside in this weather all the time."

"Well, I'm not a kid anymore and I'm freezing."

Arlene zipped her coat and raised the hood. "Fine. You stay in and warm up. I'll put these in the back and drape a tarp down over them."

"Mom, wait. What am I going to do with all of this?" Wasn't the old family home the place grown-ass kids were allowed to store their junk? Didn't her mother love reminiscing about their childhoods and having all of their awards and old school stuff close at hand to go through when she was feeling nostalgic? Wasn't that what parents did?

"What would you like me to keep doing with it?"

Cassie sighed. "Point taken, but I thought you invited me over for dinner…" She sniffed, but there were no delicious smells coming from the kitchen.

"I already ate," Arlene said, picking up one of the boxes. "If you decide to help, lift with your legs. Those are heavy—yearbooks, I think."

"Mom! I'm starving." And even if she wasn't hungry,

she was ready to stress-eat her face off. She'd purposely chosen that night to take her mom up on her dinner offer because tonight was the night Tank was introducing Kaia to Montana and Cassie was far too stressed to stay in Wild River. Not that driving to Willow Lake, distracted by the knowledge that right at that moment Kaia was meeting her mom for the first time, was a great idea. Between the rain making the roads slick and her distracted mind, she'd been a hazard on the highway.

"So was I after carrying all of these boxes down from the attic," her mother said, kicking the door open and heading outside.

Unbelievable.

Cassie put her coat back on and put her own hood up, tying it tight. Picking up the lightest-looking box, she followed her mother outside to her truck. Struggling to balance it against the back, she unhooked the tailgate and placed the box down. "So…a book on decluttering spurred this sudden purge of our family history?"

"It encouraged me to reexamine why I was holding on to some of these things and ask whether or not they sparked 'joy' in my life."

Oh good grief.

Arlene headed back inside for more boxes and five minutes later, they were soaking wet, but Cassie's truck was loaded.

"Want to take Reed's things too?" her mother asked.

"Nope. I want the food I was promised," Cassie said, heading into the kitchen. Seeing a bunch of old photos of the interior of their house, she frowned. "What are these pictures for?"

Her mother hesitated. "Oh, I was just thinking about

placing the house on the market… It's much too big for one person."

Her mother was thinking of selling? What the hell? How many times over the years had she and Reed suggested her mother sell and move into a condo with less maintenance? And how many times had their mother claimed that she would die in this house? "You love this house."

"It's just four walls and a roof, Cass. Home is where the heart is."

"Read that in a book too?"

"Actually, that little nugget of wisdom is courtesy of a Hallmark movie. Tea?"

"Yes, please… So, you're moving closer to us? To Wild River?"

"I haven't decided yet." She poured two mugs of tea, then opened the fridge and removed a stack of Tupperware containers. "I've got leftover spaghetti or chicken fettucine."

Cassie carried the tea to the table and sat. She looked around. A lot of clutter was missing. Her mother's kitchen counters were usually full of cooking appliances, but only a coffee maker and a food processor remained. In fact, the kitchen was practically empty. "Where is the side table?" For as long as Cassie could remember, the side table had sat along the wall under the window, holding all of her mother's fancy dishes and an impressive-yet-tacky collection of salt-and-pepper shakers that her regulars at the pub had given her over the years, whenever they traveled or found a unique set at a flea market… The collection had made birthday and Christmas gift ideas for their mom easy.

"I got rid of it. Don't worry, I donated it all to charity."

"Even the salt-and-pepper shakers?"

"Darling, I hated those things. Someone gave me a set from Spain once and somehow it circulated that I enjoyed collecting them. I didn't have the heart to say anything..." She gestured to the Tupperware containers. "Which one should I heat up for you?"

She didn't like the salt-and-pepper shakers—who knew? Her mother was obviously the master of fake excitement. Even if that was true, Cassie still suspected something was up. "Mom, is everything okay? Do you need money?" She'd attempted to pay her mom back for the business loan countless times over the years, but her mother refused to cash the checks she gave her.

Arlene laughed. "Of course not. Sweetheart, I'm just thinking about the future and what makes the most sense."

Cassie nodded reluctantly, feeling as though there was a lot more to this decluttering than getting rid of junk.

"Now, what do you want to eat?"

Cassie sighed. "The spaghetti, please."

"Great." Her mother put it in the microwave, then turned to her. "So, I hear Tank's ex is back in town."

"You spoke to Reed?"

Her mom nodded. "He called yesterday. I asked how you were and he mentioned it... Why is she back?"

"To have a relationship with Kaia."

Her mother scoffed.

"What?"

"That's a load of shit, that's what that is. Kaia is ten years old. Montana has shown no interest until now." She shook her head.

"She sent birthday and Christmas gifts and called sometimes. Apparently, in recent months, they've been Skyping."

"Skyping...right, 'cause that's the same as parenting."

"Mom, she had a brain injury of some sort…" Why did she feel the need to defend the other woman?

"Darlin', I'd have to be buried six feet under to stay away from my children."

Cassie swallowed hard. "So, why do you think she's here?"

"I don't know, but be careful. I wouldn't be getting too friendly with her."

So probably not the best idea to go into business with her either, then. She didn't tell her mom about Montana's offer. There was no point. She wasn't considering it. "Well, either way, she's at Tank's house right now, meeting Kaia."

"Why are you not there?" The microwave chimed and Arlene took out the food and placed it in front of her with a fork and napkin.

Suddenly, she wasn't so hungry. "Because it's a family thing… I'm not family."

Her mother rolled her eyes. "You are more mother to that little girl than anyone else. Shame on Tank for excluding you from this."

Cassie bit her lip. Was her mother right? Should Tank have asked her to be there? Would Kaia have wanted the support?

Her mother added honey to her tea and sat across from her. "What about you and Tank? I suppose this has slowed things down again?"

"I'm not sure they ever picked up." Only she knew they had. Since New Year's Eve, things had started to change between them. Tank had seemed more willing to give things a go. They'd been flirting more. The air around them seemed to have changed whenever they were alone. And then the birthday kiss… She groaned, picking up the fork. She'd desperately pushed the memory of it out of mind the thousand times it had popped up over the last few days.

She took a bite of the pasta. So far food hadn't solved anything but not for lack of trying. Lately she'd been feeding her emotions with everything edible in sight. Even Diva was starting to judge her when she caught her at the fridge at two a.m.

"Do you think Montana's here for Tank?" her mother asked.

"She says she's here for Kaia," Cassie said with a mouthful of food.

Arlene's eyes widened. "You spoke to her?"

Oh shit. Cassie shoved more food into her mouth and nodded.

Her mother waited.

She'd get the truth out of her eventually. "She came into SnowTrek Tours looking for a job."

"She plans on staying?"

"Apparently."

"You weren't crazy enough to hire her, were you?"

"Of course not!" She shoved more food into her mouth and avoided her mother's careful, perceptive gaze.

At least not yet anyway.

Arlene reached across the table, a new determination in her eyes. "Darlin', I'm only going to say this once. If you want Tank, you better get your ass in gear and go after that man before it's too late."

CHAPTER TEN

FRIDAYS, SHE PICKED Kaia up from school when Tank was on the afternoon and early evening shift at the bar. After the meeting with Montana earlier that week, Cassie had been holding her breath, wondering if she'd still be needed. Tank's text message that morning confirming the pickup had made her feel better.

She wasn't being completely replaced yet.

All week, her mother's words of advice had rung in her mind. Her mother was right. Why wouldn't Montana be here for Tank, as well? They had a history and a child together. Tank was an amazing man—kind, caring, compassionate, an amazing dad and hot as hell. It wouldn't take much for Montana to fall back in love with him. But Cassie knew one thing, she wasn't giving him up without a fight.

Walking up the stairs to the apartment behind Kaia, she shook her head. "What is in that backpack of yours?" The worn Wonder Woman–themed backpack, the one Kaia had used for years, refusing to replace it, sagged low on the little girl's back, and the straps looked ready to break.

"Books for research on different countries. We have a social studies assignment due at the end of the month."

"Oh cool…well, let me know if you need help." She'd never been a great student, but the years she'd spent traveling after graduating high school might be able to add a real-life perspective to Kaia's assignment. "I have pictures from Australia, Japan, New Zealand and Europe if you'd like to use them, and I kept a travel journal as well, so anything that might be useful, you're free to borrow."

"Thanks! I'm definitely going to take you up on that," she said as they entered the apartment.

Diva immediately rushed toward them, looking ready to pounce, but a slight hand gesture from Kaia and the dog sat obediently at her feet, though her wagging tail revealed she was having trouble not licking the little girl's face off.

Kaia laughed and bent to praise her.

"You're so good with her training," Cassie said. "She still doesn't listen to me like that." And knowing that soon enough the dog would be leaving her, Cassie hadn't exactly been all that strict with her lately.

"You just need to be consistent with her and show her who's boss."

Cassie hid a smile as she hung their coats. Sometimes, it was easy to forget Kaia was only ten years old. She acted much older.

"What is all this stuff?" Kaia said, scanning the boxes stacked everywhere inside.

"All my old junk from my mom's place," Cassie said. "She was tired of storing all of it."

"Ah…the decluttering method to a peaceful mind."

"You've read the book?"

"Dad and I watched the Netflix series. It was actually pretty insightful." She looked at all the boxes. "You might want to consider decluttering yourself."

Cassie rolled her eyes. "Yeah, I'll take that into consideration. Milk and cookies?"

"Sure. Can I look?"

"Knock yourself out." Maybe she should exchange her knowledge of world travels for Kaia's decluttering tips.

Kaia opened the lid of one of the boxes and took out several yearbooks. She flipped the pages. "Oh my God. Look at your hair. It's so curly!"

"Actually, it's called 'crimped' and it was very much in style," she said, carrying the snacks into the living room. She glanced over Kaia's shoulder and cringed at the horrible hairstyle. It had actually been in style about five years before…but they were often late to the game on fashion trends growing up in Willow Lake. And more than likely, her mother had bought the crimping iron secondhand from the thrift store. But at the time, she'd thought she looked great.

"It says you wanted to be an adventure tour guide when you grew up."

"Nailed it." She'd always known what she wanted to do with her life. It was the road to getting there that had been a mystery. And now whether it was her future.

"Also says you wanted to marry Macaulay Culkin…"

"I hear he's single again, so there's still hope on that one." Cassie opened the lids on several more boxes, but it was all mostly old clothing and survival guide books on wilderness training.

So much of this her mother could have simply tossed and she'd have never been the wiser. At least getting rid of most of it would be easy.

Kaia put the yearbook back in the box and sat on the couch, petting Diva.

"You okay?" She'd seemed preoccupied when she'd climbed into the truck after school, but Cassie resisted the urge to ask how the visit with Montana had gone. She was dying to know, but despite what her mother had said, she wasn't sure it was her place to ask.

"Yeah… I'm good…" She fluffed Diva's fur around her face into a mane. "I met my mom," she said quietly.

Cassie nodded. Admit that she knew Montana was in town or act surprised? "Wow, that's…wow. How did it go?"

"Great!" Her bright smile made Cassie happy, but simultaneously nervous.

Montana better not hurt one single, tiny emotion…

"That's wonderful."

"Yeah, she came over to our house and she didn't stay long, but I showed her my room and she helped with my homework."

Wow, really integrating herself right in there. She forced a breath. It might have gone well, but it was still Cassie Tank had asked to pick Kaia up from school that day. Her fear of being replaced was dumb. He relied on her and her bond with Kaia wasn't so weak that she had anything to worry about.

"We ate brownies and it was nice to get to know her…see her. She's so pretty."

Stunning was more like it. "Well, I guess now the mystery is solved."

Kaia looked confused.

"Of how you got to be so adorable," Cassie said.

Kaia laughed. "I do look like her… It was a little weird actually."

"But I'm sure it must be nice having her back."

"It is. I didn't tell Dad because I didn't want to hurt his feelings, but I wondered about her all the time."

"That's totally understandable and I know your dad would understand too. I used to wonder about my dad, after he went missing. A lot actually." Unlike her brother, she hadn't believed that her father had gotten lost in the outback. She'd been perceptive even then and she'd known her father struggled with alcohol. Despite their parents' attempts at shielding them from the drunken binges and fights, Cassie had known her father wasn't well.

For a long time she'd thought maybe he'd died… either an accident or suicide, but when his body had never been found, she'd started to acknowledge the more likely scenario that he'd left them.

Hearing from him the year before had been a surprise, but despite his walking out and the demons he struggled with, it was a welcome surprise. A relief to hear his voice again. She had hope that maybe someday they'd rebuild their family.

So she knew exactly how Kaia must be feeling.

"I knew you'd get it," Kaia said, finally reaching for a cookie as they heard footsteps on the grate stairs leading to the apartment.

"Your dad's early," Cassie said, fixing her hair quickly as the door opened.

"Hey," Tank said as he entered.

Diva immediately turned to the sound of his voice. Cassie noticed that a lot lately. The dog reacting and responding to Tank more and more. Working with him out in the field was doing wonders for Diva's self-esteem. It was hard to believe she was the same pup with narcolepsy that almost hadn't found a home because of her condition.

"Hi, Dad, we were just having a snack and Cassie was about to Tweet at Macaulay Culkin for a date." Kaia winked at her.

Tank looked confused. "The *Home Alone* kid?"

Cassie nodded, chewing her own cookie. "He's not a kid anymore."

"What am I missing?" Tank glanced back and forth between the two of them.

Kaia laughed. "Nothing. Inside joke. Want me to walk Diva before we head home?" she asked Cassie.

"Sure...if your dad says it's okay." She needed to talk to him. She had no idea what to say, but her mother was right. Sitting back and giving him all the time in the world to come around and fall in love with her wasn't working.

"Yeah, that would be great. Thanks, sweetheart," he said.

Diva was already standing near the door.

Kaia put on her jacket and grabbed the pink sequined collar and leash and left with the dog.

"Don't go too far," Tank called after her.

"We won't."

When the door closed behind her, he sat on the sofa. "How was she when you picked her up?"

"Fine...a little quiet at first. But she told me about the visit with Montana...and she seemed happy."

"Happy. Okay, good. That's good."

"How are you?" He looked like he hadn't slept in a while. Dark circles under his eyes, and his beard had grown much longer than usual. She resisted the urge to reach out and touch his hand on the couch between them. Too much, too fast. They needed to talk first. So instead, she grabbed a pillow and hugged it on her lap.

"Okay. Maybe not. I don't know. I mean, it's a good thing that the visit went well, but I guess I'm just surprised by how well it went, you know?"

She nodded, and he continued before she could say anything.

"I thought I provided everything she needed…and you were always there for her. For both of us."

Cassie nodded again. "About that…"

"It makes sense, I guess."

Okay, he wasn't finished.

"She's a little girl and soon she'll be a teenager with new challenges and dating and heartbreaks and then an adult, graduating high school and figuring out what to do with her life…" His voice trailed off as though he were seeing too far into the future and it terrified him. "But I didn't worry so much because…" He turned to look at her.

Because *she* was there. The stand-in role model, babysitter who longed to be so much more. But hell, if Tank had seen Cassie in all of those future events, what capacity had he envisioned? Had he simply assumed she'd be okay with a permanent platonic relationship, where she provided everything he needed, but didn't come close to getting what she wanted?

"That came out wrong…"

She wasn't sure it had and it made her pump the brakes on the feelings confession and play for him that she'd been about to make. He wasn't exactly in the right mindset to be receptive to that right now. She sighed. "Look, I don't think Kaia felt that she was missing anything…but her mother is obviously important to her and it had to be hard growing up all this time wondering about her." She'd been older when her dad disappeared. Therefore she'd at least had the opportunity to know him, had created memories with him, had something to hold on to. Kaia had only ever had her fantasies and her dreams. Chances were she'd built her mother up in her mind. "This is a good thing."

"What if Montana doesn't stick around, though? I think Kaia would be even more devastated now if she left."

Kaia or him?

"Montana said she's staying, right?" Maybe if she told Tank that Montana had come looking for a job, he'd be more willing to believe that this move was a permanent thing, but she didn't think now was the right time to bring it up. Add more stress to the situation.

And if she was being completely truthful, she didn't want to tell him yet. He'd tell her not to even consider hiring Montana or going ahead with his ex's crazy plan, and this was a decision Cassie wanted to make on her own.

Her mother wouldn't approve. Tank wouldn't approve. No one would. But it was her decision. No one else was facing losing their business, so they really didn't have a say in this. And as much as she'd like to completely dismiss Montana's idea, the big ticking time bomb that was the North Mountain Sports Company countdown had her considering it.

"Yes, but Montana's not exactly the most reliable. She says things without realizing that she may need to follow through." His voice took on an edge.

Was he referring to her promises to him, their relationship…?

"I just don't want her to get Kaia's hopes up and then disappoint her."

Kaia's hopes? Or his?

Cassie was silent. She couldn't remember ever seeing Tank this way. Montana definitely had an effect on him and his emotions…something Cassie had never been capable of. Her chest tightened and all the words she'd planned to say evaporated.

Tank reached across the sofa and touched her cheek. The gesture had her pulse quickening as she looked at him. Her heartbeat echoed in her ears and she hugged the cushion tighter. "Kinda like I did to you," he said, looking pained, troubled.

His words had her pounding heart falling into the pit of her stomach.

So that's where they were.

SITTING AT HIS DESK, Tank ordered that week's liquor delivery. One aspect of his life hadn't changed. He still had a bar to run…though he couldn't ignore the fact that that too was an issue he needed to deal with.

"Hey, why is Montana's name on the schedule for this week?" Reed asked, ducking his head in through the open office door.

So much for no one noticing. "She's going to take a few shifts, that's all. Wants to keep busy…" If he looked up from his paperwork and met his friend's eyes, the truth would pour out of him, so he kept his attention on the payroll.

"She's going to work here?"

"Not permanently."

"Why at all? I thought you two weren't exactly seeing eye to eye."

"We're not, but it was the right thing to do." As if he'd had a choice or say in the matter. Montana could use her extra set of keys to access the place anytime, night or day, and there was nothing Tank could do about it.

Reed stepped into the office and Tank sighed.

Guess they weren't done talking about this.

"So, you want her to stay in town?" Reed looked confused.

Welcome to the club, buddy. "I have no idea what I want, but I don't think it's up to me anyway. Montana can live wherever she wants."

"But you don't want her to stay in Wild River, so why are you helping her? Making it easier?"

"She's Kaia's mother, Reed. What would you expect me to do?"

Reed folded his arms across his chest, one eyebrow raised. "You're a good guy, Tank, but I wouldn't call you saintly."

He should if he knew how hard Tank had had to work all these years to keep his hands and lips and every other part of him off Cassie. And now how he was once again pushing her away so that he wouldn't hurt her any more than he already had. Damn, that was going to be the most challenging of all the shit he currently had piling up to deal with. "Fine… Montana is part owner of The Drunk Tank." The truth would come out eventually.

Reed's mouth dropped. "Come again."

"She's part owner. Fifty-fifty. She was an original investor years ago."

"And you never thought it might be a good idea to buy her out?"

"Of course I did, many times, but with her brain injury, her lawyer—her parents' lawyer—advised her not to sign the papers I had drafted. Said she might regret it and my lawyer couldn't force the issue…"

"'Cause of the injury?"

Tank nodded and went back to payroll. The situation was unfortunate, but there had been nothing he could do. His hands had been tied, but now things might be different. If she was better and able to live independently and work, then maybe she could sign the papers now too.

"Does Cass know?"

"No. No one knows besides you. And Montana has agreed not to say anything. She's just taking a few shifts to stay busy while she gets her own venture off the ground."

"Own venture?"

"Don't ask. I didn't." Whatever scheme Montana was planning was none of his concern. As long as it didn't negatively impact Kaia, she could do whatever she wanted. "I have enough to deal with right now."

"You sure do."

Tank glared at him. "Don't you have a bar to tend?"

When Reed left the office, Tank shut down the accounting program and opened his desk drawer. The old buyout documents were still in the large manila envelope he'd buried in there seven years before. Seven years ago he'd still had his savings, enough to buy out Montana's share without sacrificing the bar's profits. Now that nest egg was gone. Reinvesting the money back into the bar over the years had been a good idea, one he didn't regret. As time had passed, he'd convinced himself that Montana wasn't coming back. Sending her share of the revenue every month had been okay with him. It made him feel less guilty about not making more of an effort to help her and Kaia's relationship.

But now, he'd need a loan to buy her out and he wasn't sure he had enough equity in this place to do it. Remortgaging his condo didn't appeal to him.

He ran a hand over his beard and stared at the legal documents. Would Montana sign these now? She'd told him vaguely and without detail that she had a new plan for her future that she was working on, so maybe the buyout money would appeal to her…if he had it to offer her. He was surprised she hadn't approached him about the buyout option yet.

She'd ruined his birthday. Maybe she was waiting for Father's Day to drop another bomb on his life.

Either way, it was the only thing to do. He couldn't continue to share the bar with Montana. Sharing his daughter was more than enough.

CHAPTER ELEVEN

THREE BOOKING CANCELATIONS that day. From regular clients who booked their spring company retreats with SnowTrek Tours every year. What the hell was she going to do? Cassie counted on the business, foolishly budgeted her month with these three bookings in mind. Now she was going to have to dip into her savings to keep the lights on.

It was their reason for cancelation that bothered her most. They each had "gone a different way this year."

Translation: they'd rebooked with North Mountain Sports Company.

Cassie sighed as she shut everything down for the day. North Mountain Sports Company was already negatively impacting her business and they hadn't even opened yet.

Her spring promo wasn't working and she couldn't realistically drop her prices to match the big chain store's opening sales.

Turning off the lights and grabbing her coat from behind the door, she headed out. She was meeting Erika at The Drunk Tank that evening and she couldn't get a glass of wine in her hand fast enough.

Unfortunately, by the time Erika arrived forty-five minutes late, Cassie's day had gone from bad to worse.

"Sorry I'm late… Two back-to-back emergencies this

afternoon," Erika said, removing her coat and scarf. She eyed the empty wineglass in front of Cassie. "You started without me."

"I did," Cassie said, nodding toward the other side of the bar.

Erika squinted in the dim lighting. "Is that Montana?"

"It is."

"Is she serving?" Erika asked, watching Montana carry a tray of drinks to a booth in the corner.

"She is."

"Why? I thought Tank was upset that she's here and now he's given her a job?"

"Looks that way." Cassie drained the contents of her glass, the grapes tasting sour on her tongue. Was Tank honest when he said Montana being here wasn't what he wanted? Or was he coming around to the idea a lot quicker than expected…and would his weakening resolve result in more than just an ability to coexist and coparent with his ex? Work with his ex?

Montana's laughter from the booth had Cassie reaching for her coat. "I can't do this."

Erika grabbed her arm, stopping her. "Put. Your. Coat. Down."

"This is killing me," Cassie hissed through a forced smile as Montana's attention turned their way.

"You can't let her know that. You are here now. You can't just leave or she will know that she's gotten to you."

Cassie dropped her coat and forced a deep breath, turning in the booth so that Montana wasn't in eyesight. "Okay…let's talk about something else. Your emergencies—how'd they go?"

Erika launched into the details of her afternoon at the hospital and Cassie did her best to pay attention.

An incident with a chainsaw…a twelve-year-old's broken femur…

Two people who were arguably having a worse day than she was. Perspective. Good. Keep talking, Erika.

A few minutes later, a cold breeze made her shiver as the door opened and an old familiar face entered. Mr. O'Neilly.

"Is that Reed?" Erika asked, turning toward the door.

"No. It's Mr. O'Neilly. He used to own this place," she told Erika. She watched as the man approached the bar and Tank greeted him with a handshake.

Erika said something, but Cassie wasn't listening. She was straining to hear the conversation at the bar as Montana hurried over to join it.

"Wow, this place has changed a lot since the last time I was here," she heard Mr. O'Neilly say.

"Hope you like the changes," Tank said, placing the man's pint of cider on the bar in his own beer mug that he'd left in the bar for good luck when he sold it to Tank. No one ever used the mug and it was a customary habit of Tank's to wash it every day now in preparation for the man's visits.

"Looks great. Wish I could have had the place as busy as you keep it, but I suspect that has more to do with the person behind the bar." The older man laughed, flexing a bicep muscle. "Afraid I didn't give the ladies too much to look at, so it was mostly men in the doghouse sitting on these stools back then." He glanced toward a group of ladies sitting at the end of the bar and Tank laughed.

How many times had Cassie said the same thing to Tank? The place could be falling apart and smelling of floor cleaner and the women would still come in.

She'd gotten used to it over the years and had learned to turn her jealousy into amusement. Tank's disdain over the attention made it all that much more entertaining for all of them.

"The name is especially creative," Mr. O'Neilly said.

Cassie smiled at that. The man had to be in his eighties by now and his memory wasn't what it used to be. He made the same comment every time he came in.

"That was my contribution," Montana said.

What?

Cassie stared at Tank. Did she even know the guy? She thought she did, but over the last few weeks she was learning that the man she loved had kept a lot of life details to himself all these years.

Why hadn't he told her his ex-girlfriend had named the bar? Why couldn't he trust her enough to confide in her? Admit that his feelings for Montana had run deeper than he let on? Maybe if he'd been honest about his past relationship, it would have been easier for her to understand his reluctance to take a chance with her. Maybe.

"Well, I love the new name and all the upgrades. And it's lovely to see you two back together again," Mr. O'Neilly said, pointing at Montana and Tank.

Cassie was dying.

"Oh no…" Finally Tank was back into the conversation.

At least it was the perfect timing for him to speak up. Had he let Mr. O'Neilly think he and Montana were an item, Cassie would have been devastated. More devastated than she already was.

"Tank and I are good friends…trying to figure things out for Kaia's sake," Montana said.

"See… I know this sucks, but the two of them just

confirmed that they are only in this for Kaia," Erika said, obviously still paying attention to the conversation at the bar, as well. "Just give Tank a chance to sort all of this out."

Cassie nodded, pretending to look for her lip balm in the pocket of her jacket to compose herself as emotions combined with the wine she'd consumed, resulting in a burning sensation behind her eyes. She'd stay a few more minutes, then call it a night.

Then avoid The Drunk Tank and maybe the real Tank for a while.

When she looked up, Montana was headed toward their booth.

"Here she comes," Erika whispered.

"I can see her." She was all Cassie could see. Montana, dressed in tight jeans and a pretty pink sweater that complemented her complexion so well. Montana with her easy, inoffensive charm that made it impossible not to be drawn to her. And Montana working alongside Tank, who didn't look at all annoyed by it.

He could at least have the decency to act annoyed while Cassie was in the bar. He had to know this would be upsetting to her. The man could really be clueless sometimes.

"Hey, Cassie." Montana turned to Erika. "Erika, right?"

"Dr. Sheraton, actually."

Cassie kicked her under the booth.

"Erika is fine."

"Another round?"

"No…"

"Yes," Erika answered at the same time.

Montana looked back and forth between them. Cassie nodded. "Sure, okay."

"Hey, I know this must be hard, but they are only working together," Erika whispered as Montana headed back toward the bar.

Cassie let out a deep breath. "It's really just the icing on a shitty cake. I lost three more bookings today. I don't know what I'm going to do." She stared across the bar at Montana. There was one option...

She couldn't believe she was actually considering it, but so far nothing else had presented itself. If she had to choose between selling out and accepting a job from Miller Hartwell or jumping on board with Tank's ex's insane proposal, which one would she choose?

"I'm sorry, Cass... I wish there was something I could do."

Wade and Alison approached their booth. "Hey, Cass...gotta sec?" Alison said.

Uh-oh. "Yeah, of course. Have a seat," Cassie said.

They continued to stand. "We're about to head out, the babysitter needs to be home by eleven, but we... uh...just wanted to let you know that we have to cancel our hiking trip for next month."

What? Were they serious? They'd both been so excited about it when they planned it together in her office...for four hours the month before. It would be their first hike and weekend away since having the baby. "Second thoughts on leaving Melissa?" As much as her business would suffer another hit, she understood that. Leaving their baby was tough. New parents and all.

But Wade shifted uncomfortably, avoiding her eyes.

Alison nudged him to answer.

"Um...no. We checked out the ATV tours that North Mountain Sports Company are offering at half price and thought it might be fun to do that instead."

Now even her friends were jumping ship? So much for loyalty. "I have ATV tours. I'd be happy to switch it for you."

"I'm not sure you can beat their pricing, Cass…" Alison said.

"You can't put a price on experience, guys. Come on, you know SnowTrek's tours are so much better," Erika chimed in.

Wade nodded slowly, but Alison shook her head. "Sorry, Cass." She paused. "Is the deposit refundable?"

"It's totally fine if it isn't," Wade added quickly.

Cassie forced a smile. "Of course. Stop by the office next week and I'll process it."

"Thanks, Cass."

Wade and Alison waved as they left the bar and Erika gave them the finger behind their backs. "Can you believe those two? They're supposed to be your friends. All that talk about supporting local. Assholes," Erika muttered.

"What can I do? North Mountain Sports Company is the new shiny thing. Their opening day prices are tempting. Shit, even I was tempted to book one of their skydiving packages." Skydiving. An experience SnowTrek Tours didn't offer. Not only were they able to provide everything she did, they could give customers more. Something different…

Cassie's gaze slid across the bar toward Montana.

Something different.

It's now or never.

If she didn't jump on this opportunity with Montana, how long would it take before the woman approached Miller Hartwell with the idea? Maybe she already had.

"I'll be right back," she told Erika, sliding out of the booth.

Cassie approached the bar, resisting any remaining common sense. This was crazy, but maybe crazy wasn't such a bad thing. Maybe crazy was what she needed.

"Change your mind about the drinks?" Montana looked up as she approached.

"No. I wanted to tell you that I've given a lot of thought to what we discussed—you working with SnowTrek Tours…"

Montana nodded eagerly. "And?"

Cassie took a deep breath. "I think we should do it."

"Really?" Montana dropped the dish towel onto the bar and leaned closer. "That's fantastic! Thank you, Cassie. And trust me, this is going to put your company on the map."

With any luck.

"You won't regret this," Montana said.

She already kinda was.

"What won't she regret?" Tank asked, reappearing out of nowhere.

Seriously, where the hell did he come from?

Montana's gaze met hers and their matching horrified expressions would have been comical if they both hadn't just joined forces to do something that was sure to piss Tank off.

Now, which one of them was going to tell him?

"YOU GAVE HER a job?" Tank asked as he entered SnowTrek Tours the next morning.

Montana must have given him the "good" news. Fantastic. A heads-up would have been nice.

"So did you," Cassie said, turning away from her filing. Hands on hips, she prepared to defend her decision. Which would be so much easier if she felt certain about it. And she was nowhere close to certain. The decision had been part desperation and part impulsive the night before, but there was no turning back now.

"That's different because…" Tank paused, looking hesitant.

Cassie made the confession easy for him. "Different because she named the place?"

Tank looked like a child busted with his hand in a cookie jar. Good. He should feel guilty for never telling her.

Tank nodded, letting his head hang. "I'm sorry I never mentioned it. She was so far away and it was so long ago, I thought it didn't matter."

Of course it matters, she wanted to scream. Whatever happened to honesty among friends? True, he hadn't lied to her, but he sure as hell hadn't been completely forthcoming with certain aspects of his life. "It's your business, Tank."

"Exactly my point. All of this Montana mess is on me. I don't want anyone else feeling compelled to do things to help her out."

"I didn't feel compelled." Compelled and desperate were two different things. "You said yourself she's planning to stay."

"And you're okay with that?"

She was so far from okay with that, but what choice did she have? Montana was here. Montana was Tank's ex and Kaia's mother. There was nothing Cassie could do about that. "It's her choice, not mine."

Tank stepped toward her. "Why aren't you freaking out more?"

She preferred to freak out in private. "Because, Tank, this is life. Things happen, things change, I've learned to roll with it." Montana's choices were her own. Cassie could either learn to get used to the idea that Tank's ex was staying in Wild River or she could go insane over it. She chose the former.

"Damn, I wish I could." He ran a hand over his scruffy beard. He looked exhausted and stressed. He was always the voice of reason in their group. He said the key was to never let the highs get too high or the lows get too low…but he was looking pretty damn low that morning.

She hated that she might have added to his stress. What she wouldn't give to step into his arms and feel that beard against the top of her head. Reassure him that things were going to work out. Together they'd figure it out.

Instead, she turned away and resumed filing. "Well, anyway, her idea was actually perfect. I was looking for something to help me differentiate myself from the other adventure tourism companies, North Mountain Sports Company in particular, and her solution was great. We both get something out of this."

"What do you mean? What solution?"

"Adding BASE jumping to our activities." Cassie handed him a mock-up of the new brochures, listing the extreme sport, boasting tours coming soon for existing jumpers. Unable to sleep the night before, she'd created it to show Montana when she came in later for her first day on the job.

"I'm sorry, what?" Tank blinked rapidly.

Was he having an aneurism? Obviously this was news to him. "You didn't know that's why I hired her?"

"No. She conveniently left that detail out," he said

tightly, through clenched teeth. "I thought she was going to be a regular tour guide."

"I have too many of those already during the slower months and I'm fully staffed otherwise."

"I can't believe her." Tank paced back and forth. "I should have known she was up to something crazy."

"I take it you don't agree with this?" The fact that he was so wound up had Cassie's chest tightening. If he didn't still have feelings for Montana, why was he so annoyed right now? What did he care if she resumed her previous lifestyle?

"How could I possibly agree with this? She almost died from BASE jumping years ago. She suffered a life-altering brain injury! What the hell is she thinking?"

"That you get back on the horse?" This was different, but her annoyance got the better of her. She hadn't seen Tank this riled up since Kaia claimed she was interested in motocross...

"Don't. Don't life lesson me. This is different. She almost died. She left her daughter. Why would she want to risk that again?"

"Okay, yes, I get that. But think about it. Tank, this is what we all do. You and my brother rescue people who are thrill-seeking extremists all the time. Sometimes you have to rescue the same people more than once. Obviously Montana has decided that she isn't going to let her past or her fear rule her life anymore."

"Fear? Did she say she was nervous about jumping again?" He sounded slightly hopeful. Like maybe she wanted to do it, but wouldn't actually go through with it.

Cassie was confident that nothing—not even fear or her previous accident—could stop Montana or change her mind. The more she thought about it, hiring Montana for

SnowTrek Tours was really the best option—perhaps the only option. If she didn't, what was stopping Montana from doing it anyway? Opening up her own extreme sports company, giving SnowTrek Tours even more competition. "Not in so many words, but I'm sure it has to be a little scary."

"And she's allowed to do this? She's gotten clearance from her doctors?"

"Apparently." Why was he asking her? He and Montana seemed to be communicating just fine the night before in the bar. Why didn't he ask his ex all of these questions?

"And she's okay to lead tours, provide instruction for other less experienced jumpers?"

Cassie slammed the filing cabinet drawer. "Look, clearly you have a lot of questions about this, so why don't you go talk to her?"

"Good idea," he said, swinging the door open and leaving her alone.

Cassie took a deep breath, watching him leave, knowing exactly where he was headed.

SITTING IN A booth in the crowded Carla's Diner, Tank waved at several familiar faces. He scanned his surroundings and realized it was a lot of familiar faces. Therefore, lots of curious eyes would be on him and Montana once she arrived.

Maybe he should text her and suggest meeting at his place instead…

Though that posed its own set of issues. In a small town, gossip would fly and he sensed they were a hot topic of conversation already. Montana's presence in town had created a stir, from the whispers he'd been hearing around the bar. Most were harmless, curious questions sent his way, but he suspected there were others with strong feelings about the situation.

But their situation was no one's business and if Montana did stick around, the community would embrace her eventually...

Unless she did something stupid like reopen a BASE jumping site.

Annoyed, he checked his watch.

Come on, Montana.

He only had an hour to talk sense into her before he had to get back to the bar.

She entered the diner and most heads turned while conversations muted. If she noticed, he couldn't tell. Seeing him, she waved and hurried to the booth. "Sorry I'm late. I had to meet with my landlord. The previous tenant left a few things behind..."

"No problem." He cleared his throat and glanced around.

So many eyes were on them. He made a hand motion signaling for all the nosey parkers to get back to their own lunch, and Montana finally scanned the restaurant. "What's going on?"

"Nothing." He needed to get to the point. "Listen, Montana..."

"What's good to eat here?" she asked, picking up the menu and opening it.

"Um...everything. You can't go wrong. But actually, the reason I asked you..."

"Hey, Tank, who's your friend?" Molly Gellar, the daughter of the owner and his usual waitress, asked as she approached the table.

Damn it. From now on, he was suggesting a park or

something… They'd get no peace here. "Molly, this is Montana Banks…" Should he say it? "Kaia's mother."

Molly's eyes widened, but not wide enough. She'd known. "Wow. Hi. Welcome to Wild River…"

Montana smiled. "Thank you. I'm starving. What's today's special? I didn't get a chance to read it on my way in."

"Roast beef sandwiches and barley soup," Molly said, eyeing him suspiciously.

"That sounds wonderful," Montana said, closing the menu. "And coffee, please. Decaf if you have it."

"Sure thing," said Molly. "Anything for you, Tank?"

"No, I'm good. Thanks."

"You're not eating?" Montana asked, removing her coat and placing it on the seat next to her.

"I'm not hungry… Had a big breakfast," he added when both women looked at him as though him not being hungry was an impossibility.

"Okay then. I'll put your order in and grab your coffee," Molly told Montana.

"Thank you." Montana looked around at the fifties-style decor. "Great place. I don't remember eating here before…"

"It was Rosie's ten years ago and it was a karaoke bar."

She snapped her fingers. "Right! I remember. No brain injury could erase the sound of your awful singing…"

"Montana, we need to talk about something." They were getting off track and he wasn't there to reminisce about the past.

Her smile faded. "Okay…"

"I spoke to Cassie this morning."

"Did you get me fired?"

Shit, he wished. "No. Cassie seems to think that your insane idea is going to save her business."

"It will." Molly placed the coffee in front of her. "Thanks, Molly," she said, taking a sip.

"BASE jumping is illegal here."

"We are working on that."

He shifted in his seat. "Montana, do you really think this is the right thing to do? You almost died."

"Almost."

He shook his head. "That's usually enough for most people to quit while they are ahead."

"Look, the old BASE jumping site wasn't safe. This new location…"

He held up a hand. "I don't want the details. I want you to reconsider."

"Uh-huh. No."

"What about Kaia? You've just reconnected with her. What if something happens again?"

"It won't. But let me ask you something. When Kaia's afraid to do something, do you just allow her to give in to her fears?"

Tank jaw clenched. "No."

"And I assume she knows how to ride a bike? Skateboard? She can ski and snowboard… I think I remember seeing a picture of her driving her own Ski-Doo?" She raised an eyebrow.

He folded his arms across his chest and slumped lower in the booth. "What's your point?"

"My point is, I know you are raising her to be brave. To try new things. The only way to conquer fears is to try, and when she fails, she gets right back up, am I wrong?"

"No. But this is a little different from those activities you mentioned."

"Yes. Fewer people are injured BASE jumping every year than any of those activities you encourage Kaia to do." She leaned forward. "And what kind of example would I be if I let a setback keep me from doing something I love?"

A setback? How about a major, life altering incident that kept her out of her daughter's life for ten years? Damn. She was never going to listen to him. Talking her out of this was obviously not going to happen. And now that she had Cassie's support, it was two against one. Was no one other than him willing to think about the dangers and liabilities associated with this? Cassie was usually so much more practical about things that affected her business. She must be even more panicked about North Mountain Sports Company than he thought.

"Okay, but what if you do get injured again? Could you live with yourself knowing it could have been prevented?"

She met his gaze square on. "Yes. And you know why? Because I could get injured crossing the street or slipping in the shower. If something is going to take me out, it sure as hell better be something a lot more exciting than that."

And that was clearly the end of that conversation.

"So, LET ME make sure I understand this correctly. You are willingly going out into the wilderness with Tank's ex-girlfriend—a former criminal—who has motive and desire to see you permanently out of the picture?"

Since when did Erika have a flair for the dramatic?

"She's not a former criminal. It was a minor public disturbance," Cassie said.

"Was she or was she not in jail?"

Maybe she shouldn't have told Erika everything she'd learned about Montana.

"Look, she doesn't want to kill me. She wants a job, that's all."

Erika leaned against Cassie's bedroom wall as she packed her gear for the next morning's hike out to Suncrest Peak with Montana. "So, you are training her to be a guide with SnowTrek Tours?"

"Um…something like that, yeah." Other than Tank, she hadn't told anyone Montana's plan yet and she wasn't quite ready to. They would all have an opinion about it. One she was sure she didn't want to hear. And until things moved along, she'd been planning on keeping things to herself.

Cassie refused to feel guilty, instead choosing to think of it as a confidential business matter. A venture she was considering with a business partner. She wouldn't go announcing a new clothing line partnership before things were inked in a deal, right?

Same thing.

Unfortunately, her friend wasn't satisfied. "What do you mean, something like that? I thought you were already stressing over whether you'd be able to keep your current guides busy enough with North Mountain Sports Company stealing business. What's really going on?"

"Nothing. Montana's going to work with me and she's not familiar with these backwoods yet."

"Not buying it."

Cassie sighed. "Okay, look, she has a new idea that I

think might help SnowTrek Tours stay in business and have a hope in hell of competing with North Mountain Sports Company."

"Great. That's a good thing, but you're being awfully secretive about it, which leads me to think you're not a hundred percent sold on the idea yourself... What is it?"

None of your business.

Erika continued to look at her expectantly.

"Fine. I'll tell you, but no judgment, okay?"

"When do I ever judge?"

"She has an idea for a new legalized BASE jumping site here in Wild River."

Erika's eyes widened. "She doesn't think we're busy enough over at the hospital?"

Cassie scoffed, adding another sweater to her backpack. "See, this is why I didn't want to say anything yet. Right now, it's just an idea. We are exploring the option, that's all."

"Do you know how many BASE jumping accidents there are every year?" Erika started to pace the room. A lecture was coming.

Cassie tried to cut it off early. "From illegal jumps in unsafe areas. That's exactly why this is a good idea. This site will be a legal and much safer option, hopefully reducing the number of illegal jumps happening anyway. According to Montana, these extremists take the sport very seriously. They are basically an exclusive club and anyone who dares do something stupid like get arrested and call attention to the illegal and dangerous element of the sport is...dealt with accordingly."

Cassie grabbed her bag and, passing Erika, she headed downstairs.

"They sound worse than a cult," Erika said as she followed.

In the kitchen, Cassie opened a cupboard and retrieved several granola bars, tossing them into a side pocket of her backpack. "It's not. And I know this seems crazy, but I don't know what else to do. I've been looking for something to save SnowTrek Tours once North Mountain Sports Company opens and this could be it."

"Have you considered the possibility that you could be bringing BASE jumpers to the mountains, only to drive more business to North Mountain Sports Company?"

Cassie shook her head. "According to Montana, this group doesn't love supporting big corporations."

"What about liability and insurance?"

"Montana says most jumpers have their own insurance and they will sign waivers... I'm looking into it on my end, as well." If the extra insurance costs were too high, she'd reconsider things.

"What if someone gets injured? Are you prepared to live with that?"

"There's always that possibility, even on the safest adventure tours. And people are going to take these risks anyway. I'd rather help reduce the possibility of injuries by having the sport sanctioned and controlled." Safety was her biggest priority, but these extremists were jumping now under all sorts of conditions. She'd check out the proposed site on Suncrest Peak with Montana and she'd decide from there whether or not she was comfortable moving forward. Cassie didn't want to see anyone getting hurt either, but Montana was going to try to bring the sport to Wild River regardless of her involvement. She wouldn't admit it to Erika, but Cassie suspected Wild River was going to see new BASE jumpers in town in the near future, whether they were successful in legalizing it or not, so this was definitely the best way to go about it.

Erika sighed, obviously giving up. "Okay, well it sounds like you and Montana have thought this whole thing through."

"We have." Cassie needed to stay firm and confident about her decision. Unfortunately, no other idea had presented itself. "And I'm going out there with her because I want to make sure the new jumping spot we are presenting to Mayor Morell is a prime location. That it is a safer spot than the previous one on Canyon Ridge." They were only going to get one shot at this and it had to be perfect. Perfect location, perfect pitch presentation… Cassie stuffed a flashlight and heavier jacket into her backpack.

"I just can't believe you agreed to this."

"Look, if the site doesn't seem right, for any reason, I won't put in the request to Mayor Morell and I'll forget about the whole thing, okay?" she said.

"Sure." Erika followed as Cassie placed her hiking boots near the front door. "Just be careful out there with her. Sometimes, you can be a little too trusting…" She opened the door and stepped outside.

Cassie raised an eyebrow. "I gave you the benefit of the doubt when you first moved back here with your city slicker attitude and I wasn't wrong."

"I'd like to think that situation was a little different. We had a history of friendship and I had nothing to gain except rekindling that. Montana's motivations may be a little less sincere." Erika leaned in for a quick hug. "Call me when you get back."

"I will," Cassie said, closing the door.

Erika was right. Their situation had been different. She and Erika had been best friends for years.

But Cassie refused to believe that Montana had ulterior motives, other than wanting to get her life back on track. If Cassie and her company could somehow benefit from that, as well—what was the harm?

HE NEVER SHOULD have let Erika inside the bar. The sound of her heels echoing against the hardwood as she paced was giving him a headache. And her chosen topic of conversation wasn't helping either.

"I swear, Tank, if I hear the words 'Montana says' one more time…"

"Can you sit? You're making me dizzy."

Erika paused and placed her hands on her hips. "How are you allowing this to happen? Them working together? Pfft. Insane."

Tank's laugh was humorless. "You think I didn't try to stop this?" Having his ex-girlfriend and the woman he was in a stalemate relationship with working together was as close to a nightmare as he could envision. Not only did it solidify Montana's goal of staying in Wild River, but it added another layer of complication to his relationship with both women.

"Not hard enough obviously. They are out climbing in some remote area as we speak. I'm just waiting until the station gets a call to go save their dumb asses." The pacing continued.

"It's daylight. The weather is perfect for hiking… we haven't had any rain in days so the trails should be okay…" He wasn't thrilled about them going out into less developed areas either, but he wasn't in the habit of telling two stubborn, grown-ass women what to do.

He knew better.

"Okay…but it's the two of them. Alone."

Tank studied her. "Is this about Cassie and Montana spending time together?"

Erika's eyes would have pierced him straight through the heart if they'd been daggers. "Are you serious? You think I'm jealous?"

Seemed like a reasonable assumption. "Are you?"

"No. I just think Cassie should hate this woman or at least see her as the rival she is." She stopped pacing and sat on a bar stool across from him.

"Rival?"

"For you!"

Tank shook his head. "Montana and I are not getting back together. That's not why she's here." He busied himself drying glasses and stacking them on the shelf.

"Are you disappointed about that?"

No. Shit no. Right? "No. I am not interested in a future with her either."

"Final answer?"

Erika should have been a lawyer. "Final answer. Look, I can't stop her from having a relationship with Kaia. Truthfully, I don't want to. Kaia is thrilled that Montana is here. But I am concerned about that relationship…especially if she's planning on putting her life at risk again, running around the backwoods and jumping off cliffs. It's selfish of her."

Erika's demeanor changed. "It's selfish of her to do what she's passionate about?"

Tank blinked. "What the fuck? Two seconds ago we

were on the same side, commiserating and agreeing that this is not the right decision."

"Right, but that was when we were concerned about Cass."

"Well, it's not that easy for me. I care about both of them in very different ways but I have a vested interest in Montana's survival. Until Cass is planning on launching herself off a mountain, the bigger issue I have with this whole thing is Montana's involvement and how that could affect Kaia."

"You're right. I'm sorry. I know all of this must be driving you crazy."

He nodded. "It's been an adjustment."

"I just don't understand how Cassie could seriously be considering this. And I had to drag the information out of her, which tells me she knows this idea is risky. She's been so tight-lipped lately. I've barely seen her and reasoning with her is impossible."

"I hear you. I couldn't talk sense into either of them." A legal BASE jumping site in Wild River was just asking for trouble. Having Montana resume this crazy sport that nearly killed her was aggravating as fuck and Cassie taking on this insane liability to try to save SnowTrek Tours was just an ill-thought-out act of desperation.

He got it. He understand her desire to do everything possible to compete with the large chain store, but both women had literally gone off the deep end with this idea.

"So, you agree that it's a dumb idea?" Erika asked.

"Absolutely."

"Okay, so what do we do?"

"I doubt there's anything we can do. You've met both of them, right? There's no way we will be able to change either of their minds." He sighed. "I guess we just hope that Mayor Morell doesn't approve the jump site. As long as BASE jumping is still illegal in Wild River, Cassie won't participate in this." He wished he could confidently say the same about his ex.

As much as he tried to tell himself otherwise, this new venture of hers explained her sudden appearance in town. He'd been hoping this was actually about wanting a relationship with her daughter but he should have known there was an ulterior motive.

What happened if the site didn't get approved? Would she leave town again? Or would she stay for Kaia's sake? What did he want to happen?

Across from him, Erika's lips had curled into a smile. "That's right. They still need to get approval."

"Why do you look like that?"

"Like what?"

"Like the Grinch who stole Christmas."

"No reason…"

"Erika, what are you planning to do?"

"If I tell you, you'll be an accomplice and you've got enough heat on you right now." She climbed down from the stool. "I'll see you later. Hopefully not out on a rescue mission."

Tank sighed as she left the bar. She had one thing right—he had a ton of heat on him. Cassie was pissed with him for not being able to give her what she wanted. Montana was moving full steam ahead with her new life plans, with barely a consideration for him, and he still needed to come up with the cash to buy her portion of the bar.

He'd leave Erika to her scheming.

CHAPTER TWELVE

THE HIKE TOOK almost two hours and the terrain beneath her hiking boots left a lot to be desired. This trail was not for the average climber, but once they reached the jump spot at the top of Suncrest Peak, Cassie understood completely why Montana had chosen this particular place. "Wow, it is breathtaking up here." The smaller mountain range sat between Mount Palmer and Mount Michelson and while at an altitude of only three thousand feet, the panoramic view was phenomenal. Chugach National Forest was in sight in the distance, but below the peak was an extended stretch of valley divided by a beautiful glacier river. She'd hiked this mountain before but not this particular peak. "How on earth did you find this?"

"My first trip to Wild River was with my dad when I was ten. He was a pro skier in a former life and we traveled a lot to all of the most spectacular ski resorts around the world. We were heli-skiing over Chugach Mountain and I saw this peak. I begged him to climb it with me and we did. I fell in love with this view." Montana set her backpack on the ground and retrieved her water bottle.

"So, adrenaline junkie runs in your family, huh?" Explained where Kaia got her no-fail attitude and adventurous spirit. Cassie had thought maybe she'd been rubbing off on the little girl. A silly idea really.

"You could say that. My grandmother was one of the first female skydiving instructors in Colorado and she taught me to skydive when she was sixty-eight years old. My first tandem jump was with her. It was an incredible experience."

"I bet." Kaia obviously came from a long line of strong, confident women. It was unfortunate that she hadn't gotten an opportunity to get to know them… From the pieces she'd put together over the years, Montana's parents had chosen not to acknowledge Kaia, claiming a relationship would be too difficult, given the circumstances. Cassie couldn't wrap her mind around it. What grandparents wanted nothing to do with their grandchild?

But Montana was here now and maybe her parents would eventually come around, as well.

"You're fairly adventurous yourself," Montana said.

"Not like you." Cassie loved the outdoors and the Wild River wilderness, and while she loved the view from the mountain peaks, heights weren't her favorite thing of all. Even heli-skiing took some coaxing from her friends. The helicopter ride was the least enjoyable aspect. "I'm more of a feet on the ground explorer."

"Well, you are not the only googler on this mountain and I happen to know for a fact that SnowTrek Tours is rated one of Alaska's best tourist resources and destinations."

Why did Montana's approval and admiration mean so much to her? It was almost as though she felt the need to prove herself worthy of Tank's and Kaia's affections. "I'm really proud of what I was able to accomplish with the company. When I first opened six years ago, there weren't many guided opportunities for tourists that took them off the beaten tracks. The other company in town liked to stick to landmarks and touristy locations for their hiking and climbing adventures, and I worked for them for a year and discovered from the visitors that they wanted more. They wanted to take on more challenging hikes and venture out into untapped terrain… So I decided to start my own company."

"That was brave. You must have a business degree, then?"

"Actually, no. Just a high school education." And barely. She'd never liked school, always preferring to be outside exploring. She was smart and capable of completing her homework and tests, but she'd lacked interest. That's where Erika had been invaluable. Her studious friend had made sure Cassie went to school and graduated with everyone else. *You'll have your whole life to explore the world, but you'll only conquer it if you finish high school,* Erika had said.

She'd always remembered her friend's words when she felt like dropping out, and Erika had been right. "I did complete all of my wilderness training and safety courses and over the last seven years, I've taken a few accounting and marketing courses. Enough to successfully run all aspects of the business without having to hire outside resources."

"Well, you've obviously made all the right decisions," Montana said.

Well thought out, nonimpulsive decisions, with input from those she trusted. Until now. This was the first one that she'd jumped headfirst into.

But they were just checking the site. She hadn't fully

committed to this yet. Without a legal site, this venture wouldn't happen anyway. She took comfort in that. If the mayor approved the site, then it obviously wasn't a completely insane idea.

She surveyed the area. "Okay, so we should get both still shots and video of the area. We need to take ground measurements and altitude numbers. I'll leave the jump logistics to you…"

Montana nodded, checking her watch. "Great. Yeah, let's get started."

Cassie opened her backpack and retrieved her camera. Looking through the lens, she adjusted the clarity, focusing on the mountain peaks in the distance that extended up and into the clouds. The lighting contrast between the spring sun peeking through the light cloud cover and the dark shadows cast by the ragged cliffs on either side was a photographer's dream. This place was magical. Even if they didn't succeed in legalizing it for BASE jumping, Cassie would organize a hiking tour that explored the area. She'd arrange a staff hike in the coming weeks and route out an easier trail for the amateur hikers.

She snapped a few shots and moved a little closer to the edge.

"So, you and Tank…"

The camera nearly suffered an over-the-cliff death.

"What exactly is happening there?" Montana continued. There was curiosity in her tone and Cassie figured the woman had a right to her question about them. She was Kaia's mother and Cassie was a big part of Kaia's life.

She took a step back, readjusting the strap around her wrist. But what exactly was happening between her and Tank? They had been moving forward, but thanks to Montana's untimely arrival, they'd been yanked several feet back. "We are friends. We have been for a long time." They hadn't gone to school together, having grown up in different parts of Alaska, but Cassie felt as though she'd known Tank her entire life. He'd owned The Drunk Tank already by the time Cassie had settled back in Wild River after her travels, and while Reed knew him from their positions on the search and rescue team, Cassie met him for the first time at a Wild River community meeting two years before she'd opened her business. It was her first time meeting Kaia too. Without a babysitter or anyone in town he could really rely on, Tank had arrived at the meeting with Kaia in her baby carrier strapped to his chest. He'd sat next to Cassie and all she'd been able to focus on was this hot-as-hell single dad with the baby asleep on him.

For several months, they'd chat at the meetings and two things became clear—one, Tank and Kaia were a team and nothing was more important to him than that child, and two, they both would become important to her.

"But it's more than that, right?" Montana asked, taking a measuring tape from her backpack and measuring the running track from the edge of the cliff.

Yes. But it was complicated. This was one conversation she did not want to have with Montana. This was a conversation for Erika…though her best friend had already heard countless variations of it in the last six months. Everyone was getting tired of Cassie and Tank's issues…including Cassie. She annoyed herself with her moaning and whining over Tank's inability to commit and she was starting to see how pathetic she must look, constantly letting him off the hook and sitting around waiting to be the one he wanted. Not anymore. That ended now. Or as soon as she could get the courage up...

"It's his fear of commitment," Montana said when she didn't answer. She jotted measurements in a notebook before continuing. "Believe me, it has nothing to do with you and everything to do with his past."

Cassie's gut tightened. Montana and Tank's history was still a mystery to her, but Montana obviously knew more about Tank than Cassie had assumed. Which stole the air from her lungs. "Yeah, I know he had it tough growing up." Her family may not have had much, but they'd had one another. Tank's lonely childhood and troublesome teen years, when he'd struggled just to survive, made Cassie's heart ache. He didn't like to talk much about his past and she never forced the issue, respecting his privacy. Had he ever opened up to Montana about it?

"He had no one to depend on. No one to trust. It made him the person he is today. For better or worse..." Montana continued.

"He's an amazing dad and successful business owner— I think he's doing okay." Why did she feel the need to defend Tank? Probably because he never sought sympathy or a break just because life had been harder on him. Montana's dismissal of the success he was now irritated Cassie. The other woman had been away for a long time. She couldn't claim to know Tank as well anymore or make any judgments on situations she knew nothing about.

Montana must have detected her defensiveness. "Oh, he's doing wonderful...on the outside. In fact, he is so different from the man I knew that he's almost unrecognizable. So mature and responsible and level-headed..."

What guy had Montana known? Tank had always been that way since Cassie had known him.

"Becoming a father definitely changed him and I'm happy that he seems better adjusted…more secure and stable. I just mean, despite his strong external shell, I don't think there's been a whole lot of internal healing."

Internal healing? Probably not. Tank wasn't exactly the open, let's-talk-about-feelings kind of guy, but sometimes Cassie wondered if discussing things ad nauseam was really that beneficial for anyone. Growing up, she didn't talk much about her father's disappearance. It was easier to move on with life, focus on the good, and not dwell on the sad or troublesome aspects of life. Tank seemed to adopt the same philosophy.

"I mean, he hasn't had a relationship…since me," she said.

Cassie's chest tightened. "He's worried about Kaia and doing the right thing for her."

"*You* were the right thing for her."

Okay, her camera was totally going to fall over the side of the cliff if Montana didn't stop surprising her with these comments. "I don't… I mean…" What?

"Kaia talked nonstop about you the other night. I've seen all the photos. You two must spend a lot of time together. I'm actually so incredibly jealous of your relationship with her."

"We are close…" And Cassie was going to miss how much time she'd been spending with the little girl, now that Montana was in the equation. She hadn't realized just how much of a part of her life she was until she started to think about the things Kaia normally did with her that she might now choose to do with her mom instead. Tank wasn't going to find it easy sharing Kaia's time either.

Montana put the measuring tape back in her bag and stood. Her gaze locked with Cassie's as she said, "You've been everything I couldn't be for her and I can't thank you enough."

Then why did it sound as though she was being dismissed of duty?

LATER THAT WEEK, Tank leaned against the fire hall wall and smiled. Across the room, Kaia led a junior wilderness survival workshop for a group of kindergarten-age kids. She'd designed the program herself with smaller kids in mind and volunteered twice a month to host it. He couldn't possibly be more proud of her. From an early age, she'd been involved in the Search and Rescue's Hug-a-Tree program for older kids, helping out with the demonstration and encouraging her classmates and friends to complete the course that was designed to keep them safe in the backwoods. She was a mature and level-headed kid.

Several parents glanced his way with appreciative smiles and he nodded to them. Parenting Kaia was easy. He knew he was lucky.

She wrapped up the session and moments later, after everyone had cleared out, he helped her stack the chairs. "Great job. Was this your biggest turnout yet?" There had to be at least twelve kids in the room that day.

"Yep. Mr. Sader let me announce the program on the school announcements this morning while parents were still in home-reading with the kids. Now, I just need him to approve my workshop sign-up sheet for the afternoon students…"

Tank shook his head. "Wow. You are unstoppable."

One day, she'd make a great member of the search and rescue team, which he'd come to terms with already. There would be no deterring her. She was ten and already her ambition and determination made it difficult to tell her no. What luck would he have when she was old enough to do whatever she wanted without his permission?

Not that he ever wanted to deter that determined spirit. He loved her strong will and dedication to the things she was passionate about.

"Hey, so I was thinking…"

Oh no. He knew that tone.

"It's the weekend and I don't have anything planned—my guitar lesson was canceled for tomorrow morning because my teacher is away on vacation… Um, do you think it might be okay for me to stay at Mom's tonight?"

He blinked. "Like overnight?"

She nodded. "She said it was okay with her."

"You asked her already?"

"Well, I knew asking you would be tougher and there was no point putting myself through those nerves if Mom was just going to say no, so I texted her at lunchtime today."

She'd been worried about asking him? Shit. Now what was he supposed to do? Confirm that she'd been right in assuming he'd have a problem with it? Or agree to something he wasn't at all okay with yet? "Um… well, you've only had one real visit with her since she got here." They'd been texting a lot and even that had taken all the strength he had not to question Kaia about their exchanges. Her relationship with her mother was her business and he had to give them space to cultivate it…or at least that's what he'd read in the new coparenting book he kept hidden in his desk at the bar.

"But it went really well," Kaia said.

"Yes…but I think her apartment only has one room." Was Kaia comfortable enough with Montana to share a bed with her? Obviously if this was going to become a thing, Montana might have to reevaluate her living situation. It wasn't unheard of to postpone sleepovers until the noncustodial parents had the appropriate accommodations for the child.

Again, the parenting book.

"I'll sleep on her pullout sofa."

"She has extra blankets, pillows…?"

"I'll bring my camping stuff—sleeping bag and travel pillow."

Okay, so she'd thought of everything. Leaving him with no real good excuse to say no. Except his own hesitation and lack of trust in Montana. "You're sure you're comfortable with that? Staying in a strange house overnight?" Her sleepovers with her friends had taken months of regular playdates and Tank had developed friendships with the parents…

Kaia nodded. "She's my mom, Dad. Not a stranger."

Practically a stranger. Kaia had barely spent four hours with her. He sighed. "Okay. Sure. If you're okay with it and your mom says it's okay with her, then yeah…sure."

Kaia hugged him. "Thanks, Dad."

"Of course." He leaned back to look at her. "And from now on, don't be stressed about asking me things or telling me things. We're a team, remember?"

Kaia smiled. "I know, Dad. The best team."

The best team. One that might now have to expand to include Montana?

"Can I call her and tell her the good news?"

"Sure." Tank continued to stack the chairs as his daughter moved away to make the call, keeping an ear on the conversation. Maybe Montana had expected him to say no and that's why she'd agreed. Would she make up an excuse to get out of it? As much as Kaia might think she was ready for this step, he doubted Montana truly was.

He certainly wasn't.

"Hi…it's me. I asked him and he said yes… Great. I'll be ready. Bye." She disconnected the call and her excitement made Tank's chest ache. "She's going to pick me up at our house in an hour."

"Great." He picked up a stack of chairs and put them in the storage room.

Kaia followed behind with a stack of her own. "Hey, you should be excited too. You have the house all to yourself."

Right. "Yeah…no, it's great."

She cocked her head to the side. "You sure you're okay with this?"

"Yes. Of course." He paused in stacking the remaining chairs. "Just going to miss having you at home, that's all."

"It's no different than when I stay at a friend's house. You'll see," she said. Was that the pep talk she was giving to herself too? Was she worried about this just a little?

He was. Despite her attempt to reassure him, he knew this was definitely different than when she stayed at a friend's house.

"DON'T STRESS, WE got this."

For one ounce of Montana's easy confidence, Cassie would sell her soul. What was it about Montana that reduced her to this self-conscious self-doubter? She hadn't made it to where she was in life by being this way, so why was she struggling? "How are you so sure?"

Sitting in the reception area of the town office, Montana leaned closer, a conspiratorial grin on her face. "I did a little research on Mayor Morell. Turns out he is an expert skydiver. Completed his thirty-fifth jump two months ago near the Grand Canyon."

Cassie's eyes widened. "Mayor Morell? Are you sure?" The sixty-year-old mayor did not strike Cassie as a thrill seeker. He didn't even ski. "*Our* mayor—the grandfather of six and wearer of Donald Duck slippers around his prestigious office—you're telling me *that* mayor jumps out of planes?" Montana must have her information twisted. Mayor Morell was one of the strictest, most rule-enforcing mayors Wild River had ever had. He was the one who shut down the former jump site ten years before. Cassie didn't have her hopes up about this meeting.

But Montana was nodding. "Yep. Mrs. Kim from the post office said that Mayor Morell's sister, Mrs. Carlisle, who owns the convenience store on Jasper, said that it's his secret passion."

"Obviously not so secret," Cassie muttered. Small town and gossip. Clearly, Montana had been accepted with open arms by everyone in town if she was now privy to the gossip chain.

"Not much is around here. You wouldn't believe the stories I've heard this week. Small towns." Montana smiled as though she found Wild River charming.

Cassie squirmed in her seat.

"Okay, so Mayor Morell might skydive, but BASE jumping is different and he is the same mayor who shut down the last legal site." Could they convince him that this site was different? Safer? Appeal to his thrill-seeking nature to at least give them a chance to plead their case?

Seemed to be Montana's angle going in.

"Trust me, once we describe the location to him and show him those pictures and videos you captured, his eyes will light up like cop car lights on a high-speed chase."

Did Montana realize most of her analogies included breaking the law?

"Well, I guess we will find out…"

"Cassie and Montana, come on in," Mayor Morell said, appearing in his office doorway.

Cassie followed behind as they entered the office and took a seat next to Montana. She folded her legs at her ankles and clasped her hands together on her lap. "Thank you for seeing us."

"No problem at all. I trust business is going well after that Slush Cup performance? SnowTrek Tours was this year's winner, I understand," he said as he sat behind his desk.

"Well…" Cassie started.

"Business is not as good as it could be," Montana interjected. "But we have just the plan to change that."

The mayor met her determined gaze straight on. "By reopening the world's third legal BASE jumping location here in Wild River."

Cassie's jaw dropped. Montana's reaction was more subtle, but she was clearly derailed. She sat back slightly and crossed her legs. "Yes. Exactly."

How the hell did he know? They'd kept their plans hush-hush.

Erika had known.

Well, that mystery was quick to solve. Had Reed

and Tank gotten involved, as well? Maybe the three of them had reached the mayor first in the hopes of shutting the idea down…

No. Reed and Tank would never dare mess with her plans, but Erika had bigger balls than her brother and the man she was in love with, apparently. Cassie should never have allowed her to drag the information out of her. Her friend was a doctor and had never been particularly into athletics. Naturally, she wasn't exactly on board with some of the more dangerous sport ideas.

"I'm sorry, ladies, but I can't approve something like that," Mayor Morell said, and he actually did look sorry. Maybe the rumors Montana heard were true.

"You're the mayor. You can approve anything you want," Montana said.

Mayor Morell laughed. "Flattery will not work, Montana. The power trip of this position evaporated a long time ago. You two have no idea how much red tape we'd need to cross for something like this to get approved. There's stacks of paperwork just to initiate the process and I fear it would be just a waste of time and resources. Too many accidents happened in the past."

"My own included—yes," Montana said somberly. "Absolutely, it's a big ask, but a lot of those accidents occurred illegally on the unsanctioned launch zone once the legal site was barricaded."

True, a lot of jumpers hadn't been willing to accept the fact that they could no longer jump and instead took to launching off a few miles south, narrowing the length of free fall time, resulting in more injuries and several arrests. Cassie vaguely remembered the news stories about those injured and convicted. She'd thought the whole thing was insane.

Yet here she was now, supporting a new legalized site? Depending on one?

"Cassie and I have found a new location. It provides a longer free fall and the area is remote enough that it doesn't attract the casual hiker. It is accessible by foot and SnowTrek Tours would operate as the only company providing access for jumpers."

The mayor turned to Cassie. "You realize the liability that would be involved with something like this?"

Yes, but maybe not as much as she should have, which was why she'd agreed to it. Cassie nodded. Best to let Montana do the verbalization of their thoughts.

"BASE jumpers realize the dangers of their sport. There will be required waivers to protect SnowTrek Tours from any possible—though highly unlikely—injuries that should occur," Montana said confidently, reassuming the driver's seat.

"Financial liability and moral liability are two different things. Cassie, I know your company has a fantastic reputation for safety. Do you want to jeopardize that?"

No. Not at all.

"She wouldn't be. The clientele would be vastly different and the BASE jumping community is… Well, let's just say it prides itself on protecting the sport."

"As in the brutal way they warned you to not get caught for illegal jumping, after you were released from the hospital?"

Montana wasn't the only one who'd done their research. She visibly faltered. Slightly. "That is how we deal with things—yes. But legalizing the zone would give jumpers another location here in the US, and it would help to reduce illegal jumping and injuries…and consequences to those who might be tempted to break laws."

Mayor Morell shook his head. "I'm afraid my answer

is still no. Wild River is a family ski destination. We are a popular resort town. We don't want to bring any negative attention to these mountains."

Montana switched gears. "Yet you approved the big chain store to move onto Main Street, driving small local companies like Cassie's out of business."

"Well, I hope that won't happen," Cassie said quickly in an attempt to soften Montana's new angle. Strong-arming the mayor wouldn't work.

Montana shot her a look. "It's inevitable."

Was it?

"North Mountain Sports Company is a legitimate business and they will bring more tourists here...in a safe way. Sorry, Cassie. I know the impact on your company may be significant, but the added value they bring was something the committee couldn't deny. The added jobs for the community alone outweighed many negatives to them owning real estate in town. We voted as a committee and it was unanimous that North Mountain Sports Company was a good idea for Wild River." He turned back to Montana. "BASE jumping is illegal for a reason."

Montana sat back in the chair and a warm smile spread across her face. "Okay...obviously, your mind can't be swayed." She paused and everyone could tell there was more coming. "But before we go..."

Ah, there it was.

"I have to ask, how was the free fall over the Grand Canyon?"

The mayor's eyes widened. "How do you know about that?"

"Wild River is a small town, but don't worry, we won't continue to spread the word. Although I don't know why you want to keep your amazingly cool hobby to yourself."

"People like to know their mayor has his feet firmly planted on the ground, that decisions—like the one you've presented me with—are not made based on my own personal preference."

Point delivered, but Montana wasn't deterred.

"Really though, I bet it was breathtaking."

Mayor Morell sat back in his chair. "Look, I get it. You think appealing to my kindred spirit will help your cause, but as I just said, my own extracurricular activities don't affect my decisions."

"All we are asking is that, before you make your decision, please just come see the jump zone for yourself." Montana was definitely persistent. Easy to tell where Kaia's determination came from.

"I'm pretty sure I've given my decision—twice," Mayor Morell said, but Cassie could see that he was tempted.

She'd stayed quiet long enough. Montana couldn't carry the entire meeting. This was an attempt to save *her* company, after all. "It really is a beautiful sight, Mayor Morell. I'd never hiked that section of backcountry before Montana brought me there."

"It's accessible when you know it's there, but the average hiker won't be going near the site, which will keep it pure and serene… We will cherish and preserve the area." Montana paused. "Jumpers are nature lovers… like skydivers."

He hesitated, but Cassie knew they'd succeeded in at least getting him out of the office and up on the mountain and from there, it would be a lot harder for him to say no. "For the sake of dissuading you both from trying again, I will check out the location," he said.

Montana shot a grin at Cassie and Cassie tried to conceal her excitement.

"But," the Mayor continued, "I can't see anything changing my mind on this."

Montana's wide smile said *We'll see.*

CHAPTER THIRTEEN

"FORTY-EIGHT, FORTY-NINE...FIFTY." Tank burpee'd his body off of the floor and rotated his arms, the stiffness and creaking of joints reminding him of his age. He'd always been active, and weight training had been another outlet for his aggression as a teen, but the last few years, it was tougher and tougher to keep up the intense routines.

Pulling a T-shirt on, he followed the sound of the microwave chiming into the kitchen. A frozen dinner sizzled inside. He couldn't remember the last time he had one, but without Kaia to cook for that evening, he was going to see if they were as delicious as he remembered.

Taking the tray from the microwave, he grabbed a fork and napkin and carried it into the living room, where the latest gory thriller movie sat paused, ready to start, on the television screen.

Balancing his dinner on his lap, he hit Play.

This was good. The first night to himself in a while. Food he wasn't allowed to eat when Kaia was home, a movie he'd never get a chance to watch with her and the day off work the next day to sleep in. Shit, maybe he'd even call for an Uber Eats delivery at three a.m. The sky was the limit on his bachelor night.

Alone.

Peeling back the plastic, he nearly dropped the tray

as steam burned his hand. "They should definitely have a warn…" He stopped, seeing the words CAUTION: HOT written on the side of the tray. Right.

Well, the brownie was a little overcooked. At least, what used to be a brownie. Now it was a thick, gooey brown mess, singed around the edges.

The meat on the tray was a little harder to cut than he remembered. He bit into the steak, slathered in a thick dark gravy, and chewed the cold-in-the-middle meat. And chewed. And chewed. Okay, so it wasn't Meat & More Steakhouse quality dining, but it was good enough. The important thing was that there was no one to tell him how unhealthy the fatty slab of meat was. He was the boss of his stomach that evening.

A forkful of mashed potatoes scalded every inch of his mouth and he inhaled sharply. "Hot, hot, hot…" Kaia would have thought that was hilarious.

Focus on the movie. Don't think about Kaia. Across town at Montana's new apartment, She was fine. He'd checked out the place himself. He'd insisted on dropping her off that evening, and he'd been surprised to see Montana had put together a great bedroom, opting for the pullout sofa herself. A single bed with light sky blue bedding—Kaia's favorite color. All of her favorite snowboarder pics decorating the walls. She was even thoughtful enough to put a picture of him and Kaia that she'd snapped a few days ago at the station with Diva on the bedside table.

He hadn't been able to find fault in the setup at all. Not that he was looking.

I'm not forcing this. We will take it slow, she'd said when she'd first arrived in Wild River.

It seemed hella fast to him.

Though it had been Kaia's idea, not Montana's, and they'd agreed to go at the little girl's speed. Move forward as she was ready. He hadn't expected her to be ready for sleepovers so soon.

The first head exploded on the screen and he set the food tray aside. Maybe watching the movie and eating at the same time wasn't the best option. He barely had an appetite anyway.

And the food was disgusting.

He checked that his cell phone volume was turned up as he settled back against the cushions. But he doubted he'd be needed. Montana had said they were having a girls' night in, so there was nothing to worry about. She was cooking dinner and they were doing face masks and manicures or some shit.

What if she forgot to turn off the stove?

He needed to turn off his brain.

Being in the house without Kaia always sucked and that night it was even worse than normal. It didn't feel like his home without her there. Even when she was just hanging out in her bedroom or had a friend over, ignoring his corny jokes, at least she was there. He knew she was safe.

She was safe with Montana. This wasn't like before…

The call from the state trooper's office that horrible day ten years before had him running barefoot out of his house. He hadn't felt the ice and snow as he jumped into his truck and headed to the police station. Five minutes had never felt so long, yet he drove in a hazy trance, blowing red lights and stop signs. When he entered the station and saw Kaia in the arms of Mrs. Kelsey, the station's administrator, unharmed and safe, he finally took what felt like his first breath in minutes.

"She's okay," Mrs. Kelsey said as she'd handed him the baby.

His little two-month-old baby girl smiled as she'd reached a tiny hand up to touch his cheek. A lump in his throat had nearly strangled him. "Where's Montana?" He looked around the station but didn't see her.

"We haven't located her yet," Trooper Johnson had said, coming out of his office with a stack of paperwork. "Her car was parked in the Whole Foods lot. It was still running…"

Thank God. She'd only been gone an hour, but Kaia could have frozen to death… He shook his head, his anger at Montana combating with his concern. She'd said she was okay. She'd said the doctors said she was okay. She'd said her MRI the day before had come back negative for any signs of concern. He'd believed her. Trusted her to take Kaia to the grocery store four blocks from their condo.

Where the hell was she?

"We have two troopers looking for her. And in the meantime, I hate to do this to you, Tank, but here's some paperwork that needs to be filed. I assume you won't be pressing charges…"

He swallowed hard. As much as he wanted to blame Montana, this was his fault too. He never should have agreed to let her take the car or Kaia alone. Her attempt to prove to him that she was fine could have ended so much worse… What if there had been an accident? What if she'd parked the car somewhere that no one would have noticed the baby still inside and called the state trooper's office?

Never again. "No…she's not well."

"We know about the head injury and I'm sorry about all of this, Tank. But I would suggest reconsidering leaving Kaia alone with her anymore."

"I understand."

Never again.

Until that evening.

Turning off the movie, Tank lay back against the throw cushions, the memory of that day stealing any ability he had to turn off his worry and relax. They'd found Montana four hours later, wandering in a Walmart in Willow Lake. She had no memory of how she'd gotten there and the incident had frightened them both. She'd cried and apologized about putting Kaia in harm's way and Tank had realized that her injury was more serious than either of them had wanted to admit.

Montana's parents had arrived in Wild River the next day and she'd moved back home to get the medical attention she needed.

Tank stood and carried the tray of food to the kitchen and tossed it into the garbage. Then, turning off the lights, he headed upstairs. He hadn't gone to bed before nine p.m. since he was eight years old, but sleep was better than the alternatives.

Pausing at Kaia's bedroom door, he struggled with the sadness overwhelming him at the sight of her empty bed.

It was just one night. He could survive one night.

CASSIE CLIMBED THE stairs to Reed's place and knocked. She needed to talk to Erika. She appreciated her friend's concern, but interfering the way she had wasn't cool.

Just because they were all close didn't mean they didn't need to learn to mind their own business sometimes.

"Hey...what's up?" Reed asked, answering the door.

"Is Erika here? I went by the hospital, but they said she wasn't there." Her workaholic friend never took a day off, so Cassie hoped she wasn't sick. Giving her heck while she was under the weather wouldn't be considerate.

"No. She's in Anchorage at a medical conference this week. Giving a big presentation about the success of the clinical trials for the antirejection drug."

The one Erika and her dad had discovered to help treat organ donor patients six months ago. "Oh right... I forgot that was this week." She'd meant to tell Erika good luck before she'd left, but she'd been too preoccupied with her own issues. She hadn't even remembered to text her.

"Want to come in?" Reed asked.

"Just for a minute..." She entered the condo and saw all of Reed's personal belongings from their mother's house. "You get invited for dinner too?"

Reed laughed. "Yeah, thanks for the warning."

"At least you have a place to store most of this stuff. My apartment is crammed with boxes everywhere."

"If you need to store some things, you're welcome..."

"Thanks... Most of it is junk that I'll be donating." She paused. "So, I guess Erika told you about the new BASE jumping site proposal." The two lovebirds kept nothing from each other. Honesty was a pillar of their strong relationship. Cassie envied them that.

"She did. That's why you're here? To let me talk you out of it?"

"Hardly. Erika tried to intercept our plans by going

to Mayor Morell first and giving him a heads-up and no doubt a ton of stats about BASE jumping injuries." Knowing her friend, she'd probably put together a PowerPoint presentation. "Hear anything about that?"

Reed shook his head. "No, but it doesn't surprise me. Did it work?"

"Oh my God—seriously? You too?" She'd been hoping at least her brother would be on her side. Growing up, they'd always had each other's back.

"Me too what? Am I concerned about you and this idea? Damn straight I am."

Cassie folded her arms. "What's the big deal? No one has any problem with my company going out into the wilderness on hikes and camping trips and rappelling and all sorts of other dangerous things… How is this so different?"

"Well, for one, the other things you mentioned aren't illegal."

"We're trying to change that…"

"For two, you are the one in control of those adventures. I have all the confidence in the world in you and your experience. Montana is a stranger."

"She's Kaia's mom."

"Still a stranger. Look, you can't expect me or Erika, or Tank for that matter, to be over-the-moon excited about this. It's dangerous, it's a liability for your company, and on a selfish note, we are the ones who will be called out on rescue if things go wrong and someone gets hurt."

Her brother had a point, but she was in no mood to listen to reasoning that might have her second-guessing things. "Montana is a professional and the other jumpers are too. I'm not planning to lead a group of amateurs up there. No first timers or anyone without specific quali-fications." She wasn't stupid. They needed to start giv-ing her more credit and trust that she knew what she was doing.

"I just think you are putting a lot of faith in some-one you don't know. Montana has an agenda, Cassie. I don't fully believe for one second that she's here sim-ply because of Kaia."

Cassie didn't either. Montana wanted all aspects of her former life back, including her passion for the sport. "No, I know that too… But what's wrong with her want-ing to build a career doing something she loves, while reestablishing the connection with Kaia?"

"What's wrong is that extreme sports junkies are like addicts. They crave the high of the adrenaline rush… nothing compares to that and if they have to choose between their addiction and the people they love, the addiction most often wins. We know that more than anyone. You know that," he said.

He was comparing Montana to her father. He was right about a lot of what he said, but… "Montana had an injury that kept her away from Kaia."

"And Dad had an illness…"

"We can go back and forth making comparisons all day."

"All I'm saying is that the two situations are not so different."

"Okay, well, Dad's getting better, trying to make a new fresh start, and you're on board with that…so can't you extend the same courtesy to Montana? Give her the benefit of a doubt? Give her a second chance too?"

Reed touched her shoulder, the way he always did to soften a blow of brotherly advice she wasn't going to want to hear. "Here's the thing. A lot of people I care about could get hurt from Montana being here, so you'll have to forgive me if I retain some of my better judgment on this one, until I'm proven wrong."

TANK'S MOOD WAS as dark as the heavy late spring snow clouds as he entered the station the next day. Another night without his daughter at home had him more on edge than he'd been in a long time and given the circumstances of the last few weeks that was saying something.

It was supposed to be a one-night sleepover, but Kaia had texted the day before asking if she could spend the next night as well, and he'd been at a loss for a reason for her to come home. Besides the fact that they hadn't really discussed how things like sleepovers were going to work… They'd need to. Soon. A routine was going to be important for all of them.

His daughter's text at nine, saying she was going to spend the day with her mom shopping, had further increased his bad mood. Seems she hadn't missed him at all.

He was trying and failing to be okay with these sudden changes.

"Hey, man…how was it?" Reed asked, then seeing his face, he tapped him on the back. "It'll get easier."

"Doubt it." Tank collapsed onto the cot in the back and tried to relax. "It was just so weird not having her there. I kept forgetting and checked her bedroom twice. I don't know how other parents successfully coparent. I never signed on to be a part-time dad." Years ago, he'd been prepared for a life with Montana. He'd barely known her, but he'd been ready to commit to a future for Kaia's sake. They'd liked each other and there had

been chemistry…he'd figured they would make a relationship work, for their daughter. Montana leaving
hadn't been ideal, but he'd figured things out then too.

Now what?

"I get it, man, but just be grateful that you've had ten
years to yourself, and as hard as it is to acknowledge,
having her mom in her life is in Kaia's best interest."

Best interest. He'd heard that a lot lately. He'd repeated it to himself. But Tank wasn't so sure. Montana
could have a change of heart and leave again, and then
what? And if she stayed, and her access times and vis-
itations increased, could he really survive sharing his
daughter's time with her mother?

And damn, what if Kaia eventually decided to live
with Montana? Having visitation every second weekend, like the other divorced dads he knew, would be
the death of him.

"I want to believe that… This is just frustrating,"
he said.

"Good, you broke the news to him already," Tyler
said, entering the station.

Jesus, what now? He sat up. "What news?"

Reed punched Tyler's shoulder. "Thanks, man… I
was planning to tell him when he wasn't already looking like shit."

Tyler grabbed his training gear and ducked out, leaving Reed to deliver more bad news.

"Sorry, man…" Reed stood and handed him a new
member enrollment form.

Tank scanned it quickly, then tossed it straight into
the trash. "Nope."

Reed retrieved the papers. "Every member application needs to be accepted or rejected on merit, Tank. Not personal feelings."

"Fine. She's a liability. End of story."

Reed read from the file. "Level two avalanche training, Advanced Backwoods Safety, CPR and First Aid—all up to date. And, man, she bench-pressed more than I did at the gym the other day."

Fantastic. She had a membership at their gym now too.

"As much as it annoys me that she's convinced Cass to go along with this BASE jumping thing, she's obviously tough and strong-minded. She would be an asset…"

"I just need one aspect of my life that she's not tangled in. Just one." He was losing Kaia to her, she'd stolen the woman he was arguably in love with, claiming her as her new BFF, he still hadn't come up with the funding to buy out her share of the bar, and now this.

Wild River was suddenly feeling too fucking small. Like claustrophobic small.

"I know this whole situation sucks, but there's nothing you can do about her being here. You have to start embracing it, seeing it as a good thing. Otherwise you'll go mad."

Too late.

"And who knows? Maybe if she's part of the crew, she'll forget this whole BASE jumping idea."

Reed was underestimating Tank's ex. Nothing could make Montana forget about her one passion in life. All this other stuff was just a way to integrate into the Wild River community.

Tank checked his watch. "I'm going to get Diva for training…"

"About that…"

"Don't ask." No, he and Cassie hadn't discussed the dog living with him yet. They hadn't discussed a lot of things yet. Last time they spoke, they'd argued about Montana. "Do me a favor and find something wrong with Montana's member application."

Ten minutes later, he pulled his truck in front of SnowTrek Tours. Climbing out, he headed inside. Then immediately wanted to walk back out.

Had Montana's laugh always irritated him? Or was it just now when it melded with Cassie's?

They stopped when they saw him standing there.

Great. Now *he* was the buzzkill.

"Hey." He glanced around. "Where's Kaia? I thought she was spending the day with you, shopping?"

"She's in the washroom. We decided to stop by and say hi to Cassie and Diva on our way to the mall," Montana said, petting a sleeping Diva curled up next to her on the oversized chair.

Even the dog was a traitor.

"Oh…" He cleared his throat. "So, last night went okay? Everything's good?" Maybe forty-eight hours with her mom was too much. Maybe she was ready to come home now…

Cassie turned her attention to her laptop, an obvious attempt to give them privacy in the small space, but he knew she was listening and just as interested in how the first full weekend was going.

"It was great. We watched a full season of *Friends* and just hung out and talked. She's a really great kid."

Yes, he knew that. "Isn't that show a little old for her…?" He couldn't remember the late nineties sitcom well, but he was fairly certain it contained adult themes.

"She said she'd watched *Seinfeld* with you, so I didn't think *Friends* was any worse."

Was it him or was there a note of challenging defiance in her tone?

"Hi, Dad!" Kaia said, reappearing from the bathroom.

He smiled, dismissing the issue of the show. It felt like forever since he'd seen Kaia and he was oddly relieved to see her in her jeans and a sweater, her hair in a ponytail, a chocolate milk mustache…looking exactly as she had before the weekend.

What had he been expecting? That she'd grow up in two days?

"Hey…good morning," he said as she hugged him.

He squeezed tight, instantly feeling better about things. Maybe it would be okay.

"What are you doing here?" she asked.

"I thought I'd take Diva for a run… But it looks like she's still asleep, so I'll come back later."

Montana stood. "We have to get going. The mall is open now. Why don't you stay, Tank? Cassie can show you the pictures we took of the new BASE jumping location."

Cassie shot her a murderous look.

"You got it approved?" That fast?

"No," Cassie said.

"Not yet," Montana corrected, pulling on her light spring jacket. "I'll see you later, Cass," Montana said, obviously not wanting to stick around for the conversation. He'd talk to her later, when Kaia wasn't around. He couldn't believe they'd told Kaia about her plan. How did their little girl feel about her mother resuming the dangerous sport?

"Bye, Cass," Kaia said. "I'll see you at home later, Dad."

"The mayor is actually considering approving the new site?" he asked when the door closed behind Montana and Kaia.

"Not yet. We need to file some paperwork...but we're hoping Wild River will soon have the third legal jumping site in America." He may have imagined Montana's tone, but there was definitely an edge in Cassie's.

Why was everyone irritated with him all of a sudden?

"Wow. That's...wow." Erika's plan— whatever it was— obviously failed. Tank could only hope that the mayor had enough sense not to allow this to happen.

"Wow good or wow bad?"

"Does it matter? You and Montana will do what you want anyway."

Cassie shut her laptop with a bang. "Can't any of you just be happy that I may have found a way to help keep the doors open? First Erika tries to derail us by going to the mayor, then Reed with his big-brotherly advice, and now your attitude—I'm sick of it."

"Cassie..."

"No. When Reed was going to give everything up to pursue Erika in Anchorage, I supported him. When Erika moved here, I supported her decision. Whenever you need anything—anything at all—I am there for you. Right now, I need support and the only one willing to give it is Montana."

Tank moved toward her. "Not true."

"Isn't it?"

"No. If I remember correctly, you basically told me to butt out."

"Because you weren't being supportive."

"Because I wasn't saying what you wanted me to say. There's a difference. And I'm sorry but I'm not going to simply jump on board with a venture that relies heavily on Montana. *You* I support completely. In everything. Her? I'm not as confident."

"Her idea is a good one and she was even successful in talking the mayor into at least visiting the site and allowing us to complete the required paperwork. She really knows her stuff, Tank…"

He stepped toward her and cupped her face in his hands. "So do you. You've made this business what it is. You. Only you." His pulse raced as his thumb stroked along her jawline. Her soft, silky skin flushed from her annoyance and the fiery look in her light blue eyes made her that much more beautiful. The stress of recent events had stolen his attention, but now, standing there, touching her, staring at her, he realized how much he missed her.

Her eyes dipped to his lips and he slowly brought her face to his. "I refuse to let Montana come between us," he murmured against her lips.

Suddenly, he didn't want anything between them. Not clothes, not space…nothing. He pulled her into him. His expression scanned hers for any sign of hesitation. He found none.

His lips met hers and he kissed her. Hard. Desperate. Just like the kiss in the bar, this one had all of his emotions rising to the surface. Years of wanting combined with the intense conflict between them the last few days made him abandon all common sense.

Sliding his hand into her hair, he deepened the kiss. He was desperate for something familiar and safe to grab ahold of as the ground beneath the foundations he'd built was unsteady.

Her soft moan against his lips had his body springing to life and he held her tighter against him. She tasted like coconut flavored lip gloss and minty mouthwash and he never wanted to stop kissing her. She was the air he'd been craving and all the comfort he'd been lacking.

She was the only thing that made everything feel like it would be okay.

He pulled back slowly, reluctantly, and leaned his head against her forehead. "I want my best friend back," he said.

Cassie pulled away. The look of determination in her gorgeous eyes was almost frightening. "I want more than that."

His heart still raced and his mouth went dry. "How much more?"

"What are you prepared to give?" she asked, sliding her hands up over his chest.

He was panicking. She'd never been this forthright about her feelings before. It felt like he had seconds to make a decision he hadn't been able to make in five years. "Cassie… I don't know…"

"Right now, I'd settle for your body."

Could he take this next step with her? He sure as hell wanted to…but bringing her back to his place and crossing the line would mean no turning back. Yet in that moment he didn't give a damn about lines anymore. Life was already messy and complicated and the only thing he knew for sure was that he wanted Cassie. "Right now?"

She nodded, her gaze unflinching, her voice unwavering. "Right now."

CHAPTER FOURTEEN

TANK BACKED HER up against the wall in his hallway less than three minutes later. Bending, he scooped her up, and she wrapped her thighs around his waist. Supporting her weight with one arm draped beneath her ass, he trapped her hands above her head with the other. His mouth crushed hers and Cassie's entire body melted. How many times had she fantasized about this huge man picking her up and kissing her like this? Their difference in size might look odd to others seeing them together, but it made for one hell of a turn-on when he could bench-press her with little effort.

She returned his kiss with all the passion she'd had to resist over the last several years. All the sexual frustration coming out in what had to be the hottest kiss in Wild River history. If global warming wasn't a thing before, she was sure their chemistry could melt a few polar ice caps right now. He tasted so good and she couldn't get enough of the feel of his chest and shoulder muscles beneath his sweater. Damn, he was so freaking hot! She was going after what she wanted and no matter what happened tomorrow or next week or next month—she wouldn't regret this.

She'd only regret not getting the opportunity to be with him at all. Right now, she was giving in to what her body wanted. She'd worry about her heart later.

"You sure about this?" he asked.

Clearly he wasn't. Not completely. Not yet...

Wrestling her hands free, she gripped Tank's face, holding him even closer. He wasn't getting away. She wanted to kiss him for hours. Never ever stop. Show him their connection. Prove to him that her feelings were real and so were his. No more denying them.

His hand slid beneath her sweater, creeping upward over her stomach, her ribs, then dipping beneath the underwire of her bra to cup her breast.

Her breath caught and held. Was it possible to survive on passion alone? He massaged her hot flesh and she moaned against his mouth as his thumb slid over her nipple. It had been forever since she'd been with a man. The only one she'd wanted for years was Tank. His forced celibacy had meant she hadn't been getting laid either.

Waiting for him had been torture, but it was already proving to have been so well worth it.

He pulled back, struggling for air. "Cass...you didn't quite answer my question."

The hesitation in his voice had her nodding. "Yes, Tank. I want this. I want you. I always have."

"So...you're ready? 'Cause once we do this...for real..."

"I want this, Tank." Even if he wasn't ready to promise her any more than this right now.

His gaze locked on hers, he moved away from the wall and carried her down the hallway to his bedroom.

He pushed the bedroom door open with his foot and laid her on the bed. "Alexa, play Cassie's playlist."

She grinned. "Cassie's playlist?"

"I was hoping someday I'd need it," he said, removing his sweater and undershirt in one swipe.

Fuck, his body. She'd seen Tank shirtless thousands of times on camping trips and swimming and she'd never been so innocent that she hadn't snuck a touch every now and then, but now, his strong, sculpted, crazy sexy chest and shoulders and abs were all out there for her. She ran a hand over his washboard stomach, circling a finger around his belly button. "Keeping this body from me for so long was just mean," she said, as the sounds of her latest favorite song started to play.

"Man, you have no idea how many different fantasies I've had about yours." He reached for the hem of her sweater and lifted the fabric over her ribs and breasts and then yanked it off over her head. She sat forward to allow him to remove her bra.

His eyes took in her breasts for the first time and she felt zero shame in her body. Sure, she wasn't boasting double Ds like Erika and she didn't have Montana's ass, but she could hold her own in the sexy department. And she knew her athletic build was attractive to Tank. "Yep, as perfect as I'd imagined," he said, lowering his head between them.

Cassie ran her hand through his hair, shivering as his beard tickled the soft flesh of her cleavage. She breathed in the scent of him—mint shampoo, clean, fresh-scented body soap. All man, all Tank.

"How do you always smell so good?" he asked.

She laughed. "Am I not supposed to?"

"I just don't understand. You're always on the move. Do you not sweat?" He glanced up at her.

"Only when I'm working out hard…" she teased.

"Well, let's see if we can give you a workout right

now," he said, gripping the waistband of her leggings and her underwear and pulling them down to her ankles. His eyes grazed over her body as he knelt on the floor, removing both of her shoes. Then he slid the fabric of her clothing off over her feet, tossing everything aside. Picking up one foot, he placed a trail of kisses along her calf muscle, all the way up her inner thigh, before setting that foot down and repeating the action with the other leg.

Cassie's body trembled as his beard tickled her delicate flesh. "You still have too many clothes on."

Tank grinned as he got to his feet.

Cassie propped herself up on her elbows as he unbuckled his belt. Her heart raced. She was naked. On Tank's bed. And in thirty seconds, he would be too.

So long she'd waited for this, it didn't seem real. Yet it felt like the most natural situation on earth. He tore the belt away from the denim and the jeans dipped lower on his hips, revealing the sexiest set of oblique muscles on the planet. Tank was a big guy and suddenly Cassie's heart raced faster. Was he ultra-sized everywhere? She swallowed hard as he unzipped his jeans and let them fall to the floor.

He grinned as her eyes fell to his already hard cock straining through the fabric of his boxer briefs. "Worried?"

"Little bit," she said. Damn, as often as she'd thought about Tank's penis, she'd never really considered the logistics behind sex with a man built like a...tank. She hadn't been using her vagina much in the last ten years.

But Tank slid the underwear off slowly and then lay next to her on the bed. "Don't be. You've waited this long for me. I don't intend on disappointing you. We will take this slow." He brushed her hair away from her face, kissing her forehead.

So many forehead kisses from him over the years, but this one was different. It wasn't a "this is all I can do right now" kiss, it was a "this is just the beginning for us" kiss.

Cassie reached for him, pulling him on top of her as she lay back against the bed. "I don't think you could ever disappoint me," she said as she dragged his head back down to hers. His mouth covered hers as his hand slid the length of her body, stopping to rest on her hip. She opened her legs and he wedged himself between them. Slowly he pressed himself against her and Cassie's eyes closed. The intensity of her need was overwhelming already. The thought of Tank inside her was enough to put her over the edge, so she steadied her breathing as she raised her hips to grind against the length of his cock.

"Damn, Cassie. Slow might be harder than I thought," he growled, resting his forehead against hers.

The friction between their lower bodies grew more frantic and Tank retreated slightly. Reaching into his bedside table drawer, he retrieved a condom.

"Sure that thing's not expired?" Cassie teased.

"No," Tank said, squinting to check the expiration date. "We're good."

Cassie eyed him suspiciously. Condom shelf life wasn't that long.

"Full confession?"

"About time, I would think," she said, her heart racing. Had he been with someone else in recent years? That could change things fast.

"I bought these on New Year's Eve. We had a date scheduled and I…"

Relief flowed through her. "You thought you were going to get lucky on our first date? What kind of girl do you think I am, Tank?" she teased, but her heart swelled. He'd been wanting her too. Wanting things to move forward. This wasn't just a spur of the moment, careless abandon, impulsive move. They both had wanted this for a long time. And she might have gotten here sooner, if Reed hadn't almost died on New Year's Eve. Her brother had the worst timing sometimes…

But they were here now.

Tank slid the condom on and then, grabbing Cassie by the waist, he switched their positions, putting her on top. "You're in control of this. It's all you," he said, placing her down against his straining penis.

Cassie raised her body so that the tip of him was on the edge of her. Gripping the headboard, she slowly rocked her hips, inching him inside a little at a time.

Tank closed his eyes and his fingers gripped her waist, digging in hard. "Shit, Cass, you're so tight."

"You're so big." Would he actually fit inside her fully? She rocked her hips faster, lowering her body down over him, feeling him fill her completely. Damn, she was already close to coming. His thickness and length made the connection tight, but her wetness created enough lubrication to create an explosive, intense friction between them as she started riding him. Up and down, slow, deliberate, careful at first, then faster, more desperate, more confident and sure.

It worked. They fit together. "This okay?" she asked, out of breath as she continued to pick up her pace.

"Absolutely," Tank said. His gaze, full of love, met

hers, and she couldn't hold back any longer. Driving her hips forward, she closed any gap between their bodies as her orgasm erupted, out of control, sending her body into convulsions as she throbbed around him.

Tank held her firmly in place as he raised his hips, plunging just a little further inside her body as he came. He moaned and his body shook as they rode out the waves of pleasure radiating through their connection.

Her world sufficiently rocked, Cassie collapsed next to him on the bed a moment later and he immediately pulled her closer. "Was that okay?"

"Are you kidding me? That was amazing." She drew circles over his chest as she moved closer. She hesitated before asking, but she needed to know if this was a one-time thing or if it was the start of something real. A relationship with him. "Any regrets?"

He turned to face her, tucking a strand of her blond hair behind her ear. "Only that I waited so long."

Cassie smiled, snuggling closer to the man she'd been in love with for what felt like her entire life. Sure, aspects of their situation were complicated right now and they had challenges they were going to need to work through, but they would. She chose to believe that.

Tank didn't make decisions lightly, so if he'd finally given in to this…maybe it was the first real step to him giving in to more.

HE'D NEVER THOUGHT he'd be a cuddler. But every time Cassie tried to move away from him in her sleep, he pulled her back into him. She didn't seem to mind. Her soft moans and happy-sounding mumbling as she dreamed told him she was content being wrapped in his arms. Which was good because he didn't want to let her go.

He had no idea what this meant for them…but he didn't regret being with her. It was the only thing in weeks that had made sense.

She stirred and turned in his arms to face him. Her eyes opened slowly and she grinned. "If I'd known all I had to do was piss you off to get you into bed, I'd have done it sooner."

"I wasn't pissed…just frustrated. Seeing you and Montana working together. I'm still not sure how I feel about that."

"But you trust me, right?"

"Of course, Cass."

"Enough to support my decision to include BASE jumping if the site gets approved?" She glanced up at him.

He hesitated. "Yes. Am I worried about it? Of course. But if anyone should be taking this on, it's you. You are smart and strong and capable of creating a safe and exhilarating experience for jumpers. And I fully support you. Whatever you need." He did. She deserved nothing but his support. The same support she'd always given him.

"And Montana? Are you okay with her doing this?"

He released a big sigh. "It's her decision to make, but I feel better that she's doing this with you."

Cassie nodded, fingering the hair on his chest. "And you're sure that things between the two of you are over? There's no lingering feelings there at all?"

"You really want to talk about my ex? Not exactly pillow talk." They'd just shared a special moment together. One they'd both been waiting a long time for. He didn't want talk of his past or Montana to ruin things.

But she didn't seem upset. Just curious. "We've been talking for years, but lately it feels like we haven't really been saying anything…not important things, anyway. Your history with her is something we haven't discussed. And I'm going to need that intel to move forward if she's here and going to be a big part of our lives."

Move forward. He wasn't completely sure he was ready for that, but he knew standing still was no longer an option for them considering the afternoon they'd just spent together. "You're right. Montana is not just an ex that is in my past. She's here and we all will have to find a way to make things work." He took a deep breath. "You sure you want to talk about this now?"

"Yes… I really want to know. I'm not jealous or worried, I promise."

He hugged her tighter just in case. "Okay. Well, as you know, we met when she was here BASE jumping with a team at the old site."

"Someone got injured, right?"

"Yes. Nothing too serious, a few cracked ribs, but the search and rescue team headed out to assist and we met. She stuck around a few extra weeks and one thing led to…"

"Kaia."

He laughed at her eagerness to skip over the details. That was totally okay with him. "She went back to Aspen, and after three months without any contact from her, I get a call. She was pregnant."

"Did you freak out?"

"No. I mean, it was crazy and unexpected, but I

knew instantly that it was something I could handle. She came back and we moved in together and agreed that we cared about one another and we would see what the future held."

"Did you love her?"

He wouldn't lie to her. "Yes."

She stiffened slightly, but didn't say anything.

"She wasn't in love with me, but we were doing the responsible thing, putting the baby first, and we were in it together for the long haul... Then she had her accident. After a week in the hospital, she was released. We thought she was okay. There was some swelling, so the MRI couldn't detect the extensive damage done to her brain, but she was walking and talking and showed no signs of trauma... It felt like a miracle, really. Turns out it was too good to be true. After a few weeks, we noticed things were wrong. She was forgetful and she was sleeping a lot. At first, I thought it was postpartum. Kaia was only two months old and Montana had gone right back to her old activities without giving herself time to recover. Which was part of why she had the accident in the first place..." He paused. Until Montana had reappeared, he'd put all of these memories behind him. Over the years, he'd forgotten about the fear and uncertainty they'd faced back then. The effect the injury had had on all their lives.

"It sounds so tragic. I'm sorry you had to go through all of that," Cassie said.

As he recounted the worst part—the story about Montana forgetting and leaving Kaia in the car in the grocery store parking lot, tears gathered in Cassie's eyes.

"Hey, it's okay. She was okay." But he held her

tighter. *He* couldn't even think about the story without the fear resurfacing either. He understood the emotion.

"I just can't even imagine how scary that was…"

"It was terrifying. We were lucky things weren't worse." He paused and cleared his throat. "Then she moved back to Colorado with her parents. And you know the rest."

Cassie nodded slowly. Processing. Taking it all in.

He rolled them so that his body covered hers. He supported his weight on one hand as he looked down at her. "Montana and I will always be connected because of Kaia but that's where our entwined lives end."

The happiness on Cassie's face made his chest ache. Man, he loved her. Was falling *in love* with her. He was desperate not to hurt her and he prayed this physical relationship they'd entered into would be enough for her for now, while he figured everything else out.

He lowered his lips to hers and kissed her, hoping she could feel all of his best intentions.

CHAPTER FIFTEEN

LAUGHTER DRIFTING INTO the house as the front door opened gave Tank a sense of both relief and anxiety. Shit. He'd been hoping Montana wouldn't be staying. He hadn't seen Kaia all weekend and after his afternoon in bed with Cassie, his ex was the last person he wanted to see.

But Kaia's face was flushed with happiness as she entered the kitchen and saw him take a fresh batch of cookies from the oven.

"You made cookies?"

"Yeah…thought you might want a snack."

Montana entered and he stared between the two. How had he never noticed how much Kaia looked like her mom? Same dark hair, blue eyes, high cheekbones. Right now, he couldn't see any of himself in her.

Wait. What was all over her face?

"Yum, cookies. You know, if you ever got sick of bartending, you could open your own bakery." Montana reached for one but he moved the tray out of reach.

She frowned.

"They're still hot," he said lamely. "Um, Kaia, what's on your face?" he asked as calmly as possible. What age did kids start wearing makeup? He had no idea, but he was pretty sure ten was a little young.

"Makeup."

"Just a little blush and lipstick. She wanted to try some at the mall…" Montana looked nervous as she reached toward Kaia's lips with a napkin to wipe it off.

Good. Get that crap off of her.

Kaia moved away. "Stop. I like it. It matches yours."

Montana's cheeks didn't need blush when Tank shot her a look. "Don't worry, we didn't buy any. It was just a one-time thing… Makeup can wait a few more years."

"Good answer," Tank mumbled, fighting his irritation that Montana was setting rules already. At least they agreed on the makeup thing.

He handed them both a cookie and nodded toward the shopping bags. "So, good day shopping?"

"The best," Kaia said.

Why did that make him feel worse? He hated shopping and rushed Kaia in and out whenever she had a growth spurt and he had no other choice than to endure the torture that was the local mall. *Smarten up, man, your daughter had a great day. Be happy. Smile.*

He tried but it had to look more like a grimace. "Well let's see what you bought."

"Why don't you go try it on and show him?" Montana said.

Kaia looked at the time and squirmed on the stool. "Oh, he doesn't want to see it."

"Sure I do."

"Really?"

Clearly, she didn't really want to show him, which made it absolutely necessary that he see whatever it was. If Montana had allowed lipstick, who knew what else she'd deemed appropriate. If there was so much as a midriff showing or a skirt that needed a few extra inches added, he was vetoing any more shopping trips. "Absolutely."

"Okay." Kaia popped the rest of the cookie into her mouth, wiping off most of the lipstick with it. Then, grabbing the shopping bags, she left the kitchen.

"So, you two had fun?" he asked Montana. As long as he kept the conversation on Kaia, she couldn't steer it to more personal territory. To his afternoon...

"Would it make you feel any better if I said no?"

Damn, was his mood that obvious? "No. I'm glad she had a good day... It's just a little weird, that's all."

"It's okay. I get it. This is going to take a while to get used to. You've had her all to yourself for a long time."

And he found he couldn't help wishing it could stay that way. Selfish, yes, but their life had worked so well. Just the two of them. That's why he'd been reluctant to get closer to Cassie. To let her in. He wasn't sure what adding someone to their lives would do to the structure he'd built for himself and his daughter.

And now Montana came along and threatened that foundation, and unlike the situation with Cassie, Tank couldn't control it.

"What did she buy?"

"You'll see."

"Well, thank you for not buying the makeup. I don't think I'm ready for that quite y—" The last word evaporated as Kaia reentered the kitchen.

In a dress.

"Doesn't she look pretty?" Montana urged in his silence.

Kaia's confidence visibly shattered as she got only silence from him.

"I know it's not really me…" Kaia said, tugging at the fabric at her waist.

"It's beautiful." Damn, took his voice long enough to appear. And when the words did come out, they were hoarse.

Kaia blushed. "Really? I didn't think you'd like it."

"It looks great, sweetheart. The color matches your eyes perfectly."

Kaia smiled as she looked down at the fabric. "That's what Mom said."

Montana smiled at him and their gaze held a little longer than he'd have liked. But common ground was good. As tense as all of this was, it was better that they got along. Especially in front of Kaia.

Their daughter would never have to choose between them.

CHAPTER SIXTEEN

Tank tugged at the tie around his neck as he waited in the bank reception area. He hated dressing up, and it was kinda ridiculous, seeing how John Cartwright, the loans manager, was at The Drunk Tank at least four times a week, playing pool, and therefore knew this getup would be just for show.

Didn't matter. He was here on business. He was determined to look the part and secure the loan to buy out Montana's share of the bar. Montana's initial investment had been fifty thousand dollars. He was hoping she'd take an inflated payout of seventy thousand and sign the legal documents he'd had drafted years before.

It was fair. She'd more than made back her investment over the last ten years. He'd calculated that he'd sent her almost three hundred thousand dollars. A seventy thousand lump sum would help her buy a place here in Wild River if she wanted…or allow her to invest… There was no reason she'd want to hold on to the bar.

His only regret from the day before was not telling Cassie. He should have. Full transparency. But opening up wasn't easy for him and he had a little.

Baby steps.

Admitting to her that he'd once been in love with Montana had been a risky move in light of recent circumstances, but while he liked to keep his past in the past, he'd never lie to her.

He still couldn't believe they'd finally done it. He'd had sex with his best friend. And it was mind-blowing amazing. Surreal almost.

All these years, fighting his attraction, avoiding a commitment, he'd thought it was the only way to preserve what they had. He thought he'd feel regret or fear at the very least, but he didn't regret it and he wasn't afraid.

Funny how it took Montana's arrival, shaking up his world like a snow globe, for the pieces of his future to start falling into place. Some might still be floating in the air, but he was working on setting everything right again.

"Tank? That you?" Seeing his buddy wearing a suit and tie had Tank grinning, as well. In a small, tight-knit community like Wild River, formalities were often silly, but they couldn't all go to work in their usual camo and plaid, now, could they?

"Hey, John, thanks for seeing me on short notice."

"Not a problem. Come on in," he said, leading the way back into his office and shutting the door. "What can I do for you?"

Tank sat and folded one leg over the other. The pant leg rose, revealing his bright coral-and-purple-striped socks, the only dress socks he owned—a joke gift from Kaia. On the bottom were the words "Bitch, I'm a Unicorn." He'd laughed too hard after unwrapping them to be able to reprimand her for the unsavory language.

Despite the socks, he forced his most professional demeanor. "I'd like to apply for a bank loan… I'm sure you've heard that Montana is back in town, and I want to buy her out."

John nodded, pulling up Tank's account on his computer. "Do you have a lot of equity in the bar or your house?"

"Not really. I just bought the house a few years ago. I was renting before that. The bar makes a profit every year, but nothing sizeable." He could easily afford their modest lifestyle. They weren't going without anything and they could afford a trip once a year, but he'd be paying off his mortgage for the next thirty years and retirement didn't look to be an option unless he sold the bar eventually...

"Okay... Let's take a look at your financial health, as we call it." He scanned Tank's account. "You have the mortgage...a credit card...and a line of credit at eighteen percent interest..."

"I have it, but I've never used it." The ten-thousand-dollar line of credit was simply for emergencies. "We can close it if that helps my financial health look better."

"That's an option, but let's keep looking. Do you own any property or have any investments other than this savings bond for Kaia?"

He shook his head. "No. I keep meaning to set up a retirement plan but..."

"It's like life insurance. Everyone puts it off until they can't any longer." He continued to look at Tank's account. "How much of a loan were you looking for?"

"I was thinking seventy thousand."

John frowned. "That's a lot."

"I think it's a fair price for the buyout." Make her an offer she couldn't refuse.

"Have you talked to Montana about a reasonable price?"

"Not yet. I wanted to make sure it would be possible,

that I'd qualify for the loan first." If he didn't, there was no point in having the conversation with Montana. In fact, he'd have to keep hoping that *she* wouldn't bring it up.

"Okay...well, let's fill out the loan application. I'll have to run a full credit check, as well."

Tank nodded. "Yeah. Of course." That part was a little scary. He hadn't missed a bill payment in years, but in his earlier life he'd often struggled to make his meager salary stretch. How long could a few late payments stay on his report?

"And we may need to consider shutting down the line of credit."

"Do it." Whatever it took.

"Okay," John said, turning his computer toward Tank. "Here is the online application... Fill this out and we will see what we can do."

Tank sat forward. "Great." This had to work. Before he could consider a real future with Cassie, he had to hope that his past didn't continue to haunt him.

THE BIG FLASHY countdown clock across the street was down to its final minutes. North Mountain Sports Company would officially be open in twenty-six minutes and the line of people gathered for the grand opening celebration went all the way around the block.

The only reason Cassie wasn't stress-eating in bed right now was that she'd spent hours in Tank's bed the day before, and as worried as she was about her competitor, her anxiety was temporarily overshadowed by sheer joy.

She'd had sex with Tank. She'd fallen asleep in his arms. After an amazing experience together. He'd opened up...and not just physically, but emotionally. He'd let her in. A little bit, at least.

The day ahead might be challenging, but at least her heart wasn't as conflicted as it had been twenty-four hours ago.

Reaching for a new balaclava from a rack, she yanked off the sale tags and put it on, covering half her face.

"Are we casing the place?" Montana asked with a laugh, entering the office.

Cassie turned toward her, grateful for the fabric covering what had to be a guilty-as-shit look. Which was stupid. She had nothing to feel guilty about. Montana and Tank were a thing of the past. He'd been honest with her about his past feelings. He'd once been in love with Montana. But she believed him when he said he wasn't anymore. She'd felt their connection the day before.

"I don't want anyone seeing me over there," she said.

"Everyone expects to see you there, and participating in their opening day event shows them that you aren't afraid of the competition."

Cassie sighed, removing the face mask and smoothing her hair. "As soon as Erika gets here, we will go." As annoyed as she was with Erika for interfering with her and Montana's meeting with the mayor, she couldn't wait to confide in her friend about her mind-blowing experience with Tank the day before.

The door chimed as Erika entered, wearing a balaclava and one of Reed's oversized coats, and any lingering tension between them evaporated. That right there was why no one could replace Erika Sheraton as her best friend. "Suit up, bitches, let's do this," she said.

Cassie laughed. "I've decided to forgo the recon outfits and just walk bravely into the fire."

"Oh thank God," Erika said, removing the coat. "It's

like sixty degrees out there today. And they say global warming is a myth." She removed her face mask and hat and hugged Cassie. "I'm sorry I wasn't being as supportive as I should have been." She glanced at Montana. "I hear the jump site you two have selected is as safe as possible…"

So Montana had filled her in. Good. Erika was still going to have her reservations, but it felt great to have at least half her support in this. "It is. And nothing's been approved yet." All of them were stressed and arguing over something that might not even be happening.

"Well, I'm here to support you any way I can," she said. "Even if it means putting my professional opinion aside."

"Thank you. That's all I can ask for. Okay, let's go before I change my mind," Cassie said.

They exited the store and headed left on Main Street toward the large crowd gathered. The entire sidewalk was packed in front of North Mountain Sports Company. Cassie had seen the crowds lining up since earlier that morning. This was a big deal. "There's so many people here," she said.

"Don't worry. Once locals realize these 'grand opening sale' prices are still double what they would pay online, and that their adventure packages aren't worth the outrageous prices, this store will be a ghost town," Erika said.

Hopefully before the store had too much of an impact on SnowTrek Tours.

"She's right," Montana whispered. "A store like this does well in Aspen, where tourists are prepared to spend more, but Wild River is not their usual clientele. From what I can tell, people here are not impressed with name brands. They want practical and functional."

"Thanks." Cassie appreciated their attempts to make her feel better.

As they stopped near the crowd, Mayor Morell appeared on the sidewalk on a raised platform in front of the store with two North Mountain Sports Company execs. Two people the community would never see again beyond that opening week. They'd already staffed the store and Cassie could at least appreciate the hundred jobs the store had provided the town. She'd be even more grateful if it didn't ultimately cost her her own.

"Hello, everyone! I want to thank you all for coming out to the grand opening event of Wild River's very own North Mountain Sports Company store! Since Mr. Hartwell first approached us with the opportunity to have one of their locations here in Alaska, we've all been excited about what it will mean for Wild River's economic growth and the increase in tourist satisfaction, so I want to be the first to welcome Mr. Hartwell and North Mountain Sports Company to our town."

A round of applause erupted around them. Cassie begrudgingly clapped along.

"With no further ado, I'm going to leave it to the executives here, Mr. Ralph Harrison and Mrs. Kimberly Mitchell, to formally introduce the store's brand, and then we invite you all inside to check it out."

More applause as the store executives stepped up to the microphone.

"Hello, everyone," Mr. Harrison said. "Thank you, Mayor Morell, for the warm welcome. We've had the pleasure of getting to know a lot of you already during the construction over the last few months, and I've been honored to have been accepted into the community. We know big box stores can create some anxiety within close-knit communities, but our goal at North Mountain Sports Company is simply to enhance…not detract from the vibrancy of the communities where we launch our brand." He stepped away from the mic and Mrs. Mitchell stepped forward.

"That's right. We want to add value to your existing economy by providing more jobs and opportunities for growth, as well as offering something more. I think as you explore the store, you will clearly see our vision and what North Mountain Sports Company is all about."

Erika rolled her eyes next to her and Montana continued to pretend not to be eager to get a look inside. They really were good friends, and having them standing on either side of her gave her even more strength.

"But before we open the doors, we have a special guest here to say a few words," Mayor Morell said, taking back the microphone.

Lance Baker appeared from behind a barrier and the crowd roared.

"Should I know him?" Montana whispered.

"He's a professional snowboarder. Won gold at the Winter Games and the Olympics. He's from Alaska, so he's as close to a celebrity as we get," Cassie told her.

Montana nodded, turning her attention back to Lance. Gone was the steely, unimpressed look of solidarity. Replacing it was one of unconcealed attraction.

Great. Even Montana was being won over by the company's impossible feat of bringing in the local snowboarding god.

And was he wearing North Mountain Sports Company gear? Logo'd ski pants and jacket, hat and gloves… Holy shit. It made sense now. They were his new sponsor.

"Guess that solves the mystery of how they got him here," Erika said, realizing it, as well.

"Hey, everyone! Thanks for coming out. I'm happy to formally announce that I will be partnering with North Mountain Sports Company, designing a new brand of snowboards to launch next winter. I look forward to meeting everyone and I'll be signing autographs on the first floor."

The crowd cheered and Cassie's heart fell into her stomach.

If Wild River's golden boy said North Mountain Sports Company was the best, everyone would believe it. She felt ill. "Maybe we should go…"

"No. We need to stay. We are not afraid of competition, remember?" Montana said, but Cassie suspected her desire to see this through stemmed more from wanting to meet Lance herself.

Mrs. Mitchell appeared at the mic. "So, now we'd like to invite Mayor Morell to help us cut the ribbon and invite you all inside!"

Mayor Morell picked up the ceremonial oversized scissors and held them on the ribbon. Mr. Hartwell and the other executives positioned themselves on either side for the promo picture, and then the ribbon was cut.

"Alright, let's check this out."

"I've already seen everything at the VIP event. You two go on without me," Cassie said, but Erika and Montana refused to let her bail.

"Head held high," Erika said.

"Smile," Montana added.

Head up, best fake smile plastered on her face, Cassie headed inside with her friends. They were swept along with the crowd as they walked through the first floor showroom.

"Shit, those mannequins are creepy," Erika said.

Cassie laughed. "That's what Tank said when he saw them." A memory of their afternoon together had her cheeks flushing.

Erika noticed. "Okay, we're talking about those red cheeks later," she whispered.

Cassie nodded, not wanting Montana to hear. They might all be getting along. Friends even. But girl talk about Tank would be reserved for Erika alone. She squeezed her friend's hand, grateful she was there.

As they headed toward the women's clothing section, Montana glanced over her shoulder before ducking behind a rack of skis and pulling Cassie and Erika with her.

"What's wrong?" Cassie asked, catching several skis before sending them all crashing in a domino effect. No one would believe her destroying the place was an accident.

"Why is that guy watching me?" Montana said, motioning to the right of the rack.

Cassie didn't even have to look to know who Montana was talking about. She'd sensed Eddie following them throughout the store the moment they walked in. At first she'd thought nothing of it, but why else would he be in the women's section of the store?

"That's Eddie," she said.

"Is Eddie a stalker?"

Erika laughed. "No, he's a cop."

"And he's been following me because…?" Montana's irritation was evident.

"He's been following you?"

"Yes. I've seen him around town—the grocery store, the post office…and even at my apartment building once."

"Coincidence?"

"No way. I've caught him watching me…like this." She peeked around the corner. "He's still there. Checking out women's sports bras."

"He's a new cop. He's overzealous," Cassie said. Though he was being really weird…

"What does he think I'm going to do? BASE jump off of the top floor of the building?" Montana moved out from behind the rack and shot Eddie a look.

Which he pretended not to see.

Cassie sighed. "I'll talk to him."

"Seriously. The guy's everywhere I turn." Montana said, dipping out of sight again behind several mannequins.

Eddie turned in a circle, looking for her.

Shit. The guy really was keeping an eye on Montana. "Hey, Eddie, what is your deal?" Cassie asked as she approached him.

"Oh hey, Cass… I didn't see you."

"Quit it, Eddie. Montana said you've been following her around town. What are you doing?"

He lowered his voice. "She's an ex-con."

Cassie scoffed. "Hardly. Her 'crime' was an extreme sport, not shoplifting."

"You're defending her?"

"No. Just clarifying things for you so that you can relax and give her some space," Cassie said.

He looked at her suspiciously now. "You two are friends now?"

"Yes. And she's going to be working at SnowTrek Tours with me."

"So she's sticking around?"

Cassie couldn't tell if he was irritated or pleased. Was there something more to Eddie's attention toward Montana than just serving and protecting? "Yes."

"And you're really okay with that? What about the fact that she's Tank's ex?"

"Not a big deal."

"And she's Kaia's mom…and you've been that maternal role model for Kaia for so long. Someone else stepping in is okay with you?"

Why was she suddenly being interrogated? She wasn't such good friends with Eddie that he needed to know her business. "Eddie, Montana is Kaia's mother. Not some stranger or new girlfriend Tank has brought into their lives. It's in Kaia's best interest."

Eddie looked concerned. "Kaia's maybe. Yours, I'm not so sure. Protect yourself, Cass…and I don't mean your wallet," he said, casting a glance toward Montana.

Cassie shrugged off his concern. "Everything's fine. Please stop following her," she said, walking away to rejoin her friends. She forced Eddie's concern out of mind. Everything *was* fine. It was more than fine, actually. She and Tank had finally taken the next step.

Erika was browsing a rack of snowboards, but Cassie didn't see Montana. She scanned the store and spotted her near the camping gear… She headed toward her, but stopped, noticing Lance Baker.

The two were smiling and flirting, perhaps? Montana's body language certainly suggested it… The head tilt, the eye contact… And Lance was definitely feeling her. His lean in was obvious.

See—Eddie didn't know shit. Montana's demeanor around Tank had never even come close to this obvious attraction toward Lance. At least not when Cassie was around. If she was still into Tank, she wouldn't be flirting with Lance.

Cassie's shoulders relaxed as she moved a little closer, pretending to browse the thermal sleeping bags. She wasn't being nosy, she just wanted to keep an eye on Montana. These mountain snowboarding gods had a reputation for being playboys and she didn't want Montana getting hurt. The woman was here to finally get her life back on track. A casual fling was cool but Cassie would hate to see her get invested in a guy like Lance and have her heart broken.

Though, who was kidding?

Montana was more than likely quite capable of breaking her fair share of hearts.

Her ears pricked up as she heard Montana mention the BASE jumping venture, and she moved a little closer.

"I knew I recognized you," Lance said. "So, that's what brings you to Wild River? Isn't it illegal?" Lance asked, sounding even more intrigued that Montana might be the bad girl her former misdemeanor offence suggested she was.

"Hopefully not for long."

Cassie listened as Montana explained their plan to Lance and told him about the new site. She felt slightly uneasy with Montana's confidence in the whole thing. She was talking as if this was a done deal. Which it certainly wasn't just yet. Cassie had been tight-lipped about the venture because locals would have mixed feelings about it and until things were confirmed, there was no point spreading the rumor all over town.

Shouldn't Montana have spoken to her about how

much they were going to say right now? After all, they wanted this venture to make a big splash if they did follow through with it. Lance Baker could post it on social media and half the world would know within minutes.

"Then, I take it you're moving to Wild River?"

Cassie started to move away, but stopped when Montana hesitated.

"Well… I'm not really sure yet. Not a hundred percent anyway."

What? Hadn't she told Tank she was here for Kaia? That situation wasn't dependent on this new venture's success… At least, it shouldn't have been.

"It depends on whether you are successful in this or not?"

Cassie's heart pounded as she waited. Would Montana still stay if the mayor rejected the proposal for the jump site? Was that really the only reason she was here?

"That…and a few other things. For now, this is temporary."

Temporary. Shit. Tank was right not to fully trust Montana and her motivations.

And now, this knowledge was on Cassie's shoulders. Should she confront Montana about what she'd just heard? Should she give Tank a heads-up? For Kaia's sake?

Damn, Eddie might not have been too far off the mark after all.

Cassie moved away, having heard more than she'd wanted to. Glancing across the store, her face flushed, seeing Tank and Reed approach. She quickly moved further away, out of earshot of Montana and Lance. She wasn't sure how Tank would feel about witnessing his ex flirting…and that made her even more uneasy.

Seeing Erika, Reed headed toward her, while Tank continued straight toward Cassie.

"Hey…you guys made it."

"Sorry we're late. We had a call to assist ski patrol this morning," he said. "Was that Eddie you were talking to?"

"Yeah…apparently, he's been following Montana around." She should at least tell him that much.

Tank frowned. "He's been what?"

Cassie forced a laugh. "You know Eddie. He's just taking the job a little too far…"

Tank looked beyond her toward the guy. His chest got slightly puffy and Cassie's stomach knotted again. Protective much?

"Seriously, it's nothing. I talked to him. He'll quit it."

"He better," Tank said and the note in his voice had Cassie's stomach twisting. But a second later, his hand reached for hers. "I've been thinking about you all day," he said.

That made two of them, but she looked around to see if anyone noticed the hand hold.

"Do you want to spend next weekend with me?" Tank asked.

Um, yes. But, "What about Kaia?"

"She's going on an overnight camping trip with her Girl Guide group."

"She is? They didn't need me to volunteer this time?"

Tank looked sheepish. "I may have told them you were unavailable for this one." He took a step closer and the look in his eyes had her body on fire. A whole weekend together. Not just one afternoon…

"That's a white lie I can live with."

CHAPTER SEVENTEEN

THE REST OF the week dragged on and Cassie's productivity was next to none. Tank's invite to spend the weekend with him was the only thing she could think about.

Weekend. Shit. Two full days and nights with him. Uninterrupted. No Kaia. No work—they'd both booked it off. He had Reed filing in at the bar the entire weekend. Would they even leave the bed? She'd be okay if they didn't. They could order in food if they were hungry.

Other than emergency calls or texts, she was unplugging from the real world and enjoying the time with him.

Pulling into his driveway a little past five, she checked her reflection in the rearview mirror before reaching for her overnight bag from the back.

A sleeping Diva woke immediately and her tail wagged seeing where they were. The dog whined, unable to contain her excitement.

Cassie laughed. "I feel the same way, Diva."

They got out of the car and headed inside.

The smell of garlic and spices had her stomach growling and her mouth watering. She'd suggested picking up dinner along the way, but Tank reassured her that he was already on top of dinner plans.

She hoped they had the same idea. Eat early and move on to other appetite-satiating activities. "Hello…?" she called out as she closed the door.

"In the kitchen," he called back.

Diva took off toward the sound of Tank's voice.

Cassie moved a little slower, dropping her overnight bag into his bedroom on her way to the kitchen. She suddenly felt anxious, yet nervous...as though she hadn't been friends with him for years, hadn't spent countless evenings in his home. This was different.

Maybe she should have worn jeans...stayed casual... but the spring sun and unusually warm temperature that day had tempted her to wear her new navy slim-fitting skirt that came just above the knee. It matched her white shirt with the pale blue feather pattern on it perfectly.

Diva was already curled up on her mat near the door, destroying a new bone, when she entered the kitchen. "Smells great in here," she said.

Tank turned, and seeing her, he nearly dropped the spatula he was using to flip the ground beef. "Wow."

Cassie gave a nervous laugh. "I'll take that as a compliment."

Tank reduced the heat of the pan on the stove and within two big strides, he was next to her. His arms went around her waist as his mouth crushed hers.

Cassie gripped his face between her hands and stood on tiptoe, closing the gap between their bodies. She'd been waiting for this, craving it, since he suggested they spend the weekend together. He tasted so delicious and smelled so tempting. She was only hungry for one thing in this kitchen.

Tank's hands slid lower over her hips and ass as he lifted her off the floor. Her legs went around his waist as he hoisted her higher. Her arms wrapped around his neck as she deepened the kiss. She wanted him... couldn't wait to have him again. Couldn't wait to be naked with him again. How had they ever been around one another before *without* being naked? It would certainly be a challenge now.

Tank lowered her onto the kitchen counter and separated her knees, wedging himself between them. He broke the contact between their mouths and buried his head into her neck, kissing gently along her exposed skin.

Cassie moaned as goose bumps surfaced all over her body. For someone who was out of practice, Tank was stirring up all sorts of amazing sensations within her. Maybe sex was like riding a bike.

When his hands slid up her thighs beneath her skirt, her body trembled with desire and anticipation. There was no denying what either of them wanted right now. They had all weekend. Just the two of them…but luckily neither of them seemed interested in wasting a single moment of it. "I'm glad you're here," he murmured against her ear as his fingers reached the edge of her underwear.

"I couldn't wait to see you," she said, wrapping her arms around his neck and pulling him closer. She kissed him softly, her gaze locked with his, and then she ran her tongue along his bottom lip.

He growled as he pressed himself closer. "I want you, Cass…"

"Here?" she whispered against his mouth. He could have her anywhere he wanted.

"I don't think I can wait long enough to get you into the bedroom," he said, unbuttoning his jeans. He slid the fabric down over his hips and she took in his erect cock, straining against his underwear.

She swallowed hard at the memory of him inside her. She longed to feel all of him deep inside her body. She reached for his underwear and lowered them, then lifted her skirt higher around her waist. She was so ready for him. So willing to give him all of herself. Over and over again that weekend.

Tank pulled her body closer, his cock pressing against her body through her underwear. "Shit, Cassie... I've never wanted someone so badly before."

"So, what are you waiting for?" she asked.

His grip on her waist tightened, but then he stopped. "A condom..." he said, taking a deep breath and moving slightly away. "I'll be right back."

He was. In record time.

Cassie laughed as he rejoined her, tearing open the condom and sliding it down over himself. "That was fast."

"This will be too," he said gruffly as he gripped her ass and moved her to the edge of the counter. He pushed her underwear aside with one hand as he guided himself into her ready, wet body with the other.

Cassie gasped and her eyes closed as he filled her. Her body trembled and she held on tight as Tank plunged deeper and deeper inside her.

Her folds tightened around him and her pulse raced as he moved faster and harder with each thrust of his hips.

All weekend. They had all weekend to do this. She wasn't sure it would be enough. Her desperate pace grew frantic as she rode up and down over his cock. So hard, so big, so fucking incredible. Her body pulsated as the first ripples of pleasure washed over her. "Tank... I'm coming already," she said, wrapping her entire body around him. She couldn't get close enough as her orgasm erupted, stealing her breath.

Gripping her hips, Tank rocked forward a final time, his head falling against hers as he came seconds later.

"Told you I wouldn't last," he said, a satisfied smile in his voice.

"Next time," she said, kissing him again. "And the time after that…"

"And the time after that," he said, kissing her forehead.

Good to know they had the same agenda for the weekend.

"Quick or not, it was definitely the best thing I've had in this kitchen," he said.

"Looks like it might stay that way—the meat is on fire," she said, wide-eyed at the sight of flames coming from the forgotten pan on the stove.

"Shit." Tank yanked up his pants quickly and reached for the fire extinguisher on the kitchen wall. He sprayed toward the stove and the flames immediately went out.

Cassie climbed down from the counter, readjusting her own clothes. Then, wrapping her arms around his waist, they stared at the destroyed frying pan and charred meat. "Never thought I'd be able to say I'd had sex so hot, it caught a kitchen on fire."

Tank laughed as he turned in her arms. "Let's order in for the rest of the weekend. Just to be safe."

Cassie's head on his lap, asleep on his couch hours later, Tank stared at her. Diva was curled up at her feet. This—her being there with him—felt so natural, so right. Being with her had always felt that way, and despite their relationship turning physical, things didn't feel a whole lot different.

That both relieved and worried him.

He thought taking this next step with her would have changed things. It should have. If things still felt the same, was he really opening up to her? Was he putting his heart on the line again or was he only giving in to the physical?

She'd said she was willing to accept whatever he was ready for. They'd move forward slowly...as long as they were moving forward.

But he knew eventually this wouldn't be enough. Weekend sleepovers when they could sneak them in wouldn't be enough for either of them...or fair to expect. Cassie wanted a commitment from him. Deserved a commitment from him.

His cell phone vibrated on the cushion beside him and Diva opened one sleepy eye. Not wanting it to wake Cassie, Tank reached for it quickly.

The station.

Shit. So much for an uneventful weekend.

"Hello?" he whispered.

"Tank, that you?" Tyler asked loudly into the phone.

Diva must have heard Tyler's voice because she immediately jumped down off the couch and sat at attention at Tank's feet.

Tank lowered the call volume. "Yes."

"Why are you whispering?"

"What do you want?" Please let the guy just need the Wi-Fi password again.

"We just received a call from the state trooper's office—a bunch of tourists booked ATV tours with North Mountain Sports Company earlier today and ran into mudslide territory on the side of Canyon Mountain. The company called for assistance in getting them out."

"Any injuries?"

"A few minor ones reported...mostly from trying to get the vehicles unstuck."

"Can you guys handle it?" This wasn't a real emergency and even something serious would have him hating to leave Cassie right now.

"We could…but seeing as how you are the only one on crew who could possibly just lift the ATVs out of the mud, we thought it would be faster if you came along."

"But you *can* do it without me?"

"I know Kaia's away with Girl Guides. What else you got to do?"

Plenty. He gazed down at Cassie's soft blond hair and flushed, glowing skin. Nothing that he wanted circulating around the station. The guys would all know about him and Cassie soon enough. They would think it was long overdue, but it still wouldn't prevent the razzing… and he wanted to keep all of this to himself for a while.

"Fine. I'll be there in fifteen minutes."

"Bring your muscles," Tyler said before disconnecting.

Just once he was tempted to let someone else do the heavy lifting. Literally. But if the crew got stuck out there themselves in the mud, he'd only be called to help get all of the vehicles out later.

Better to get this over with as soon as possible so he could resume his weekend.

He carefully slid his leg out from under Cassie's head, supported her head with a hand, and placed it gently on the sofa. Then, standing quietly, he bent and lifted her into his arms. She stirred, but didn't wake, just cuddled into his chest.

Damn those ATV'ers. Booked with North Mountain Sports Company. That was their first mistake. Well, good. At least this event would put a question mark next to the corporate company's safety record and once news spread around town, the hype surrounding them would die down.

Diva followed him into his bedroom, where he placed Cassie on the bed and pulled the bedsheets up over her.

"Mmmmm...hi," she said, opening her eyes.

She looked too freaking cute with her sleepy expression and messed-up hair. He resisted the urge to climb in next to her. "Hey, go back to sleep..."

"Where are you going?"

He sighed. "I just got a call from the station. Some ATVs are stuck in mud out at Canyon Mountain... They need me for obvious reasons," he said, flexing his biceps.

Cassie smiled, but then her eyes widened. "ATV tour? Did I have a tour scheduled today?"

"No, you didn't. North Mountain Sports Company did."

"Great, they are stealing my business already."

"Yeah, and look what happened. Don't worry, I'll be sure to toss out a dozen times that this wouldn't have happened if they'd booked with SnowTrek Tours."

Cassie relaxed. "Perfect. Thank you." She pulled him down toward her and kissed him.

Soft, simple...yet it had the opposite effect on his body.

Gripping her face, he deepened the kiss. A bad idea. He was hard within seconds. How had he managed to keep his erections under control before? Now just the sight of her, a simple touch or a passionate kiss had him wanting her.

"Sure you have to go?"

He growled. "No... Yes. You know if I don't go out now, I'll just have to go out later." He stood and pulled the blankets all the way up to her chin to cover her beautifully tempting body. "Stay here. Sleep. I'll be back as soon as I can."

"Hurry," Cassie said.

Oh, he planned to.

CHAPTER EIGHTEEN

TANK RESTED HIS head against his arm as the hot water steamed the shower doors. Searches always wiped him, even the easy ones. After every one he thought maybe he'd quit the crew. This one had been non-life-threatening, but going out during the more dangerous situations when he was a single dad, with a daughter to think about, seemed foolish.

Unfortunately, his loyalty to Wild River ran deep. This place had saved him. Coming here had changed his life. He owed it to everyone to do his part, keeping the backwoods safe. His size and strength made him a valuable asset on the crew and he'd never feel right letting his best friends head out there alone.

Kaia looked up to him and respected him for it.

Hell, it gave him a sense of pride in himself. Something that had taken a long time for him to feel.

Once Diva completed her training, there was no turning back...

Shit. They were getting so close and he still hadn't talked to Cassie about what that meant for the dog. He needed to have that conversation soon. He'd let it slide to the backburner with everything else going on, but he wanted to give her enough of a heads-up to adjust to the idea of Diva living with him.

He put his face in the spray and ran his hands through his hair.

A soft knock on the other side of the glass had him grinning as he opened the shower door. "Hey, you."

"Can I join you?" Cassie asked, already sliding her underwear down over her hips beneath his oversized T-shirt.

His exhausted body sprang to life again. Maybe that was the trick. Maybe he just needed a new surge of adrenaline after each rescue. Keep him on the high.

He watched as she stepped out of the underwear, then slowly lifted his T-shirt up over her head.

Damn, her body was fantastic. How he'd resisted having her for so long was a miracle, really.

Sainthood awaited him in death.

He moved aside as she entered, letting her stand beneath the stream of water. She inhaled sharply as the heat of the water hit her back. "Too hot?" Tank asked, reaching around her to adjust the heat.

"Better," she said, reaching up to wrap her arms around his neck, turning them slightly so that they both enjoyed the spray. "You were in here for a long time. I was starting to think you'd fallen asleep."

"Almost," he murmured against her lips. He had been tired, but he was wide awake now. He wrapped his arms around her, pulling her body into his. Their wet slickness was arousing and he was instantly hard.

Her lips met his and he closed his eyes as he devoured her mouth. She tasted like a breath mint and coconut lip gloss and her skin was smooth and soft beneath his touch as he slid his hands upward, over the strong muscles in her back and shoulders. Her strength was a huge turn-on for him. There was nothing she couldn't handle.

Except maybe the idea of losing her dog...

Nope. He refused to think about that right now.

He massaged the muscles along her spine as he lowered his hands back down to cup her ass. Firm and tight, like the rest of her. Lifting her slightly off her feet, he held her against his hardened penis.

A soft moan escaped her as she deepened the kiss and slid her hand in the tight space between their lower bodies to touch him.

Steam from the heat of the water had surrounded them and beads of sweat gathered on his body as she started stroking him. Slowly. Torturously slow.

How many times had he fantasized about her in the shower? At least several times a week, and now she was really there. Naked and incredibly sexy, her mouth and hand driving him insane. Better than anything his imagination could have come up with.

Dipping his own hand between her legs, his thumb massaged her clit as he inserted a finger inside her body. So wet, so ready for him.

Her tongue separated his lips and her stroking grew faster, her grip on his shaft tightening. The moisture inside the shower provided an arousing amount of lubrication as they pleasured each other.

His breathing grew heavy as he backed them toward the wall, lifting Cassie's legs around his waist, giving him better access to her. Lowering his head to her neck, he placed a trail of desperate kisses along it, down her collar bone, dipping low to capture a nipple between his teeth. Her breasts were perfect—small and round and perky. He sucked hungrily, then bit gently, and her legs gripped him even more. "That feels amazing," she said, her own breathing coming in short pants as her hands reached out for support along the shower wall.

"You feel amazing. Man, this body is incredible." He could run his hands over her all day. Now that they'd crossed this line into a physical relationship, there was no going back. He'd never survive without her touch, her kiss, her body… Words and emotions were not something that came easy to him; he wasn't sure they ever would…but maybe he could show her how he felt. Maybe she'd be okay with what he was able to give.

But for how long?

"Put me down," she said, lowering her legs from around his waist.

"Am I hurting you?"

"Not at all," she said, grinning as she moved away from the wall and dropped to her knees in front of him.

Holy shit. His penis throbbed in anticipation.

Cassie moved closer and gripped his ass cheeks as she lowered her face to his erection. The feel of her tongue along his shaft made him shiver. His knees weakened, and he grabbed the shower door handle for support. "Fuck, Cassie…you sure?"

"Absolutely." She smiled up at him before taking him into her mouth. Slow, seductively, her beautiful eyes locked with his as she sucked him, rotating her tongue along the shaft as he slid in and out of her mouth.

With one hand, she massaged his balls, while the other held his body close. He couldn't remember ever feeling this good. He couldn't remember being with anyone who could turn him on and have him craving more, the way Cassie could.

His grip tightened on the door handle and he supported his weight against the wall as she sucked and teased him with her tongue. Her mouth was so wet and warm…

His breathing was labored and the water was cooling off, but all he could focus on was the intense sensation coursing through his body at her pleasuring him. He swallowed hard, feeling himself close to the edge. "I'm coming…"

She didn't stop. Keeping the demanding tempo with her mouth, she continued to suck and lick and tease him into orgasm.

"Fuck." He was dizzy as the overwhelming sensations of pleasure rippled throughout his body. His legs nearly gave way beneath him as he came. He closed his eyes, and his head fell back into the now cold stream of water.

Cassie slowly removed her mouth and got to her feet.

Gripping her face between his hands, he kissed her. Hard. A new longing ache developing for her even before the first one had completely faded… He was ready for her again immediately. No recovery time needed. He'd never get enough of her.

Reaching behind his back, he shut off the water. Then, opening the door, they stepped out. In one fell swoop, he lifted her into his arms and carried her into his bedroom.

"I'm soaking wet," she said with a laugh as he placed her on the bed.

"You'll be even wetter soon," he said, lifting her legs and placing them over his shoulders as he buried his head between her legs.

He slowly licked her opening, savoring the taste of her. How many times had he fantasized about going down on her? It was one of his favorite ways to think about sex with her. He loved the idea of pleasuring her, making her feel amazing…like she'd just done for him.

She moaned, her hands tangling in his wet hair. "Tank…you're killing me."

He grinned as he pushed against her thighs for better access. His mouth teased and his fingers slipped inside. She was so wet, so ready, but still so tight. He felt himself harden as she lifted her hips higher. Sex with her was incredible. He'd always known it would be. What surprised him was his own inability to be satiated.

After so many years without sex, his body was making up for it now.

His fingers applied pressure as his tongue circled her clit. Flicking faster against it.

Cassie's moans grew more frantic and he knew she was close.

"Tank, please, Tank, don't stop…"

He had no intentions of stopping. He wanted to feel her body pulsate around his fingers.

Seconds later, her back arched and he could feel the intense throbbing inside her body as her orgasm rose. She let out a cry as her body fell back against the bed, and she slid her hips away, freeing his fingers.

He crawled across the bed to lie next to her, taking in her look of spent contentment. "That okay?"

"More than okay… Had I known you were capable of that, I would have successfully seduced you years ago," she said playfully, rolling him onto his back and straddling him.

His rock-hard erection between them made her laugh. "Wow, ready again so soon?"

"What do you say? You up for it?"

"Oh hell ya," she said, leaning down to kiss him.

Holy shit. This woman was going to be the death of him.

IT HAD TO be the warmest May on record. Tank unzipped his search and rescue jacket as he climbed out of his truck late on Monday morning. Or maybe he was still heated from his weekend with Cassie.

He opened the back tailgate to let Diva climb out. She still had a dog pout. She hadn't exactly been impressed to be cooped up inside all weekend, but in their heated state, neither he nor Cassie had wanted to leave the house unless it was absolutely necessary. Short walks and not enough attention from them had Diva acting truly dejected. "Are you going to stay grumpy all day?"

She refused to look at him.

He took her favorite ball out of his pocket. "Well, if you're not in the mood to play…"

She yipped and her wagging tail said he was forgiven. "Good girl," he said as she jumped down from the truck.

He whistled an undeterminable tune as he led the way to the training clearing. The dog eyed him with suspicion.

"What? I'm in a good mood."

Now a knowing look spread across the dog's face.

"Don't look like you know anything about it. You were passed out most of the time."

A mischievous glint.

The dog had serious personality.

"Alright, smartass. I got lucky this weekend, now let's see if you do."

Woof, Diva took offence.

"Not luck. *Skill*. I know, it was a figure of speech," Tank said as he bent to remove her sequined leash. "Looks like we're the early ones today." Damn, he could have spent more time kissing Cassie goodbye. He'd arrived extra early to pick up Diva and it had taken all his strength not to drag her into her own bed.

Lying next to her in bed, waking up to her, spending uninterrupted alone time with her had been a long overdue experience. They fit together perfectly and she was everything he'd thought she'd be and so much more. They were best friends, which had to contribute to the mutual trust and respect they had for one another between the sheets, but it went so much deeper than he'd imagined.

But did it go far enough? Could he really open himself up to her?

Taking the ball, he tossed it as far into the clearing as he could, feeling the burn in his bicep. He grinned, knowing the muscle tension was from holding Cassie up against the wall in the shower. She was a featherweight. He had to start working out harder.

Diva returned with the ball and he threw it again.

But hearing Frank's truck pull into the clearing, Diva immediately sat at attention at Tank's feet, ignoring the ball, even though it took all of her willpower not to chase after it.

"Someone looks ready," Jimmy said as he and Frank approached.

"She's determined to get it today," Tank said. "It's okay, girl. Go get the ball."

Diva took off across the clearing.

"So, is she living with you yet?" Jimmy asked, nodding toward Diva.

Tank squirmed, the question making him even more nauseous than before. He'd had all weekend to have that conversation with Cassie, but he hadn't wanted to ruin things. The weekend had been going so perfectly.

"Not yet," he said as Diva returned with the ball and dropped it at his feet.

Frank grinned. "Time's running out, buddy."

He was far too aware of that.

"What's the holdup anyway?" Jimmy asked.

"Cassie will be devastated to lose Diva. I mean, sure she will still see her all the time, but it's going to be hard on her," he said.

Jimmy shrugged. "So, ask her to move in with you too."

Diva barked her agreement.

"Things are still complicated…" They weren't ready for that. He wasn't ready for that. His ex had been back less than a month. Things were still up in the air regarding parenting between him and Montana…how could he start living with Cassie, having her in their lives full-time, in the middle of everything else? "We're not there yet."

The two men just shot him looks of disbelief and impatience, so he felt the need to say something more. "Look, we just started moving forward…but no one else knows right now."

"In that case, you may want to remove Cass's bra from the hood of your jacket," Jimmy said.

Diva grinned her agreement.

HAD A GOOD hike always made her feel this fantastic? Or could she credit Tank for her euphoric feeling that morning? Everything just felt right with the world.

They'd finally taken the next step in their relationship and while she wasn't crazy enough to start hearing wedding bells in the next decade, it was difficult not to get ahead of herself. She'd always been able to see a future with Tank, and being in his house with him all weekend, being intimate physically but also sharing their daily routine, every moment, had just reconfirmed for her that this was what she wanted. He was what she wanted.

"You're glowing this morning… I take it you had a nice weekend off?" Montana said as they reached the top of Suncrest Peak. Mayor Morell was heli-lifting in and would be there any minute.

"Yeah…the break was nice." Luckily her glow could be blamed on exertion. She and Tank had agreed to keep things between them for now…and Montana was probably last on the list of people Cassie wanted to recount the details of her weekend with Tank to.

How would Montana feel about the two of them together? So far, she hadn't made a move to get Tank back herself, so maybe she really was there just for Kaia and to get her life back… Was that too much to hope for?

"This weather is perfect. Conditions couldn't be better," Montana said as she set her pack on the ground and opened it.

Cassie agreed. They'd picked the perfect day to show him the site. "I could sit up here and look at this view forever," she said. Whether this peak was legalized as a jump site or not, she wanted to bring Tank up here. A romantic picnic would be nice…and maybe they could bring a tent and sleeping bags…

What on earth did they do together *before* they started having sex? That was all she could think about doing now.

Montana eyed her. "Okay, you are definitely different today. You are radiating happiness."

There was nothing wrong with Montana's instincts. But she couldn't exactly confess the reason she was on such a high.

"I just have a good feeling about this, that's all," Cassie said, opening her canteen and taking a gulp of water.

"Me too. Get your video camera ready," she said, opening her backpack.

"What are you doing?" Cassie could see the jump suit inside and her heart raced. What the hell was Montana doing? She hadn't told her she was planning on jumping. It was still illegal. The site wasn't prepped yet. The mayor would be here in minutes.

"Look, the only way we will convince Mayor Morell that the site is safe is if he sees it for himself."

"But we haven't triple-checked the height or the running distance…"

"Trust me, I got this."

"But it's still illegal. He could have you arrested." *Them?* Would she be guilty by association?

"He won't." Montana arranged the chute behind her on the ground as the sound of a chopper approached in the distance, then slipped into her suit, attaching the straps.

Holy shit. This was not what Cassie had been expecting that day. If they were going to go into business together, Montana couldn't pull these crazy surprise stunts on her. "How do you know?"

"He's an adrenaline junkie. We get each other."

"He's also the mayor," Cassie hissed, glancing over

her shoulder, seeing the mayor's helicopter coming over the peak. Shit, shit, shit…

Montana saw him too and strapped into her harness quickly. She put on a helmet—thank God for that at least—and a pair of sunglasses.

"Montana, I don't think this is a good idea." Correction: she *knew* this was not a good idea. They were trying to get the mayor to trust them and this was not the way to do it. Impulsivity and recklessness was what got the first jump site shut down.

"Stop worrying," she said.

Worrying was an understatement. Her heart pounded and her palms were sweating…this was a full-on anxiety attack. She was rethinking this entire thing. Tank was spot-on when he said the part of this venture that made him uneasy was Montana's involvement. She understood clearly what he meant now.

"Montana, this is your first jump in years…are you ready for this?" This jump was premature. There were so many things they needed to go over again before this was a good idea.

Montana's eyes shone with excitement as the mayor's chopper hovered directly overhead, giving him a clear shot of the action.

"Camera, Cass…come on. We may only get one shot at this."

Before they both went to jail. Right. Fantastic. She'd just started having sex with the man of her dreams. Of course fate had to try to screw with that. She let out a big, nervous sigh as she got her recording equipment.

Seconds later, Montana started to run toward the edge and Cassie hit Record with a trembling hand before noticing the tangle in the strings connecting Montana's chute.

"Montana, stop!"

The sound of the chopper overhead drowned out her words and Cassie rushed toward the strings, untangling them just as Montana pushed off.

Shit, that was close. This had to be what a heart attack felt like.

A glance at the mayor in the chopper revealed he'd seen the close call, as well.

Both Cassie and the mayor watched with their own mix of admiration and fear as Montana soared over the edge and gracefully flew over the canyon below. She maneuvered the chute perfectly to glide across the breathtaking landscape, and now that the initial shock of it all had subsided, Cassie felt almost envious of the experience. Montana was as close to flying as a person could get.

Still, she held her breath, capturing the flight on camera, and released a sigh of relief as Montana settled on the ground two minutes later. Safe.

Montana waved from the ground, with a triumphant holler that echoed loud against the canyon, above the noise of the chopper.

Cassie glanced at the mayor in time to see his own look of relief, then his unreadable expression before signaling the chopper to turn around and head back down the mountain.

Shit. They might have pulled off a successful stunt but now it was time to face the music.

CHAPTER NINETEEN

"I TAKE IT you had no idea she was planning to do that?" Mayor Morell asked, turning to Cassie the minute they were seated in his office an hour later.

Cassie clutched her hands in her lap. "Of course…"

"No. She didn't. The jump was my idea and I would have done it with or without Cassie's agreement," Montana said. Her face was still flushed from the adrenaline rush and Cassie might have been the one radiating happiness before, but now that honor went to Montana.

"We know it was drastic, but…"

"It's okay, Cassie," the mayor interrupted.

It was?

"I understand that Montana felt the need to show me in order to convince me."

He did? Could they actually be getting away with this?

"Of course, what you did was still illegal and as I suppose you plan to use the video of the jump for promotional purposes, I will have to fine you," he told Montana.

Montana nodded. "I understand. It was worth it."

Maybe a fine, but would she have accepted jail time as worth it? Cassie liked to think herself hardcore in pursuing her goals, but Montana took things to a whole new level. A dangerous level?

Could she really put her business's future in Montana's hands like this? They needed to talk and establish some serious ground rules. Fast.

The mayor sat back in his seat and stared at them. Finally he spoke. "The site is fantastic. I can see why you wanted me to see it. I take it you've done all of the necessary calculations for safe jumping?" The question was directed toward Montana.

She nodded. "Yes, sir..."

Please don't let him mention the mishap with the strings. Cassie knew he saw it from the helicopter. Would that be a strike against them? Make him think they weren't as ready as Montana thought? Cassie had her own doubts now.

"We received a new application to reopen the old location two days ago," Mayor Morell said.

Cassie's jaw dropped.

"Let me guess...from North Mountain Sports Company?" Montana sounded unimpressed.

Mayor Morell nodded.

"But that's not fair. This was our idea..." Cassie said. How had the other company found out about their plans in the first place? Lance Baker. Montana really needed to start discussing things with her if they were going to be partners in this.

The mayor held up a hand. "Slow down. We aren't approving their application."

If the mayor wasn't going to even consider the application of the bigger, more established company that could easily absorb liability cost, what chance did her company's application have of getting approved?

"I can't believe they even tried. No one on that corporate team has even ventured out into the Wild River outback areas..." Montana shook her head.

"Well, believe it or not, their application has only strengthened yours," the mayor said.

"Really? How?"

"They pleaded a rather compelling case for a new legal jump site as well, so now when I present the idea to the committee, I have strong backing—not only from SnowTrek Tours, but also from North Mountain Sports Company... I know it may be slightly disappointing that your application may not have been enough on its own, but the good news is, the site now has a much better chance of getting approved."

Montana smiled. "Good. Then we will have to send a thank-you gift basket to North Mountain Sports Company."

The mayor laughed. "Don't get too far ahead of yourselves." But when he paused and a dreamlike expression appeared on his face as he turned to Montana, Cassie's confidence soared. "So, tell me...how many more skydives do you think I should complete before attempting that jump you did today?"

Five minutes later, Cassie excused herself from the meeting. The conversation had turned to all of their adventures and they'd barely noticed her leaving. She headed down Main Street and, seeing Tank's truck parked in the alley behind The Drunk Tank, she unlocked the back door with the spare key he'd given her and slipped inside.

Her pulse picked up speed as she quietly walked down the hall. She'd been missing him all morning and part of her needed to see him, make sure things between them were still strong, that the light of day had yet to change his mind or give him a reason to retreat. They were making progress, but she knew the emotional side of things would still move along slowly. She wouldn't push for too much, too fast and spook him.

Cassie knocked once on the partially open door to his office, then peeked inside. He was alone.

"Hey…" He glanced up from paperwork on his desk as she entered. "What are you doing here?"

"Was on my way to the office and saw your truck outside. Wanted to stop in and say hi." She grinned as she shut the office door behind her.

Then locked it.

Tank's eyes widened in surprise. Then he was immediately on his feet.

Cassie's breath caught as a second later, he grabbed her and pulled her into his chest. His hands immediately cupped her ass, lifting her from the ground, and her legs went around his waist. "Hi," he said before his mouth found hers.

Wrapping her arms around his neck, she pressed her body to his, her hands creeping higher into his hair, still damp from a shower. He smelled of musky cologne and manly scented body soap, and his threadbare T-shirt had the shape of his pectoral muscles on full display. He hoisted her slightly higher as he broke contact with her lips to bury his face into the opening of her jacket. "Mmmmm," he moaned, breathing her in.

"Was I interrupting anything important?" Cassie whispered. "'Cause I can go…"

Tank tightened his hold on her. "Not a chance. Do you know how many times I've wanted to drag you back here and rip your clothing off?"

Seemed they'd shared a lot of fantasies.

Thank God they were finally starting to live them out.

"So, what are you waiting for?" she asked, feeling her entire body come alive with anticipation. The beautiful day, the energizing hike, the near heart attack caused by Montana's stunt and the early confirmation from the mayor that they were getting closer to approval for the site had a feeling of euphoria washing over her that day, and being with Tank right now would only make a fantastic day even better. Getting back to the office could wait. Another round of sex couldn't.

Tank carried her back to his chair and sat. Cassie's legs straddled him as he removed her coat, placing a trail of kisses along her neck. "You smell like the outdoors," he said, lowering his head to her breasts.

His beard tickled her flesh. "Just came from a hike." He didn't need to know details. She moaned as she reached for the buckle on his jeans. She undid them, then pulled down the zipper. Tank was rock-hard already.

Good, because she was ready for him, as well.

Climbing off him, she removed her top and leggings, then watched as he freed himself from the fabric of his underwear. She climbed back onto his lap and he slid his fingers into her panties. "Damn, Cass, do hikes always make you this wet?"

"I may have been thinking about you."

"I had a similar problem. Had I known I was going to get this unexpected visit, I wouldn't have taken care of myself in the shower this morning," he said.

"Doesn't look like it's posing a problem," she said, staring at the huge erection between them.

"It's not." He stroked himself and closed his eyes. "Shit…this won't last long."

So far, they hadn't been able to make any session last long. So many years of foreplay had them both ready to go at all times. She wasn't complaining. It just meant multiple orgasms.

"You didn't happen to bring protection by any chance, did you?" he asked.

Damn. Impulsive sex had its one downside. "I don't usually carry condoms on hikes... You don't keep any in your wallet?"

"Kaia goes through my wallet," he said, stroking himself with one hand and sliding a finger inside her body with the other. "I think we can work with this," he said, his breathing slightly labored.

They could definitely work with this. She lifted her body slightly and then lowered herself back down over his fingers. Then she pushed her hips forward so that her clit rubbed against his shaft. "Oh my God, this feels incredible."

His fingers plunged deeper, adding more pressure, and she felt herself tighten around them as she rocked her hips back and forth and slid up and down against him.

Circling the tip of his cock with her thumb, she massaged the pre-cum over him before stroking him... slowly at first, then faster as his own fingers picked up their pace inside her.

"Grind faster against me, Cass. I'm going to explode."

Instead, she slowed her pace.

Tank's head fell backward. "You're driving me insane."

"Good," she said with false bravado. She could pretend to be in control, but her body told her otherwise. She was at his mercy. She pushed her hips forward and rocked faster, coming so close to the edge...then backing off.

Tank's breathing was heavy and his hands gripped her ass, holding her against him. "Cassie..."

There was no holding off her release any longer. She moved her hips faster, harder...and seconds later, she collapsed against him as her orgasm rippled through her body.

Tank moaned his own release as his lips found hers again. Passionate, demanding kisses that had her pulsating even harder. He removed his fingers slowly from her body and took her face between his hands.

"I could get used to you stopping by to say hi," Tank said, staring into her eyes.

"Me too," Cassie said, snuggling into him as her body still enjoyed the final tremors of her orgasm.

Tank's arms went around her and he kissed her forehead. "So, how did your morning go? Your hike was out to the jump site, right? Wasn't the mayor meeting you out there today to see it?"

Cassie hesitated. "He loved it. He thought it was as fantastic as we do."

"That's good news... So, your application?"

"Not approved yet, but I think we're definitely closer." Should she tell him about Montana's jump? If she didn't and Montana did, he'd wonder why she'd kept it from him...and if they were in a relationship, they couldn't keep things from one another. But she was still partially naked on his lap and they'd just gotten one another off... Was bringing up his ex-girlfriend right now really necessary?

"Montana jumped." Better to just say it quickly.

Tank frowned. "She did what?"

"She jumped. I had no idea she was planning it..."

Tank stood, lifting her off his lap and setting her

on the ground. He reached for a tissue, then readjusted his underwear. "Classic Montana. Didn't she realize she could have gotten you both arrested…or worse, she could have gotten hurt?"

Obviously the latter was the main concern.

He pulled up his jeans quickly and retrieved his belt from the floor.

"She got a fine, that's all."

Tank shook his head. "This was what I tried to warn you about. She's not the most trustworthy."

Cassie couldn't argue but she felt the need to defend her business partner…if for no other reason than to continue to justify her decision to do this. "I agree that she shouldn't have done it and at the very least she should have given me an opportunity to talk her out of it. But you should have seen Mayor Morell's face. While I know it wasn't the right thing to do, it might have been the only thing to push the pendulum in our favor…" She pulled on her sweater and then her jeans. Getting dressed this quickly put a damper on their impromptu escapade.

Tank still didn't look pleased. "She's not planning any more of these surprises, right?"

"I still need to talk to her." Cassie had no idea what Montana would do next. But in that moment, she wasn't thinking about Montana…

"Yeah. You and me both," Tank said and Cassie wished she'd kept that day's excitement to herself.

CONFRONTING MONTANA ABOUT her stunt that day had to wait.

The search and rescue team was scheduled for a two-day training course on drone technology. Tank preferred the physical training to anything technical, but he understood the value these drones could provide in performing aerial searches without the expense of helicopters and to help navigate terrain that ground teams just couldn't reach safely by foot.

Any additional training or support they could get was appreciated, but his mind wasn't in it that afternoon.

As soon as Cassie had left his office, it had hit him how bad he'd messed up. Letting his annoyance over Montana, his concern over her, overshadow the moment they'd just had was a boneheaded move. He was an idiot. The look on her face when she'd left his office had told him he'd be lucky if he ever got her naked again.

And he desperately wanted to get her naked again. So he'd better smarten up.

What his ex did and didn't do was out of his control. He might not like it, but he refused to let it come between him and Cassie again.

Climbing out of his truck, he joined the rest of the team on the training field.

"Question," he heard Tyler say, raising his hand.

"We haven't even started yet," the instructor with the nametag Ken said. "But go ahead."

"When do we get to fly those bad boys?" Tyler said, nodding to the Zenmuse XT drones, visible in the back of the SUV.

"As soon as you learn enough not to crash them," Ken said. "But there will be two flight sessions in today's course. A thermal imaging flight as soon as we cover those lessons and then a night operations flight once it gets dark."

"Awesome," Tyler said, looking eager to get started.

As the instructor set up for the lesson, Reed approached. "You okay?"

"Yeah…just got a lot on my mind." Like how to make it up to Cassie for disappointing her earlier that day.

"About that… I, uh…stopped by the bar this morning. I was surprised to find your office door locked." He put his hands on his hips and eyed him suspiciously.

"Oh, um…" Shit. Reed would be happy for him and Cassie, but would the guy really want to know that Tank had been with his sister earlier that morning?

He didn't have a sister, but he was going with no.

"Look, your business is your business," Reed continued, "and if you and Montana have reconnected, and you're happy, then that's cool, but I just think Cassie deserves to know." Big brother protection was on full display and it was obvious that if he and Montana were hooking up, it was definitely not "cool" with Reed.

Tank shook his head. "Reed, nothing is going on with Montana and me…"

"But I heard… There was definitely a woman in there."

Shit. It was either tell him the truth or risk getting punched in the face. Actually the truth might spur that reaction, as well. "Your sister."

Reed looked slightly ill. "What? Oh shit…seriously?"

Tank nodded. "Feel better?"

"I'd say more disgusted, but definitely relieved," Reed said, punching him in the shoulder.

Better than the face.

CHAPTER TWENTY

THE ANCHORAGE ADDICTION Treatment Center number lighting up her phone had her hesitating before answering. Cassie never knew what to expect when she answered her father's calls.

Some days were good. He was sticking to the detox program and making progress. Other days he threatened to quit the program—again—and walk away from his third attempt at getting sober.

She checked the calendar on the wall before answering.

Day eighty-nine of his ninety-day program. He was so close this time. One more day. If he bailed now, it would be the hardest one to deal with.

"Hi, Dad," she said, answering just before the call went to voice mail.

"Hey, Cassie Lassie…"

The nickname he'd always used for her. She smiled, relieved that he sounded happy, relaxed. This was a good day.

She pushed all of her stress aside. "How are you?"

"Better than the last time we spoke…"

At day sixty-four, when he'd yelled and cried and demanded that they all love him for who he was and not insist on him changing. He was who he was, he'd said. Why couldn't they accept that? Accept him?

She remained silent when he would rant like that, knowing it was part of the process. The addictions center had provided her with her own support line and had equipped her with the tools she needed to survive the ninety-day journey as her dad's major source of support.

His words during those calls were a reflection of his disease, the struggles he was facing and the demons he battled, so she took nothing to heart. She simply told him she loved him and was there for him. Repeating that support throughout his treatment was important.

But today was a better day.

"One more day," he said, sounding hopeful, something she hadn't heard from him before.

"Nothing. A blink." One more day to complete the program, but then that was when the real hard journey started. Leaving the clinic ninety days sober was an amazing accomplishment, but outside of the clinic, living each day without alcohol would be the greatest test. He'd be challenged constantly. Was he strong enough to resist being pulled back under?

"I wanted to talk about my plans for when I leave here…"

Was he coming back to Wild River? Did he need a place to stay? Admittedly, she hadn't been confident that he would complete the program, so she hadn't really planned for what came next.

Of course whatever he needed, she'd provide. He was her father.

"That's probably a good idea. What are your plans exactly?"

"Point Hope."

She blinked. "The dry village in Northern Alaska?"

"Yes. I know staying sober isn't going to be possible

if I come to Wild River. I'm so, so sorry. I know I said I wanted to get better to come back to you all, but I don't think it's the right step for me…not yet anyway. But you can come to Point Hope anytime. I've spoken to a company there and arranged lodging and a job—it's just maintenance work, but it's honest work and I'll be around people who can help me stay on track. Temptations won't be there, so I have a chance. Once I'm stronger, then I can look at coming back…to Wild River or Willow Lake."

Cassie was speechless. This was the last thing she'd expected when she'd answered the call. Her dad had a plan. A real one. Lodging and a job. She wasn't sure how to respond… He really was determined to get better this time. Live a better life.

"You're disappointed…"

"No!" She cleared her throat. "No. I'm the complete opposite of disappointed. I'm proud of you, Dad."

Silence on the other end of the line, except for the sound of him swallowing hard. Tears gathered in her own eyes.

"You'll visit?" he asked finally.

"Of course. And so will Reed and Mom if you want…" They would. She may have been his main source of support, but the whole family had been praying for his success.

"Actually, Cass… I've been talking to your mom—just through letters that I'm allowed to send."

Yes, she knew about the letters to her mom and to Reed. It was part of the process and it was good for all of them. Helping them move on from years of hurt and sadness…

"She's planning to move to Point Hope too. With me."

Okay, now she was really in shock. Her mother hadn't said a word. "Really?"

"Yes. She said I could tell you. I don't want to take her away from you..."

"Dad, she's all yours," Cassie said with a laugh. Her mother would be the strength her father needed in his journey. This explained the decluttering and selling the house... It filled Cassie with only joy. She'd miss having her mom close, but she'd visit them both in Point Hope.

"You're sure?" her dad asked.

"Absolutely."

"Okay, gotta go. I'll call you soon. I love you."

"Love you too, Dad. Stay strong."

She disconnected the call and sat back in her chair with a smile. Her parents were going to make a go of it. In a safe, healthy community. Their best chance at making a future work. Her dad wanted that. They both did. There was a reason her mom hadn't filed for divorce all these years.

And having her parents back together was any kid's dream, right?

Her heart sank as the thought hit her and only an image of Tank and Montana came to mind. It had always been a dream of Cassie's... Was it also a dream for Kaia?

TANK HAD BEEN banished to the living room by his ten-year-old. "What are you doing in there?"

"You'll see. Have some patience," came Kaia's reply from the kitchen.

Tank grinned as the smell of grilled cheese reached him. "Be careful using the stove!"

"Dad, shhhh... I got this."

She had this.

Tank didn't doubt it. His little girl was nothing if not determined. She'd always been stubborn and headstrong and while at times it was challenging, when she was challenging *him*, he loved those traits about her. They would serve her well in the future.

Grabbing the television remote, he flipped to the basketball game and sat back against the couch cushions.

"Dinner's almost…" Kaia stopped when she saw him. "What are you wearing?"

Tank glanced at his old Gold's Gym sweatshirt he'd had since he was eighteen. Tattered, full of holes and threadbare. Comfy. "My sweatshirt."

"You have to change for dinner."

"Why?"

Kaia rolled her eyes. "Because I don't want to dine with you smelling like old gym socks."

"Hey, this sweatshirt is…" He sniffed it. "Okay, you have a point." Standing, he pulled the sweatshirt off over his head.

The sound of the doorbell had Kaia's eyes widening. "She's early."

Tank's narrowed. "Who's early?"

Kaia pushed him toward his bedroom. "Don't worry about it. Just go get a shirt on. A nice one," she said.

Ahhhhh, so she was up to a little matchmaking. He grinned. Grilled cheese sandwiches were *Cassie's* favorite. She would be touched that Kaia remembered. Maybe tonight would be the perfect opportunity to let his daughter know that he and Cassie had been making strides forward on their own. "Okay, okay… I'll get dressed."

Kaia closed his bedroom door behind her and a second later, he heard the front door open.

Tank surveyed the possible choices for a nice shirt in his closet. He only had two dress shirts. A white one he wore to weddings and funerals and one covered in multicolored surfboards that he wore on beach vacations.

Reaching for the white one, he put it on, leaving the top few buttons undone and rolling the sleeves for a more casual vibe. Then he ran some gel through his hair, washed his face and left the bedroom.

He hadn't spoken to Cassie since the awkward way they'd left things earlier that day and he should have been smart enough to plan a dinner. His daughter might well be saving his dumb ass.

Kaia was clanging away in the kitchen, the sound of plates and cutlery revealing she was setting a nice table for them. And noise from the living room told him she must have blocked Cassie from seeing the surprise, as well.

"You've been exiled from the kitchen too?" he asked entering.

"Yes. What is she up to in there?"

Shit. "Montana?"

Her smile faded. "Expecting someone else?"

Yes. Was she in on this? Kaia's matchmaking? Damn, this was not what he'd been expecting. At all. "I thought it was Cass at the door, actually."

Montana looked slightly confused. Then, taking in his white dress shirt and gelled hair, she assessed the rest of the situation quickly. "Oh shit. She's making dinner for us?"

Tank nodded. "You didn't know about it?"

"Of course not. Did you think I put her up to this?" Montana hissed.

Not anymore. His ex looked as panicked and uneasy about this turn of events as he was. "What are we going to do? We can't exactly go through with a romantic candlelit dinner together."

Soft music started to play throughout the house. Oh shit. He tugged at the collar of his shirt, sweat pooling on his lower back.

"But you could have with Cassie?" Montana asked, her tone unreadable.

He nodded. May as well be honest. They all needed to know the truth. He and Cassie were together. It might be complicated and slightly messy at times. He might fuck things up along the way as he had that morning, but they were together.

"So, things between you two…?"

"None of your business, but yes. We're together."

"Right." Okay, there was definitely disappointment in her voice now.

What the hell? He ran a hand through his hair. How the hell did they get out of this? And what was the meaning of Montana's one-word response just now? She knew he and Cassie were more than just friends. And shit, she hadn't said anything about him and her getting back together. He'd assumed they were on the same page about that. The past was the past. He didn't have those feelings for her anymore.

She'd never really had them for him. So, why this reaction now?

"Okay, you guys can come into the kitchen now," Kaia called out.

Did they have to? Maybe he could fake a call from

the station or maybe Montana could fake an illness. "How do you want to play this?"

Unfortunately, her expression softened. "I think we just go through with it."

"I'm sorry—what?"

"She went to a lot of trouble. We will break her heart if we tell her we won't have dinner together."

"Leading her to think that something—that feelings—exist between us is wrong." He needed to talk to Kaia about the situation with Montana. Clearly she'd come to her own conclusions. Damn, he'd been so concerned about her feelings and her reconnecting with her mother, he hadn't thought to clarify their own relationship.

"We're still friends, Tank."

"Or close proximity thereof…"

Montana scoffed. "It's only one dinner. We will turn off the music and blow out the candles. When I leave, you can talk to Kaia…explain things."

Oh good. Once again, it would be all on him. That was probably for the best, though. He wouldn't want to hand off tough conversations to Montana. Unfortunately, he didn't see any other way around this. "Fine."

Tank followed Montana to the kitchen and forced a smile as he entered. Indeed, the kitchen lights were dimmed. On the center of the table were two flickering candles, and a bouquet of multicolored daisies in a glass vase Tank had forgotten he even owned. Glasses of lemon water and a pitcher of the same sat on the table in front of two place settings with grilled cheese sandwiches and apple slices.

Two place settings. Only two.

"Wow, this is wonderful!" Montana said. "You cooked by yourself?"

Kaia beamed. "Do you like it, Dad?" she asked, turning to him.

"Yes! It's…yeah, it's wonderful!…like your mom said." Damn, he sounded like a moron. His daughter would see straight through the fake enthusiasm. "Um… where's your plate?"

"Oh, I'm not staying."

"What? Where are you going?"

He heard a truck pull into the driveway and his heart raced. A hip-hop song on blast could be heard drifting in through the open windows.

Kaia grinned. "There's my ride. I'll let you two enjoy dinner." She hugged them both quickly and left the kitchen.

"Just a second…" Tank called out after her. "You called Cassie to come get you?" Had she told Cass about all of this?

"Yeah." Kaia's expression changed as her face fell. "Is that okay? I just wanted the two of you to have some time alone together. To talk."

It appeared she was hoping for more than just her parents talking. Tank sighed as he forced another smile. "It's fine, but you and I need to chat later, okay?"

He followed Kaia to the front door and opened it. His gaze met Cassie's behind her steering wheel as Kaia ran out to the truck. The way her pained expression took in his appearance, he knew he was in the doghouse. Damn! Not breaking his daughter's heart meant digging him an even deeper hole with Cass.

He waved.

She ignored him.

Yep, he was screwed.

Closing the front door, Tank reluctantly returned to the kitchen. The lights were back on and the candles were blown out. A little less awkward at least. Montana was leaning against the counter, a bite of a grilled cheese sandwich in her mouth. "Couldn't wait, huh?" he said in an attempt to lighten the mood.

Montana swallowed the food. "Was Cassie pissed?"

"I'm sure she will be fine once I explain this misunderstanding."

Montana nodded but her expression made him nervous as she said, "What if this is more than just a misunderstanding?"

His pulse raced. "What do you mean?"

"Kaia obviously wants us to reconnect. She's asked me about us a few times—wanting to hear the story about how we met, how we…fell in love."

Tank coughed. Only *he* had. For her, their relationship had been a fling. Even when she returned, pregnant, she hadn't been in love with him. They'd only agreed to try to make things work for the baby's sake. "She's asked me about us over the years as well and I usually focus the story on her—how lucky I am to have her."

"That's really great. You're a wonderful father, Theo." The intimacy in her voice told him she'd called him by his real name on purpose.

His spine stiffened as he started clearing the table. "What did you tell her?" He hoped she hadn't given Kaia the wrong ideas about them. He may have loved Montana years before, but he'd healed from that experience and moved on.

"I wasn't sure what to say. I told her how we met,

that we were amazing friends..." She took a step toward him and touched his forearm. "Maybe now things could be different...there could be more."

Was she serious?

Tank took a step away from her and her hand fell away. "No. There couldn't." He was struggling to open up and be vulnerable with a woman who had always been there for him and Kaia, a woman he loved, his best friend... Montana had broken his heart twice and they were barely friends anymore. Did she really think they would be together again?

"Because of Cassie?" she asked.

"Yes, and also because you and I are a thing of the past..."

"We have a daughter together," she said.

"And that will never change, but that wasn't enough before." He dumped his sandwich in the garbage, his appetite vanishing, and put the plate in the sink. He needed to keep moving, the nervous energy coursing through him making his hands shake slightly.

"We need to think about Kaia," Montana said.

Tank blew out a deep breath. "That's all I've been doing. For ten years, I've always put our daughter first." At the sacrifice of a relationship with Cassie. His own chance at love. A real love, not the casual way Montana had approached their relationship.

Cassie loved him. And he put his and Kaia's feelings before her. All the time. His fear of commitment and fear of being hurt again all came before what Cassie wanted. The realization made him feel even worse.

"I know that," Montana said softly. "I'm just saying, if there's a chance...if you have any feelings left for me..."

He shook his head. "I don't."

Obviously she hadn't expected his response. But what had she been expecting? To come back here and find that he'd never gotten over her, had never moved on?

Maybe in a way he hadn't, but in that instant, he knew whatever feelings he'd had—both the love and the hurt—were gone.

"I'm sorry, Montana. The last thing I want to do is hurt Kaia, but you and I are not getting back together."

"What if things don't work with Cassie? What if you try and that relationship doesn't work out?"

"For years, I've let those excuses stop me from even trying…but I'm done with that. I deserve to be happy and so does Cassie." He paused. "So do you. And I'm here to support your starting over—with your career, with Kaia…just not with me."

Montana nodded slowly. Unfortunately, she didn't look entirely convinced. "Okay…but let me ask you one thing. If you're really in love with Cassie, why has it taken you so long to take this leap with her?"

His jaw clenched and he took a deep breath. "Because I'd taken a leap twice before and it was a long way down."

Montana lifted her chin. "You think it will be different this time?"

All he could do was hope. Unlike Montana, Cassie loved him. "I do, yes."

Grabbing her purse, she walked past him on her way out of the kitchen. "Okay…well, for your sake and Kaia's, I hope you're right."

A moment later, he heard the front door close as he stood there, staring up at the ceiling. His ex was like a tornado with an uncanny ability to blow through his emotions, sending them up in a spiral, just when he thought he'd finally figured them out.

"WHERE'S MOM?"

Tank turned off the television as Kaia entered the living room two hours later. "She went home."

Disappointment was evident on her face. "Why? Did you two argue?"

Not exactly. "No…she just had to get home."

"So you both had a good time, then?" Her hopeful expression was almost harder to handle than the disappointed one. Obviously his little girl was hoping for a reunion between her parents, but that wasn't what he wanted. Unfortunately, that was easier to remember when he wasn't left alone with his thoughts and his ex's words echoing in his mind.

Damn, Montana!

He'd been struggling enough with the idea that he was having to share his daughter's time, with the uncertainty of their future now that Montana was in it, but then she dropped a bomb of a solution on him that solved those issues. If they did try again to be a family for Kaia's sake, he wouldn't have to be faced with the potential of eventually being a part-time parent. But that's not where his heart was leading him, even if it might be an easier solution. He'd loved Montana at one time, but he knew those feelings were long gone.

"We did have a good time. We did a lot of talking," he said.

"Great! I'll cook again tomorrow night." Kaia started to leave the living room.

"No. Wait. Come back, please."

Kaia sat on the couch next to him and frowned. "I don't have to make grilled cheese again. I can also make spaghetti as long as you help strain the noodles once the water boils…"

"No, Kaia, honey, it's not about the food." He turned to face her, summoning the balls to be as honest as possible. He couldn't leave any room for doubt. She had to understand that he and Montana weren't getting back together.

He'd been hoping to tell her that he and Cassie were together now, but that conversation would have to wait. One thing at a time.

"Kaia, your mom and I love you. Very much. We both do. But we don't love each other."

"That's because she's been away for so long. You two just need to spend more time together."

"No… We're… I'm certain that we will only ever be friends. Great friends." Eventually. "And I'm willing to support your mom in anything she needs in order to be in your life. I'm glad you have her back."

"But you loved each other before. When you had me."

Damn, how did he explain the less than fairy-tale reality of unrequited love to a ten-year-old? He took a deep breath. "We care about each other. We did then. We do now. But love…that's complicated."

"I trust you two are smart enough to figure it out," she said confidently, unfazed by his attempts to clarify the situation.

He pulled her closer for a hug. He'd been honest with her and she'd see for herself that they weren't getting back together, and in time she'd be okay with it. They'd all fall into a new routine and things would be easier for her to understand. "We will figure it out—figure out this coparenting thing so that you get the best of both of us." Couldn't possibly explain it any plainer than that.

She frowned. "But that's what I'm trying to avoid. As much as I like spending time with Mom…it's weird being away from you."

She was already feeling the impact of the sleepovers and time with Montana.

"So…if the two of you got back together, I wouldn't have to do that. I could be with both of you…all the time."

Tank sighed as he touched her cheek. "I'm just not sure that would really be the best thing…"

"Just promise you'll think about it?"

Damn, he hated disappointing her. He had to tell her about him and Cassie…but would that make her feel better or worse? "It's getting late… We'll talk about this again, okay?" He chickened out. It had been an exhausting day and he needed time to process things.

"Okay," she said, standing and wrapping her little arms around him. "'Night, Dad.'"

Hearing her bedroom door close down the hall, Tank leaned back, resting his head against the cushion on the couch.

Shit. For once in his life, could he go after what he wanted? Do what would make him happy?

At the risk of denying his daughter what she wanted most?

"AH, MAN…POOR KAIA," Erika said, curling a leg under herself on Cassie's couch later that evening.

"Poor Kaia? How about poor me?" Cassie said, shoving her fourth piece of peppermint-flavored fudge into her mouth.

Erika took the box of chocolate away and put the lid on it. "The only thing I'm worried about with you is you getting sick from all this sugar."

"The sugar is the only thing keeping me from freaking out right now." For two hours, she'd sat in the diner listening to Kaia go on and on about how awesome Montana was and how her dad just needed to see it. Then she'd felt guilty for being relieved when Montana's vehicle was no longer there when she'd dropped Kaia back off at home.

"You have nothing to be worried about. Believe me, we can all see the change of heart in Tank the last few days…or him finally following his heart at last."

"Really?" She'd sensed the change in him too, but past experience had taught her to be careful about getting her hopes up.

"Yes. Even Reed says he's never seen the guy so happy, and with everything going on in Tank's life right now, that's a true testament to you and his feelings for you."

Cassie nodded. "He does seem happy when we are together." Though lately, whenever they were together, they were mostly naked… Was Tank's good mood a result of getting laid or was he truly ready to go all in with her?

"It's Kaia who will be the disappointed one when she finds out."

Cassie cringed. That hurt. The idea that Kaia would be upset made Cassie's stomach hurt more than the sweets did. She'd always thought that Kaia would be happy if she and Tank were more than just friends. Had she always read things wrong? Tank had always been reluctant for Kaia's sake. Maybe he'd been right.

But Cassie loved Tank and Kaia and she was desperate to make this work. No matter how difficult it would be now. She just hoped that across town, Tank felt the same way.

"I know it has to be hard on all of you. Everyone involved. Families are complicated," Erika said, opening the lid on the box of fudge and handing her one more piece. "Does Montana know about you and Tank?"

"I'm not sure." Cassie hoped that Tank had seized this opportunity to tell Montana. How would she react? How would working together be affected by all of this?

Erika waved a hand. "Well, ultimately it shouldn't really matter what Montana thinks."

Yet it did. Cassie wholeheartedly believed that Tank was over Montana, that there were no more feelings for her, except mutual respect and caring. But it would make Cassie feel a whole lot better if she was as certain that Montana didn't still possess feelings for Tank.

Had Montana been the one to put the idea of her and Tank getting back together in Kaia's head? Had she alluded to it being a possibility? Cassie swallowed the chocolate fudge and reached for her wine. "Things are so much more complicated now than they ever were."

"But at least in this version of complicated, you're getting laid," Erika said, raising her wineglass toward her.

"At least there's that," Cassie said as they clinked their wineglasses together.

CHAPTER TWENTY-ONE

FLOWERS ARRIVED FIRST thing the next morning. Three dozen roses in red, yellow and white. Red for love, yellow for friendship and white for forgiveness, the card read. He must have gotten help with that from Mrs. Cartwright, the owner of Wild Blossoms. There's no way Tank would know the meaning of different flower colors, but Cassie appreciated the effort.

No doubt he also got quite a lecture on love from the eighty-three-year-old florist who'd recently hit a bestseller list with the real-life relationship advice book she'd self-published the year before. As the town's local love expert, Mrs. Cartwright could be credited for saving a lot of marriages in Wild River.

Cassie sighed as she smelled the roses.

She'd already forgiven Tank. He had nothing to apologize for. He'd had nothing to do with the dinner setup and he had already texted to reassure Cassie that everything was fine and that he'd explained to Kaia that he and Montana weren't getting back together.

Unfortunately, she'd just realized how shitty this situation was for Kaia. Erika was right. The little girl was the one who would ultimately be disappointed by this. Which continued to break Cassie's heart. As adults, the three of them could work things out. But Kaia was ten. She wouldn't understand or be okay with this.

Kaia expected to have her family back. Wanted her family back.

Cassie slumped in her chair. Not even the text messages from Reed with photos of the dirty North Mountain Sports Company ATVs and the helpless-looking tour guides stuck in the mud had made her feel better. She knew what she wanted and for the first time she had a glimmer of hope that Tank wanted the same thing... but she worried about Kaia and what all of this transition meant for her.

Filing the stack of paperwork that had piled up over the last few weeks, her thoughts a frazzled mess, she barely heard the bell chime above the door.

"There's my Cassie Lassie," a familiar voice said.

She whipped around so fast, she whacked her elbow on the open file cabinet drawer.

"Ow...shit...oh my God! Dad!?" Tears brimmed in her eyes and she wasn't sure if it was from the intense ache in her elbow or the sight of her father.

"Hi, sweet girl," he said, smiling.

Her mother stood next to him. Beaming. Absolutely beaming.

Now the tears definitely had nothing to do with her elbow.

"What are you doing here? When did you get in?" He'd finished his treatment. He looked so much better than she would have expected. Older. Much older than when she'd last seen him, but healthier. He'd gained weight and his graying hair was cut short... He'd always worn it long, but this suited him better. In jeans, a new ski jacket and hiking boots, he looked great. Best of all, his eyes looked clear and bright. Not bloodshot from hangovers or tired from the pressure of trying and failing to quit drinking.

"I just caught the train into town a few hours ago and your mom picked me up from the station. I said this was my first stop."

Cassie nodded, swallowing the lump in her throat. She stepped forward and he outstretched his arms. She hugged him tight, savoring the familiar scent of his old cologne. He'd worn the same one since she and Reed were kids. But this time, the lack of whiskey mixed with the musky scent had fresh tears gathering in her eyes. "Hi, Dad, you look great."

"Not as beautiful as you. Look at you." He held her at arm's length and took her in. "Amazing. Hard to believe you're the same little thing…" He shook his head. "Lots of years…"

Her mother joined in the hug. "And lots more to come," she said, tears of happiness in her own eyes.

They both looked so happy. As though the years in between the day he disappeared and now no longer mattered. They didn't. The past was the past and her parents would focus on their second chance at a future together, because they both clearly wanted one.

Her father stepped out of the embrace and looked around the store. "Your mom was telling me about this place on the way over. Wow, Cass…it's really fantastic."

She blushed at the praise, wishing she'd had time to organize better. But it didn't matter. Her father was standing there, finally getting to see her accomplishment.

It meant a lot more than she'd ever thought it would.

"Thank you. I didn't do it all on my own."

"Everyone needs help to achieve their goals, but the determination in you was what made it happen," he said, scanning the photos along the wall. "So many years…" The tinge of regret in his voice tugged at her heart. She didn't want him to regret the past…just keep moving forward. That's all anyone could do.

"When do you leave for Point Hope?" Not that she didn't like having him in town, but temptations were there. Hell, her boyfriend owned a bar. Boyfriend? Was Tank her boyfriend? What were they exactly?

No time to think about that now.

"We head out there tomorrow morning," he said. "Your mom's all packed and I start the new job the day after tomorrow."

Hitting the ground running—good. Acting while his motivation was high would help him be successful.

"Yes. We wanted to take you kids out to dinner tonight before we left," he said.

Cassie froze slightly. What would Reed think seeing their dad again? They'd been communicating through letters, but face-to-face was stirring so many emotions in *her*, Reed was going to be a whirlwind of thoughts and feelings… "Have you talked to Reed?"

Her father nodded. "Called him from the truck. He was…surprised. But happy, I think."

"I'm sure he was," she said quickly. Reed had been waiting for this for so long.

"Him and that lovely surgeon of his will be meeting us at Meat & More Steakhouse in an hour," he said.

Cassie glanced at the clock. If she locked up now, she had just enough time to shower and change.

"If you want to invite a guest, you're welcome…" her dad started.

Arlene was shaking her head. "Cassie's situation is a little complicated."

"Complicated?" Her father frowned. "What have I always told you? What do you do when boys give you trouble?"

"Kick them in the nuts," she said with a laugh. Unfortunately, in this case she was quite fond of Tank's nether regions.

"That's my girl," her father said with a wink.

Her mother checked her watch. "Okay, well, we should get going, darling. We have a few things to pick up for the trip tomorrow. We will meet you at five?" she asked Cassie.

"I'll be there."

Cassie watched as her parents left the store. In complete awe. She'd never imagined the day she'd see her parents back together again. So happy. So in love. So committed to starting a new life together.

Could she really prevent Kaia from having this feeling?

Tank might claim he was over Montana, but the two had been determined to stick things out and make it work for Kaia's sake before… Would they again if Cassie wasn't in the picture?

She knew what she wanted, but was she willing to continue chasing it if it meant hurting Kaia?

Damn. Two days ago, things seemed to be going in the right direction. She'd been elated and confident in her feelings and the progress she and Tank were making. So why did she suddenly feel like a roadblock?

An hour later, she'd showered and changed. As she opened the door to Meat & More Steakhouse, Cassie could hear laughter and Reed's voice to her right, and she released a deep breath as she headed toward their table near the window. Before they saw her, she took a second to stare at her family. Her mother, father and

Reed at the same table. And Erika, fitting in perfectly, sat next to Reed, his arm draped over her shoulder, the smile on his face telling the story.

Good job, Dad.

He'd made it back to them.

Seeing the love at the table… Erika and Reed and her parents… Cassie struggled to compose herself. Would she ever really have that? Could she be selfish and continue to fight for what she wanted?

Reed turned and saw her. "Ah, there she is," he said with a wave.

Forcing a smile, Cassie joined her family, refusing to let her own conflicted, tortured heart destroy this moment.

CASSIE'S DAD WAS BACK.

Tank was happy for her and Reed as he glanced at the photo she'd just texted him of all of her family together for the first time in so long. Too long. He hoped her father's road to recovery got easier with time and the loving support of his family. Tank only wished he could be a part of that. This was the first Reynolds family dinner in years he hadn't been invited to and it made him nervous. But the fact that he wanted to be there, by her side on this special occasion, told him a lot. All day, he'd been thinking about Montana's words and Kaia's wishes…but he kept going around in circles of indecision.

He knew what he wanted…to be with Cassie. But at what cost?

"Hey, Dad, can you text Cassie and ask her if she can come over to help me with this social studies homework?"

"Cassie's busy tonight," he said, opening the fridge and taking out two cans of soda.

"Doing what?" Kaia looked shocked as she glanced up fróm her homework, as though Cassie didn't have a life of her own.

Tank could understand. He too had taken Cassie and her schedule for granted over the years. There was so much he was regretting about their previous one-sided relationship. "Her father is back in town and they are having a family dinner together."

Kaia pouted. "But she promised she'd help. This assignment is due tomorrow."

"I can help."

"You're no good at this stuff. Cass always helps."

Right. She did. And yet, since Montana was in town, his little girl had given Cassie the cold shoulder, unless she needed something from her...like now.

He sat and ran a hand through his beard, choosing his words carefully. Kaia wasn't at fault for taking advantage of Cassie, *he* was. He'd allowed it. He'd done it himself. "Well, I think we can figure it out."

"It's due tomorrow and I haven't even started it."

Whose fault was that? "I'll help. But maybe next time, you should start working as soon as the work is assigned." He couldn't be hard on her right now. She'd had a lot going on lately. They both did. Normally, he kept on top of her school assignments better too.

"Cassie was supposed to loan me some pictures of the different places she's traveled, though."

"We will find some online." He reached for his laptop on the table and opened a search engine. "Okay. What are we looking for?"

Kaia pushed her assignment away and folded her

arms. "They won't be as good as the ones Cassie has. I'd rather wait for her. Do you know when she'll be done with dinner?"

Tank's teeth clenched. "Cassie is busy. In fact, I'm sure she's often busy, but she agrees to help you because she cares about you." It was unlike his daughter not to realize that and be appreciative.

"Obviously not enough to remember that this assignment is worth twenty percent of my grade," she mumbled.

"Hey!" Tank said, a little too loud.

His daughter's eyes widened.

He took a deep breath. "Sorry to raise my voice, but that's enough of the attitude. Cassie must have forgotten. And this family dinner is important. It's the only time she'll get to see her dad before he and her mom move to Point Hope. I'm sure she would be here helping you under any other circumstances. You know that too."

Kaia nodded, immediately embarrassed. "You're right. I was being selfish. Family is important."

"It is, and Cassie hasn't seen her dad for a long time."

"He went away when she was a kid, right?"

"Yes. He had some problems he needed to work through, help he needed..." He didn't want to get into it in too much detail with Kaia. Over the years, she'd put together the bits and pieces she'd overheard about Cass's dad.

"Like Mom," she said, staring thoughtfully at her pencil.

"Something like that—yes." It wasn't exactly the same, but in a way she was right. Both parents had needed to go away in order to come back stronger, for any chance of being a good parent.

"You know, I never realized that Cassie and I had so much in common," Kaia said.

"Yeah, I guess you do." He reached across the table and bopped her on the nose. There was his sweet, understanding little girl…

"And you know… Cassie never thought her parents would get back together either," she said slyly with a pointed look at him. "But now they have."

Oh, fuck my life.

CASSIE HURRIED DOWN Main Street, dodging puddles on the sidewalk and careful not to wipe out on her heels. She'd forgotten about Kaia's social studies assignment.

Please let her still be awake.

It was just after nine…

Her cell phone battery had picked the worst time to die during dinner, so she couldn't even text to let Tank and Kaia know she would be stopping by. She'd left the restaurant as soon as she'd remembered and hurried home for the photos she'd promised Kaia. Luckily, she'd dug them out the week before and had been waiting for the little girl to start the assignment.

But she hadn't asked her for them… Shit, maybe she hadn't needed Cassie's help after all.

Out of breath, she knocked on Tank's door.

The light in the hallway came on, illuminating his shape through the window, and her heart raced even faster. Would her body ever not react to the sight of him? In five years, her attraction had only grown stronger and since being with him, she was helpless against the overwhelming emotions she'd fought hard to suppress for so long.

"Hey…" he said, surprised and happy to see her.

"Hi. Is Kaia still awake? I completely forgot about the social studies project," she said, entering the house and struggling to catch her breath. "Dad's arrival caught me completely off guard today. I don't even know if she still needs my help or not…"

"Hey, hey… Don't worry. We understand."

Cassie nodded, her heart rate slowing. "Is she still awake?"

"Just went to bed about ten minutes ago."

"Damn it. Sorry, Tank…"

He smiled, touching her shoulder. "Don't stress about it. I know a thing or two about geography and Google images might not match Cassie Reynolds's quality of photographs, but we figured it out. Besides, it was her assignment."

True, but… "Yes, I know. I just feel bad for bailing on her."

"You didn't bail. You had a family thing come up."

"Was she upset?"

"No." He paused. "Actually, she had a revelation. She realized that maybe she often took you for granted. She felt bad about that." He took a step forward.

Cassie shook her head. "No, I love helping her…"

"She knows that. But we both realize that in the past we relied on you for so much and that wasn't fair to you."

Cassie swallowed hard. Great. She let Kaia down once and now they were trying to let her down easy. Sugarcoating the fact that they didn't need her around as much anymore. Her chest constricted.

"Tank… I'm not sure that all of this…you and me… I think Kaia isn't ready for this yet." She was panicking in the worst way. She was in love with Tank, but she also loved him and Kaia, and loving people meant doing what was best for them. Maybe Montana was what was best for them…being a family again. The way Kaia wanted.

He studied her. "What's happening here? I thought we were both on the same page. Moving forward. Being together. It's what we both want."

"I know…but you just said yourself that Kaia doesn't really need me as much now."

He laughed. "That's what you got from that? Hell, no, that's not what I meant. What I was trying to say is that we were both being assholes—expecting so much from you and not giving close to enough in return. We were being selfish and that needs to change. We want to offer you as much as you've been giving us."

"Really? But I thought Kaia was wanting you and Montana…" Had the little girl had a change of heart? Had Tank told her about them? Her hope rose.

"She still does."

Hope plummeted.

"But that's why I think we need to tell her about us. Right away." Tank stepped forward and wrapped his arms around her. "There's no point in hiding the truth from her. Everyone around town shouldn't know before her."

Cassie sank into his arms. "You sure?"

"Yes." He pulled away and bent low at the knees to kiss her.

All the stress of her day melted away. His lips were so soft and inviting, and in his strong arms was the only place in the world she wanted to be.

Cassie wrapped her arms around his neck as she felt herself lifted from the ground. He headed down the hall and she looked at him. "Are you sure about this? Kaia's home," she whispered as they passed the little girl's room. "We should probably tell her about us first…"

"She sleeps like a log and I'll make sure we're up before she is." Tank kissed her again and any and all arguments died on her lips.

She was desperate for him. Emotionally exhausted, but physically awakened, she needed to be with him right now.

Tank carried her into the bedroom and softly closed the door behind him. He set her down in front of him and unzipped her jacket, lowering it over her shoulders.

She slid her arms out and reached for the base of her sweater, pulling it off over her head.

Tank reached for her face again, pulling her into him for a long, torturous kiss that had her body tingling with desire. She wanted him. He wanted her. All of her worry over whether or not they were doing the right thing evaporated. She raised his T-shirt up over his stomach and chest, and he raised his arms into the air.

She stood on tiptoe in her heels, but still couldn't reach high enough. "You're too tall."

He grinned as he lowered his arms out in front of him to allow her to remove the shirt. She tossed it aside and went for his belt. Suddenly, she couldn't get him out of his clothes fast enough.

She unbuckled the belt and tore it from around his waist. Her fingers fumbled for his button and zipper. He took over, removing the jeans at lightning speed and kicking them across the room.

Cassie slipped out of her heels and removed her own dress pants, then led the way to his bed. Sitting on the edge, she climbed backward until she reached the pillows, then lay back, staring at him as he removed his underwear and tossed them aside.

He was hard already. How on earth had they been

successful at curbing their intense attraction to one another for so long? They certainly couldn't now.

She wouldn't think about the missed opportunities or lost time. It really hadn't been. Without the physical all those years, their connection had deepened, strengthened, in every other way...which made sex with him that much better now.

And they had the rest of their lives to discover even more truths about how deep their connection was.

Tank climbed onto the bed and lay next to her. "I'm glad you came over."

"Me too," she said, shivering as he trailed his fingers lightly across her stomach.

"I really am sorry about the other night...dinner..."

"I got the flowers," she said. "And I was never upset with you."

He grinned. "So that murderous look you shot me from the truck..."

"Okay, so maybe I was a little upset."

"Well, let me make it up to you." He slid a hand beneath the waistband of her underwear and she opened her thighs as his fingers crept lower and lower. Tickling and teasing, they inched toward her opening, which was already desperate for his touch.

His gaze locked with hers and she reached for him, drawing his mouth to hers as his fingers stroked along the folds of her vagina.

Her entire body trembled, wanting him. Her tongue slipped between his lips and he hungrily devoured her, their tongues frantically exploring one another.

His fingers dipped inside her body and she felt herself tighten around them. She could come so easily with just a simple touch from him. The affection and trust they had for one another made giving all of herself to him so easy. Loving Tank was easy.

She traced the shape of his abs as she moved lower to wrap her hand around his cock, so hard and big. Her breathing grew more labored, just at the thought of him inside her. She had nothing to worry about with him… she was safe.

He moaned against her mouth as she stroked the length of him. Up and down, slowly at first, then faster as his own fingers picked up their pace, moving in and out of her body.

Her legs spread even further and he dared to dip another finger inside. The tightness and pleasure had her pumping him harder now. She craved release already.

He broke away slightly, panting as she felt him harden even more under her touch. "Cassie, you're killing me… I was hoping to make this last," he whispered.

"Okay, let's slow things down a little," she said as she experienced the first warming sensations of orgasm along her inner thighs. It felt so good. Slowing the rippling effect that continued to build throughout her body was nearly impossible.

She rolled him onto his back and lifted her body to straddle him. His hands gripped her hips as she lowered her body to his. The feel of his penis against her wetness had her swallowing hard. This wasn't helping to slow things at all. She wanted him inside her right now.

"I'm so close, Cass," he said, sitting up and burying his head between her breasts. The warmth of his breath against her skin sent shivers throughout her core.

"Condom…" she whispered. "Quick."

Tank reached into the bedside drawer and retrieved one. Ripping it open, he handed it to her.

Cassie slowly rolled it down over him, marveling at the size of his erection. "Where do you even find these big enough?" she whispered.

Tank laughed. "You already have me naked. You don't have to continue stroking my ego." He flipped them so that he was on top. Holding his weight on his arms, he wedged himself between her legs.

The tip of him pressed against her opening, and Cassie wrapped her hands around his biceps as she lifted her hips and took the length of him inside her body. Damn, the sheer size of him made everything that much more intense. "Make love to me, Tank," she whispered, her gaze locked with his.

The intensity in his expression as he started to rock his hips, plunging deeper and deeper inside her, left no room for doubt about how he felt for her. They hadn't said the words to one another, but Cassie felt his love, she could see it, feel it…

She stared into his eyes as he thrust faster and harder. Their gazes locked and held as the friction between their bodies grew more and more intense. She was so close. She held him tighter as she fought to control the urge to cry out.

Tank lowered his face and drowned a moan of his own in her hair as he plunged deeper. His fingers tangled in the pillow and she heard his breath catch as his body trembled above her. "Shit, Cassie…" he whispered.

She arched her back and rocked her hips forward, her own orgasm erupting. She bit her lip in an effort to restrain her pleasure as her head fell back against the pillow.

Tank collapsed next to her a second later and stared at the ceiling, as though trying to catch his breath and gather his surroundings… She knew the feeling. She still pulsated where his penis had filled her, and a euphoric feeling had her floating.

"Holy hell, Cass…"

She rolled to her side, draping one leg over his. "Thank you."

"Thank *you*."

She slapped him playfully. "I meant for what you said before…about wanting to tell Kaia about us." She knew that would be a big step for him…for them.

"She deserves to know."

"I really am sorry I wasn't here to help her tonight."

"She understood." Tank pulled her closer and kissed the top of her head. "Your family dinner went well?"

"Really well. Dad looks great. I hope he can stay on the right track."

"Me too." Tank trailed his fingers up and down her arm. "And Reed? He was cool?"

"I've never seen him so…complete. Dad was a missing piece for him for so long."

Tank squeezed her tight. "Families come in all different shapes…the key is making everything fit."

Cassie nodded, as her eyes drifted closed. She hoped they could make all the pieces of their relationship fit somehow, because now that she was in Tank's arms, she never wanted to let go.

CHAPTER TWENTY-TWO

HE DID NOT wake up before Kaia.

Tank was in the middle of the best dream of his life when the sound of Kaia's scream had his eyes snapping open.

The scene in front of him moved as if in slow motion, but happened in milliseconds.

"What is going on?" Kaia asked, still looking horrified, glancing between him and Cassie. Tank jumped out of bed and hurried after Kaia as she left the room and ran down the hallway.

"Cassie came by after you went to bed last night to help you with your homework." Damn, that sounded so lame.

"It was a social studies assignment, not sex ed! What the hell, Dad?"

"Hey, watch your language!"

"Hey, how about putting on some more clothes?" she yelled, slamming her bedroom door.

Tank hesitated…then marched back into the bedroom.

"Shit, shit, shit," Cassie was muttering, sitting up and reaching for her discarded clothes on the floor.

"Sorry… I forgot to set my phone alarm," Tank said, reaching for his own jeans and T-shirt. It was inside out, but he pulled it on anyway.

"I'll get dressed quickly and leave," Cassie said, yanking her sweater on.

"No. You don't have to. We will all sit down and discuss this." Did he sound calm? Because he was absolutely fucking terrified by the idea, but he'd told Cassie the night before that they needed to tell Kaia the truth about them right away in order to move forward.

Of course this wasn't the way he'd envisioned it happening, but here they were...

"Are you sure? Maybe you should talk to her first...?"

He wavered. "No. Maybe... I don't know. Just give me a sec to figure this out," he said. He went to leave the room, but then turned back and jumped over the bed to Cassie. He gave her a kiss and held her chin up to look into her eyes. "This is going to be the hard part. We'll get through it."

As she dressed, Cassie listened to Tank trying to coax Kaia out of her bedroom. "Kaia, come on out, let's talk about this."

"Go away!"

"No, I can't do that. We need to talk about what you saw."

"I saw you and Cassie in bed together. Pretty sure there's nothing to talk about."

Cassie winced as she leaned against the door frame of Tank's bedroom. His shoulders slumped as he rested his head against Kaia's bedroom door. They had a strict "respect of privacy" policy in this house. He wouldn't go into the room unless invited. If Kaia refused to come out, there would be a standoff through the door.

Unfortunately, Kaia must have forgotten about the come-in-by-invite-only rule that morning.

"Sweetheart, I was going to tell you about Cass and

me, but you had a lot going on… We were planning to have a chat with you today. We are sorry you found out this way."

Very sorry. This situation was tough enough. Now they'd possibly made things even harder. She wished she could regret staying over the night before, but unfortunately, it was exactly the reassurance she'd needed from Tank.

"Kaia…"

Silence from the other side.

Tank glanced at Cassie, shooting her a desperate look. Unfortunately, she had nothing to offer. Which was like a brick to the forehead. Here they were, moving forward with a real relationship, and she was determined to integrate more fully into their lives. She was a role model and confidant to Kaia already, but she was quickly realizing that stepping into a more serious, more permanent role in the little girl's life wouldn't be easy.

Especially now with Montana back. Before, it had been just whether or not she'd make a good stepmom… now it was almost a competition to see if she could measure up to Kaia's real mom.

Shit. How had she never considered what it would mean to be a stepmom to Kaia? Had she never fully believed she and Tank would make it that far or had she obviously thought that Tank would still parent and she would just be…Cassie?

Right now, she had no idea how to deal with the situation and that was speaking volumes.

Mostly that she was going to have to try even harder. Cassie had always committed to being there for her. Now she needed to prove that her commitment went even further. She didn't just want to be Kaia's friend, someone she could rely on, someone who babysat her when necessary and took her shopping or helped with homework. She wanted to be family. To think long-term and plan a future with Kaia and Tank.

And she wanted to believe that eventually Kaia would want that too.

Tank turned back to the door, knocking gently. "I'll give you some time to process what you saw. But after school, we do need to talk."

Silence.

He slowly walked away from the door, looking slightly hopeless.

Cassie hugged him tight. "As you said, this was never going to be easy." But she wasn't willing to retreat this time.

A FULL DAY of silence later, he was dying.

Of all the ways he'd been planning on telling Kaia about him and Cass, this was never one of them. Mortified that she'd found them in bed, he was mostly terrified of the psychological damage it could cause her.

Shit. And he'd been doing so well keeping her from needing therapy as an adult.

This had to be the longest they'd ever gone without talking to one another. She'd even forgiven him faster that one time he said he could trim her bangs to avoid the cost at a salon and she ended up wearing a baseball hat for a month until they grew out.

He was going crazy.

He knocked on her bedroom door just before dinner. "Hey, Kaia, I think it's time to talk now."

Silence on the other side of the door had him sighing. "Kaia, I know we have rules and boundaries in this house, but if you don't come out, I'm going to have to come in. We don't ignore problems in this family."

Nothing. She was calling his bluff. Fantastic.

"Okay, I'm really coming in now." Turning the door handle and stepping inside, Tank caught a chill, as though someone had walked over his grave. Spidey senses tingled as he scanned the empty room. "Damn, Kaia." Her bedroom window was still slightly ajar. Her safety fire rope ladder hung over the edge.

The note on her desk had his heart hitting the pit of his stomach.

Dad,
I'm happy for you and Cassie. Clearly, she's the one that matters most to you now, so I'm going to live with mom.
Love, Kaia

Jesus, seriously? When had his daughter developed a knack for the dramatic? It seemed like overnight, Kaia had become a moody preteen, and thinking that he now loved Cassie more than her? What the hell had happened to his no-nonsense, mature, practical little girl?

Montana's arrival in town and in their lives had happened.

Frustrated, he reached for his cell phone and started to text Montana, but then stopped, seeing one from her, letting him know that Kaia had arrived at her place safely and that she would call him soon.

Great. He should be the one with Kaia right now. Talking all of this through, making her feel better... He sighed, running a hand over his beard.

What was the right way to deal with this? He wanted to drive straight over to Montana's and bring Kaia home, but was that the right thing? His daughter was upset. Clearly she needed space. Acting like a caveman and forbidding her from leaving the house was never his parenting style… As she got older, raising her would only get more challenging and he didn't want to push her away.

So, ignoring his every instinct, he folded the letter and tucked it into his pocket. Leaving the house, he headed straight to the bar. There was only one thing to do while he waited this whole thing out. Those damn darts weren't going to throw themselves.

"OH MY GOD, what are you doing here? Let's go get her." Reed indeed looked ready to kick everyone out of the bar, whether they'd finished their drinks or not.

And Cassie totally agreed with her brother. She re-read Kaia's brief running-away letter and looked at Tank in disbelief. Why was he so calm right now? When she'd left his house that morning, he'd been a mess—understandably so—and all day she'd been waiting on an update about how his discussion had gone with Kaia.

This letter and Tank's lack of freaking out wasn't what she'd been expecting.

"That's not the game plan," Tank said, casually stacking beer glasses behind the bar.

"You have a game plan for this?" If it was up to her, they would drive straight to Montana's, take Kaia home and bar the bedroom windows until she was thirty. Montana was in town for a month and the little girl was jumping ship already.

Cassie had felt the intense sting of being replaced in the little girl's heart, but it couldn't possibly even come close to how upset Tank must be feeling right now. Leaving him on his own to deal with it earlier that day hadn't sat well with her, but she'd had work obligations, and with North Mountain Sports Company now open and business across the street booming, she had to pick up the pace on her own bookings and incentives… She couldn't put all of her hopes into the approval of the jump site.

"Yes. I've been texting with Montana about it…"

Oh good. He and his ex were working together on this game plan.

"Kaia arrived safe and sound. She begged Montana not to send her home." Heartbreak was evident in his voice and Cassie felt horrible that she was partially to blame for the little girl's running off. "We decided to let her stay the night and Montana will bring her home after school tomorrow," Tank said, leaning against the bar and reaching for Cassie's hand.

Cassie sighed, stroking the back of Tank's hand. "That's probably for the best."

"I hate to be the voice of dread," Erika said, "but Tank, have you thought about what you're going to do if Kaia continues to want to spend more time with Montana? What if she decides she wants to live with her mom? For real?"

"It's all I've *been* thinking about. I'm not sure what legal rights Montana has, but I'm sure she has some, and if Kaia decides she'd rather be with her…" He ran his free hand over his hair.

Cassie understood his fear, and she wanted to reassure him that she was pretty certain that wasn't what Montana would want. After the conversation Cassie had overheard at the North Mountain Sports Company grand opening event, Montana's real intentions for being there were starting to shine through. Cassie wasn't sure it was her place to tell Tank…and for Kaia's sake, she hoped she was wrong, but she suspected Montana wasn't interested in parenting full-time. "I say we not get ahead of ourselves yet. Let's just take it one day—one outburst and crisis—at a time. Kaia is angry right now, but I'm sure once she has time to cool off and really think about things, she'll realize that she's being hasty," Cassie said, hating seeing Tank look so unsure. She squeezed his hand tight.

But his gaze drifted past her and he gently released her hand and straightened as John Cartwright approached the bar.

"Hey, John," he said. "What can I get you?"

"A beer, please," John said, avoiding Tank's eyes as he rummaged in his wallet for cash.

"Put it away. It's on the house," Tank said, pouring the pint.

"I insist…" John put the money on the bar and shifted from one foot to the other while he waited.

What was going on? The two men were usually bickering about basketball by now. But tonight, John looked uncomfortable and Tank seemed to be taking a long time to pour that beer.

"Hey… You haven't been in here in a while. Starting to think you're trying to dodge me." Tank laughed, but the look Cassie caught on John's face confirmed it was true. She looked back and forth between them, feeling a thick tension around them.

"My loan's not getting approved, is it?" Tank asked.

Loan? What loan?

John sighed, lowering his voice. "I was planning to call you about coming in to the office to discuss…"

"Now's as good a time as any for bad news," Tank said.

Bad news? What was he talking about?

"I'm sorry, Tank. We just couldn't make the numbers work," John said. "Wish I had better news. I hope you can find another way to buy out Montana's share of the bar." He took the beer and headed back toward the pool tables.

"Thanks for trying, man," Tank mumbled after him.

Montana was part owner of the bar? What the actual fuck? When was Tank planning on telling her? *Had* he been planning on telling her? She stared at him now, but he avoided her gaze.

He removed his apron and tossed it onto the bar. "Reed, can you watch the bar for me for a few minutes?"

"Sure thing, man," Reed said.

Tank disappeared toward his office and Cassie climbed down from the stool and followed him. This may not be any of her business, but if she was hoping for a future with Tank, he had to stop keeping things from her and avoiding tough conversations.

He glanced up as she entered and a look of guilt spread across his face. "I'm sorry I didn't tell you."

She took a deep breath, unsure of what to say. Up until a few days ago, this really was none of her business, but after opening themselves up to more than friendship, she expected full transparency, honesty… He had to start trusting her. "Why didn't you?"

"Because I was hoping I'd get the loan and be able to buy her out and then it wouldn't matter."

He was so missing the point. "Of course it would matter. Tank, obviously you and Montana share more of a connected past than you've ever admitted. You two share a child. You've admitted to being in love with her years ago…and now she owns the bar with you?" Cassie's emotions were in a whirlwind. In the grand scheme of things, maybe this shouldn't matter, but it did. The fact that he didn't tell her hurt the most, but emotions aside, she had to face the fact that logically, there was every reason in the world for Tank and Montana to be together. Their lives were interconnected in more ways than he'd let on. Kaia wanted her parents to reconnect... The little girl's running away was a clear indicator that she wasn't happy about Cassie and Tank acting on their feelings... This was a mess.

"I'm sorry, Cass. I shouldn't have kept this from you," he said, coming around the desk and wrapping his arms around her.

She folded her arms across her chest. "If we're going to do this...be in this together, I need you to be open with me. Tell me things, let me in, let me help."

He nodded. "I know... I'm trying, Cass. This isn't easy for me."

She swallowed hard. "I know, but this relationship can't work if you don't try a little harder."

He kissed her forehead and she heard him sigh as the disappointment of the reality of things settled in the air around them.

"Theo was my father's name," he said.

She studied him. "What?"

"My full name is Theo Alexander. And no one knows that." He took a breath. "After growing up in foster homes, I learned not to get close to people..."

Cassie wrapped her arms around his neck, relaxing just a little.

"So...when I fell for Montana and gradually opened up, learned to trust and then things ended... I guess it just reconfirmed that the only person I could rely on, count on in life, was myself."

She kissed his forehead. "I can't imagine how tough

growing up was for you and I'm sorry you had your heart broken in the past...but I want to know you. The real you. All of you." She raised her lips to his and kissed him softly.

"Be patient with me...even more patient, okay?" he said.

She nodded slowly. What choice did she have? She couldn't expect him to change overnight. Baby steps were still progress and she just hoped everything started to fall into place soon... The uncertainty and upheaval of their lives in the last few weeks were starting to take their toll on her. "On one condition—no more secrets, okay?"

He kissed her again and pulled her in to him. "I promise. No more secrets."

SEEING MONTANA'S NEW Jeep pull into his driveway early the next morning, Tank quickly moved away from the window. He took a deep breath and blinked exhaustion from his eyes. Sleep had eluded him and worry about Kaia and what Erika had said had him going crazy.

If Montana wanted shared custody and Kaia voiced her desire to live with her mom, what could he do? What did he want to do? He hated the idea of not having Kaia with him and it seemed brutally unfair that Montana could waltz in like some fairy tale and win his daughter's affections so easily.

Unfair. So many things were unfair.

He couldn't help the bitter disappointment he felt about the bank loan falling through. He'd been putting his hopes on it. He should have told Cassie about the bar, but he'd wanted to tell her when he had good news... that the situation would soon be resolved. He'd wanted to tell her once he was full owner of the bar and that particular tie to Montana had been severed.

But he knew she was right to be upset. The bar thing was just an example of his struggle with vulnerability, his inability to fully trust and be open.

He thought he was making strides in that direction, but they obviously weren't big enough, fast enough.

He stopped pacing as the front door opened. "Dad?"

Rushing into the hallway, he hugged Kaia tight, any anger or annoyance melting away at the sight of her.

"Hi, Dad… I'm sorry about leaving without telling you," she said, the words coming out on a grunt as he squeezed her.

He glanced at Montana as she entered. Her expression was unreadable, but something was definitely not right. "I won't say it's okay, but I understand you were angry. I'm glad you're back."

Kaia stared straight into his eyes as she delivered her next blow. "I'm not back. I'm just here to pick up some stuff, and then I'm going back to Mom's."

Tank blinked.

Montana looked panicked behind Kaia.

"I'm sorry…what?" *Keep calm. Don't raise your voice. This is a misunderstanding.*

"Mom said it's okay with her," Kaia said, a note of defiance in her tone.

She what? Tank stood and cleared his throat. "Kaia, could you go to your room for a moment, please?"

"Sure. I have to pack up some stuff." She turned to Montana. "Don't leave without me."

Montana simply nodded.

When Kaia was out of earshot, Tank turned to his ex. "What the hell, Montana? We said one night." They had a deal. If she thought she could join forces with Kaia against him, they were both wrong. He loved his daughter and he respected her right to a relationship with her mother, but moving in with Montana after only a month was not happening.

"Calm down," Montana said. "It was the only way I could get her to come back here. She was furious last night, then she was upset, then mad again... She's disappointed that you being with Cassie means you won't be with me."

Did that fact also upset Montana? He couldn't read her, but she looked tired...not her usual vibrant self. "Why didn't you explain things to her? Tell her that you and I aren't getting back together. With or without Cassie in my life."

Her voice and expression took on an edge. "Look, Tank, I'm not exactly used to this parenting thing."

"Exactly why you should continue to just let me do it!" Too loud, too harsh, but the words were out. He meant them. Montana being in Kaia's life might be good for her, but in what quantity? Certainly not full-time. He knew that now. Not if she couldn't be honest with the child. Misleading Kaia hadn't been the right thing to do. "I'm sorry, but you shouldn't have given her false hope about us...or about her living with you. That's not going to happen." And he'd fight to make sure it didn't. His daughter needed stability and a strong role model and while her mother had a million admirable traits, she wasn't fully committed to parenthood. She lacked the knowledge and experience he'd gained from years of raising Kaia alone.

"I don't want that to happen. She belongs here with you," she said quietly and relief flooded his body.

Unfortunately Kaia wasn't relieved. "You still don't want me?"

He whipped around at the sound of her voice and his stomach dropped. Shit.

Montana was silent, looking to him to deal with it. Of course. "Kaia..." he started.

She folded her arms and glared at Tank. "This is your fault. You kept Mom away so long, now she doesn't want me."

"That's not true. Things were never your dad's fault," Montana finally said.

"Why would I believe you?" Kaia asked, her eyes filling with tears. "You lied to me. You said I could live with you. You said you were happy to be back in my life." She swiped at the frustrated tears running down her cheeks.

Tank longed to hug her, comfort her, but any attempt wouldn't be appreciated at that moment. It broke his heart to see her like this.

"I'm sorry, Kaia, but this is your home," Montana said.

To her credit her tone was firm, resolute, final. Man, he felt like an asshole to be relieved that he wouldn't have to battle this out in court with Montana, that they were both on the same page. Especially when Kaia looked so devastated.

"I hate you both," Kaia yelled, going into her bedroom and slamming the door.

Montana's eyes immediately filled with tears and she looked as if she'd been kicked in the stomach.

Tank knew that feeling quite well. He walked toward her and held out his arms.

She stepped into them and his T-shirt was instantly wet from her tears. "She said she hates us."

"Welcome to parenting."

CHAPTER TWENTY-THREE

MONTANA LOOKED A MESS, which was completely off-brand for the woman.

"Rough day?" Cassie asked carefully as Montana entered SnowTrek Tours later that morning. She'd heard from Tank that Kaia was home, but not entirely happy about it.

"Update. She hates us. All of us."

Cassie handed Montana a cup of coffee as she slumped into the chair next to her in the office.

"Sorry about my part in that…" Why did she feel so awkward all of a sudden? She had nothing to apologize for. Montana and Tank were a thing of the past…but still, working together now would be slightly awkward for both of them. Hopefully not so awkward that they couldn't still make this venture work.

Montana squinted and rubbed her temples.

"You okay?" She looked pale and the dark circles under her eyes hadn't been there before. Cassie had assumed it was just the stress of the Kaia crisis, but maybe there was more to it.

"Yeah. Fine. Just a headache," she said, opening her purse.

Cassie tried to pretend she wasn't looking, but she caught sight of various prescription-labeled bottles inside. Montana bypassed them and reached for a bottle of over-the-counter painkillers. Shaking several into her hand, she washed them down with the coffee.

"You sure you're up for this?" They were planning on launching the first newsletter to the jumpers that day, a teaser that something exciting could be on the horizon. Drum up buzz and interest, without giving all the details. Montana had suggested it and Cassie could see how it was a good idea.

She didn't want to get ahead of themselves, but the minute the site was approved...if it was...they wanted to hit the ground running. Summer was coming and putting Wild River on these athletes' radar early was a good idea, before they booked trips overseas to jump in other destinations. They weren't promising anything just yet, so Cassie didn't think it could hurt to reach out. At the very least, it might drum up other business for her company.

"I'm fine," Montana said. "These painkillers should kick in at any moment." She reached for the laptop, turning it to face her. "Okay, so the newsletter blast should reach about three hundred and seventy people. That may not sound like a lot, but these are serious jumpers. They will all be intrigued and even if we get ten percent of them interested in our inaugural jump tour package, it will be hugely successful for SnowTrek Tours."

"Can we even handle ten percent?" They really were moving forward before things were finalized. They could pull together a tour package quickly if the site got approved, but she was worried about being able to safely accommodate a tour of more than ten or twenty people.

"Absolutely." Evidently the painkillers had kicked in in record time because Montana's determination was back in full gear. "So, here's the draft of the teaser promo I want to send out," she said, turning the screen back toward Cassie as the promo loaded.

Cassie held her breath as she watched the twenty-second video, a snapshot view of Wild River, the beautiful picturesque scenery shot she'd captured from the jump site…and then Montana running toward the edge.

It cut off just before Cassie had ditched the camera to untangle Montana's chute strings, and the footage switched to a GoPro shot. Cassie clutched the chair arms as a 3-D sensation of soaring over those mountains herself made her eyes widen. "You were wearing a camera that day?"

"It's built into my suit," Montana said, her eyes on the video.

The ending was a flash sequence of SnowTrek Tours' current spring promo, featuring the Slush Cup race and a group shot of Cassie and her tour guides.

"Wow. This looks professionally done. You could go into business making promo videos."

"No way. Jumping videos are the only ones I'm passionate enough about to put the work into, and I couldn't sleep last night, so I had plenty of time to work on it… You really think it looks good?"

"It's amazing. Maybe a little crazy…" But she needed crazy. She'd been looking for crazy. She'd just never expected it to come in the form of Tank's ex.

"Do it," she said. "Quick, before I change my mind."

Montana gave a sheepish grin. "Okay, so I may already have."

Cassie frowned. "What?"

"Like I said, I couldn't sleep. And after I made the video, I was excited…" She logged into YouTube as she spoke. The video appeared. With thousands of views already. "Look! Amazing, right?"

That was one word for it. Unfortunately, her irritation with Montana overshadowed any excitement she could feel. "Um…you posted this without telling me?"

"Yes. But I knew you'd be okay with it once you saw how many views it was already getting."

Right. Just like she'd known Cassie would be okay with the illegal jump once she saw that it worked to impress Mayor Morell. What other decisions would Montana continue to make without her?

Before she could say anything, Montana continued, "And the best part…" She opened an email and turned the laptop toward Cassie. "Look at the interest."

Hundreds of unread emails sat in an inbox for a new BASE jumping site.

Cassie blinked in disbelief. "You created your own website?" How much time did she have the night before?

Montana shook her head quickly. "No! Of course not…it's not live, anyway. I just created a template so that I could create an email address to attach to the YouTube version of the video. I knew you'd freak out if you started getting emails overnight to the SnowTrek Tours email. But don't worry, we can link this new site…"

"Montana…stop. Please," Cassie said, her annoyance rising. She'd launched the promo, posted it to YouTube, created a new site… Montana had made all of these decisions without even consulting her. They were supposed to be doing this together. Slowly. Cautiously optimistically. Not recklessly full speed ahead. She cleared her throat. "While I appreciate the enthusiasm and focus… I think you should have waited to talk to me about it before doing all of this. The jump site's not even approved yet."

Montana looked genuinely confused. "But you just said to go ahead and send out the buzz email."

"Right. Together." SnowTrek Tours was still her company. Montana was going to be a big part of this new venture. They'd be partners in it, in fact, but she couldn't just take over completely when Cassie's company's reputation was on the line.

Montana sighed. "I don't see the problem here."

That *was* the problem. "I just think big decisions regarding and affecting my company need to be discussed with me. I mean, the jump the other day was risky as hell."

"It worked. So did this," Montana said, pointing to the inbox as another email appeared.

"That's not the point," Cassie said.

Montana studied her. "What is this really about?"

"You acting on things without talking to me!" What did she think Cassie was annoyed about?

Montana nodded slowly. "This is about Tank."

What?

"Look, I didn't know you two were more than friends. I would never have done it if I'd known that you two were…together now. Officially."

Cassie's heart raced. Done what exactly? And why the hell was she hearing this from Montana—whatever this was. Her annoyance gave way to severe irritation… no longer at Montana, but Tank.

What was he keeping from her now?

She was desperate to find out, but not from Montana. She refused to let Montana know that obviously her and Tank's relationship wasn't strong enough for him to be open and honest with her. Cassie took a deep breath. "This has nothing to do with Tank." It was true. She was professional enough to be able to separate her personal and professional lives. "But, Montana, I need to think about if this—you and I working together—is going to work." She wanted to save her company, but Tank had been right about his ex.

Montana was too impulsive to be trusted with Cassie's future, her career and obviously her love life.

NORTH MOUNTAIN SPORTS COMPANY's opening had succeeded in one thing. Flooding Wild River with a bunch of tourists who would normally prefer the trendy Aspen scene to the real wilderness. Tank surveyed the crowd in his bar. Or rather the clothing choices and turned-up noses.

Mountain ruggedness wasn't for everybody. But if they thought he was changing his drink menu to accommodate all the fancy-named cocktails they were requesting all evening, they were in for a rude awakening. "The place is full of Pre-Wild-River-ized Erikas," he mumbled.

Reed laughed. "Do not let her hear you call her that."

"What? It's a compliment. Your girl's adaptation to life here has been a one-eighty transformation. I don't think any of these people have ever used paper napkins or spotty glasses before."

"True. But they have cash," Reed said, showing him the tips he'd collected all evening.

"Stuck-up money is as easy to cash as any other," he said, sliding the money from the too-full cash register into a bag to put in the safe out back. If business kept this pace, he might actually be able to solve his financial dilemma. Six months of profits like this, combined with a lot of restructuring his budget, and he just might be able to pull off a buyout offer for Montana. Maybe not the seventy thousand he'd originally planned, but close… "Watch the bar for a sec. I'll be right back."

Reed nodded. "Hurry. These people aren't used to waiting for service."

Taking the bag, Tank carried it into his office and secured the money. The influx of visitors would eventually taper off, but Reed was right. The money these tourists were bringing to his business was certainly appreciated. Though, he hated that something that benefitted his company was hindering Cassie's.

Grabbing his cell phone, he took the opportunity to text Kaia. She was still giving him the silent treatment, but his rule for letting her spend the night at a friend's house was that she had to answer his text messages.

So he was using it to his advantage and texting her more than normal. He was dying from the silent treatment at home and while he was determined to give her the time and space she needed to get over the initial shock of things and disappointment that he and Montana obviously weren't getting back together, he missed talking to her. Missed her smartass jokes and hearing her sing off-key in her bedroom.

This tension between them had never happened before and it needed to end soon. He had to find a way to talk to her.

Just checking in... Everything good?

He waited.
A minute later, she replied.

No change from the last ten times you asked.

Most parents would be irritated by the attitude, but he grinned. She was coming around. Otherwise she'd just have replied yes...like the last ten times she'd replied.

"Hey..." Cassie's voice in the office doorway made

him smile. Then it faded when he saw the look of irritation on her face.

Shit. What had he done now?

"Got a sec?" she asked, entering the office and closing the door.

"Of course." Something told him she wasn't closing the door with the same intentions as when she'd visited the office the week before. Unfortunately. "What's wrong?"

"Did you kiss Montana?"

His eyes widened. "What? No! Shit, no. Where is that coming from?"

Her shoulders relaxed as she released a sigh of relief. "Well, what *did* happen the other night...when Kaia made dinner for you both?"

"Nothing. Montana and I just cleared the air about a few things."

"So then why was she apologizing to me today for making a move to be with you?"

Tank sighed as he walked around the desk and reached for her.

Cassie backed away.

Damn it. She was pissed. He ran a hand over his beard. "Look, it was really nothing. She just admitted that maybe the two of us together wasn't such a horrible idea...for Kaia's sake."

"And that's nothing?"

According to Cassie's expression, he was quickly realizing it might not be nothing. At least not to her. "Okay, so it's not nothing, but I shut it down immediately." He touched her shoulders and bent at the knees to look her in the eyes. "I told her there were no feelings anymore. That we wouldn't be trying again...not even for Kaia."

Cassie stared at the floor. "Why didn't you tell me?"

Damn, it seemed like she was asking him that question a lot lately. A lot more than she should have to. "I guess I should have, but I handled it and it was over. I didn't want to upset you…especially when you two are going to be working together. I didn't want things to be awkward."

She scoffed as she moved away from him. "All of this has been awkward…and challenging…and heart-wrenching. Working with her was never going to be the most comfortable situation, but at least when I thought I wasn't in competition for you, it was a little less awkward."

"There's no competition…"

"But she loves you?"

"No. She just wanted to *try* to love me for Kaia's sake." Like before. A relationship of convenience that could never truly work. He knew that now. Montana had ample opportunity in the past to develop feelings for him and she never did… She wouldn't now. And more than that, Tank realized he didn't want her to. He was falling hard for Cassie. Harder than he'd ever fallen for Montana… Now might be the time to tell Cass that.

Nope. The words got stuck somewhere in his throat. Deep in his throat. What the hell was wrong with him? Why were feelings so hard for him to express?

"Do you want her to love you?" Cassie asked.

Oh Jesus. "No! See, this is exactly why I didn't mention this. I didn't want to make it worse." He paced back and forth in his office, annoyed with himself for not having the balls to just say how he felt. It would certainly defuse the situation right now, but then again, he didn't want the first time he confessed his love to be in the middle of an argument to prove he still didn't love his ex.

"You have to stop thinking that you're protecting me by not telling me things, Tank! I'm a grown-ass woman—I can handle hearing the truth. What I can't handle is feeling like your ex has all the control... She's holding all the cards and she knows you better than I do."

The pain in her voice killed him. "That's not true. You and I are so much closer than Montana and I ever were."

"She knew your real name," she said, sounding defeated.

He sighed. They were back to that again? "It's really no—"

"If you say 'it's nothing' one more time, I'm going to lose my shit."

"Okay, okay...you're right." Tank released a deep breath as he sat on the edge of his desk. He ran a hand over his face. Cassie was so right. About everything. He'd kept things from her over the years...not just to protect her but to protect himself. They couldn't move on with a real relationship, though, unless he opened up to her, let her in...the way he'd let Montana in years ago.

Cassie wasn't Montana. She wouldn't hurt him.

Still, he wasn't a freaking machine. Able to just bring up all the shit from his past without feeling the emotions he'd felt back then—hopeless, lost, confused, angry...

Cassie still waited for him to say something, but he had no idea how to give her what she wanted. "I don't know what you want from me, Cass."

"I've been here for you and Kaia for a long time. I've never expected anything from you but I deserve to have someone who is willing to go all in with me. I need someone who wants to share their life with me—the good and the bad—and I'm not sure you're ready for that," she said, sounding sad and defeated.

He stood and folded his arms across his chest, his annoyance with his own inability to be vulnerable making him take it out on her. "Tell me, then, what old wound would you like me to reopen for you?"

"Tank…"

"How awful it was to know that my mother didn't care enough to push through her own pain and suffering to take care of me? How shitty life was moving from one foster family to another?"

"Tank, stop, please."

"This is what you wanted, though, right? You want me to talk about my past so that you can feel as though you know me. Because knowing the person I am now isn't enough."

Cassie shook her head. "That's not it. I'm just frustrated that Montana seems to know you so much better than I do. She shares your past, your present, and she'll continue to share your future."

Tank swallowed hard. He wanted to reassure her. Make her feel better. He was confident about them, but she was right about Montana, and in that moment, he was tired of disappointing her. "I'm not sure I'm ever going to be able to be the person you want me to be, Cass." He stared at the floor because looking at her would break him. He'd been selfish regarding her for too long and until he could be what she deserved, that had to stop.

"I'm not asking you to be something you're not… I was just hoping someday you'd let me in the way you…" Her voice trailed off.

The way he'd let Montana in. "And I guess I was hoping I wouldn't need to."

His defeated gaze met her devastated one, before she nodded slowly, turned and left the office, leaving him alone with a million instant regrets.

CHAPTER TWENTY-FOUR

DIVA CUDDLED NEXT to her on the sofa late the next morning. Cassie was going insane replaying their argument in her mind. She'd gone back and forth between feeling justified in her emotions to convinced she was in the wrong and then back again all evening.

Was she pushing for too much? Could she really expect Tank to flip a switch and become vulnerable just because she thought that's what she needed to move forward?

Or was it perfectly acceptable to want to know him—truly know him—inside and out? She didn't know why he was so worried about opening up. She'd only ever been there for him in the past. Did he really think she'd judge him or love him less if she knew him better?

But did his past define him? Did she need to know those painful parts of him or was it because someone else did?

She reached for her laptop and hit Play on Montana's YouTube promo video… What the hell did she do about Montana? This video was amazing and all the work the other woman had put into this new venture gave Cassie confidence that with Montana's help, it would be a great success…

But communication was the issue. And trust.

Just like with Tank.

Damn! Maybe *she* was the one with the problem. Maybe actions outweighed the need to talk about things all the time. Montana shouldn't have gone ahead and posted this without her, but ultimately, did Cassie need to be in control of every little detail? Going forward, she was going to have to have faith and trust in the partnership. After all, Montana was the expert in this case.

She sighed.

Similarly with Tank, did she need to dig deep into his soul to feel like they were connected or was the passion and commitment she'd felt growing stronger from him each day enough? Moving forward with a real relationship with him meant having faith that they'd grow together, learn more about one another over time.

As she watched Montana soar over the mountainside, tears of frustration and uncertainty blurred her vision.

Montana was helping her save her company. Tank was giving her more than ever before.

So why couldn't she just be grateful that she might finally be getting everything she wanted?

Tank's number lighting up her cell phone on the sofa next to her made her pulse pound and her mouth go dry. She'd been wanting to reach out to him, but she hadn't known what to say or where his head and heart were now after their argument… She stared at the ringing phone and answered just before the call went to voice mail.

"Hey you," she said, nervously. "I'm happy you called."

"I wasn't sure if I should, but…" Worry filled his tone.

Cassie's heart raced as she sat straighter. "Everything okay? Kaia?"

"Kaia's okay…I think. She's at school. It's Montana."

"Is *she* okay?" Remembering how pale the other woman had looked the day before and the painkillers she'd been swallowing like candy, Cassie bit her lip. She hadn't seen her since then…since their argument.

"I don't know. That's why I'm calling. She's not picking up or answering texts from anyone. Have you seen or heard from her today?"

"No… Actually, I haven't seen or spoken to her since yesterday morning." When she'd left SnowTrek Tours, she hadn't looked well…but not sick enough to be worrisome or to warrant telling Tank about it. With everything going on with Kaia, and their disagreement over the video, Cassie had assumed Montana had needed some time to herself.

"Me neither," Tank said. "Did she mention going anywhere?"

"Not that I can remember… Do you want me to try her cell?"

"Could you?"

"Sure. Of course. I'll let you know if I reach her."

"Thanks, Cass…"

"Hey, don't worry, I'm sure Montana is fine. I'll call you as soon as I talk to her," she said with more confidence than she felt.

Disconnecting the call, she immediately dialed Montana's number. Voice mail.

She texted her,

Worried about you. Call me.

Turning up the volume on the cell phone, she placed it on the sofa and stared at it, willing a reply. But hours and several more attempts at calling and texting later, there was still nothing from her.

Montana, where are you?

Tank pulled into a parking stall in front of Montana's apartment building six hours later. Climbing out, he went inside and buzzed her apartment. No one had heard from her. She hadn't returned any calls or texts.

Something was wrong.

No answer from inside the apartment.

He buzzed again.

Come on, Montana.

A man leaving the building looked at him. "Tank?"

Eddie…in his police uniform. He nearly choked on his heart. "Are you here for Montana? Is she okay?"

The guy frowned. "No. I live here."

Tank's pulse steadied. "Oh, sorry. I'm looking for Montana… Kaia's mom. You've seen her around town." Had been following her…or maybe not. The guy lived in the same building. It could have been a coincidence that Montana had noticed Eddie as often as she had. "She lives on the second floor, apartment…"

"Nine. Yeah, I know. We're neighbors. I actually haven't seen her coming or going in the last few days…"

Shit. If anyone should have seen her, it would be the guy who lived next door and who admitted to keeping an eye on her. "Hey, I know it's against building rules to admit nonresidents, but do you think we could go up there? I'm worried about her. She's not returning any calls or texts from anyone. No one has seen her since yesterday afternoon." He'd even asked Kaia to try calling…without letting her know he was worried, of course, and she'd had no luck getting a response either.

Montana might ignore him and Cassie, but he didn't believe she'd ignore Kaia.

"Lucky for you I'm allowed to bend the rules," Eddie said with a grin, pointing at his badge. "Police."

"Great."

Eddie unlocked the door and, taking the stairs two at a time, they went to Montana's apartment.

Tank knocked and waited. Nothing.

Putting his ear to the door, he listened, but all was silent inside. No music, no television, no sound of footsteps... He dialed her number, but no sound of her phone ringing came from inside.

"She's not in there. I haven't even heard water running or anything all day," Eddie said.

Seems the guy was keeping close tabs on Montana. Must be driving her nuts. "Can we go in?"

Eddie hesitated. "Only if we have cause for concern...foul play or something..."

"She could be in trouble. Like I said, no one's heard from her since yesterday morning, which is unusual." Damn, he was an asshole for not having called this in sooner. "What if she fell and hit her head or something in there?" She could be really hurt inside. Or somewhere else.

"I think that's just cause," Eddie said. "Stand back."

Tank eyed him as he got ready to charge the door. All one hundred and sixty pounds of him. "Um...Eddie, want me to do this?"

Eddie looked determined as he shook his head. "Are you kidding? I've dreamed of this moment my entire life. I've got this."

And surprisingly, he did.

Seconds later, the door flew open so hard it nearly came free of the hinges and they were inside the apartment.

It was a furnished rental, so there was a couch, a TV and a small dining room table in the open concept seven-hundred-square-foot floorplan, but little else.

Montana's things were littered about—several books and personal items. A coffee cup still sat on a counter in the kitchen. Eddie picked it up. "Coffee stain looks old."

So she hadn't been there that day. The place had a chill about it like she hadn't been there in a while. No lingering scent of perfume or a cooked meal...

Tank scanned the room for a note or any indication of where she'd gone and couldn't decide if it was a good thing or not to not find one.

He followed Eddie into the bedroom. Nothing. Just an unmade bed and clothes spilling out of her suitcase. Some of Kaia's things were in the closet and the picture of him and Kaia sat on the nightstand.

Nothing else.

"Well, her suitcase is here, so she probably didn't leave town," Eddie said.

"Right..." So where had she gone?

"Did she know anyone else in town? Could she be visiting someone?"

"I don't think so." He ran a hand over his beard as he scanned his mind for where she might be.

"Well, what do we know about her? What clues about her whereabouts might we get by considering her hobbies, her passions...?"

Her passion. Shit. He knew exactly where she was... or at least where she'd been heading.

STARING AT THE map of the backwoods area where Cassie and Montana were planning to open the jump site, Tank's palms were sweating. Had he known the two of them were running around out there in these less traveled areas, he would have fought harder against the idea. No wonder the two of them had kept the exact location to themselves...until now.

Cassie looked guilty and worried, pacing the station, as the crew discussed their plan. Tank didn't doubt Montana's survival skills...*if* she was actually better. But if not, who knew where she might be or what danger she might be in?

"So, we have eight of us ready to start the search near Suncrest Peak, where we suspect she would have headed," Reed said.

Montana wouldn't have gone anywhere else. They were all fairly certain of that. It was better to have more hands on deck in the most likely location than to separate into two teams and search elsewhere.

Eddie had called in the missing person report to the Wild River state troopers' office and was there, offering his support.

Tank's cell sounded and his heart raced, seeing Kaia's number. What the hell was he going to tell her? He'd already asked one of her friends' parents if she could stay at their place for the evening, but they hadn't spoken properly in days and he didn't want her worrying... How was he supposed to answer without giving something away?

Luckily Cass took the phone. Despite the awkward tension still lingering between them, she held his hand tightly in hers as she answered, "Hey, Kaia... It's Cass... Oh no, he's fine. Just got a call at the station, so he's in briefing with Reed and the crew. I'm acting as secretary." She forced a laugh.

Thank God for her. As soon as they found Montana, they needed to talk. The night before in his office, he hadn't known how to respond to how she was reacting, how she was feeling, but he was desperate to find a way to communicate with her. Apologize. Make things better between them.

But first they had to find his ex.

"Yeah... No worries. I'll come get you and we can hang out tonight, if that's okay."

Having Kaia with Cass was the only thing that made sense and he was so grateful that she'd simply assumed she'd be with the little girl during the search. He paused for a second, realization hitting him. Was that the reason Cass had never applied to be on the crew? Had she known that he needed her?

Maybe her adrenaline-craving spirit had a balance he hadn't fully realized was there. Seems he'd worried about a lot of things he shouldn't have for too long.

"Okay. I'll be there to pick you up soon," Cassie said, disconnecting the call. Handing the phone back to him, she added, "She said to be careful and she loves you."

His daughter loved him. She might still be upset with him, but she loved him. He'd take it. Was the same true of Cassie? "Thank you for that...and for stepping in to get her." He kissed her forehead.

"Of course."

"Okay, I think we've mapped our in and out. Suit up and let's meet outside in five," Reed said, photocopying their routes for the team.

Tank grabbed his gear and three minutes later, he waited out front for the rest of the crew.

Diva sat at his feet, looking at him expectantly. "No, girl, I know you want to go, but you're not quite ready yet," he said, petting the dog.

Diva yapped disobediently, obviously disagreeing with his assessment.

"Soon…" Though he'd love to have her out there. An extra set of eyes and super sharp nose would certainly be appreciated. It was a shame she wasn't fully certified yet.

Cassie hesitated before saying, "You know, maybe it's not a bad idea. You said she was doing really well."

"But she's not certified yet and these backwoods are dangerous. For a first mission…"

"Every mission is dangerous. We both knew Diva would have to face this eventually. She wants this. Look at her."

The smart husky was sitting, alert, waiting for her commands. No trace of a playful puppy anywhere.

"I, for one, would appreciate the backup," Reed said, joining them, putting on his reflective jacket.

"If nothing else, she could provide a sense of comfort to the crew. They are all a little stressed about this one," Erika said, zipping into her own gear.

Tank looked at the dog. She stared right back at him.

"Okay, Diva, let's get your vest," he said, uneasy about the idea. Already, one person he cared about was lost out there. And now his closest friends were heading out with him to find her…

"I think this is the right idea, but I can't watch you all leave. I'm going to go get Kaia…" She paused. "What do you want me to tell her? Anything or just wait?" Cassie asked him.

Shit. His little girl was going to be worried enough. If she tried reaching Montana again and got no response, she was smart enough to put the pieces together. "Wait for now. But if she asks about Montana…be honest with her."

"Okay." She looked hesitant for a fraction of a second, but then stepped into his arms. He breathed in the scent of her, savoring the comfort and security of her arms wrapped around him. She was always his rock, his best friend, the woman he was falling in love with... already loved. They really needed to talk. He needed to tell her and he hoped it might put all her doubt to rest. "Be careful," she whispered.

"We will be back soon."

She bent to hug Diva, then her brother and Erika. "Everyone be safe," she said.

He walked her to her truck and hugged her again quickly before she jumped into it and drove away.

Ten minutes later, the crew gathered at the base of the trail leading toward Suncrest Peak. Along the way, Eddie had gone back to Montana's for an article of hers for Diva to get the scent. He jumped out of his squad car now and hurried toward them.

"I brought her pillowcase. All of the clothing looked clean and I wasn't sure how helpful it would be."

Pillowcase. Genius. "This is great—thanks, Eddie." Tank introduced Montana's scent to Diva. She pawed at it and sniffed it for several minutes, then sat back on her hind legs and waited. "Find!" Tank gave the official command.

Diva stood. Ready to go.

"She looks confident," Reed said.

At least one of them was. "Okay, let's go."

A misty rain started as they headed into the woodsy area at the base of the unworn, unfamiliar hiking trail. "This weather had to pick now to start?" Tank mumbled. It had been sunny and mild all week. That day had seen a change in temperature—a cold wind and overcast clouds.

"I don't like it either," Reed said, scanning the sky in the distance. "It looks like storm clouds to the west."

The forecast hadn't predicted any thunder and lightning but by the looks of the clouds, they were going to be in for some unexpected weather that evening.

"Have you been through these woods before?" Tyler asked, zipping his coat higher over his neck and pulling his hood up.

"No. These trails aren't great for hiking."

"How on earth did Montana even discover the jump site out this far?" he asked.

"Cassie said she'd seen it on a heli-skiing trip with her father years ago," Tank said. How she'd remembered the site for so long was a mystery. Clearly it had left an impression on her back then.

Tank pushed through an uncleared section of the forest, holding back the large tree branches for the rest of the crew to make it through to the clearing on the other side.

Diva walked through first, barking once she'd reached the other side to announce everything was safe ahead.

And the search for Montana began.

"THEY'VE BEEN OUT there for a long time," Kaia said, her attention obviously not on the new Disney movie that Cassie hadn't been paying attention to either. "Has Dad checked in yet?"

The crew had only been out for eight hours but it felt like days. It was after three a.m., but Kaia had insisted she couldn't sleep. Their mutual worry had eased any lingering tension between her and the little girl. "Um…not since just before midnight." When Reed had reported in to the station that movement inland was slow because of the weather that had hit. Heavy rain and thunder in the distance. "But you know how cell service is."

Kaia bit her fingernails—something she only did when she was nervous. "I wish I hadn't been so mad at him. I've barely even talked to him in three days."

Cassie knew the feeling. She hated that their last real conversation was an argument and she desperately wanted to tell him that she'd been wrong to push him for more than he could give, wanted to give. She couldn't wait for him to be back. Safe. "Don't worry. You two will have plenty of time to talk as soon as he gets back. And he knows you love him," Cassie said, wishing she'd said those words to him before letting him go, as well. It hadn't felt like the right time...but now...

"Yeah, I know... Can you call the station for another update?"

It was the same every rescue. Kaia was always as nervous as she was, if not more so, but this one had Cassie more on edge too. So far, she'd dodged having to tell Kaia that they were out looking for her mother, but not telling her was taking its toll. Knowing both of the little girl's parents were out there was driving Cassie to the brink of insanity. "Sure... I'll call and check in," she said.

Dialing the station, she listened to three rings, then Riley's stressed sounding voice. She knew before asking that there wasn't an update. Not a good one anyway. "Hey, it's Cass...just checking in."

"Sorry, Cass. Still no news. Reed radioed in about three hours ago, but I haven't been able to make contact with him since."

Right. That was their last update. "Okay...thank you. Let us know..."

"You'll be my first call," Riley said, disconnecting.

Rescues were hard on the crew member back at the station, as well. They were waiting for good news and having to field the update calls to the family and friends. All the positions on the search and rescue crew were challenging and she admired everyone who put their lives at risk.

It worried the hell out of her that too many of them were her close family and friends...and the man she was in love with. She should have told Tank she loved him before he'd left. What if...

No. She wouldn't go there. There would be plenty of time to tell him how she felt once they were all back safe and sound.

"No news?" Kaia asked. She'd paused the movie and had been listening intently.

"Not since the last update. But everything was okay then, so I'm sure things are fine."

"We're hitting critical time..."

It sometimes sucked having the little girl know so much about the search and rescue procedures.

"Hey, don't worry. Reed's leading the crew and you know he won't sacrifice everyone's safety." Cassie paused. In this case, putting the crew's safety first and turning back would mean abandoning the search. Abandoning Montana.

"Is it okay if I try calling my mom? I know it's really late, but I think she should know that Dad's out there."

Damn it. It was unfair to keep this up. The little girl deserved to know... "Kaia, there's something I need to tell you." She sat on the couch and turned to face her.

"What's wrong? Is Dad okay?"

"I'm sure he is, sweetheart. The thing is…" She paused for a deep breath. "The crew is out looking for your mom."

Tears and fear filled the little girl's eyes and Cassie swallowed a lump in her throat. "My mom is lost out there?" she whispered.

Cassie nodded. "We think she may have been headed up to the jump site yesterday…"

Kaia got up from the couch. *"Yesterday?"*

"We don't need to worry yet. We both know your mom wouldn't have ventured out there unprepared." If she was fully aware of what she was doing. How much did Cassie tell Kaia? For now, just what she needed to know.

"What if she's hurt?"

"The search and rescue team will find her. I'm sure she just got turned around… The trails up there are a little confusing…"

Not helping. Kaia paced in front of the television. "This can't be happening. I just got her back in my life… I can't lose her again." Tears were streaming down her cheeks now.

Cassie stood and hugged her tight. "Hey, you're not going to lose her. She's going to be fine. They will find her."

Kaia wasn't relieved. "But you said yourself, Reed will do what's best for the crew. If things get too dangerous, he will turn back and leave my mom out there."

There was no right thing to say. Her brother's priority was the crew. If they didn't find Montana in the next few hours, they would head back, get the crew rested and head out again in the morning with volunteers…

But the objective of the next mission was a little different and the outcome not so promising.

"Cassie, you have to tell them not to leave my mom out there." The little girl was practically hysterical and Cassie hugged her tighter as tears fell down her own cheeks. "Please, Cassie, please…"

Sitting on the floor, Cassie pulled the little girl into her arms as she leaned back against the living room wall. She said the only thing she knew to be true. "Don't worry. Your dad won't give up until he finds your mom and brings her back."

CHAPTER TWENTY-FIVE

HEAVY, UNRELENTING RAIN had the ground slippery beneath their boots as they trudged along the path. Mud and slick tree branches cluttered the trails along the mountains. Wind had picked up out of the northwest, piercing through their wet clothing. Searching familiar territory posed its own risks. This more remote area of the mountain was somewhere none of them, besides Cassie, had really ventured into before.

Most tourists stuck to the familiar trails and even the more adventurous locals, familiar with the outback, rarely hiked these woods. Why Montana had ventured out here alone was a mystery. And especially without letting anyone know her plans.

"Ten more minutes in this direction, then I suggest heading east along the Chugach Mountain range. There hasn't been any trace of her having gone this way and we have no idea what to expect further up," Reed said next to him.

Normally Tank didn't question the lead rescue's advice. Reed's gut instinct in most cases was always spot on. But he knew Montana and where she'd been heading. She may have gotten turned around—however unlikely—but she wouldn't have taken the east trails back toward town.

No, she'd stubbornly keep moving up the mountain.

What if she had made it? What if she'd made the jump?

They had to keep going until they reached the peak.

"I think we need to move further north. According to Cassie's map, the jump site was at the top of that ridge…" He pointed to the north in the distance. "Montana would have continued to head there."

"Even if she was lost?" Reed wasn't convinced.

"Especially if she was lost. She'd use the jump site as a landmark, something familiar, and keep moving toward it, knowing we'd look for her along the trail headed there."

Reed looked uneasy as he surveyed the rest of the wet, exhausted and worn-out crew. "Tank, we both know these trails in these conditions put us all at risk…" His gaze fell to Diva, her fur dripping with rain and mud as she sat obediently near Tank's feet. "And Diva must be struggling to find the scent. She's taken us in a circle twice now."

The dog wasn't certified yet. She wasn't ready for this. But having her with him did provide some comfort and he believed if they continued to move higher and Diva could catch the scent, away from the heavy, dense forest, she might be able to put them on the right path.

It was really their only hope.

"Look, I know the crew's safety is your main concern, and I understand that, but we can't just head back toward town. We are reaching forty-eight hours missing… Montana could be in danger." Two days out there would be challenging for anyone, especially in this current weather. He hoped she'd had enough sense to bring food and water… The medication Cassie had mentioned seeing in her purse—had she brought that along? Had she taken it?

"I'm just suggesting we take the safer trails, at least until this torrential downpour stops," Reed said, glancing at Tyler and Tiffany struggling to get traction on the side of the steep mountain. Two steps forward, then they'd slide backward several feet. They weren't getting anywhere fast.

But retreating would be worse. "If Erika or Cassie were lost out here, would you be suggesting that?" he asked Reed.

Reed shifted uncomfortably. "Look, I get it. We will go a little further, but if Diva can't pick up a scent, anything at all to let us know we are headed in the right direction, we need to reconsider things."

Tank nodded, but he knew he wouldn't be turning back. Reed had to look out for the safety of the crew. He understood that. And the crew included Diva. Soon, they could all start heading down the safer trails… and he would continue on. There was no way he could return to town without Montana safe and sound and look his daughter in the face again. He'd never forgive himself if something happened to her.

Slick terrain grew more challenging to climb the higher they went. Every step forward made little progress as their boots slipped and the footing shifted.

"This has to be the worst hiking conditions I've ever attempted," Tyler said after another twenty minutes. "Extreme athletes or not, is Montana serious about these BASE jumpers being so hard-core that they'd tackle this hike for a thirty-second adrenaline rush?"

Tank nodded. "These guys are nuts. Hence the passion for free-falling from a cliff," he muttered.

"Crazy, man…"

Reed stopped the group a few minutes later as they

finally reached a small level clearing, still about five hundred feet from the peak. He gestured for everyone to gather around. The wind and rain in the clearing were even worse without the shelter of tree branches and overhang, so he had to yell to be heard. "Unfortunately, I think we've gone as far as we can safely go..." He glanced at Tank, and Tank avoided his friend's eyes. "I suggest going back for the drones. Had I known this area was this challenging, I would have brought them along. I think they might be our best hope."

Only hope.

Everyone looked defeated as they agreed with Reed.

They could all turn back. And they should. But Tank couldn't. His buddy understood that. And he understood the choice Reed was making. No hard feelings. But he was out there until Montana was found.

"Sorry, Tank," Tiffany said, patting him on the shoulder. She looked pained at the outcome of their attempts, but relieved that they were planning to move into safer zones.

"Montana may have realized the same thing we have and headed down there herself," Wade said, repeating Reed's sentiments from before. "She could have gotten turned around on the east trails headed back toward town."

Unfortunately, Tank knew his ex too well. He handed Diva's leash to Reed. "I'm going to keep looking."

Reed didn't try to talk him out of it. He simply nodded.

Diva's sad, low-toned whine reflected Tank's feelings perfectly. He bent to pet the dog. "You did good. Real good. But it's time to head home."

"We will be back at sunlight with the drones and more volunteers," Reed said.

Sunlight. About four hours from now. He was on his

own until then. Tank stood and watched as the crew carefully headed down the slope.

But the dog refused to budge as Reed attempted to head down after them. "Come on, Diva. Let's go see Cass."

The dog was unmovable. Her butt glued to the ground, she refused to leave Tank's side. She turned her head from side to side, sniffing the air.

"Go on! Follow Reed," Tank commanded in a gruff voice. Or at least as commanding as he could manage when emotions had him choking. Diva was such a great dog, and someday she might be an amazing search and rescue member, but he'd barely given her the chance needed to succeed. He'd been unfair to her. "Diva! Go!"

She continued sniffing the air. Then she stood up. Alert. Three sharp barks before pulling Reed slightly west of where they'd been searching. "She's got something," Reed said. He handed the leash back to Tank. "I'll let the others know we are moving west."

Tank nodded his gratitude at his friend. Thank God he'd have their assistance a little longer. "Whatta you got, girl?" he asked Diva as he unleashed her and followed her toward an overgrown path to the west of the mountain. Wet slabs of evergreen branches and moss covered the ground as they moved further into the bush. Slow, calculated, careful steps.

Diva stopped and sniffed some more. Tank held Montana's pillowcase close to her nose, letting her confirm the scent she was following.

Three sharp barks, then she was moving again. All business. Serious. Dedicated.

Tank heard the cracking of tree branches ahead on the trail before he glimpsed Montana, but seconds later, she turned and saw them there. Diva hurried toward her target, Tank close behind her.

Montana was weak, wet and cold. No backpack and just a thin spring jacket that was now soaked all the way through. She was disoriented as she stumbled along the path toward them. He heard Reed call in to the station as he moved closer. "Montana… it's okay. We're here to help you."

Wild-eyed, she looked panicked, scared…lost. Never had he seen her look this way. Her hair was soaked and matted to her face. Makeup stained her cheeks and her yoga pants were dirty and torn. She frowned, recognizing him. "Tank?" Her voice was hoarse—either from lack of fluids or from calling for help…either was gut-wrenching.

"Yes, I'm here. We're going to take you back to town. Get you warmed up, food and water… You're okay now," he said. Thank God they'd found her. His own relief had his exhaustion setting in…but they still needed to hike back out on these uncertain trails.

Diva sat at his feet, waiting. Obviously sensing her job wasn't over.

"I got turned around, that's all," Montana said, looking worried. "I swear I was headed in the right direction…" Her voice trailed off.

"Happens to the best of us," Tank said, checking her for signs of injury.

Reed moved closer with a heated blanket that wouldn't stay dry and warm long, but would at least offer some instant comfort to Montana. He opened a canteen of hot water and helped her drink from it.

Immediately, Montana looked less frightened, seeing everyone around her. "I'm okay?"

Tank nodded. "Yes. You're okay. But we need to hike back out. Are you hurt?"

"No," she said. "I can make it." She drank more of the water and accepted a granola bar from Reed with a shaky hand.

"Okay, slowly, we move out along the east trails," Reed said to the crew. Then to Tank, he said, "Let's get her home."

Tank supported Montana's one arm, and Tiffany supported the other as they started the hike back out of the bush.

Diva, the world's best search and rescue dog, was never more than a pace ahead of Montana, providing comfort and security on her first successful rescue.

CASSIE HAD BARELY parked the truck when Kaia had her seat belt off and the passenger side door opened. The search and rescue vehicles were parked in the hospital emergency lane already, so she said, "Go on ahead. Be careful."

Kaia ran toward the hospital and Cassie moved at a sprint right behind her seconds later.

Inside, Reed and Tank stood at the triage desk, filling out paperwork and answering the questions posed by the nurses. When Reed saw them enter, he turned to Tank and said, "Go ahead, I'll finish taking care of this."

Tank patted him on the back. Then he and Diva approached them. They were both caked in mud. Rain had Tank's clothes and Diva's fur soaked and dripping. They both looked exhausted, but they were safe. Montana was safe.

Kaia rushed to hug Tank and normally Cassie would

have held back, giving the father and daughter some space, but that morning she was more relieved than ever to see him, so she rushed into the three-way hug. Once they'd gotten the update that Montana had been located around four thirty a.m., she and Kaia had tried to sleep, knowing the crew were hiking back toward town. But neither of them had been successful in catching even a few minutes rest. Now, at eight thirty, they'd caught a second wind.

"We were so worried," Kaia said.

"It's all okay now, sweetheart," Tank said, hugging them both in one arm.

Diva whined at their feet, wanting her own attention and affection.

Cassie bent to pet her. "Hi, girl… We were worried about you too."

"It was actually Diva who saved the day," Tank said, pride in his voice.

Cassie looked at him in surprise. "For real? She was able to pick up Montana's scent?"

"It wasn't easy but she pulled it off in the nick of time," Tank said, looking affectionately at the dog.

Kaia bent to wrap her little arms around Diva's neck. "Thank you, Diva. You're my hero…"

"Hey!" Tank said, teasing in his voice.

"After you of course," Kaia said, still cuddling the dirty, tired but pleased-looking dog.

"How's Montana?" Cassie asked.

"She's okay. No major injuries. Just dehydration. She was wet and cold and disoriented when we found her. Erika's in with her now, assessing any less obvious injuries."

"Can I see her?" Kaia asked.

"Soon," Tank said. "Why don't you take Diva for a quick walk outside? I'm sure she must have to pee by now."

"Okay," Kaia said reluctantly. She headed for the door with the dog, but then ran back to give Tank another hug.

"Everyone's okay, sweetheart," he said, kissing the top of her head.

When the little girl went outside, Cassie asked, "Montana was headed to the jump site?"

"From what we can gather, yes. She had her jump gear with her originally, as well as food and water for one day, but she got turned around on those south side trails that all look alike and ditched her gear as the provisions ran out and exhaustion set in."

"A legitimate accident or…was it because of her brain injury?"

"We're not sure. Hoping Erika can help with that." He ran a dirty hand through damp hair and released a big, heavy sigh. "Man, it was a close one, Cass…"

She didn't have to ask what he meant. She suspected there had been more than one difference of opinion out on those mountains that day.

"If Diva hadn't caught the scent when she did…" He shook his head.

"It worked out. Everyone's safe," she said, wrapping her arms around him. Now wasn't the right moment, but as soon as he was rested and relaxed, she needed to tell him she loved him. She always had and she wanted him to hear it. She longed to hear the words back. Whenever he was ready.

Erika appeared in the waiting room. "Hey, Tank,

can I talk to you?" Her friend waved to her and offered a small, tired smile.

Her best friend was a superstar, trading in her search and rescue gear for her scrubs without even taking a break.

"Sure," Tank said, slowly releasing Cassie and heading toward Erika. "She okay?"

Cassie strained to hear, but Erika led Tank down the hall for privacy, so she had no other choice than to wait. She approached Reed as he finished the paperwork. "You okay?"

He nodded as he turned to her with his own exhausted expression. "Nothing a hot shower and a twelve-hour nap can't fix. You and Tank okay?"

"Yeah... He wasn't willing to give up on the search, was he?"

"No, and I understand where he was coming from out there. I'm just relieved we found her when we did. Leaving him out there alone would have killed me."

"No doubt," she said.

Reed touched her shoulder. "Hey...don't for a second read anything more into Tank's unwillingness to give up. He couldn't leave his daughter's mother out there. He wouldn't have been able to face Kaia."

Her brother's reassurance helped keep things in perspective. And if it had been *anyone* that Tank cared about out there, he'd have dug in his heels just the same.

"I can't believe Erika's treating her. She must be exhausted."

"She's planning on heading home as soon as Montana is stabilized."

Tank returned and he seemed more at ease.

"So?"

"Erika says she's doing great. They want to keep her overnight, but she will be released in the morning. She said after talking to her, she believes it was a simple mistake that caused her to lose her way. She's scheduling an MRI in the morning to get a baseline for Montana if she's going to be her physician from now on. And she's already requested Montana's medical file from Colorado General Hospital." They saw Kaia approach the hospital doors, and Tank took Cassie's hand in his. "Montana's not up for visitors yet, so I think the best thing to do is get out of here and come back in the morning."

Cassie nodded, hugging him tight, relief overwhelming her. They were all safe.

They would all be okay.

CHAPTER TWENTY-SIX

"THANKS FOR THE RIDE," Tank said as Cassie pulled her truck into his driveway ten minutes later.

Kaia was passed out in the back seat, with Diva curled up beside her. He glanced back at her and released what had to be his millionth sigh of relief.

What the hell would he have told her if they hadn't found Montana? What if he hadn't made it back to her?

He wouldn't think about it. Everyone was safe.

"She's out cold," Cassie said with a small smile.

Tank reached across and touched her cheek. "Thank you again for staying with her and being honest with her and making her feel safe." He owed so much to Cassie. She was *his* rock when he had to be at his strongest. He didn't know what he'd do without her. He never wanted to be in that position.

"There was no other place I would have wanted to be. She was so scared, but she was also very brave. I'm not sure I could have held it together as well as she did if my parents were both out there."

Tank's chest was full of emotion when he glanced back and forth between the two women who held his heart. "Do you want to come in?"

Cassie hesitated. "I do, but…" She paused. "She's had a rough night already. You have too. And while she was okay with me last night, she might still have an issue with us being together."

He nodded. He understood and she was probably right, but that didn't stop him from wanting to be with her right now. Needing to be with her. The last forty-eight hours had been hell and he longed to hold her. Longed to feel safe. Longed to reassure her that his feelings were as strong as ever. Even stronger. "Okay, but tomorrow, we talk to Kaia. Together. And we figure all of this out, okay?"

"I'd like that," she said.

He leaned toward her, pulling her face to his. He was dirty and gross and he hoped she didn't mind because he needed to at least kiss her before letting her go. She tasted like peppermint and coffee and her mouth was soft, warm and inviting. Even though he could barely keep his eyes open and every muscle in his body ached, he wanted her. There was so much he wanted to do with her, so much he wanted to say.

On the hike back to town, she'd been the only thing on his mind. Getting to her and telling her all the things he'd never said.

He loved her. He had always loved her.

Kaia stirred in the back seat and Cassie reluctantly pulled away from him. "You two should get inside and get some sleep."

"Okay…but I'll see you later?"

"You can count on it," she said.

Climbing out of the truck, he opened the back door and quietly unbuckled Kaia's seat belt. Then carefully, he lifted the little girl out of the truck. She didn't wake up. Her limp, deadweight body just sagged into him as he closed the door with his elbow.

Cassie waved and smiled at him as he made his way up the stairs. He unlocked the door and Kaia woke as they stepped inside. Her eyes flew open and a wild, scared expression appeared as she flailed...uncertain of her surroundings. "Shhhh...it's okay. Everyone is okay," Tank said.

Kaia blinked the sleep from her eyes. "Where are we?"

"We're home now."

She looked past him into the house. "Where's Cassie?"

"She just dropped us off."

"She's not staying?"

Tank swallowed hard. Damn, he'd wanted her to. "No...we thought it would be better..."

Kaia squirmed out of his arms and headed back toward the front door.

"Where are you going?"

"To get Cass," she said, rushing outside.

Tank followed her, leaning against the door frame as she flagged down Cassie's truck exiting the driveway. He watched as his daughter approached the window and said something to Cassie.

He saw the look of pleasant surprise on Cassie's face before her truck pulled back into the driveway and she climbed out.

Kaia took her hand as they made their way up the stairs toward him.

"Guess I'm staying..." Cass said.

"Good," he said, stepping back to let them in and closing the door behind them.

"Sleepover in the living room?" Kaia asked, suppressing a yawn.

Tank smiled. "Best idea I've heard all day. Why don't you get your pj's on, I'll shower quickly, and then Cassie and I will grab blankets and pillows from the closet."

Kaia nodded, hurrying into her room.

Tank turned to Cassie. "This was...unexpected." Maybe they wouldn't need to worry about their talk with Kaia. Maybe she was coming around to the idea on her own.

"Tell me about it. She said she wanted me to stay..."

Tank wrapped his arms around her. "I wanted you to stay first." He kissed her forehead.

Cassie smiled. "Go shower. I'll get the blankets."

Ten minutes later, with Kaia sleeping soundly between them in their comfy blanket and pillow fort and an exhausted Diva snoring near their feet, Tank looked over at Cassie. Their gazes met and held and he finally let himself relax as a tired smile formed on his lips.

Everyone was okay. They were okay.

He reached across and took her hand in his and moments later, after Cassie's eyes drifted closed and she was breathing softly, fast asleep, Tank rolled onto his back and closed his own exhausted eyes.

CASSIE COULD BARELY keep her eyes open the next day. Sleeping on Tank's living room floor on a mountain of blankets and pillows may not have been the most comfortable sleep she'd ever had, but the situation had made it quite possibly the best. Snuggled up next to two of the most important people in the world to her, everything had been right with the universe.

Kaia had invited her to stay. It was a step in the right direction at least. And despite her exhaustion, Cassie was happy. Happier than she'd been in a long time. They still didn't know if their BASE jumping venture would happen and Montana's incident might deter the mayor from approving it, but she'd figure it out. Her company wasn't going anywhere.

As if to confirm her thoughts, her landline rang on her desk. "Hello. Thank you for calling SnowTrek Tours, how may I help you?"

"Hey, Cassie Lassie…"

She sat back in her chair. "Oh hey, Dad, how are you?" She hadn't heard from them since they'd left for Point Hope.

"Great. Your mom and I are all settled."

"That's wonderful. How's the new job?"

"It feels good to be working again. And your mom has already joined a new book club and knitting group."

"Wow, sounds like you two are fitting in nicely." That was a relief. She'd worried that her mom would miss her life in Willow Lake, that she might second-guess giving it all up…but it sounded like she'd worried for nothing.

"We're doing great. I wanted to call and check in with you and Reed. Everything okay?"

"Yeah. Things are good. There was a rescue last night, but it all turned out okay." Luckily it had, but Cassie couldn't squash the uneasiness in the pit of her stomach. Montana was okay, but what happened now?

Tank and Kaia were heading to the hospital to see her. Erika had decided to keep her a day longer to make sure she got enough rest, but she reassured them Montana was fine. Kaia had invited Cassie to come with them, but she thought maybe it was best to give Montana some space with just her daughter for now. Let her sort things out.

"Yeah, I saw the report online. Congratulations to that pup of yours—great job. Your mother has shown me countless photos of Diva, by the way," he said with a laugh. "Oh, hang on, your mom wants to say hello..."

Silence on the other end of the line, then her mom's voice. "Hi, darling!"

An unexpected lump rose in Cassie's throat at the sound of her mother's voice. It had only been a few days since she'd seen her, so the emotions rising in her chest surprised her. Having her mom in the next community, she'd always been close when Cassie had needed her. Now, it felt like she was a million miles away. "Hi, Mom..."

"Oh sweetheart—are you okay?"

Cassie laughed at the silliness of her tears. She brushed them away with the sleeve of her sweater. "Yes. I'm fine. Just missing you, I guess." Turned out no matter how old, a girl still needed her mom.

Cassie just hoped that after her terrifying experience, Montana was still willing to stay in Wild River and be here for Kaia.

CHAPTER TWENTY-SEVEN

THEIR SCHEDULED CONFERENCE call with the mayor was the next day and they were about to find out if they'd received the jump site approval. Montana's disappearance and rescue were things everyone in town knew about by now, and Cassie's hope for approval was wavering. The search and rescue crew's report clearly stated how difficult the hiking trails were to get to the top of Suncrest Peak and Cassie couldn't argue with that. Unfortunately, her company didn't have a budget for helicopters to airlift jumpers to the site.

She busied herself with her filing as she waited, her shaky hands making the tedious process even worse.

Montana was coming in to be on the call so they could get the news together—for better or worse—and Cassie kept checking outside for the other woman.

Her landline rang, the mayor's office number lighting up the display, and she hesitated, checking down the street for Montana before answering the mayor's call. "Hi, Mayor Morell... How are you?" She'd try to stall his decision until Montana got there.

Maybe she wasn't coming. Maybe after their disagreement, she wasn't sure they could work together. Maybe after her experience in the woods, she'd lost hope in this venture and couldn't bring herself to be there for the bad news.

"Great, Cassie, just great... Is Montana there with you?"

"Um...she's just..." From the window, she saw Montana a block away. "Yes, she's here." She waved at her to hurry up and Montana jogged the last few paces.

"Sorry I'm late," she whispered as she entered.

Cassie smiled, giving her a quick hug. Then she put the call on speakerphone.

"Okay, so I have to tell you ladies, this was not an easy decision and the vote from the committee members wasn't unanimous..."

Montana wasn't breathing and Cassie reached out to take her hand. "We understand we are asking for something a little extreme," she said.

"Yes, well...what is Wild River if not a haven for extreme sports enthusiasts and offering tourists things they can't get anywhere else?"

Cassie's eyes widened and Montana's expression was one of shock. Neither answered what they assumed was a rhetorical question.

"So, I'm approving your application for a legal BASE jumping site in Wild River," the mayor said, sounding as excited about it as they were.

Holy shit. They were approved.

"That's..." Cassie cleared her throat. "That's wonderful. Thank you. Thank you so much, Mayor Morell." She squeezed Montana's hand and it seemed to snap the woman out of her trance. She smiled but it wasn't the full-on excitement Cassie would have expected.

Please, God, Montana, don't bail on me now.

There was no doubt that the site had only gotten approved because of her. And while they did need to set some ground rules moving forward to work together effectively, Cassie needed her for this to be a success.

"Yes, thank you," Montana said.

"There is still a lot of paperwork to fill out and work to be done. Because of the unsafe trails leading to the site, the town is planning on developing a road wide enough for motor-terrain vehicles in so far as the midway point. From there, we will put up the required signage and protective measures to make the hike to the jump site safer."

"Perfect. Yes, that all makes sense." The city was going to invest time and money into this venture to help it succeed. Cassie's heart was full of gratitude.

"Unfortunately, that means the summer will be spent on construction, so we estimate a fall opening date."

"That's totally fine." She was still staring at Montana, who was yet to say anything more.

"Okay, ladies. Well, congratulations! I'll have the first of the documents couriered to you at SnowTrek Tours, Cass... As the only official company authorized to coordinate tours, I'm sure your business won't have anything more to worry about with North Mountain Sports Company."

Cassie grinned. "North Mountain who?"

"That's the spirit. Talk soon," Mayor Morell said.

Cassie disconnected the call and sat back in her chair. "Wow. We did it."

Montana nodded, clutching her hands in her lap. "Yeah...crazy. But in an amazing way. Congratulations."

"Congratulations to both of us! I wouldn't have dreamed of doing this on my own." She paused. "You okay?"

"Yeah, just a stressful week…but this is going to be great for your company."

"But…"

Montana gave a soft, sad-sounding laugh. "Cass, as much as I was hoping for it, I'm not completely better." She took a deep breath. "The truth is, I'm never going to be allowed to BASE jump again. My doctor in Denver and ten other second opinions have refused to sign any release for me. I mean, I can do it anyway…hell, I already have…but while I can help bring jumpers here, I won't be allowed to do it myself."

Cassie's heart ached for her. "I'm so sorry, Montana." Being involved in all of this, facilitating, organizing the launch, knowing she wouldn't be able to enjoy her passion herself had to be torture.

"It's just something I'm going to have to learn to live with. And don't think for a second that I'll be leaving you high and dry. I'm still with you on this."

Cassie squeezed her hand again. "Are you sure?"

She looked worried. "That is, if you still want me to be."

"Absolutely."

Montana smiled for real for the first time, reaching for Cassie's laptop. "Perfect… Then, let's send out that email blast with the good news." She paused. "Here… you should do it," she said.

"Go ahead. I trust you," Cassie said, suddenly not as exhausted as she moved her chair closer to Montana's and they started compiling the email.

Montana's smile was wide as she started to type. "Fall 2020—Prepare for the experience of a lifetime… only from SnowTrek Tours."

"SORRY, THE BAR'S NOT… Oh, hey," Tank said as Montana entered. He knew she'd gone to see Erika about a program at the hospital—a research trial Erika was leading that might be able to help her further, and they'd agreed to work out some sort of visitation schedule for Kaia. Despite her scare in the woods, she was staying in Wild River. And he was happy about it.

They were all in this together now. Montana was an integral part of SnowTrek Tours' growth with the jump site getting approved that morning and she was still part owner of the bar until he could save enough money to offer to buy her out. He'd figure out a way, but for now he was rolling with it. One day, one new challenge at a time.

"Hi. Sorry to just pop in. I would have texted, but I don't have anyone's numbers programmed into my new cell phone yet."

"You're welcome anytime. What's up?" She looked much better that day—rested, refreshed, ready to start her new life. Her dark hair was slicked back and, dressed in a pair of jeans and white blazer, she gave off the same air of confidence she always had, but looking closer, he could see the slight apprehension and uncertainty in her demeanor. He hoped in time she'd get her self-assurance back.

"That's actually why I'm here." She sat on a bar stool and opened her oversized bag. She took out a manila envelope and his heart raced.

Shit, was she planning to go through the courts to gain access to Kaia? He thought they were on the same page with coparenting in a positive way. He'd loaned her all his parenting books and promised not to micromanage how she developed a relationship with Kaia. Promised to try his best, at least.

But his shoulders relaxed as she laid the legal documents on the bar. The ownership buyout papers he'd drafted years before. She still had a copy, as well?

"Give me a pen. I think it's about time I signed these," she said.

Damn, wouldn't he love that? "Unfortunately, Montana, I can't afford this deal anymore. Back when I'd drafted these, I had savings…but over the last ten years…" His voice trailed off. He wasn't ready to detail the list of expenses that owning a bar and raising a daughter on his own had cost.

"Give me a pen," she insisted.

He took the one from behind his ear and handed it to her. "Look, you can sign, but I can't. I'm sorry, but the money just isn't there and my bank loan wasn't approved." He'd calculated that with some cutting back, he might be able to buy her out the following year, and he was determined to make it happen.

But as he watched, she amended the buyout clause and turned the papers toward him. The fifty thousand dollar amount had been changed to a dollar. She reached into the tip jar on the bar and took out a dollar bill, folded it and grinned. "There. Done."

If only he could allow her to do that. "This is an amazing gesture, but I can't ask you to just sign over the rights to the bar like this without being compensated."

"You're not asking and Tank, you've been sending me money, profits, for ten years. You've more than repaid my initial investment. And I did nothing. I did put that money away…and you're not getting it back," she said with a teasing grin, "But you don't owe me anything else."

She scrawled her signature at the bottom of the page.

He hesitated, staring at her. "You're sure about this?" She couldn't possibly understand what she was giving him right now.

"Yes. Absolutely. You can't build a future with Cassie when you're still financially tied to me."

Okay, so maybe she knew exactly what this meant to him. And she sounded perfectly okay with the idea of him building a life with Cassie, which was a relief because that was the only life he wanted moving forward. Montana was right—he needed to be free of the financial ties with her. He cleared his throat. "And me and Cassie…together…" He didn't need Montana's seal of approval on his relationship, but he wanted it.

"Long overdue. Now sign it!" she said, checking her watch. "I'm meeting with the lawyer to file these in twenty minutes."

He laughed, huge relief flowing through him as he signed. "Thank you. This means a lot."

"Trust me, it's nothing compared to what you and Cass were able to give me," she said, touching his hand quickly on the bar before gathering the papers and standing.

"Um…and about Kaia and the visitation?" Was this an olive branch just to hit him up for more than he was prepared for on that front? Life had taught him things were never this easy.

"Every second weekend she spends with me…and I'm included in all of her important life events… Sound good to you?"

Shit. Had he really hit the lottery that it could all be

that easy? Then, thinking of Kaia, he nodded slowly. "With the clause that if Kaia wants more time…we allow it…work with it?" Their needs, their daughter's needs, would change over the years, but as long as they could work together on this, Kaia would reap the benefits. And it was her they needed to think about.

"I like that," Montana said. "I'll see you both tomorrow at the Passing of the Leash ceremony," she said with a wave as she left the bar.

Tank released a deep sigh as he stared after her.

The Passing of the Leash ceremony and his and Diva's official certification was the last loose thread on his list now…

And he knew the perfect way to wrap that up.

CHAPTER TWENTY-EIGHT

"OH MY GOD, this is so silly, but I can't stop tearing up," Cassie whispered to Erika as they sat in the Wild River fire hall the next day. Chairs were set up in front of a wooden stage and dozens of people had gathered for the Passing of the Leash Search and Rescue Dog ceremony.

Diva's successful rescue had been her passing test. Frank Jennings had said that her actions under the pressure of a real-life situation proved far more than any simulated rescue he could have challenged her with in training.

All over town, Diva was receiving the star treatment she deserved that week.

A row of soon-to-be-retired search and rescue dogs and their human partners, dressed in their S & R gear, lined up along a wooden stage. Dutiful canines sat at attention, looking proud and slightly sad, knowing the significance of the ceremony. On the other side, eager expressions lit up the faces of the younger pups, though they also waited respectfully as the ceremony started.

Erika lowered her sunglasses to reveal teary eyes of her own. "I don't know how that dog did it, but she certainly weaseled her way into my heart."

"She has that effect on everyone," Kaia said, sitting next to Cassie.

Montana nodded. "She certainly does. And I for one am eternally grateful for her. She saved my life."

Cassie's pride was at an all-time high as her friends praised her dog.

On the other side of Erika, Reed sniffed and Cassie shot him a look.

"What? Allergies," he said.

"Sure," she said with a laugh. They were all such saps. She was so happy for Diva and Tank, but a little sad for herself. She'd known this day would come, when she'd have to be selfless and allow the dog to move in with Tank, but she'd been hoping...

She sniffed and wiped a tear from the corner of her eye as the head of ASARD, Mitch McDonald, stepped up to the microphone. "Hello, everyone. We are once again honored to perform this ceremony of passing the leash from one generation of rescuers to another. As these new teams follow in the foot and paw prints of the brave rescuers before them, we wish them safety and confidence..."

He continued on, but Cassie's attention was on Tank and Diva. They looked so great up there. They made a wonderful team and her heart was full seeing them reach this incredible achievement. Tank had really helped Diva reach her potential and the dog's loyalty to Tank rivaled Cassie's own.

Frank Jennings approached the new teams, a certificate in one hand and a new official vest for the dogs in the other.

Tank looked a little nervous being the center of attention, but Diva sat proudly, soaking it all up when it was her turn.

"As Diva comes full circle from rescue to rescuer..." Mitch continued, "we are proud to announce Wild River's newest canine rescuer and her partner."

A round of applause echoed through the fire hall and Cassie clapped loudest of all.

Kaia stood on her chair and let out a whistle that had all the dogs turning to look. "Oops, sorry," she said, climbing down and sitting back on the chair.

Cassie smiled and held her hand.

"Thank you to everyone for being here today as we honor our new ASARD Team—Theodore 'Tank' Wheeler and Diva. They have completed their training and excelled with flying colors, and we are proud and excited to have them on the team." Frank handed Tank the certificate and shook his hand. "Great job, man."

"Thank you. Couldn't have done it without you," Tank said.

Frank handed Tank the new vest and leash for Diva. "You can do the honors," he said.

Tank bent on one knee and fastened the new vest to the dog. Then he petted her head and hugged her affectionately.

The lump in Cassie's throat nearly choked her and she heard Kaia's heavy sigh.

"Yeah, I can totally see why you love him," Erika whispered.

"Right?" Cassie whispered back.

"And you're totally fine with Montana staying in Wild River?"

"More than fine," she said, wiping a tear from the corner of her eye as Tank smiled at her. She was. She was confident in her relationship with Tank. She loved him and he loved her. No one could come between them.

An hour later and barely a dry eye in the room, everyone dispersed.

Cassie hugged Tank and Diva as they joined her in the back of the room. "Congratulations. You did it,"

Cassie said, petting Diva's head. It was hard to believe this sixty-pound hero sitting in front of her was the same little pup with narcolepsy that she'd found on the side of the highway a year before.

So confident and special.

"You did great too," she said to Tank. He looked amazing and she longed to crawl into his arms and kiss him, but there were still a lot of people around. And this moment was about him and Diva.

"I was nervous as shit up there and man, it was heart-wrenching watching those other dogs retire."

"Well, you two have a long career together before that happens." Cassie cleared her throat. "Speaking of which, I have some of her things in the truck outside if you want to grab them." It was easier to do the hand-off now. If she'd brought Diva back home with her that day, she might never let the dog move in with Tank.

Erika had reminded her that she could adopt a new puppy, one that needed a good home and lots of love, and maybe she would eventually, but no one could re-place Diva.

Tank led the way outside and Diva hung back, walk-ing next to Cassie. To reassure her that things would be okay, and maybe also a little sad knowing what was happening. Either way, it did give Cassie comfort.

She was such a great dog. Cassie would miss her, but so many other people would benefit from Diva's gener-ous spirit and determination of heart.

At the truck, Cassie opened the back and handed Tank the bag of Diva's belongings. "Her bowl and fa-vorite bed, and a bunch of toys…"

Tank smiled as he took the bag from her and put it in the back of his truck. "Well, it appears she's all set to come live with me."

Cassie refused to cry. The dog was just going to be staying at Tank's house. She'd see her every day. She was practically at Tank's all the time now. This made sense for everyone. Especially Diva. Cassie couldn't be selfish.

"Now we just need to get your things all packed up," Tank said.

She blinked. "What?"

Tank took a step toward her. "Did you honestly believe I was going to steal your dog and not you, as well?"

Cassie stared at him. Was he serious? "You want me to move in with you?" They'd never discussed it before. Things had only just recently moved out of friend territory. Was Tank really ready for that?

"With me, Kaia and Diva."

"Eventually..." He couldn't mean right now. Could he?

"Nope. Now." He took a step toward her and wrapped his arms around her waist. "I've given this a lot of thought, Cassie, and I want to start a real life with you."

"What about Kaia?"

"She's thrilled about it."

"Really? But she wanted you and Montana to be together."

"She understands that isn't for the best and it's not what I want. A relationship of convenience is not the message of love and what a union looks like that I want Kaia to experience." Tank touched her cheek gently, but his words were sure and strong.

"Wow." When had Tank gotten so intensely deep about this? Clearly, he was better with emotions than he gave himself credit for.

"I want Kaia to have a relationship with her mother and with me, but trying to pretend to be a family isn't in anyone's best interests. Not Kaia's. And definitely not mine."

He wrapped his arms around her and she moved in closer. "For the first time in ten years, I want to consider what I want," Tank continued. "And I want you. And I honestly believe that you and I together is the best thing for Kaia. We can provide an example of what real love looks like."

Cassie's mouth dropped. She barely recognized the man standing in front of her. The changes in Tank and his attitude about them over the last few days had turned everything upside down...in a fantastic way. "And Montana?"

"I think she was about ready to kick my ass if I didn't ask you." He kissed her nose. "So? What do you say?"

She could barely speak above the emotions strangling her. This was more than she'd ever expected. Getting Tank to open up and be committed to her was enough... This was everything she'd ever wanted. "I say yes. And it's about damn time."

"I love you, Cassie Reynolds," Tank said.

Too many emotions that day. Many wonderful, amazing, long-overdue emotions. She hugged Tank tighter and kissed him hard. She never wanted to stop. The last few months had been full of twists and turns and life's uncertainties, but now their future looked better than she ever could have hoped.

"Well?" He pulled back to look at her, tucking her hair behind her ears.

"Well what?" she teased.

"Do you love me?"

"Only for the last five years...and only for the rest of my life," she said, jumping into his arms as he lifted her off her feet and into the air. Sometimes, life was full of the unexpected...in all the best ways.

* * * * *

If you've fallen in love with Jennifer Snow's
Wild River series, you'll want to keep reading for
a special preview of her next novel,
Sweet Alaskan Fall*!*

PROLOGUE

SHE'D DONE SOMETHING TERRIBLE.

Fear wrapped around her heart the minute Montana Banks opened her eyes and scanned the familiar surroundings of her bedroom. How'd she get here?

She shut her eyes tight, clenching her fists at her sides. *Remember... Come on, remember!*

The last memory that flashed in her mind was driving into the parking lot of the grocery store. A familiar song had played on the radio. She'd felt good...happy... She had parked the car in the spot and glanced in the rearview mirror...

"Kaia!" She sat up straight in her bed "Kaia!" She looked around the room but she was alone.

Footsteps sounded down the hall, then the bedroom door opened and Tank entered. Montana jumped out of bed, a wave of dizziness and nausea hitting her like a freight train. She swayed off balance, the room swimming around her, the floor wavy beneath her feet.

Tank's arms went around her as her legs gave out from beneath her. "Hey...relax," he said soothingly, but there was fear and pain and unease in his voice.

It terrified her. Struggling to focus, to rebalance herself, she gripped his arms and stared up at him. "I left her in the car...in the parking lot." How long? Outside it was now dark. The clock numbers blurred. What day was it? Where was Kaia?

Tank held her close, but his sigh was deep, resolute... "I know. She's okay. We found her."

Before it was too late. Before something terrible had happened to her baby girl. Her precious baby girl.

A sob escaped her throat and tears left a deep pool on Tank's shirt. She'd done the unforgivable. She could have lost Kaia. This wasn't the first time her injury had caused her to black out...to not remember... She wasn't getting better since her fall out of the sky; she was getting worse. She couldn't keep pretending to be okay. Or that she wasn't a danger to her daughter.

"I'm not okay," she whispered.

"I know," Tank said, holding her tight.

And they both knew what that meant.

CHAPTER ONE

Ten years later...

"Hello, I am Montana Banks. And I am addicted to BASE jumping."

Obviously not what they'd expected her to say. Eighteen pairs of eyes stared at her with varying degrees of judgment.

Safe space my ass.

"Um...okay. Well, welcome, Montana," the director of the Addictions Support Group, Jane, said in the awkward silence. "I'm not entirely sure you're in the right place..." She gestured to the manual on her lap as though searching for the rules. Or a reason to ask Montana to leave.

"This is a group for people addicted to things they shouldn't do, right?" Montana asked.

Jane glanced around the room. "Not things we *shouldn't* do...more like, things we are trying not to do, things that negatively impact our lives or the people around us."

"Well, I'm in the right place then," Montana said. Though whether she'd come back next week was still up for debate. It had taken three months of living in Wild River, Alaska, for her to get enough courage to walk into the Addictions Support Group and this reception was precisely why. No one was going to take her challenges seriously. Not when her "issue" seemed a lot less serious than everyone else's.

Unfortunately, there was no group to support extreme athletes with brain injuries that prevented them from fulfilling their life passion.

As different the demons of everyone in this room were, they all shared the same storm cloud over their heads every day. One no one else saw. One they constantly battled against to find a ray of sunshine. Montana wasn't so different.

For her, that ray of light was Kaia, her ten-year-old daughter. Staring at the picture of the two of them on her cell phone, Montana released a deep breath. Moving to Wild River had been the right thing to do. She'd let her injury keep her from her daughter long enough. No matter how hard living in the small ski-resort town got, she would not abandon the little girl again.

But maybe the group wasn't the right place for her. She gathered her things. "It's okay, I'll leave."

"No, please stay," Jane said, her warm, welcoming nature returning. "Everyone, meet Montana."

"Hi, Montana!" the group said in unison.

"Why don't you tell us about yourself?" Jane said. She checked her watch.

Everyone was given the floor for ten minutes, and pressure to sum up thirty-four years of life made Montana's heart race. Where did she start? With the BASE jumping injury ten years ago that had derailed her future? Or further back to the incident that rocked her existence?

"I'm new to Wild River," she said. "I have a daughter here and I am trying to reintegrate back into her life."

Nods. They all understood that. Alienation from family members and the struggle to find a way home again was a common thread in the group.

"I've started a new career with an amazing business partner and I've made a lot of new friends here in town." Settling in had been disturbingly simple. Her new apartment was cheap and close to everything in town and her landlord had no problem with her not signing their usual one-year lease, instead allowing her to pay month by month. Her new job at SnowTrek Tours launching a new legalized BASE jumping location in Wild River had gone a lot smoother than she ever could have predicted, thanks to the local mayor, who was an extreme sports junkie himself. She'd made friends—including Cassie, her ex-boyfriend's new girlfriend and the owner of SnowTrek Tours. And she was coparenting like a superstar with Kaia's father, Tank. Life was… simple. And easy.

Unfortunately, *simple* and *easy* weren't enough for her.

"But every morning when I wake up, the first thing on my mind is jumping off a cliff." Wide eyes made her add quickly, "With a parachute." A wingsuit actually, but she knew they didn't care about the details. "And the persistent temptation doesn't go away. It used to be a big part of my life. It was everything, actually. An adrenaline rush like no other, it was highly addictive." She'd started skydiving with her grandmother at age thirteen, then BASE jumping at eighteen, when she was barely old enough to sign a waiver. She'd traveled all over the world with other extreme athletes and had soared over the most breathtaking scenery. She was among the top jumpers in the world and had even done a short stint in jail for an illegal jump-off from a city building…until the accident changed everything.

She cleared her throat and continued. "But I know it's not the right path for me anymore." Her unpredictable brain with its rare form of transient global amnesia and impaired judgment couldn't be relied on for a safe jump anymore. "What's that saying? Those who can't, teach… Well, that's where I am."

With her BASE jumping fundamentals course booked solid all month long at the cost of $3000 a week, SnowTrek Tours no longer had to worry about the competition from North Mountain Sports Company opening their big new chain store and claiming some of their usual adventure-tour clients. Cassie's business was thriving in the other store's shadow, and Montana was happy that she'd been able to help Tank's girlfriend and the woman who'd been her daughter's primary role model in Montana's absence all these years. But she couldn't deny the ache in her chest whenever she stood at the top of Suncrest Peak, staring down into the breathtaking valley, knowing she'd never be able to soar over it again. It was too much of a risk when she wasn't sure what triggered her random bouts of amnesia and if one were to happen midjump, it could be devastatingly dangerous.

"Thank you for sharing that," Jane said. "So, what do you do to help get you past the tougher days? The challenging times when you're tempted to give in?"

I see my dead sister and she talks sense into me.

"I'm still figuring that part out," Montana said, taking a seat quickly before she could verbalize the thought and have them think she was even crazier than they did already.

Half an hour later, the meeting wrapped up and she collected her things to head back to the office. The next day was the first day of her BASE training program. The four-day course would teach wannabe jumpers the fundamentals…while keeping them safely on the ground. It was the best place to start with the new venture. Fall was only two months away and winter would shut them down until spring, so Montana would have at least a year before the advanced courses started and she'd have to actually watch other people jump. Cassie thought her idea to use their first few months in operation to introduce athletes to jumping and hook them early for their first jump next year was a brilliant way to build their business. Montana accepted the compliment and didn't reveal that she just wasn't ready yet to see other people doing what she loved.

She tied her short hair into a ponytail, laced her running shoes tighter and set off at a fast pace through town toward Main Street.

Breathe in. Breathe out. Exercise was supposed to help with the pent-up energy she had inside, but five miles a day and an hour of weight training barely took the edge off. The mountain air and the breathtaking view of the wilderness just made the itch stronger. Her parents had thought moving back to Denver was the best thing for her. They hadn't been supportive of her decision to come to Alaska, hesitant to believe she was well enough to live completely on her own, a million miles away from them. And some days, she wanted to agree with them, but after reconnecting with Kaia, she couldn't leave her. Skype chats and phone calls and letters may have worked in the past, but now that she was there, actually spending time with her daughter, she didn't want to lose that closeness they were forming.

Kaia was almost eleven now. She was growing so fast. Montana had spent years trying to get well enough to be in her life without putting her safety at risk. She wouldn't live another day without knowing Kaia and being there for her in whatever capacity she needed.

Even if it meant struggling every day to face her own limitations and learn to eventually accept them.

Ten minutes later she opened the door to SnowTrek Tours.

"No... I'm sorry, that course is full until May of next year," Cassie said, the landline phone pinned between her shoulder and ear while she typed on her laptop. Several other lines were lighting up and she shot Montana a desperate look through a veil of blond hair falling across her face.

Dropping her things onto her desk, Montana picked up the phone and hit one of the lines. "Thank you for calling SnowTrek Tours, can you hold for just a moment?" Twice more she repeated the action, then returned to the first caller. "Hello, sorry about the wait. How can I help you?"

"Hey, I'm calling about the Fundamentals of BASE course." Who wasn't? She'd been right about her prediction that legalizing the sport in Wild River would have SnowTrek Tours turning adventure seekers away. But even *she* hadn't known how much things would have exploded for the small local company.

The site wasn't even officially open yet and they were booked solid for tour groups with experienced professional jumpers in the spring, her advanced courses were already full and the fundamentals course was even more popular.

Who knew there were so many adrenaline junkies in the world?

She was happy that things were going well, but being surrounded 24/7 by talk of the sport she loved and couldn't do was making her crazy. But at least she was involved somehow. It was the next best thing and she couldn't complain. For nine years in Denver, she'd gone completely insane, holed up in the city, being treated like a child by her overprotective parents.

Baby steps.

She was living on her own and hadn't burned the place down yet.

She answered the third call. "SnowTrek Tours, how may I help you?"

"Well, you could start by going to dinner with me Saturday night."

Montana felt her face flush at the sound of Lance's voice. In the last three months, she'd been out with the local snowboarding god three times   two dinners and a coffee date. But he'd been away for three weeks and had obviously been so busy he'd forgotten to text. She wasn't that woman—the one who couldn't take a hint. Clearly, he just wasn't that into her. Yet, here he was calling again. "I'm sorry, who is this?"

He laughed. "I deserve that."

"Yes, you do," she said.

"I'm sorry I was MIA. New York was insane. Back-to-back meetings and promotional events…"

Dates with countless groupies, casual hookups with no strings attached…she knew the lifestyle. She'd once been a professional athlete, traveling the world, meeting new people, getting involved temporarily then moving on. Hell, Kaia had been the result of that lifestyle. For her, at least. Tank on the other hand had been in love with her back then, but Montana hadn't had a real connection with anyone, not having allowed anyone in her life to get too close in a very long time. Not even her daughter's father.

Maybe more than just her brain was broken.

"And I left my cell in a taxi," Lance was saying, "that's why I'm calling you at work."

Lost cell phone. Not exactly the most creative excuse. "It's fine. I get it." It *was* fine. She *did* get it. They'd had three dates. They weren't exclusively seeing one another.

"So, is that a yes to dinner?"

Montana hesitated. She liked Lance, and she wasn't ready for a relationship, which made him the perfect man for her right now...but on the other hand, she wasn't interested in a fling either—not exactly the right example she wanted to set for her daughter. Therefore, that left a semicasual thing that could potentially turn into more and leave her with a broken heart. The guy was a major player. He'd ghosted her for three weeks and would no doubt do it again.

But what was her Saturday night alternative?

Hanging out at The Drunk Tank, the local bar she'd previously owned with her ex, with two couples very much in love? Or Netflix and takeout, while trying to drown out the sound of her next-door neighbor's attempt at learning to play guitar?

"Seven o'clock?" she said.

"I'll pick you up."

Montana disconnected the call and stared at it.

"Going out with Lance again?" Cassie asked, ending her own call.

"Yeah…" She paused. "I know, I'm a sucker, you can say it." Hadn't she gone on about the fact that if the guy said he was going to call and didn't call, it was a clear sign to move on? Hadn't she claimed she was done with Lance? Several times now.

Cassie laughed. "I'm the last person on the planet to lecture you on giving second and third and fourth chances."

Cassie did get it. For years, she'd played the same cat and mouse game with Montana's ex, Tank. The two had finally gotten together, and Montana liked to think she'd been a part of Tank's eye-opening. Cassie was too amazing to find fault with. She was a successful career woman, the partner Tank needed in his life and a wonderful role model to Montana's daughter. Whoever said women couldn't build one another up and celebrate successes was wrong. The two of them were proof of it.

"He's just exciting and I desperately crave excitement." Lance's adventurous, no-fear attitude was a reflection of her own, but she worried part of his waning interest in her was because she was no longer the extreme athlete she used to be.

Hell, she was a disappointment to herself.

"Just be careful fraternizing with the enemy," Cassie said, pulling up the window blinds and nodding to the chain store across the street.

Lance was the new poster boy for North Mountain Sports Company—images of him and his new line of snowboards decorated their exterior windows—therefore Montana was careful what she revealed to him regarding the BASE jump site and SnowTrek Tours' future business plans.

She bit her lip. "You don't think that's why he's dating me, do you?"

Cassie shook her head. "Oh my God—no! That's not what I meant. I was totally kidding. He's dating you because he'd be an idiot not to. Look at you! I'd hate you if you weren't also the best business partner and co-mom I could ask for."

Montana nodded. They *were* amazing business partners and co-moms to Kaia. They were enough alike to agree on most things, and Montana was desperate to believe that they were different enough to both add value to the little girl's life.

Unfortunately, some days she questioned whether that was true or if Cassie could handle both just fine without her.

EDDIE SPRINTED FROM his truck to the entrance of the Alaska Department of Public Safety building in Anchorage. He yanked the door open and hurried down the hall toward the auditorium, his wet shoes squeaking against the tiled floor as he scanned the packed room for his family. All the chairs were occupied and it was standing room only. He spotted them in the front row on the left and apologized his way through the crowd.

"You're late," his sister Katherine hissed as he took the saved seat next to her.

"Just got off shift an hour ago and had to turn on the lights to make it here in time." He hadn't even had time to shower and change out of his uniform for the ceremony honoring his mother's career on the force, but he'd made it.

"You still on rotating shifts?"

"Yes."

"Bored stupid yet?"

"As a matter of fact, things have been busy." Not that he was happy about the recent string of break-ins in town, but in six months as a state trooper he'd answered only domestic-dispute calls, bar fights and busted several teenagers for graffiti. He wasn't proving himself or moving up the ranks within the force quickly with those kinds of calls.

"Any leads on the break-ins?" Katherine asked as she dialed their younger sister's cell.

"Not yet. It's odd. Nothing stolen. Just broken glass to be an annoyance to the store owner. Captain thinks it's vandals."

"There's more to it," Katherine said.

"Well, if you say so, I guess the head of the department must be mistaken." His older sister was a homicide detective. She'd seen the worst and was trained to think the worst. It made her good at her job. Terrible at relationships. She once pepper sprayed a blind date who was simply reaching into his pocket for his inhaler when her intense questioning spurred an asthma attack. Unfortunately, her gut was almost always right. About just about everything.

She tucked her shoulder-length blond hair behind her ear as the call continued to ring. "Look, I'm telling you. Keep looking into it."

Leslie's face appeared on Katherine's phone screen, a view of sand, surf and palm trees in the background behind her, ending their conversation. His younger and older sisters could pass for twins they were so much alike. On the outside at least—same blond hair, same blue eyes, same tall, sturdy build. In comparison, Eddie looked like he was adopted into the family with his dark hair and brown eyes. As a kid he often wondered, but as he got older, he recognized the features he shared with his father.

"Hey…has the ceremony started?" Leslie asked.

"Not yet," Katherine said.

"Where are you?" Eddie leaned closer. Looked like the beach on Santa Monica Pier, but all of those West Coast beaches looked alike to him.

"Can't say." Leslie was jogging. He could tell by the way her ponytail swung back and forth and her breathing was controlled and steady. His sister was a firm believer in not wasting a second of time. If she had to be on a FaceTime call to see their mother awarded with the State Trooper Hall of Fame Award, she'd work out while doing it.

"Who are you protecting these days?" he asked.

"Can't say."

Eddie grinned. "Can we guess?"

"Nope."

They did anyway. It was a game they loved to play with their baby sister. Once a state trooper herself, Leslie had quickly opted for the more lucrative profession of private security detail to the rich and famous in California, refusing to admit that the sudden death of her fiancé had anything to do with the drastic life change.

"Is it Cameron Diaz?" Katherine said. She always started with her favorite actress.

"No," Leslie said.

"Dwayne Johnson?" Eddie asked. He always started with the most unlikely.

"Why the hell would the Rock need private security

detail on a beach?" Leslie's annoyance at this game never grew old.

"So, you're on a beach," he said.

"It's California, Eddie. It's one big beach. And I'm off duty."

"Dating anyone?" Katherine asked.

"Next question." Leslie was as tight-lipped about her personal life as she was about her job. She'd moved to LA two years ago and had been home only once. She took her NDAs seriously and revealed nothing to them. It was fun irritating her with questions though.

"Are you coming home for Gran's nuptials?" Katherine asked.

Leslie rolled her eyes. "It's her third marriage. Why is she having a big wedding?"

"She likes the attention," Katherine said.

"When you get to be my age, you need to pull these kinds of stunts to get your grandkids to come back from their famous clients to visit once in a while." Their grandmother had a unique ability to pop up when they least expected her, whenever she knew they were talking about her. In his rush to his seat, Eddie hadn't noticed her and her fiancé, Melvin, seated on the other side of Katherine. He smiled warmly at them now as his grandmother leaned over to join in on the call.

"Hi, Gran," Leslie said, lighting up at the sight of the older woman. "You know I'll be at your wedding… again." Their grandmother had practically raised Leslie, after their mother and her youngest daughter had had a falling out when Leslie was thirteen and she'd gone to live with the matriarch of the family.

They'd all thought it was teenage rebellion, but the stubborn streak in the Sanders family ran deep. Neither woman would apologize, so Leslie stayed with Gran and their mom pretended she was okay with it. It had been tough not having their sister at home, but the peace in the household with Leslie gone had been appreciated.

Having Leslie on FaceTime for this important milestone in their mother's life but live in person for Gran's wedding was just another way the two women continued to hurt one another, but…at least their sister had agreed to appear on the cell phone screen.

"You look tired. You sleeping?" Gran asked Leslie.

"Yes, I am."

"*With* someone?" their grandmother asked.

Eddie hid his grin. There was no question where their joy of razzing one another came from.

"Is the ceremony starting yet?" Leslie asked, checking her Fitbit on her wrist.

No one would tell their mom that Leslie had scheduled her run around the event.

"Any minute now," Katherine said. Sensing Leslie had had enough family bonding and was ready to disconnect, his older sister turned the phone toward the stage.

"Have you gone for your tux fitting yet?" Gran asked him.

"I'll do it next week, I promise." He'd completely forgot…and well, part of him still wasn't convinced his grandmother was going to go through with it. She was eighty years old and divorced twice already. She really did pull stunts like this for attention from all of them.

"Young man, if you show up to my wedding to give me away in your dirty uniform, smelling like the night before's heat…"

"Oh, don't worry, Gran," Katherine interrupted.

"Eddie's not getting any heat. He's still patrolling the ski resort."

He sighed. Being around female members of his family always made him desperate for an escape. Sure, it had taken him several attempts to pass the police entrance exam, his dyslexia making the written component challenging. And sure, out of the three siblings, he had the least dangerous job on the force. But the lack of respect from his very female-dominated family drove him crazy.

"I'll get the tux…and if you're lucky, I'll even get a haircut," he told his grandmother with a wink. He wasn't sure what the rush was. The wedding wasn't until November. Plenty of time.

"Do you have a date yet?" Gran asked. "I need to confirm final numbers with the event organizers."

As if one extra person either way would make a huge difference. She was just trying to get his relationship status out of him. Unlike Leslie, if Eddie was seeing someone, he'd be shouting it from the rooftops, not trying to keep it a secret. His dating life was also something he struggled with. Growing up and living in the small town of Wild River, everyone knew everyone. He'd dated just about every single woman in town. Once.

It was hard to find a spark with women he'd known his entire life, and he wasn't like some of the other guys who could hook up with tourists for a few nights. Therefore, his Facebook status said Relationship: nonexistent. He'd give anything just to be able to change it to It's Complicated. "Nope. No date yet," he said.

"Shhhh…ceremony is starting," Katherine said.

They all turned their attention to the front of the

auditorium and a silence fell over the room as the ceremony began.

His mother sat on the stage dressed in her uniform, her medals and badges of honor proudly displayed as the head of the State Troopers of Alaska talked about her many accomplishments over her forty-year career.

His mother has been the second female state trooper in Alaska. Graduating from the academy top of her class in the sixties, she was a trailblazer for all women in the force. His sisters owed their own careers to the work their mother had put in.

Growing up without their father, who'd died of cancer when Eddie was eight, meant his mother held double duty as both parents. She worked long hours on the job, but she was always there for her kids. She may have missed birthdays or Christmases…or softball games, but she was there in the ways that really mattered—raising them to be respectful, considerate people who gave back to their community. Her pride in her family had made them *want* to be people she could be proud of.

On the cell phone screen, even Leslie's face beamed with unconcealed admiration as their mother was inducted in the State Trooper Hall of Fame and handed her plaque commemorating the event.

His mother was a true hero. One who had no trouble giving him shit.

"Why are you still in uniform?" she asked immediately when she joined them after the ceremony.

"Hey, look! Leslie's on FaceTime!" Deflect. It was a defense mechanism they all employed with their tough-as-nails, take-no-shit mother. If she was focused on someone else, she left you alone.

And it worked.

She took the phone from Katherine, but Eddie couldn't listen to the strained conversation, quickly announcing his exit. "I'm out. Got to get back to Wild River before my evening shift."

Katherine checked her watch. "That's eight hours from now." She glared at him.

He shrugged. "Traffic might be bad."

His grandmother looked disappointed. "I thought you were joining us for lunch." She looped her arm through Mel's and the older man's expression screamed "Don't leave me alone with the three of them." But Eddie could handle the women in his family only in small doses.

"Next time." Eddie hugged his grandmother tight and shook Mel's hand. Then he hugged his mother quickly while she was still distracted by Leslie.

Unfortunately, she wasn't going to let him sneak off.

"Hey, hold up…" she said and Eddie sighed, slowing his pace.

His mother said goodbye to her youngest and fell into step with him as he walked across the parking lot. "Have you heard anything about your transfer yet?"

"How do you know about that?"

His mother pointed to the badges on her uniform. "I'm retired, Eddie, not dead. I still have my finger on the pulse of things around here."

As long as she wasn't using that pulse-finger thing to pull strings to secure his transfer. He'd applied to the Alaska Bureau of Alcohol and Drug Enforcement division without telling his mother and sisters precisely for that reason…and to avoid their disappointed expressions if he didn't get the promotion.

But it had been weeks since his last written exam and physical and still no word. "Not yet."

"When did you first apply?"

"Two months ago."

"It's taking longer than usual, but give it another few days… Keep me posted." She touched his shoulder.

A simple, casual gesture to most people. In his family, that gesture meant "Don't get your hopes up." He wasn't even sure if his mother realized it was her tell when she didn't have faith in them for something. She'd done it since he was a kid. When he'd wanted to play football but hadn't made the team. When he'd wanted to ask Carla Spicer to the winter formal and she'd said no. When he'd failed his written driver's permit test twice. Each time, his mother's shoulder touch had predicted the outcome. Or was it the negative energy he associated with it that became a self-fulfilling prophecy?

He hoped this time its predictive powers and ability to upset his karmic balance were wrong.

"Will do. Enjoy lunch." He hugged her again. "Congrats, Mom. I'm proud of you." He waved to the rest of his family as he headed toward his car.

Someday he hoped his mother would finally have a reason to say those words to him.

* * * * *

"Hi, my handsome boy." Lee couldn't resist her chubby
feline. She rubbed his head. After a moment, Chester sat
down contentedly, arms under his body so he looked like
an oversize bread box, closing his eyes with a happy sigh.

Colt took his seat again. "He needs a ramp."

"I know," Lee agreed. "I've looked online for steps
that are tall enough, but I need to have something custom-
made for him. It's on the list."

Colt nodded, his hands resting on his knees, looking
too large for her flea-market armchair. "I know I've heard
about this place before—maybe from my brother or even
Callie's mom, Kate. Now that I think about it, you must
know Kate...?"

Lee nodded, her hands folded on top of his file. "She's
donated some of her time to train my therapy horses. And
I know your brother Liam, too. He takes care of all of

the horses' annual physicals and only charges me for the shots, so he's been a big asset to us ever since we opened ten years ago."

"It seems like you and I have been living our lives with just one degree of separation. It's kind of surprising that the two of us haven't run into each other before."

Lee didn't respond, smoothing her hands over the file. It didn't surprise her in the least that they hadn't crossed paths. In her experience, young cowboys like Colt weren't focused on serving others. They were focused on serving themselves and their whims—bouncing from rodeos to line dancing at the bars to hunting and fishing and then back again. It wasn't necessarily a harsh judgment against him—it was just the observable truth of the stark differences in their lives. She didn't spend her time at rodeos or line dancing in the downtown Bozeman bars. She wanted her life to have more purpose than just drifting from one amusement to the next.

"Now I wish I had paid this place a little more attention." Colt's eyes pinpointed on her face in a way that made her self-conscious enough to reach for her locket with a free hand.

"Well—" she tucked her hair behind her ear "—you're here now."

Get 4 FREE REWARDS!

We'll send you 2 FREE Books _plus_ 2 FREE Mystery Gifts.

FREE
Value Over
$20

Both the **Romance** and **Suspense** collections feature compelling novels written by many of today's bestselling authors.

YES! Please send me 2 FREE novels from the Essential Romance or Essential Suspense Collection and my 2 FREE gifts (gifts are worth about $10 retail). After receiving them, if I don't wish to receive any more books, I can return the shipping statement marked "cancel." If I don't cancel, I will receive 4 brand-new novels every month and be billed just $6.99 each in the U.S. or $7.24 each in Canada. That's a savings of at least 13% off the cover price. It's quite a bargain! Shipping and handling is just 50¢ per book in the U.S. and $1.25 per book in Canada.* I understand that accepting the 2 free books and gifts places me under no obligation to buy anything. I can always return a shipment and cancel at any time. The free books and gifts are mine to keep no matter what I decide.

Choose one: ☐ **Essential Romance**   ☐ **Essential Suspense**
                          (194/394 MDN GNNP)   (191/391 MDN GNNP)

Name (please print)

Address   Apt. #

City   State/Province   Zip/Postal Code

Mail to the Reader Service:
IN U.S.A.: P.O. Box 1341, Buffalo, NY 14240-8531
IN CANADA: P.O. Box 603, Fort Erie, Ontario L2A 5X3

Want to try 2 free books from another series? Call 1-800-873-8635 or visit www.ReaderService.com.